Just Two Weeks

Jenn Lynn Adams

ISBN: 979-8-9869860-7-4 (paperback)

ISBN: 979-8-9869860-6-7 (ebook)

First edition, October 2024

Edited by Nice Girl Naughty Edits

© Cover design: Ya'll That Graphic

www.jennlynnadams.com

Also by Jenn Lynn Adams

Daughter of the Underworld

Daughter of War & Witchcraft

There's nothing more beautiful than the way the ocean refuses to stop
kissing the shoreline, no matter how many times it's sent away.
-Sarah Kay

Four Years Ago

CHAPTER ONE

Jack

"*All units in the vicinity of Moores River Drive and Pattengill Avenue, please respond to a 10-50 possible PI.*"

A sigh of sheer exhaustion escapes my lips as I click the button on my radio. "Dispatch. Unit 67. I'm 10-5." I roll my neck as I pull away from the copse of trees where I'd been patrolling-slash-napping. Today was another 16-hour shift, and I'd snuck away to catch a few winks just before evening rush hour. My lunch, a burger and fries from a greasy fast-food joint, sits untouched on the passenger seat. The caffeinated soda drips condensation onto my vest as I bring the straw to my mouth and take a pull.

The radio on my shoulder sparks to life again. *"10-4, Unit 67."*

Luckily, I am only a few streets away from the mansions and bespoke estates that sit along the Grand River and Moores River Drive. As I navigate along the scenic route toward the accident, I can't help but gawk at the palatial homes.

What would it be like to live there?

My phone rings, jarring me from the moment of daydreaming. Eyes flicking to the device on top of my in-car computer, my mom's name flashes across the screen.

I slide my thumb to accept the call and then click the speaker function. "Hi, Ma," I answer cheerily, but also preparing myself for some new chaos. "I don't have long. I'm on my way to a crash." The radio trills with another accident, this one across town.

"Jacks, I can't find the butter, and I need my keys to drive to the store to get more. Can you come by the house?"

If I had a free hand, it'd be rubbing my temple. "Ma, there's plenty of butter in the fridge. I just picked some up from the store yesterday." I want to add, "*Remember?*" But I don't. Because of course she doesn't. "And your keys are hanging on the hook by the back door."

I listen closely as the rattling of glass bottles sounds through the phone. I imagine her opening the refrigerator door and scanning over the contents I carefully organized. "Oh, there it is!"

"Ma, did you remember to take your medicine this morning?"

"Yes, Jack, I took my medicine. You don't need to treat me like I'm old, son."

Pressing my lips together, my eyes roll into my brain. I love my mother, but her recent diagnosis has not been easy on her. Or me, if I'm being honest.

"I'll stop by tonight if I get a chance, okay?" I try to temper my voice. "But it'll be late when I get off duty." The dispatcher calls out a hit and run.

Ever since our department moved to the new schedule to compensate for the lack of manpower, my availability to help Ma has dwindled. I'm lucky if I make it over there once every few days at this point.

"I'm fine, Jacks. Besides, that old bat next door keeps stopping by to check on me and gossip about the neighbors."

"Be nice to Mrs. Whitberry. She's doing both of us a solid. And she's your *friend*."

I'm pretty sure my mother mumbles something about Mrs. Whitberry being a nosy bitch, but I'm too distracted by the scene I'm driving up to.

A black BMW coupe completely torn to pieces while a white Porsche SUV sits smoking next to it, the front bumper thoroughly destroyed.

Two men screaming at one another.

And a dark-haired woman sitting on the curb, her eyes shiny with emotion as blood drips from a cut along her hairline.

"I gotta go, Ma. I'll call you back soon." I click the red button on the phone and flick on my lights as I pull into the roundabout. I'm grateful traffic isn't too backed up, and most cars are able to navigate around the accident.

"Dispatch. Start me an ambulance."

"10-4, Keaton."

As I exit the patrol car with the first aid kit, I keep my right hand on my weapon. Especially with two men involved in a verbal disagreement, an officer can never be too prepared for something to go south. I approach slowly, my gaze straying to the woman on the curb. Her lip quivers as she watches the argument.

"Gentlemen, if you could stop yelling at one another, I'd like to get statements from both of you, but I need to check her out first, seeing as she's bleeding. Can you both return to your vehicles for a moment?"

They oblige, but not without sending one another narrowed glances. When they're both clear, I crouch down beside the woman. "Other than your head, is anything else injured?" I rip open a pack of gauze from the kit and pass it to her.

"N-No, nothing else hurts," she answers shakily. She presses the gauze to her forehead, wincing as she does.

"Can you tell me what happened here?" The moment I hit the lights on my car, my body cam activated. It means I can treat the woman's injuries without taking copious notes.

"My boyfriend and I were driving and that guy T-boned us." She points to the man near the white Porsche.

"Which car is yours?" I ask, hoping to clarify more of the story.

"Neither. I was driving my b-boyfriend's BMW." My gaze catches on the younger man leaning against the trunk of the black coupe. I don't miss how his eyes narrow as he watches us. The way his jaw clenches.

I'm trained to see these things. To catch the smallest details.

"Sir?" I beckon him over with a wave of my hand. As he walks toward us, I clock his designer shoes and hoodie.

I wonder which mansion belongs to his parents.

"Yeah?" he answers as he stares at the injured girl. His girlfriend, apparently.

I stand and turn, directing my camera at him. "Can you confirm who was driving and what happened?"

"She was driving, Officer. Did she say she wasn't driving? It was totally her! She was the one who—"

"Whoa, calm down, sir. I'm just asking for—"

"I told him I was driving, Malcolm! He just wants your side of what happened. Jesus fucking—"

"She wasn't the one driving, Officer! It was him!" I tear my focus from the now-bickering couple and walk over to the white SUV. "He was speeding through the roundabout, and I thought I had enough distance, but—"

"You're blind, old man! She was driving the whole time!"

Taking a deep breath, I tilt my gaze skyward just as a gull flies overhead and releases a massive shit. It lands on my shoulder with a juicy thud.

Just perfect, I think as I place my hands on my hips and decide how I'm going to deal with the screaming trio in front of me.

Only eight more hours to go.

"Keaton, call for you on line two! It's the governor." The intercom clicks off.

"The *governor*?" Elijah Jenson, my partner and best friend from the academy, raises his eyebrows from the cubicle next to mine.

Ignoring him, I turn away from the desktop computer and glance at the blinking red light on the office phone. I rarely receive calls in the office, as I am rarely *in* the office. But after discovering that the woman in last week's car accident was Savannah Smith, daughter of Governor Paul Smith, I'd been summoned to the precinct to discuss the case with my supervisor.

"I know I don't need to tell you this, Jack, as your reports are always top-notch, but ensure this one is above reproach. Especially since the governor will certainly want a copy."

I'd nodded along, all the while knowing that what I wrote—what I did on a daily basis—was by the book. So I submitted the case report and thought nothing of it.

Until now.

I lift the phone from its cradle and press the flashing button. "Jack Keaton."

"Hi, Officer Keaton. This is Miranda Abbot, Governor Smith's personal secretary. Please hold for the governor."

I wait only a moment before the line picks up again. "Hello there, Officer. Paul Smith here. I just wanted to personally thank you for handling the little accident my daughter was involved in last week."

"Oh, uh, it's just part of the job, sir." My voice comes out raspy and muddled, so I discretely try to clear it, but the noise amplifies over the phone lines. I can feel my face turning red. Beside me, Elijah snorts a laugh.

"Listen, I want to invite you over for dinner sometime this week. I'd love to thank you in person. Our cook makes a fabulous steak. What d'ya say?"

"Oh, that's really not necessary. I'm sure you're busy and—"

"No, no, I insist. I'll have my secretary provide you with the details. See you soon!"

Before I can get in another word, the line briefly goes silent before it's picked up again by the secretary. "Do you have a pen, Officer?" I reach into my vest pocket and jot down the information as she rattles it off at breakneck speed. Then she hangs up with nary a goodbye.

As I replace the phone, still shocked and wondering how I can somehow get out of this dinner, Eli just stares at me.

"What?" I ask as my gaze slowly slides back to the computer.

His shit-eating grin gives me nothing.

"What?" I repeat, my voice growing louder. "He just invited me over to dinner. To say thank you for working the crash involving his daughter."

He simply shakes his head. "I don't think you're getting invited to dinner as just a thank you, Jack."

I swallow the lump forming in my throat. The anxious feeling brews in my stomach and rises to my chest.

What else could it be?

CHAPTER TWO

Savannah

"And you remember my daughter, Savannah." My father beckons to me like I'm a prize on a game show and, like the good little governor's daughter I am, I smile brightly and consider sinking into a curtsy like some debutante on a Regency-era Netflix show.

Get it together, girl.

Except I can't because the man standing in front of me is nothing short of gorgeous. I didn't exactly notice Officer Keaton's attractiveness when he showed up in his patrol car and uniform at the accident a week ago. I'd been too focused on my idiot boyfriend—*ex*-boyfriend now. Malcolm had been the one driving but, with too many accidents on his record, he was worried his parents would take away the new Beamer they'd just bought for him.

"C'mon, Sav, just tell them you were driving. *Please*?" The way he *begged*. The way he looked so *pathetic* and immature as the tears welled in his eyes. And, the final straw, when he screamed at me in the middle of the street while the paramedics cleaned blood from my face... well, I knew then that Malcolm Shepherd was *not* the one.

Not like we were going to get married or anything.

But you know, the one to lose my v-card to. The one to finally *be* with.

But as my gaze travels over Jack Keaton, I don't feel a lick of sadness over dumping Malcolm. *Malcolm who?* my brain asks. The man standing in front of me is another level of hot. I drink him in like a parched survivor in the desert. His dark brown hair is brushed away from his sharp features. Rolled shirtsleeves allude to a tattoo hidden beneath the crisp cotton. And did I mention he's also at least six feet tall? The cop towers over my father, who at 5'11" is still taller than I am.

"What?" I blink dumbly as three sets of eyes turn to me. My father's, Officer Keaton's, and Miranda's.

"Officer Keaton just asked how your healing was going. I assumed it was going well, but now I'm not so sure," my dad responds with a wary look.

"Oh," I laugh lightly and gently tap the bandage still covering the gash on my forehead. "It's fine. The doctor said I shouldn't have a scar, so yay." I pump my arm across my body in mock glee.

What the actual hell am I doing?

"Anyway, dinner is through here." My father turns away from my awkwardness and leads our guest of honor into the expansive dining room. I follow behind Miranda, who seems hellbent on worming her way next to Officer Keaton. She even goes so far as to situate herself right next to him at the table.

Normally, when she's here, she's at my father's side. Ready to talk his ear off about some political alliance or work-related issue.

As though regularly interrupting our family dinners isn't enough, she now shows up to intrude upon dinners with hot guests?

Great. I'll likely not get a word in edgewise.

I take the seat across from the hot cop while my father seats himself at the head of the table.

At least I'll have a side of eye candy with my juicy steak tonight.

"So what do you say, Officer?"

The man across from me is speechless at my father's proposition.

And in all fairness, I am too.

"Why do I need a-a bodyguard?" My nose scrunches up at the word. To me, it's nothing more than a burly babysitter. Someone to watch my every move and report back to daddy dearest.

"Savannah, we've put this decision off long enough. With you at school just across town, it was easy to keep tabs on you. But now... Now it's clear to me that you need more protection. Especially at college in the fall."

"Protection from *what*?" I sound shrill. Hysterical. I hear it, and I know everyone else in the room does, too. But that's what I am right now. Hysterical with confusion bordering on rage. "I've only ever been the good daughter who does everything right. Why would I need someone to shadow me all day, every day?"

"It's for your safety. Most political families have security." My father's tone is cold. Calculated. It brooks no arguments. Except I'm fired up and ready to rumble.

"You chose this—this *lifestyle*. This *job*. *You* chose to be governor. Not me. So why do *I* have to suffer for it?"

"We will discuss this later." He turns away from me and, just like some across-the-aisle politician, I'm dismissed.

So rather than sit here and continue to play my part—the perfect daughter to the perfect politician—I stand and dismiss myself from the table.

"Savannah, wai—" My father's voice echoes in the dining room as I push the swinging door to the kitchen.

The chef has already cleaned and cleared away the remnants of the meal, everything wiped down and pristine.

Not a single crumb left. The perfect house, perfect kitchen, perfect daughter.

My gaze falls to the small liquor cabinet in the corner of the room. The gleaming amber and honey-colored liquids beckon to me, and I approach, like Eve to the forbidden fruit.

Being the good girl got me assigned a bodyguard. So what's the point of doing everything right?

I slowly unscrew the cap of the nearest bottle and take a whiff. It smells of vanilla and cinnamon.

Why not? I lift the bottle and take a deep pull. The liquor scorches my throat and I cough loudly before covering my mouth.

Once my throat reopens, I take a deep breath and try again.

This time, the swig goes down smoother, but still tastes like nail polish remover mixed with essential oils.

How do people drink this? I replace the bottle and wipe my eyes. Definitely not for me.

I stalk across the kitchen and through the other door, my thoughts on heading straight to my room and pouting there instead. Only, as I enter the hallway, I come face-to-face with Officer Keaton exiting the washroom.

I gulp, praying he can't smell the vanilla-cinnamon liquor on my breath.

"Miss Smith." He acknowledges me with a formal nod. "I want to let you know that I've accepted the position as your bodyguard." His eyes fly over my face. *Can he smell the alcohol?* My cheeks burn, surely turning bright red. He clears his throat. "I hope we can work together in a professional manner."

I blink up at him. "Yeah. Right, Officer Keaton." He may be hot, but I'm less than thrilled to be assigned a babysitter. I duck my chin and attempt to walk around him, excusing myself from his presence with the least amount of awkwardness as possible.

Pleasedon'tsmelltheliquor. Pleasedon'tsmelltheliquor.

"Miss Smith?" he says, just as I reach the stairs, stopping me in my tracks.

"Yes?" My voice comes out all squeaky, like a cartoon character with a big secret. I flash a toothy smile to deflect.

"I'd like it if you could call me Jack. After all, we'll be spending a lot of time together." He steps closer to me, filling the room with his presence. My eyes flick to his, the color of the Michigan leaves in late September. Just as the green is fading to a light brown.

"Y-You can call me Savannah." I try to breathe out as little as possible, but something catches in my throat and suddenly I'm coughing and exhaling all over the place.

Officer Keaton—*Jack*—edges closer as his gaze darkens with concern. But, as though hit with a wall of alcohol-infused perfume, he suddenly stiffens. Stepping back slightly as his jaw tics, those same autumn-leaf eyes narrow as they assess me. "Have you been—"

"See ya around, Jack!" I say quickly as I sprint up the stairs.

Because even though I'm certain that drinking isn't my thing, there's got to be some way I can ditch the good girl badge I've worn for eighteen years.

Chapter Three

Jack

Savannah stomps toward the black town car, and by the look on her face, she is anything but happy.

"Fuck this place," she mutters under her breath as she rips open the door and falls into the passenger seat.

It's been a few days since I officially started my job as her bodyguard, and in that time, Savannah has only uttered two words to me.

"Drive" was the word yesterday, while "What?" was the word the day before.

"Something wrong?" I ask casually, pulling the car away from the curb.

She's silent. Staring out the window with her arms crossed over her chest, her bottom lip worried between her teeth.

"C'mon. Did your boyfriend ignore you or something? Best friend troubles? It wasn't too long ago that I was in high school."

She uncoils from her seat, looking me up and down with the kind of contempt the youth have for those even slightly older than them. "I don't have a boyfriend anymore, but that's not why I'm upset." Her eyes slink to the passenger window once again. "Not that it helps," she murmurs.

I ignore the desire to ask about her *ex*-boyfriend. It's not my place. It's not appropriate for someone in my position to concern himself with that.

Right?

I've never actually been a bodyguard, let alone for an eighteen-year-old girl. I'm in totally new territory here.

"Well, you only have a few days left. Then you're officially graduated and an incoming college freshman. That must be exciting?" I grasp at anything to talk about.

"That's what I thought, too, until my psychology teacher informed me that I'm not passing and have to take summer school to make up the credit."

As we drive down the road, the houses grow larger and larger. But Savannah seems to shrink smaller and smaller into her seat. "I take it you haven't told your father."

A snort escapes from her nose, and she shakes her head. "The whole situation will just be one more reason for him to say, 'I told you so.'"

"What do you mean?"

She shifts her body, turning to face me. I'm pleased she's opening up.

"My dad *hated* my ex, and he's the reason I'm failing. He logged into my drive, made a copy of my final paper, and submitted it under his name. So then when I tried to turn *mine* in, the psych teacher claimed I was pla-giarizing! She told me I was lucky she wasn't pursuing further disciplinary action beyond the F, which dropped my overall grade."

As my grip on the steering wheel tightens, my knuckles turn white. The urge to find out where this kid lives and show up at his house with a K9 in tow skyrockets through my veins.

Someone should show that little punk a lesson.

Especially after he clearly forced Savannah to lie about that accident. The traffic cameras had proven he was the driver.

The overwhelming sense of justice and...dare I say, rage, has me second-guessing myself. As a police officer, I never became emotionally involved in petty car accidents. Minor criminal offenses. Sure, I cared about making the world a better place, but I never wanted to seek vengeance against any of the offenders.

But the way Savannah looks, slumped in her seat like someone just kicked her puppy? It has me riled up. "I-I just can't believe I'm not going to graduate on time. After how hard I worked for *four* years..." Her voice cracks, and she flicks her gaze out the passenger window as she adjusts herself away from me.

Fuck, is she crying?

What do I do?

Without another thought, I pull the car over, blocking the bike lane, and hit the hazards. Shoving the car into park, my suddenly clammy hands fall to my thighs. I track Savannah's movements, from her shuddering shoulders to the quick swipe of her cheek with the back of her hand.

"Hey, everything will be fine," I say, with as much helpfulness as I can muster. I've never had to deal with a teenaged girl crying in my front seat. It's oddly off-putting. And my chest feels strange and warm.

She sniffs and shakes her head, her eyes still trained on something beyond the passenger window. "You don't know that."

I run my hands through my hair and press my lips together. "You're right. But you're clearly smart, so the psych class will be no problem. It's just a minor bump in the road."

As she glances down, a few tears fall onto her uniformed skirt. The fabric turns from navy blue to nearly black. "I used to be smart. Before..." Another tear streaks down her cheek.

"Before? Before what?" I search with my eyes for something, anything, to hand her to dry her tears. When I come up with nothing, I seriously consider offering my sleeve, but just then, she grabs a tissue from her bag and wipes at her eyes.

"Before I started dating Malcolm. I'm so stupid for not seeing it sooner."

I blink slowly, still completely confused as I navigate this new path of female emotion. Sure, I've dated. But my time in high school was spent focused on sports. My friends. My grades. When I graduated from the academy, getting hit on by "holster sniffers" was a given, but I'd steered clear, unlike my partner Elijah.

I wonder if he'd know how to handle a sobbing high school senior.

I sincerely hope not.

"It's obvious that Malcolm character was no good for you, so it seems you're much better off."

She chuffs and rolls her eyes. "That's exactly what my dad said."

Hm... I try again. "It's just—"

"Are you also going to tell me I'm too pretty to date a punk like him?"

I swallow the lump in my throat as my eyes widen. What exactly is the protocol here?

"I mean, that's what my dad said." Her cheeks turn a soft pink as she glances down at the balled-up tissue in her palm.

My hands return to the steering wheel, and I click off the hazards as I prepare to return to the roadway. "Well, your dad is right, Miss Smith—Savannah. That kid seemed like a real piece of work."

Her eyes watch me as we merge into the traffic, and I try not to notice. Have I made her feel better?

"For the record, I really wasn't driving. You know, when—"

"I know," I interrupt, pulling the car into the driveway. My heart stutters at the little nugget of trust I've built with her.

"How'd you know?"

"He wasn't smart enough to adjust the seat. There's no way you could reach the pedals," I lie. My gaze travels down her legs to the low-top sneakers she wears today. The same pair she was wearing during the accident.

Shame flares in my chest. Why didn't I tell her about the traffic surveillance?

Because you want to impress her, a small voice hisses in the back of my mind.

She snorts as I bring the car to a stop at the top of the driveway. "He is pretty dumb."

"Then you're *definitely* better off without him. You deserve better." I offer her a friendly smile and shift into park.

"Thanks," she says as she turns to me. My smile dips as she glances at me through tear-stained lashes, heart pounding as sudden tension thickens around us. Yet I don't cut the engine or move to leave. I'm frozen. And I'm not sure if it's by choice. She slides her hand over mine, which lingers on the gearshift. Her fingers press into the ridges of my own as she tries to interlace our hands.

Body stiffening, I instantly sit up straighter. My hand tingles under her touch. "Savannah, I-I'm your personal bodyguard." I gulp, considering my word choice carefully as my pulse pounds in my ears. "I was hired to protect you. I'm employed by your father."

Her eyes shutter, her expression turning to granite. "My father's employee," she repeats.

"Yes."

"I see."

She doesn't remove her hand. She doesn't exit the car. She stays like that, although her fingers tremble slightly, for only a moment longer. But it seems like forever in this small, enclosed space.

Until finally I pull myself from her grasp and kill the engine.

"My apologies, Officer Keaton, for forgetting your place." Her eyes drop to the gearshift before she flips her hair and turns away. Then she opens the door and stands, leaving me staring at the empty seat next to me.

It's only when she slams the car door that I take a deep, shaky breath, as though my lungs were starving for air.

What have I gotten myself into?

Chapter Four

Savannah

His eyes flash with desire as he takes my hand and pulls me closer. I crash into his wide, sturdy chest, our lips nearly touching. My core pulses and throbs, and a moan slips past my glossy lips. An ache echoes deep in my belly as another needy whine escapes me. We inch closer. Closer. Until our breathing syncs and our exhales become one another's inhales. I gulp down the desire simmering in my gut and press forward—

"Savannah." His voice is distant.

"*More,*" I beg as the aching continues, but somehow becomes less intense. It flickers and fades just beyond the ether. My ears pop.

"Want it." I'm agitated. Unfulfilled. I seek a return to the depths where the dark-eyed god resides.

"Savannah." Smooth, whiskey-soaked breath edges against my neck. My nerves stand on end as the timber slides down to my collarbone, making my nipples pebble with desire.

"Yes." My fingers reach out for him, but he's gone. It's dark and I'm alone, left with only a thrum in my belly. A fire that can't be quenched. I whimper.

"*Savannah*." The softness is replaced with irritation. Aggressiveness and frustration tinge the air as something hard presses against my temple. Another jolt jars me back to the present and a familiar *ding* sounds overhead. My eyes snap open, and I inhale sharply as everything comes into focus.

An airplane.

Turbulence.

Drool.

Oh God, so much drool.

Wiping my mouth with the back of my hand, I squeeze my eyes closed and beg for this to be part of the dream. Or is it actually a nightmare?

"Savannah, are you listening to me?" Sterner now, I slowly turn my head toward my seat mate. Not *quite* the god from my lust-filled vision.

But close.

My eyes immediately catch on the giant puddle of saliva wetting Jack's crisp white collared shirt.

Oh fuck.

I gulp.

My tongue is fuzzy with sleep and stickier than the Florida heat into which we're descending. I continue to stare dumbly at the wet spot as my face heats and my fingers curl around the skinny armrest.

"Did I... Did I say anything while I was asleep?" Dear God, please say no.

"No."

Thank fuck.

I may have uttered the last bit out loud, as his dark eyebrows lower over dirty dishwater eyes. He reaches across and grazes my lap. It's like a strike of lightning straight between my legs.

Oh.

My body goes rigid before my brain comprehends that he's fastening the belt across my hips, cinching the dingy fabric with large hands until I'm properly restrained.

"They turned the fasten seatbelt light on, for God's sake." I catch an annoyed eye roll before he turns to the window and slides the shutter all the way up, blinding me with the sun.

I swallow and blink back the wetness pooling in my eyes. From the brightness. Not from *him*.

Never from him.

Because he's nothing more than an employee.

My *father's* employee, to be exact. As he so casually reminded me just a month ago.

And since then, we've both tiptoed around one another.

With shaky hands, I reach beneath the seat and pull a stick of gum from the pocket of my carryon. I'd offer a piece to my travel companion, but he couldn't even be bothered to give me the window seat. Instead, as the spearmint floods my taste buds and my ears pop once more, I'm stuck staring at his back.

He cranes his neck back and forth, blocking my entire view of the tiny oval. Rather than focusing on the way his muscles ebb and flow under his ironed dress shirt, I again reach into my carryon and dig out the smutty romance novel I'd brought for the beach. Then I purposefully take up the entire armrest with my "stabby, pointy elbows," as he'd called them earlier.

Because Jack Keaton isn't going to ruin my last two weeks of summer vacation before college.

Even if he does look surprisingly like the man in my dream.

"Savannah, you'll take this room here." Miranda dips her chin toward the brightly painted guest room at the back of the beach house. Next to the garage. Perfect for sneaking in and out as needed.

Lucky me.

I blow out a puff of air, the sweaty fringe along my hairline fluttering from my face.

"Is something wrong with the room I've selected for you?" Her sickly-sweet smile pulls at her hollow cheeks, making her look like some kind of cartoon villain.

"It's fine," I answer in a monotone. I just want to get inside and wash away the plane germs.

"And Jack? You're across the way." She points with a pale arm to a second room adjacent to my own. "Close enough to keep an eye out," she adds. This room is smaller. Darker. Built-in bookshelves line the far wall, and a large wooden desk takes up most of the space.

Jack hums in assent from behind me. Like he can sense my plans and is already thwarting them with his presence. I squish myself against the wall, sucking in my stomach, as he squeezes past with only a duffel bag slung carelessly over his shoulder.

At least the drool spot dried.

"You're sleeping in an office? Where's the bed?" The questions are out before I can stop myself, and I feel the familiar blush creeping onto my cheeks.

Miranda's overly plucked eyebrow quirks at my interruption. "The couch pulls out. I hear it's quite comfy." Her eyes stray to Jack.

"Just fine for me," he says as he tosses the duffel onto the couch. He then begins to loosen his tie and promptly closes the door in our faces.

My lips flatten in acceptance even as I refuse to meet Miranda's eyes. The perfectly coiffed woman barely has to move her stick-figure frame as I wheel my luggage past and into my room.

"And of course I'm just next to Jack in case you need anything, *sweetie*." She offers me a close-lipped smile that doesn't reach her eyes, and I cringe inwardly at the moniker. Miranda used to be my nanny, but now that she's become my father's assistant, she still can't quite drop the toddler-esque nicknames. I'm not a child, even though both she and my father only see me as such.

I pull my suitcase into the room, and as I turn to close the door behind myself, I catch Miranda knocking on Jack's door.

He opens it, exposing his completely bare chest to both me and Miranda. My eyes go wide.

Those muscles...

My thighs clench together.

Miranda must be thinking— or feeling— the same thing, as her hand rises to her mouth.

But then they exchange a few words.

Just as quickly, the door closes, and both of us are left in the dark hallway with dual dreamy smiles.

I clear my throat and avert my gaze.

Shit, I knew my bodyguard was hot, but I didn't realize he was *that* hot.

As I close my door, I remind myself that he's nothing but an employee.

He works for me. For my father.

And, most importantly, he would never balk at his duties. Duties that don't include entertaining the yearnings of a soon-to-be college freshman.

I unzip my bag and drop my airplane sweats. Digging through the luggage, I pull out a pair of cutoffs and a skimpy tank to change into. I hold the strappy top against my shoulders as a renewed smile pulls at my lips.

Tonight, I'm off to find the man from my dreams. One who will entertain my yearnings, perhaps. And this time, he won't look like a thing like Jack Keaton.

"So he, like, touched your crotch?"

"No! He buckled me in because I was *asleep*," I explain to my best friend, Delia, rolling my eyes. Not that she can see me over our FaceTime conversation in the darkness.

"Hm," she hums before cracking her gum. "Where are you going now? I can't see shit."

"I'm just gonna take a walk on the beach. See if I can find a friend or two while I'm here. Maybe replace my future roommate."

"Hey!" she squeals as I laugh. "You've got two weeks away from me and then we're tied at the hip for the next four years."

My flip-flops slap against the walkway's wooden planks as I descend to the sand below. "Two weeks is plenty of time to change my mind."

"You wouldn't dare, Sav. We've been planning this since we were kids. Attending Emerald Coast University with you as my roommate? I, for one, cannot wait. I'm just jealous that you're down there first."

As if I had a choice. My father's attendance at an annual energy conference, which just happens to coincide with dropping me off at college, was nonnegotiable. He'd flown a skeleton staff down to northern Florida but swore he'd make time for the two of us to have some father-daughter time.

We'll see.

He already missed the flight. "Something came up," he said over the phone as I boarded with his assistant and my babysitter. "A meeting went longer than expected. I'll catch the next flight."

As usual, I accepted the excuse wordlessly, even as he ended the call before I could say goodbye.

"Sav? Are you paying attention, or did I lose you?"

Discarding my sandals, I step onto the cool sand. "I'm here," I sigh as my toes sink into the softness. I've always felt like half a person most of the year. Like I'm in the wrong place. Michigan can be cold and unforgiving. I hate fishing. Bird watching. Meandering in a forest. Even with the sandy beaches of the Great Lakes within driving distance, I miss the warmth and smell of Florida's Gulf Coast. Give me a beach towel and a book and I'm set. In the summer, when my father attends the annual energy conference—first as a member of Michigan's public service commission and now as the current governor—and the ocean's undulating before me, I'm whole again.

"You're doing that weird thing with your feet, aren't you?"

I snicker and wiggle my feet farther down. Burying myself to my ankles. There's just something healing about soft sand between the toes.

"Well, enjoy your dirty feet and call me tomorrow. I want to hear more about this crotch touch."

"Ugh, there's nothing more to tell. He's literally paid to watch me like a child. He was just doing his job. Besides, my other nanny is here practically tucking me in—"

"Stick Lady is there, too? Wow, you're really going to have a great time... Too bad I missed out this year." I used to be allowed to bring a friend on our yearly trip. "To keep her entertained," as my father reminded Miranda. But this year, Delia needed to spend the last vestige of summer with her family. And I was promised father-daughter time, too.

So here I am. Alone at the beach for the first time.

"Yeah, right." I roll my eyes again. "Anyway, I see a bonfire down the shore. I'm going to check it out. Talk to you tomorrow?"

"Be safe, *sweetie*," Delia singsongs, purposefully using the moniker she knows I hate.

"Ew," I growl before hanging up the call. Tucking my phone in the back pocket of my cutoffs, I traipse through the sand. The waves methodically roll up and down the shore, the sound a balm to my haggard soul. My father had not been pleased with my summer school requirement. What I'd gone through over the last few weeks had been my own personal version of Hell. Stuck in a summer school class with a bunch of burnouts and truant seniors who were completing a "victory lap." Listening to nightly lectures from my father about my choices and their consequences. *And how it would look if the media found out.*

"The governor's daughter should be above reproach," he'd chastised, as though it was my fault. As though I was the one who plagiarized. As though I wasn't trying hard enough to make him proud.

"Hey! Can you toss me the ball?" I snap to attention as a cute blond raises his arm in my direction, his tan bicep flexing as he wiggles his fingers.

"Oh. Um, sure." I try to remember how to throw a football without looking like a complete idiot.

It takes me a moment to find the ball in the dusky evening light, but as I retrieve it from the surf and toss it back, I'm granted a dazzling white smile and a backward glance.

The blond throws the ball to his friend and then immediately jogs to me, his pecs dancing under his worn t-shirt.

I wipe my sandy hands on my shorts and make sure to close my gaping mouth. Then I school my features to look welcoming. Normal.

Not like a horny eighteen-year-old who's dying to forget about the hot bodyguard assigned to protect her. The girl desperate to lose her virginity.

And as I check out the buff blond with an award-winning smile traipsing toward me, I think I may have found a way to pass the next two weeks.

CHAPTER FIVE

Jack

Florida in July is fucking hot.

After ensuring the camera system is active and there are no blind spots around the perimeter of the house, I close the laptop before interlacing my fingers and stretching out the tension in my forearms.

I stand from the computer chair and roll my neck and shoulders. The flight's whiskey had loosened me up, but the effects are long gone by now.

I've certainly earned my bottle of Michelob. Hours of hooking up the surveillance cameras' electrical wiring through the new property's attic and duct system has left me dirty, sweaty, and tired. Not to mention, I've got something itchy in my eye. Growling, I rub roughly until I run into something on my way to the kitchen.

Nope, not something.

Someone.

Miranda, in fact. The boss's tight-ass personal assistant.

"Oh! I'm so sorry, Jack." She bats her lashes as her hand floats to her throat. Like I don't know exactly what she's doing. This woman has been after my dick since the day I started working for the governor. Unfortunately for her, I'm not interested. "Are you okay?"

"Fine. Just got something in my eye after installing all the cameras." I move around her and continue my path toward the refrigerator. That ice-cold beer is calling my name.

"Let me help you." She follows in my wake, her hands now fluttering a little too close to my face.

"*I said I'm fine*, Miranda." If turning my back on her won't stop the unwanted attention, maybe my stern tone will. There's no way I'm getting involved with a co-worker. Not a chance, lady. Sleeping with the governor's all-too-willing assistant would certainly be grounds for removal.

And I'm not about to risk losing my dream job for someone like Miranda Abbott.

"Oh," she says quietly. Her footsteps falter and, against my better judgement, I glance back and spot her crestfallen features.

Damn it. I meant to be closed off. Not downright rude. I may not be interested in her like that, but I still need to be professional. We work together. I exhale heavily, my midwestern upbringing getting the better of me, and stalk to the fridge to grab two beers. I hold one out to her, my eyebrows raising in a wordless invitation.

Her face lights up like a kid on Christmas as she accepts the cold bottle. After all, it's after work hours for her.

"Allow me." I twist off the top and pocket the cap before returning the drink to her waiting hands.

Brushing her fingers along mine as she takes the longneck, she smiles slowly before moving toward the bar top along the kitchen island. Hitching herself into a seat, she curls inward over the beer. And waits.

"Hoping it'll turn into some kind of fancy girly drink?" I ask after swallowing a mouthful of the carbonated beverage.

"Oh, um, no. I love beer." She lifts the bottle tentatively to her thin lips and takes a pull. Her throat doesn't move as she holds the liquid in her mouth. Eyes watering, she blinks quickly.

She hates it. I press my lips together to avoid cracking a smile.

Another beat goes by before her body shudders as she swallows the beer. "Yum," she lies, a fake smile plastered on her face. "So, have you eaten yet?"

I shake my head—because who actually says "yum" after drinking a low-calorie beer—and chug the remainder of the drink before tossing the bottle into the recycling bin. "Was just gonna head out to find a bite. Boss's flight lands in a few hours, so I'll have to head back to the airport anyway."

Her back straightens and her face perks up. "I'll come with you!"

I squint at her, searching for any reason to deny the company. "What about Savannah? She shouldn't be left alone."

"She's not even here."

Something thuds loudly in my chest, and I stiffen. How did I not know she'd left? "Where'd she go?" *And why did nobody tell me?*

She shrugs. "Left hours ago. I think to take a walk?"

"Has she checked in? Did she say when she'd be back?" Savannah has been avoiding me like the plague ever since that day in the car, most of the time refusing to even acknowledge my presence.

Until the plane earlier when she fell asleep on my shoulder. *"Did I say anything while I was asleep?"* My throat tickles. What could she have said, or dreamed of, that would cause her to ask that question?

From a professional standpoint, it's certainly important for me to understand my protectee's head space. After all, if she's worried about something, I should know and be made aware.

Just in case.

And now terrible scenarios spiral through my mind as I imagine all the horrible things that could have already happened to the innocent eighteen-year-old we've been entrusted to keep safe until her father arrives.

Miranda pulls out her phone and scrolls, the light doing nothing to hide her pinched expression. "Nope. No texts." She slams the phone back onto the island. Face down.

I swipe her unfinished beer and empty the contents into the sink before throwing it away. "Text and find out where she is. *Now.*"

"I'm sure she's fine, Jack. She's a teenager. This is what *they do.*"

With a rough swallow, I meet her gaze. "Regardless, part of our duties is to keep an eye on her. That means knowing where she is at all times. What will Governor Smith say when he shows up tonight and his daughter isn't here? We'd have no explanation for where she is either."

She shrugs. "I guess you're right." She sounds less than convinced. Thumbing her phone to life, she shoots out a quick text before shoving the device into her back pocket.

"Let's go," I instruct as I grab the keys from the counter and usher her toward the garage.

Her face brightens like I've invited her to dinner. I tamp down the urge to groan in exasperation.

The only thing on my mind is finding Savannah.

Just so I can keep my job.

"*Stooooop it!*" Savannah's voice trills before the line goes dead. My body chills, and I instantly see red. I grip the phone in my hand, wanting nothing more than to toss it out the window, but I know that won't help the situation. Especially as I need it to track her whereabouts.

"She didn't say where she was going?" My hand grips the wheel of the black SUV as I look left and then right, scanning the road and sidewalk for Savannah. But the town is crowded with vacationers moving in and out of the eateries and bars along the main drag. Even with the location-enabled applications I've installed on the Smith family phones, computers, and watches, it'd be impossible to know her *exact* position.

"Nope." Miranda stares at her phone, not even bothering to look out the window and help search.

"And you didn't think to ask her where she was going? Didn't you used to be her nanny?" My gaze slides away from the road, and I squint into the darkness of the vehicle, looking for any sign of contrition.

Huffing, she tosses her phone into the bag on her lap. "That was ten years ago. It's not exactly my problem anymore. My job is to organize the governor's schedule, not babysit his daughter." I don't miss the annoyed tone or the way she rubs her temple and scowls.

I grind my teeth and rethink my retort. As Ma says, "If you don't have anything nice to say, don't say anything at all." And I definitely don't have anything nice to say to the lady sitting in the passenger seat, who is clearly not concerned that she allowed an attractive eighteen-year-old to go out by herself in a town full of strangers.

"Oh my gosh!"

An excited squeal raises my spirits slightly, and I slam on the brakes, turning to her with a flutter in my gut. "What? Did you spot her? I dip my torso to see out the passenger window.

Miranda ignores my inquiry and leans forward to turn up the radio. "I *love* this song!" She proceeds to hum along as she digs through her bag, and then, finding a shiny lip gloss, applies it with the visor's lighted mirror.

I take a deep breath and return to grinding my teeth until I feel them nearly eroding to dust.

My phone dings. I brake again, slowing down, and look at the text.

> Governor: Plane landing in 45 minutes. Gate 18.

I type out a quick response, acknowledging the information, then toss the device into the center console cupholder. Miranda's phone pings next. "It's probably Mr. Smith. He just texted me, too."

She bites her lip and shrugs, leaving her phone unchecked.

"You still need to check it," I direct sternly. "It might be Savannah. We need to find her in the next 45 minutes."

Grabbing the device, she briefly looks at it before plunking it back into her bag. "You're right. Just confirming the gate number."

I hold in the growl that I'd like to release into Miranda's face, but at that very moment, I spot Savannah.

Falling down as she exits a bar with some guy holding on to her hips.

"Hey!" Miranda shrieks as I yank the wheel and curb the vehicle. She bounces and smacks her head against the window with a thud, but I hardly even notice as I immediately slam the car into park, rip the door open and, in a breath, grab the random dude by his fraternity letter-emblazoned shirt.

"Let go of her, you little punk!" With my fist raised, ready to pummel him, Savannah—crouched on all fours—vomits all over the sidewalk.

And my shoes.

I release the guy, who looks like he's my age, and immediately reach for Savannah's hair. Holding the sweaty brown strands back from her face, I lean down and rub my palm up and down her back as a sob racks her body. She hurls again. "Let it out."

"I've got her, bro. We were just—"

When I turn a murderous gaze toward the "bro boy," he instantly backs away, his hands held up in the air. "How old are you?" I grit out between clenched teeth.

"Tw-twenty-two. She said she was eighteen, man!" He moves even farther as his eyes scan the crowd that's started to form around us. "Nothing happened, I swear!"

"I *am* eighteen!" Savannah manages as she lifts her head and eyes the guy—her date?—retreating. Scowling, she shrugs me off and stands.

"Savannah, let's go. Now," I command.

She wobbles on shaky legs, her eyes assessing me. From my baseball cap to my dirtied Henley and ripped jeans, her gaze travels down until she reaches my puke-covered shoes. Pushing her shoulders back, she rolls her tongue in her mouth. "No," she finally states as she wipes her lips on the back of her hand.

"Who is this guy?" the frat boy asks as he returns to her side. Probably feeling slightly more comfortable, having her age confirmed.

"He's nobody," she replies and grabs his hand. She doesn't notice the way he cringes at her vomit touch, but I do.

I don't bother looking at the chump. Another beat passes, and she doesn't move. "Get in the car, Savannah." My fists clench. Does she really think I won't hoist her over my shoulder and carry her ass to the SUV?

She narrows her eyes in challenge. "No."

But I'll give the dude credit. Before I can haul her off, he releases her hand and nods toward the vehicle. "You should probably go. I have your number, though. I'll call you."

His gaze shifts to the left. We both know he won't.

"Oh. Okay," Savannah says as her shoulders slump. She gives him a small smile and then raises her chin and struts past me to the waiting SUV.

As I turn and follow her retreating figure, Savannah stumbles over the curb. I'm there, my arm around her waist and our faces mere inches apart.

Her lips part as her pupils dilate. Darkness fills the spheres from edge to edge as we both catch our breath. Her inhaling my exhale and vice versa. "I'm gonna be sick again," she says, pushing away from me.

She leans against the SUV and retches. Once again, I grab hold of Savannah's hair as my palm instinctively presses against her back to soothe her.

"Good girl," I mutter, my eyes focused on the delicate skin beneath her ear.

I blink and press my lips together, averting my gaze. And that's when I notice Miranda in the front seat. Her expression pinched and her arms crossed over her chest as she glares daggers in my direction.

CHAPTER SIX

Savannah

"**I**'m *fine!*" I proclaim as Jack helps me through the garage. The SUV's headlights roll over us and then disappear as Miranda reverses down the driveway. She was adamant about picking up my dad from the airport.

"I've got important scheduling details to go over with our boss. I don't have time to babysit an eighteen-year-old who can't hold her booze," she stated snottily as we pulled into the drive. "Besides, it's not my job to watch her anymore. That's all you."

"You don't have any shoes. Where are they, Savannah?"

I shrug. I don't owe Jack any answers, especially after he scared off my date tonight. I'm certain Beau, or Bryan—or whatever his name was—would've been down to help me shed the good girl badge. Help me lose my virginity, "become a woman" and all that. I can't say I've ever believed in that nonsense. My v-card is nothing more than a symbol of being the governor's untouchable and prissy daughter, and it's got to go if I'm ever going to make a fresh start at ECU. Now I'm back to square one.

No prospects and one day down. I navigate through the garage, around folded beach chairs and a large umbrella, when I stub my toe on something large and made entirely of metal. The grill.

"Shit!" I squeal as tears well in my eyes. I hiss as the pain intensifies. Bending down, I rub the tender digit and feel wetness. The earth tilts. I'm going to be sick again. "I think I cut my toe off!"

"I doubt it," Jack mutters, then adds, "But this wouldn't happen with shoes." Coming from behind, he swoops down and lifts me into his arms.

"What are you doing? Put me down!" I'm not the kind of girl who wants to be carried around. Although being held against his solid frame does feel…nice.

"You'll get blood all over the floor, or worse, get an infection from this dirty garage." His deep voice tickles against my ear and ignites something low in my gut. That same feeling I dreamed about on the plane. "And how will you explain that to your dad?"

I swallow down a smart-ass retort. I suppose he's simply protecting me from getting into even more trouble. Disappointing my father more than I already have.

He opens the door to the house without even adjusting my weight and turns us sideways to fit through. I never noticed just how wide his shoulders are, but as we slide through the doorway and the glow from my room accentuates the outline of his chest, the flame in my core heats up another notch.

He carries me past the bed and into the adjoining bathroom before depositing me onto the edge of the tub. "Let me see." Kneeling down, he pulls my foot into his large hands and assesses the damage.

Deft fingers tickle along the arch, and I practically gasp as the pleasure turns to a sharp pain that makes me wince.

"Sorry," he mumbles, gently pulling the injured toe away from the others.

As he examines my foot, my gaze runs over his face. His eyes aren't exactly the color of dirty dishwater. Rather, they're more a combination of gold and brown. Like tea mixed with warm milk.

I lean back slightly, quite enjoying the view, and immediately notice my wet bra and panties hanging from the shower curtain rod. *Shit*! "I can handle it from here. Thanks again," I stammer, pushing against his solid form and hoping he'll take the hint and leave.

His eyes follow mine overhead to the delicates, and then return, dancing over my face. "Nothing I haven't seen before." He bites his bottom lip. "Stay put. I'm going to get the first aid kit."

As he strides from the room, I instantly do a one-legged reverse squat and pull the offending underwear down. I look around for any place to stow them, but come up with nothing.

"Ugh," I growl under my breath as I spy my opened suitcase outside the bathroom. Halfway across the bedroom. I'm not a great shot, but even if I miss, at least the items are out of sight. I ball them up and go for it, launching the damp panties and bra into the air.

"Fou— What the hell?" Jack stutters as the makeshift basketball hits him square in the face. He stops dead in his tracks because—*of course*—the universe sends yet another *fuck you* my way as the unmentionables cling to him.

Wet panties hanging off his ear.

Damp bra slung across his shoulder.

Now would be the perfect time for one of those famous Florida sink holes.

"I'm so sorry! I was aiming for my luggage." I dip my chin and cover my face with my hands. How much worse is this night going to get?

Returning to the bathroom without my underwear attached to him, he ignores my embarrassment. "Sit."

I oblige, shame searing hotly over my scalp, and he begins tending to my wound. The toe can be saved, thank God, but the cut is deep.

Through spread fingers, I watch as he runs the tap, testing the water temperature with the flick of his hand. Something about the way he massages the liquid between his fingertips as he waits for the tap to warm sends a shiver down my spine. After a few moments, he douses a washcloth and brings it over to clean my dirtied sole.

"No idea where you left your shoes, then?" he asks as he swaps to my other foot.

A shiver vibrates in the base of my spine as his wet fingers wrap around my ankle.

"No," I admit. "Probably on the beach." To be honest, I can't remember how we got from the beach to the bar. How many drinks did I even have at the bonfire? Jack presses his thumb against the soft spots on either side of my heel. I almost slide right off the edge of the tub; it feels that heavenly.

"Not your first drink either. Or, at least that I know of," he says smugly, likely alluding to the night he was offered this job. Turning, he tosses the used washcloth through the air. It lands in the sink.

I narrow my eyes at him and yank away my foot. "You're not my parent."

"Never said I was," he responds as he uncaps the antibiotic ointment and begins rubbing it into the cut. I wince again, but bite down on my lip, refusing to allow him to see me in pain. "But I know what it's like to tiptoe around a parent. Avoid causing waves. My mother..." he pauses and takes a breath, his brow furrowing as his gaze meets mine. I listen raptly, waiting for a single nugget of Jack's story.

But it doesn't come.

"You need to be more careful, Savannah. You're not like every other girl. You're—"

I roll my eyes and interrupt. "Are you going to give me the '*your dad is important*' speech? Because I've already heard it. From Miranda. And my dad. Oh, and my teachers. So save your breath."

He runs the tip of his tongue along the bottom of his lip. Stops talking and then swallows. "I guess you know better than me, so I'll take your advice." Pulling open the bandage, he gently lays it across the torn skin. "All done."

"Thanks." My tone is purposefully cold as I try to ignore how much I'm enjoying his hands on me. It says what I can't make myself say, which is 'get out.'

He holds his hand out and I take it reluctantly. Rising to my feet, I move past him and stand at the door of the bathroom, ready to put this night behind me.

Taking the hint, he snaps the first aid kit closed and exits. As he pads through the bedroom, his footsteps falter and he stops. "Savannah?"

"What?" I ask, keeping my arms crossed over my chest and my gaze trained on the carpet. I'm so used to being lectured, I've started just tuning it all out. I don't need another person telling me how my behavior could fuck up my dad's career.

With an audible exhale, he hesitates. My eyes snap up to him. He's working his bottom lip between his teeth. "It'll be hard to keep that cut clean."

"Right," I manage to say without a huff. And then I close the bathroom door and bury my head in my hands.

So many emotions and thoughts run through my mind.

I feel like such a fool after the way I acted around Benson. Or was it Branson?

But more importantly, what am I going to do about Jack Keaton and the way he makes me feel?

CHAPTER SEVEN

Jack

I sweep the sand with my foot and finally touch upon what I believe are Savannah's forgotten flip-flops. Spotting the sandals with my phone flashlight, I reach down and pull them from beneath their hiding place tucked under the planks of the walkway. I clap the flimsy plastic together and tuck them into my back pocket.

"What are you doing out here, Keaton?" Paul's voice echoes over the roar of the surf.

"Just taking in the view," I call out in return. He struts down the worn stairs, his loafers plunking and his hands tucked into the pockets of his khakis.

"It's a beautiful night. Looks like the weather will be perfect for the next several days."

"Hm." I nod and dip my eyes to the ground. He quickly discards his shoes and trudges closer.

"Take a walk with me."

It's not a request. The governor rarely makes those anyway. I eye the house in the distance, wanting nothing more than to get back to the property and put the day's events behind me. Instead, I hide my heavy sigh in the sound of a wave crashing against the shore and follow in my boss's stead.

The moon is hidden behind a large gray cloud, dimming the world enough that I can watch my employer without him being any wiser. He's on the younger side for a politician, but clearly old enough to have a college-aged daughter. While his hair is still dark at the top, the sides have begun to lighten as hints of gray pop through. He's also shaved since I saw him last, losing his trademark trimmed beard. Rubbing his smooth chin, he stops in his tracks and stares out into the ocean's darkness.

"Miranda filled me in on why you couldn't pick me up," he says as both hands drop to his hips.

If I've learned anything while working for a politician, it's to never admit something before you have all the facts. I clasp my hands behind my back. And I wait.

"I appreciate your concern for Savannah. Her safety and well-being."

I exhale slowly and wonder where this conversation is going. How much did Miranda tell him?

"You're always one step ahead with your planning and preparations, Keaton. Keeping an eye on my wayward daughter. Immediately knowing how to help, to solve the problem. That's why I like you. You've done a great job throughout the last few weeks, and I want you to know that I am extremely happy with the progress we've made together."

As it stands, Paul Smith is in his second term as governor. He's very popular, both with the ladies and with his constituents. Chances are, he will continue to rise through the ranks, with his next stop being Washington. I've already started helping with other security needs as things ramp up, and I'm hopeful for additional responsibilities as time goes on.

My hand whips from behind my back and meets his with a firm shake. "Thank you, sir. I'd be honored to continue in whatever capacity you see fit." He releases my hand and turns to leave before stopping and turning back to face me.

"You know, Savannah wasn't always like this."

"Sir?" Is he finally going to provide insight into his puzzling daughter? My chest bubbles with interest.

"She wasn't always such a... well, such a challenge. She used to be bubbly. So outgoing and involved. An honor student." He pauses and rubs his hand along his jaw. "But the boys she chooses are just nothing but trouble." I wait as he inhales deeply and then exhales a heavy breath. "It must be hard for her not to have a mother to confide in. I even asked Miranda to check in on her, thinking perhaps a motherly figure might invite her to open up."

I withhold my opinion about Miranda showing any kind of maternal instinct. It's no wonder Savannah has kept her mouth shut.

"I wish I knew what was going on in that mind of hers, but women...am I right?" Even in the darkness, I see the flash of his pearly whites. A politician's smile. He turns to leave, but I stay rooted in place, simply excited to know that I am still employed.

Paul reaches the stairs and bends to retrieve his shoes. As he stands, he turns and hollers back at me. "Don't stay out too late, Keaton. We've got a lot to plan tomorrow."

I set the pink box of pastries on the counter and flick open the lid. Pulling a warm palmier out and plopping it onto a plate, I then grab a mug from the cupboard and pour myself a cup of coffee. I take a swig once I'm sitting on a stool, savoring the rich flavor.

Uncurling the newspaper from its rubber band, I flip through the sections, settling on sports. Finally, I take a filling bite of pastry before spreading the paper out on the counter.

The buttery flakiness melts in my mouth, and I push down a contented sigh. I love starting my mornings slowly. Taking my time to eat, catch up on the news, and enjoy my coffee in peace ensures that I can remain focused the remainder of the day.

Focused on Savannah, the woman who—

"Oh, thank goodness! You got breakfast." Miranda pads into the kitchen on socked feet, her dress pants dragging on the tiled floor. She peers into the pastry box and frowns. "You didn't get any gluten-free bagels?"

"All out," I mumble through a second bite of rich bread. I bring my mug to my lips and take another pull of coffee before returning to the NFL's prospects.

Loudly grabbing the coffeepot and pouring herself a cup, she then swirls in milk and sugar until the concoction is a creamy shade of beige. Her eyes continue to peek at the pink box. I watch from beneath heavy lids as she finally relents and grabs a pain au chocolat. She plates the confection and sits down next to me with a fork and knife.

I attempt to read about the chances of the Buccaneers taking the Super Bowl, but the scraping of the knife as Miranda digs into her pastry and extracts each chocolate chip makes the hair on my neck stand on end. On a heavy sigh, I close the paper and take my dishes to the sink.

So much for starting my day peacefully.

I turn from the sink just as Savannah rounds the corner, her eyes going wide as she spies the box of treats.

"Oh! You went to Blaine's for breakfast?" She scurries forward and gently lifts the lid. "How did you know these are my favorite?" Her eyes narrow as she pulls a pain au chocolat from the box and takes a healthy bite. The chocolate leaves a trail along her lip as she chews. But with her eyes closed and the look of pure ecstasy on her face, I'm not sure she cares.

"Uh, your father told me," I mutter as I lean against the counter. Apparently, she's back to talking to me. Who knew I only needed a healthy dose of chocolaty breakfast treats? I try not to stare at the fact that she's wearing a thin tank top or fleece pajama pants that sit low on her hips. *Eyes up, Keaton.* It's the same top she had on last night when I'd cracked open her bedroom door to drop off her flip-flops. What I found was Savannah tossing and turning, murmuring in her sleep. The covers tangled and twisted. Her arms thrown out and clenching the emptiness.

I watched helplessly from the doorway until she calmed and her breathing returned to normal.

The continued scraping of cutlery pulls me from my memory. Savannah spins around, her eyes crashing to Miranda's plateful of chocolate chips. "What are you doing?" she asks as her brow furrows.

"I don't eat chocolate." Miranda crosses the fork and knife over the plate, the remnants of the chocolate pastry looking like a surgery gone wrong.

Savannah's lip curls. "Since when? You ate it when you were my nanny. In fact, you used to stuff your face with—"

Miranda's eyes narrow to slits and her mouth pinches so tightly it resembles a puckered butthole. "I don't eat chocolate *anymore*."

"Why?" Savannah blinks blankly as she cocks her head. I hold back the smirk playing at my lips and instead cross my arms over my chest, ready to hear about Miranda's newest fad diet. Or trendy social media campaign. Whatever she's worked up about, it's surely as ridiculous as she is.

"Because, *Savannah*, chocolate is the root of all our problems as a society. Not only is it filled with processed sugar and unwanted chemicals, but the way in which our government obtains the cocoa bean from—"

"And what about your coffee?" Savannah interrupts, tipping her chin toward the steaming mug next to Miranda's elbow. "Or the sugar you've ladled in there by the spoonful?"

"Well—"

"I mean, if you're going to go for ethically sourced chocolate, you should at least consider the ramifications of your coffee and refined sugar consumption, too, right?" She licks the last bit of pastry from her finger and then returns to the box. Going for seconds.

My kind of girl.

The voice inside my head comes out of nowhere, and I choke on my own breath. Hacking and pounding on my chest, I earn a frown from Miranda.

"Savannah!" the governor booms eagerly as he enters the kitchen. I immediately snap away from the counter and grab a mug, filling it with coffee and nothing else. *The darker, the better.* We've chuckled over our mutual lack of coffee accoutrements.

"Dad! How was your flight?" Savannah lifts to her toes and plants a chocolaty kiss to her father's cheek. I catch Miranda rolling her eyes and handing him a napkin, indicating he should wipe his face. He shrugs off her nagging and, instead, grabs Savannah's chocolate pastry from her outstretched hand.

"Hey!" she squeals as he takes a bite. But the look of love in her eyes tells me that she's not mad at all. Simply happy to have the next few days with her dad.

"My flight wasn't nearly as exciting as your night," he admonishes as Savannah's cheeks redden. "We'll talk about your behavior later."

"Good morning, sir," I greet as I pass him the mug. I swipe the business section from the bar top and follow him to the dining table. Pulling out his chair for him, he takes the seat with a murmured thanks.

"Now don't forget, Keaton, that the north versus south volleyball game is this afternoon. I need you putting those police academy muscles to good use for our side. And don't worry about being professional. The game can get...heated."

Savannah snorts from the kitchen. "Last year, a fight nearly broke out, Dad."

"And rightly so. That Georgia aide was a horrible referee." The governor sets down his coffee and flicks open the newspaper. "What's on the agenda today, Miranda?"

Miranda discards her surgically altered pastry and slinks to his side, taking the seat I'd been standing over. She whips out her phone and scrolls through her calendar. "Unfortunately, you'll miss the volleyball game due to the meeting you have with Ohio's governor."

I back away, leaving the two to talk business. While Savannah lounges by the pool this morning, I'm entrusted to chauffeur the governor to and from the conference. And then it'll be time to showcase my athletic ability. I'm eager for a change of pace and to have some fun.

After all, beach volleyball with a bunch of aging politicians can't be too competitive, right?

CHAPTER EIGHT

Savannah

"Where did these come from?" The flip-flops dangle from my pointer finger. From the doorway, I raise my eyebrows at Jack, but his gaze stays stuck to his laptop. It gives me a precious moment to look him over. His hair is wet and the smell of his cologne wafts across the room. There's a wrinkle in his black tee, from his shoulder down to where the fabric ends just above his tattoo-covered bicep.

A tingle flicks across my chest as my eyes trail down to capable hands and the memory of his fingers pressing into my foot last night.

Yet he still doesn't look up. "Where did what come from?"

"*These!*"

A sigh escapes his parted lips, and he finally raises his eyes to meet mine, but not before his face turns beet red.

I frown and glance down at my bikini top and cutoffs. "I'm laying by the pool," I add unnecessarily. He certainly already knows my schedule for the day, considering he's paid to be my shadow most of the time.

Those honeyed eyes trail from my collarbone down to my naval and then snap back up. Now *I'm* the one blushing. I cross my arms over my chest but still manage to hold out the sandals. "Where did these come from?"

He shrugs and returns to his laptop, the clacking keys destroying my good mood one at a time. "Maybe your boyfriend dropped them off?"

I glare at him. "I don't have a boyfriend. And I highly doubt Brett, or Benji, or whatever his name is, knows where I live. Or cares to find my shoes for me," I mutter.

"I take it he hasn't called then?"

My cheeks now burn hot, and I shake my head. "He's probably scared my male nanny will threaten to beat him up again."

That observant gaze of his snaps up, locking me in place as we hold eye contact. "I'm not your manny, Savannah."

"Could've fooled me. And him, evidently." I drop the sandals— and my gaze— and slide my feet into them, the cut on my toe stinging as it scrapes against the cheap rubber material, making me wince.

"Do you need—"

"No." I hold up my hand. "I'm fine. I'll be here until you're ready to leave for the volleyball game." As I turn to leave, I catch myself. "And thank you for finding my shoes," I toss out as quietly as I slink from the room.

From the corner of my eye, I catch his small smile behind the glow of the laptop.

I think I like when he smiles.

"Come on, Smith. We just need a few more points to make a comeback." Jack's encouragement is irritatingly cute. And while the way he smacks his hands together—like a cheerleader on crack—is obnoxiously loud, I can't help but like the attention.

I focus a menacing glare across the net at a group of older politicians and their younger employees. Men and women who either appear to not have played any sport other than golf in the last decade or are sucking on asthma inhalers to combat the oppressive Florida humidity. And yet, somehow, they're up by two points. They wear matching red visors while our team wears blue armbands. I swipe my band across my forehead, soaking it through with my salty sweat.

My eyes stray to Jack's muscular bicep, which is directly in my line of vision. Maybe it's just the heat getting to me. But the way the sweat streaks down his arms also has me melting into the sand, drip by core-aching drip.

"C'mon, Sav, don't embarrass yourself," I mutter under my breath. Jack may be as strait-laced as they come, but he sure is attractive. So attractive that it's costing me my concentration. We can't lose to a bunch of geriatrics and asthmatics. I swallow around the thickness in my throat. My gaze strays to the sidelines, where the boy from last night watches with an older woman. Likely, his mother. She's wearing a red visor.

The enemy.

Bryan—or was it Barrett?—catches me staring and offers a subtle wave. If I'm not mistaken, Jack's shoulders tense slightly.

"I'm your personal bodyguard. Hired by your father."

But the way he caressed my foot last night. Almost opening up. Dropping the tough guy act.

The way his face heated at seeing me in a bikini this morning.

Forget volleyball. I've got a high-stakes game to play. And it involves giving my personal bodyguard a little taste of the green-eyed monster... So I smile and giggle, offering the guy a wink and a wave before returning my focus to the game.

"Oh my gosh," I hiss at Jack. He turns, giving me his full attention. "Did you see who came to watch?" I play up the affection I feel for the dude whose name I can't even remember.

Jack doesn't say anything. But I see something in his eyes before he sets his jaw and returns his gaze to the net.

Biting my lip, I suck in a deep breath, the thick air coating my throat and doing nothing to calm my nerves as I stand behind the serving line. I'm not a great volleyball player. Hell, I can hardly even serve over the net. But with Jack and everyone else watching, I need to *not* embarrass myself.

"Let's go already!" shouts a bald man on the opponent's side. His dome is starting to match the color of his visor. I squint in his direction, trying to place him from the introductions made earlier. I think he's the lieutenant governor of Oklahoma.

I suck my lips between my teeth and attempt a serve to their weak side. Directly at the red-skinned bald man. The ball slices through the air and barely makes it over the net. A younger woman tips it with her fingertips while her teammate comes up from behind and spikes it over to our side. Jack is there before I can blink, getting in a dig. A second teammate, this one from Pennsylvania, gets an off-speed hit that volleys back over the net. A red-visored enemy hits a cross-court shot, which Jack sets up for me to spike. My palm slaps against the ball. Across the net, it hits their sand—*yes!*—and, before I know what's come over me, I leap into my bodyguard's arms. My teammates' cheers ring in my ears as I wrap my arms around his neck.

For a brief moment, those ripped arms tighten around me as I drop my nose to his neck, hugging him close. Inhaling the lingering cologne mixed with the scent of sunscreen.

He stiffens slightly, his muscles flexing against my body as his hands fall to my lower back, just inches away from my butt.

"Savannah, I shouldn't—"

"Oh, lighten up, will you?" I laugh in jest as his jaw tics. The artery in his neck beats to the cadence of my heart.

Feeling every single muscle of his chest against my own, I slide down his sweat-drenched body, my gaze hooked to those hazel eyes, his hands bracketing my hips, feeling elated and so—

"*Out!*" the referee calls, his whistle blowing through the cacophony.

"What?" Jack's tanned face turns a nuclear shade of crimson as he releases me.

"That was a perfect line shot, and it was *in*," I add, pointing at the spot in the sand, a noticeable round hole marking the ball's landing.

The red team begins to celebrate, high-fiving all around and already discussing where they're getting drinks once they've clinched the game.

I turn to my bodyguard. "Jack, I—"

"I got you, Savannah," he says as he trudges over to the ref. The two look serious, but it's Jack I'm focused on. He's pointing. Shaking his head. Narrowing his eyes and crossing his arms over his chest.

He's got me.

I roll my lips to suppress a smile and step back to the corner spot to prepare for their serve. Jack stalks back to the position in front of me, his face still a cloud of anger. "Blind-ass ref," he murmurs under his breath. But loud enough for me to hear.

"I thought I had it," I mumble as my eyes meet his, then fall to the tops of my bare feet. They have turned an unhealthy shade of pink, and I surely need to reapply sunscreen before I'm burnt to a crisp.

Jack's toes appear beside mine, and I glance up, the sun stabbing me right in the eyes as I attempt to assess his expression.

"Listen," he says, turning me away from the sun. "That point was ours."

I nod and glance at my foot again, the skin starting to sizzle.

Jack's eyes follow my line of vision. "When was the last time you applied sunscreen, Savannah?"

The ref's whistle trills. "Let's hurry it up, folks!" Jack ignores the warning and pulls a tube of sunscreen from his swim shorts.

"Forget him. He probably can't even see us. Here, put this on before you're completely burnt." He hands me the tube, and I squeeze out a glob. I rub it between my hands and bend, slathering it on the tops of my feet, my kneecaps, and my shoulders. Then I slick the last bit onto my cheeks, rubbing my face to ensure it's properly soaked in and there are no white smears.

Except now my hands are all slimy from the lotion. Like I need another reason to suck at this game. I hold them away from my body just as Jack grabs my wrists.

"What are you—" But he's already pulling my hands into his shirt and wiping off my palms. My brain short circuits as my fingertips graze his bare torso. It's like touching a wall, but softer, which makes absolutely no sense. His own hands are strong, swiping the sunscreen from in between my digits and then letting me go much too soon.

"Wait, you've got a little..." He wipes under my eye. The pad of his thumb drags along my skin gently.

Before I can register what's happened, he's jogging back to his position. And I'm a puddle of desire in the sand.

"C'mon, blue team!" He claps way too boisterously as he attempts to rally our troops and I have to roll my eyes, even if I find myself smiling. "Let's hit 'em where it hurts!"

I'm mentally preparing for the game-winning point to come to our side. I try to keep my gaze trained on the net, but having Jack in my sights isn't helping. I can't stop my gaze from straying to his calves. How he spreads his legs and dips his hips lower to get into position.

The bald red visor steps up to the serving line and, with a force that no man as old as he should possess, launches a rocket right in my direction. I hardly have time to react before I swing my arms in an attempt to hit it. Sadly, I misjudge, and the ball slams me in the face. I fall to the sand with a thud.

"Ace, ace, in your face!" one of the asthmatics from the red team cheers.

"Jesus, Savannah, are you okay?" Jack hoists me to my feet and pulls my hand away from my cheek. "Does it hurt?"

"I-I'm fine," I mumble as embarrassment flushes my body from my sizzled feet to my hot scalp.

"Did the sun get in your eyes?" His fingers dance around the injury as his palm cups my opposite cheek. His face is so close I could...

I gulp. "Something like that."

He takes my hand and pulls me along to the lineup, where we shake hands with the other team. "Good thing you're pretty, darlin'," the bald man says as he shakes my hand.

"Bless your little heart for trying so hard," another southerner drawls.

Once we've made it down the line, Jack guides me away from the crowd. "C'mon, let's get some ice for that cheek."

I wish the ball had just knocked me out cold.

CHAPTER NINE

Savannah

I skid to a stop just outside my room, my sand-covered and sunburnt hand on the doorknob, as my dad's voice reaches me from farther down the hallway.

"Savannah, what are you wearing?"

I roll my eyes. Turning slowly, I compose my features into a beatific smile. I'm still waiting for the 'we'll talk later' discussion and hope this isn't it. "Dad, I'm wearing a bikini. It's not too revealing. I'm eighteen. I can choose my own—"

"Why are you wearing a bathing suit when we've got dinner reservations in twenty minutes?"

"What are you talking about? The volleyball game just ended."

"Savannah." My father adopts *the tone* with me. That tone that an adult only takes with babies or the feeble-minded. I hate that tone. "Miranda shared a very detailed schedule with you. This dinner is one of the few we can have together."

I grit my teeth, but don't have the heart to tell my dad that his incompetent assistant most certainly did *not* share a detailed schedule with me. She's probably growing forgetful from lack of proper sustenance. A life without chocolate chips and carbs will do that to a person. "Of course." I flutter my lashes and shrug stupidly. "I must have forgotten. Silly me. I'll go shower."

He checks his watch and taps his foot. "Make it quick. We don't want to lose our table."

I plaster a smile back on my face and, jaw clenched, practically yank the doorknob from the door. But even as I take the quickest shower known to man—forget exfoliating and shaving—I still stumble from the bedroom sporting the Florida frizz. No way was I blow-drying *and* straightening my long hair *and* keeping the reservation.

As I wrestle to zip up the back of my spaghetti strap dress, sweat beads across my hairline and runs down my temples. I crane my arm as far as possible behind and up my back, but the zipper stays put. Reaching over my shoulder and grasping at air, I eventually give up. I'm sweating, stuffed into a tight black dress that won't zip properly, and my hair is all over the place. I swipe on a coat of mascara—as though that will cure my ailments—and, grabbing my tallest wedges, swing open the door and run right into a wall of muscle.

Jack.

His mouth actually falls open at the sight of me.

I must look worse than I thought.

"*Ineedyoutozipmeup!*" I spew all at once, coiling my rat's nest hair around my hand and holding it out of the way as I expose my naked back to him.

I wait.

And wait.

And wait some more.

"Jack?" I turn slightly, catching his eye. Is he mad because I cost us the volleyball game? He's biting his bottom lip, but as he hears his name, he snaps into action and pulls the zipper up. "Can you hook it, too?" I ask.

As he leans in, his breath tickles the top of my shoulder. Goosebumps break out along my collarbone, circling around the back of my neck. His fingers brush along the sensitive skin just beneath my shoulder blades as he pulls the tiny clasps together. He fumbles with the fabric, his breaths coming in puffs as he tries and fails a few times. Finally, the mechanism slides into place.

"There," he whispers against my nape. My lips part on an inhale.

"Finally!" My dad's footsteps echo behind us as he traipses down the hallway. I jump away from Jack just as he releases my dress from his hands, but I still manage to notice the way his eyes look everywhere but at me.

If I wasn't burning up before, I certainly am now.

"Ready?" my dad asks, his face turning from mine to Jack's.

"He's coming? I thought it was going to be just us." I ask, my voice rising an octave.

My dad chortles. "It is just us. Just *us*," he indicates, waving his hand between the three of us. "Miranda has the evening off. Some kind of Zumba-yoga thing." He shrugs.

Jack's jaw clenches as he nods to the door. "Shall we go?"

With a halo of frizz and a sheen of sweat dripping between my boobs, I follow my father through the door, as though I have a choice.

"I'll take the filet, medium rare, and a side of the garlic smashed potatoes with butter and sour cream on the side." My father snaps the menu closed and passes it to the waitress as a smile lifts his lips. He turns his attention to the table. "I've been waiting for a steak from here for a year!"

"I can't wait to try it," Jack replies. He lifts his glass of wine to his lips and takes a sip, his facial features pinching.

"Is there something wrong with the wine?" Dad takes a pull from his own glass and rolls his jaw as he savors the vintage. His eyebrows crinkle. "It seems fine to me."

"I'm not well-versed in wine, sir. I suppose it's my unrefined palate. I'm more of a beer and whiskey man myself."

"Ah," my father sighs. "Well, there's hope for you yet. You're still young enough to figure out how to enjoy the finer things in life. Stick with me; I'll convert you!" He releases an uproarious laugh. When my father used to work as a foreman for the energy company, he'd come home after a long day and kick back in his La-Z-Boy recliner with a Budweiser and a TV dinner from the microwave. Now, in his suit jacket that probably cost more than the mortgage of my childhood home, he orders fancy grape juice from the restaurant's sommelier and pretends to know the top notes of berries, barley-sugar, and bullshit.

I sip my water and keep my eyes trained on the place setting in front of me. I'm afraid if I look up, I'll catch Jack's eyes and feel his soft touch on my skin as he zipped up my dress. His breath tickling the small hairs that escaped from my hands. I'm mortified that I look like a troll in a tight dress.

"Savannah? Are you feeling all right? You look flushed, dear."

"Probably got too much sun today," I mumble unconvincingly.

"That's right!" he responds as he brings his glass to his lips. Taking a dainty sip, he sets it back down. "How was the game? Did we beat the south again?" It's been a running joke for years that the blue north team consistently beats the red southerners every year.

Except this year. All because of me.

"Well—" I start, but Jack interrupts before I can continue.

"The damn ref was blind as a bat. Savannah had a perfect line shot, but the fool called it out when it was clearly in."

My father reaches across the table and places his hand on mine. "Ah, there's always next year!"

I pull away and grab a roll from the basket the waitress sets down. "Thank you." I'm grateful for something to do with my fingers as I pull apart the roll and pinch off tiny pieces. "Yeah. Next year." I flick my gaze to Jack and find his eyes already on me, his thumb running along his bottom lip. Saliva floods my mouth, and the small piece of bread instantly melts. Swallowing heavily, I drop my hands to the napkin I'd placed in my lap. My fingers dig into the fabric as I twist and press it into my thighs beneath the table. As I cross my legs, the heat in my body somehow spreads deeper.

My father's phone rings loudly, startling me from the intensity surging in my gut. "Oh, I need to take this. Excuse me." Tapping the screen, he holds the device to his ear as he stands. I watch his retreating form as he strides purposefully from the dining area and out into the lobby.

Damn it.

My face flames as I return my gaze to the table. To Jack. He's no longer rubbing his thumb across his lip, but is now leaning back in his seat. Arms crossed. Watching me.

"What?" I blink.

"Your cheek. It looks better. Does it still hurt?"

My fingers itch to palm the subtle bruise I'd considered covering up. "No. It's fine. Just wish we could've won." I shrug.

"You played really well."

"Thanks," I reply, glancing around at the patrons in the restaurant. Focusing my sole attention on Jack is just too much. "I wish there were more chances to let loose like that. Have some fun."

"So do I." He offers me a small smile.

And I wonder if he's thinking of the way he held me in his arms. The way his eyes creased when he smiled up at me before he tensed and shut down. The way my body felt against his in the Florida heat.

Because, when I look at him across from me, it's all I can think of.

CHAPTER TEN

Jack

She'syourboss'sdaughtershe'syourboss'sdaughtershe'syourboss'sdaughter.

I have to repeat that to myself as my mind returns to Savannah throwing herself into my arms during the volleyball game. The way her smile lit up her entire face, transforming her from the sullen protectee to the fun-loving woman I was eager to spend more time with and get to know.

I look to the entrance of the restaurant, willing Paul to return and either save me from this awkwardness or put me out of my misery.

"He's not coming back."

"What?" I snap to her.

"This happens all the time. I'm surprised you haven't noticed." Her face falls.

I haven't noticed how long he's been gone because I've been too distracted. Even though Paul isn't my main priority to look after, as a professional—a police officer capable of assessing situations involving multiple protectees—I should be observant and aware at all times. "Stay here, Savannah." I stand with as much gallantry as I can muster with a semi-hard on in my pants. I was supposed to be watching the governor and his daughter, not ogling her. Jesus fuck, what an inappropriate, amateur mistake.

I hurry to the lobby. There are groups of families waiting, milling around and chatting.

But no Paul.

Sweeping my hands through my hair, I yank open the door to the sidewalk. A few bystanders hang around smoking. I pause, wishing I had a cigarette right now to calm my nerves.

But no Paul.

"Shit," I growl under my breath as I reenter the restaurant. I stalk past the hostess, sneak a quick peek that Savannah is still at our table, and make my way to the men's room. Shoving open the door, I quickly scan the open stall and empty urinals.

Still no Paul.

Even as my mind is going to the worst-case scenarios, my body guides me out of the restroom and through the bar.

There.

I audibly sigh as I spot the governor with a female companion. She has her hand resting on his arm and is leaning in, listening intently as he appears to wax like a king among his consorts.

Spotting me, he waves me over. "Keaton, meet Laurel Prescott. She's one of the commissioners from the energy panel and is our neighbor for the next two weeks. She's staying just a few houses down from ours." He turns to the woman at his side. "I poached Officer Keaton from the East Lansing Police Department. He's keeping an eye on my daughter for the most part, but I believe he'll have more duties before long." Paul winks at me.

"Nice to meet you," I mumble as my heart rate finally slows. "I'll just let Savannah know you'll be another minute."

"Savannah is my daughter," Paul adds as Laurel's eyebrow cocks slightly. "She'll be attending university here."

"How lovely. My son is with me as well. He's twenty-two. Perhaps we should introduce the pair of them. See if they hit it off." She chuckles, and I blanch. Twenty-two is much too old for Savannah.

Except *I'm* twenty-seven and can't stop thinking about her in that tight black dress.

"I'll meet you back at the table, sir." I smile flatly. "Pleasure to meet you, ma'am."

The thought of introducing Savannah to some politician's son sends a sour taste up my throat. I hurry back to the table and the glass of wine I'd hardly touched. Maybe I can get the waitress to bring me a beer. Or a shot of something stronger.

"There you are!" Savannah's cheery voice greets me as I approach, but it's not until I tear my eyes away from hers that I see who's taken a seat at our table. The douche from last night.

Brett.

Or Benji.

Or whatever the hell his name is.

"You seem tense, Keaton. Did dinner not suit you?"

My grip tightens on the steering wheel and my foot hovers over the brake as I navigate through the traffic. There're so many damn people out that I'll be lucky to make it back to the house without hitting someone.

"Jack?" My boss's voice breaks through my thoughts, and I slide my eyes over to him. He's scrolling through his phone, glasses down to nearly his nostrils.

"What? No, dinner was fine, sir."

Paul tucks his phone away in his suit coat pocket and turns to me. "Then what, exactly, is the problem? And more importantly, should I be concerned?"

My lips thin as I fight to control the anger simmering just beneath the surface of my skin. How can I confess to my employer that I'm worried sick about his daughter? His eighteen-year-old daughter. I have no place thinking of her outside of work, let alone picturing myself *un*zipping her little black dress.

"Nothing to worry about. Just a little indigestion." I rub my sternum for good measure and blow a breath out to add to the ploy.

"Ah, that happens more frequently with age, I'm afraid. There'll be Tums in the first aid kit at the house." He returns to his phone without even realizing he's crushed me even more.

With age.

Because that's what I am. I'm of an age where men get heartburn and need special medication. I'm not the young *Brett* who whisked Savannah from the restaurant with the promise of dancing and a night of college-aged debauchery.

A growl escapes my lips just as I slam on the brakes, nearly mowing down a family with two lanky teenagers glued to their phones.

"Whoa! Do I need to drive or what?" Paul's dark eyebrows lower as he grips the *Ohshit!* handle.

I press as hard as I can onto the brake pedal as I lean back and rub my forehead. "Sorry, sir." The family moves out of the intersection, and I ease off the brake and tap the gas.

But I still can't focus, and as my mind returns to dinner, I wonder if the Tums will be enough.

"What's he doing here?" I practically snarled, reclaiming my seat and immediately motioning for the waitress. "Whiskey, please," I ordered as soon as she was within earshot.

"Brett's staying with his mom at a property just near ours and—"

"Is your mother named Laurel?" I asked, interrupting Savannah. She frowned, her bottom lip pursing so seductively that I suddenly had the urge to suck it.

"Yes," Brett answered warily. "Laurel Prescott. She's around here somewhere." He scanned the room, probably remembering how I was ready to knock him out last night. I'd want some potential backup or a quick escape route too, if I were him.

"Just perfect," I muttered as my drink arrived. I took a healthy slug and sat up straighter as the liquid courage coursed through my blood. "How convenient for everyone."

Savannah's face tightened as her lips thinned. "What's that supposed to mean?"

"And what do you do, Mr...?" Brett leaned forward, his shrewd eyes and fake blue blood smile the perfect picture of southern hospitality.

"Keaton," I added without extending my hand across the table. I wasn't from the south, and even if I was, I still wouldn't shake this cocky asshole's hand.

"Jack is the family's bodyguard," Savannah answered as she glanced at me, a challenge flickering in her eyes.

"*Your* bodyguard," I clarified as my gaze settled on hers.

"Why does your family need a bodyguard?"

Jesus, did this kid really have no manners at all? *None of your fucking business*, I wanted to reply. But before I could explain—perhaps in a way that wouldn't get me fired—Paul and Laurel approached the table, dual smiles of encouragement beaming at their progeny.

"Brett, I'd like you to meet Governor Smith of Michigan. Paul, this is Brett, my son I was telling you about." Laurel gestured between the two men, and Brett rose to shake my boss's hand.

"Nice to meet you, sir. Thank you for returning my mother to me. I was beginning to worry." Everyone at the table chuckled—*har har har*—except for me. I didn't trust this little fucker. I especially didn't trust the way his hand lingered along the back of Savannah's chair, mere inches from her bare shoulders.

"Laurel, this is my daughter, Savannah. She'll be attending ECU this fall with a major in political science and international relations." Savannah's skin turned a pretty pink hue as she shook hands with Brett's mother.

"You know, Paul, we shouldn't keep these two kids cooped up with us old folks on a beautiful night." She turned to her son and Savannah. "Why don't you two go enjoy yourselves?"

"I'd love to," Savannah chirped as her face lit up. She looked at her father through thick lashes. "Could I, Dad? Without...?" With raised eyebrows, she tipped her head in my direction.

"Savannah hasn't eaten," I inserted, my gaze trained on her. All eyes turned to me as though I'd just let out a wet belch.

You're not getting away from me so easily, I wanted to say.

But Brett, that smug fucker, looked me straight in the eye as he said, "Don't worry. I'll take care of her." Then his hand descended from the chair and trailed down her bare arm. I watched that hand, wanting nothing more than to reach across and snap it right off at the wrist, as it took Savannah's and pulled her to her feet.

"You kids have fun!"

I gaped at the governor. Then, before I could utter another word, they were walking away. Out of the restaurant.

His hand dipped dangerously low on the small of her back.

"Don't forget to take those Tums, Jack, or you'll be hurting tonight." I'm pulled from my reverie and look around, startled to find that we are already in the driveway. Parked. Paul exits the SUV and saunters through the garage and into the house.

And what do I do? My fingers thrum against the steering wheel. My breathing becoming more and more shallow. Imagining that asshole's hand sliding to the small of Savannah's back. And inching even lower.

Fuck the Tums.

I'm going to find Savannah.

CHAPTER ELEVEN

Savannah

"So, are you hungry?" I immediately regret leaving the restaurant. I was really looking forward to that filet I'd ordered. A juicy steak covered in butter, salt and pepper, with a side of pomme frites? I'm practically salivating on the sidewalk. Hell, I didn't even fill up on bread.

"Not really. My mom and I had just finished eating when she saw your father at the bar. Why, are you?"

I'm too embarrassed to admit my stomach is about to cave in on itself, so instead I shake my head and look down demurely. After all, isn't this how one goes about getting an older guy interested? Being carefree, agreeable, and, apparently, hungry?

We walk another block in silence. Or, rather, I'm silent while Brett tells me all about his fraternity and the parties he can't wait to get back to once the semester begins. "You'll have to come by sometime. And bring your roommate."

I feign a jolly smile and nod stupidly. What else am I supposed to say? *My best friend would likely hate you because she despises the frat bro vibe and, in her opinion, you are clearly the epitome of everything wrong with Greek life?*

"So how long have your parents been divorced?"

The question catches me off guard, and I nearly stumble. "Oh, my parents weren't divorced. My mom died when I was little." Sometimes I forget that people outside of Michigan don't know about my family. That my father is some bachelor governor who attracts the adoration of women.

Brett pales. "Oh, fuck, Savannah. I'm so sorry."

"Thanks." I shrug, like I always do, but don't offer any additional details.

"I just figured your parents were divorced like mine." He runs his fingers through his hair and shakes his head again, as though doing so will clear the air. It doesn't.

"Nope." My feet are starting to ache. These shoes weren't meant for hiking down the boulevard. "So where are we going?" I'm more than ready to change the subject. And get something in my stomach.

"I thought we'd stop at this little hole-in-the-wall place with great music. Does that sound okay?"

"Sure! I love live music!" I perk up, if only for the opportunity to add to my growing list of singer-songwriters to follow on Spotify.

After all, music is a hidden passion of mine.

"Yeah, the DJ is really good. He spins at a lot of parties on campus."

My face falls, but I manage to recover as I swallow and murmur "cool." I blow out a puff of air and wish I'd stayed back in the restaurant. Let's be honest, I'd be elbow deep in a juicy cut of meat and have better eye candy than the current company.

As I slyly glance at Brett, I can't help but compare him to Jack. Whereas Jack's thick brown hair curls at the nape when it gets a little too long, Brett's hair is shaggy. Unkempt. I wonder when he brushed it last. I purse my lips and look at his clothing. He's wearing a fitted polo that hugs his biceps and shows off his muscular pectorals, paired with a pair of pressed Dockers and boat shoes.

Not bad.

But I can't stop myself as I envision Jack's crisp black dress shirt tucked into slate gray slacks. At dinner, he'd rolled up the shirtsleeves, showing off his tattooed forearms. I'd been taken aback by the designs delicately decorating the tendons. I'd wanted to ask him about the ink, but then he'd stalked off unexpectedly. My core throbs just thinking about what those tatted forearms could do.

My gaze slides to Brett's forearms. Blond-haired and freckled from lack of sunscreen.

"Here we are— Is everything okay?"

Ripping my eyes from his weak spindles, I lift my lips into a smile as I take in the "hole-in-the-wall." I gape like a fish as the bass thrums through the doors. Lights flash and, if possible, it's darker inside than out here on the sidewalk.

A rave.

This frat bro has brought me to an actual rave.

"Oh, it's bigger than I imagined and so... loud."

"I know, right? Come on!" He grabs my hand and pulls me into the darkness.

Looks like my Spotify playlist will be as empty as my stomach.

This music isn't so bad, I think as I ignore Brett's roaming hands. If I close my eyes, I can picture he's someone else. Someone with wide shoulders and hazel eyes. Someone I want but can't have. With my nearly empty drink in hand, I writhe against him as he runs his palms down my back and cups my rear. He pulls me closer, our lips nearly touching, but I bring my drink to my mouth and take a deep sip from the plastic straw. I'm not drunk, but I'm definitely not sober.

It makes what I'm doing so much easier.

Letting someone I hardly know grip my ass cheeks and pull me against his hard-on while his gaze stays trained to my chest.

In the end, we'll both get what we want, and I'll finally be able to move on from this little crush on Jack.

It's exactly what I need to do. Besides, nobody wants to go to college a virgin.

"Want another drink?" Brett interrupts the thumping bass as he leans in and yells in my ear. I open my eyes for the first time in what feels like minutes, the flashing strobe lights jarring. Bringing me back to the here and now.

"Sure!" I yell with gusto. I hand over my empty glass and he retreats into the crowd surrounding the bar. A new song comes on, this one with a familiar beat and popular lyrics. I sway unsteadily on my wedges and make eye contact with a group of girls next to me. We sing aloud to one another, pumping our hands into the air.

"I love your dress!" one of them shouts over the music.

"Thanks!" I move closer and we link fingers. We shake our hips and shimmy our chests, laughing as the music moves through us. I spin around and dip it low as the girl wraps her arms around my waist.

"That your boyfriend?" She points to Brett, who is practically frolicking toward us as he thrusts his hips, two drinks raised high to avoid spilling.

"Nope, just a friend."

"Oh, he's cute. Looks rich, too."

I snort and shake my head. When did money become a reason to be with someone? I'd much prefer a down-to-earth blue-collar worker if it meant I was happy and in love.

Like my parents were before my mom died. My dad was just the foreman at the electric company and my mom sold insurance.

Accepting my drink from Brett, I give him a grateful smile. Rather than move away from my new friend, I invite him into our private dance party. He moves in between us and, facing me, waggles his eyebrows as the other girl drags her long, pointed nails down his thighs.

I simply take another deep pull from my drink. This one must be stronger, as I can immediately taste the alcohol as it hits my throat. "Whoa! The bartender made this one *strong*!"

Brett simply shrugs and gulps from his own glass. "Drink up."

I do as he commands, taking lengthy slugs and bouncing to the beat and, before the new song ends, my drink is completely gone. I pout as the room tilts. "All gone," I hiccup as I shove the empty glass into his chest. Except the man in front of me isn't Brett. And the girl I'm dancing with is someone I don't recognize. "Where's Brett?"

The girl blinks. "Who's Brett?"

I stop dancing and stand in the middle of the floor, looking around for him and the girl we were just with. But he's gone, and so is she.

Digging into my purse, I search for my phone, and realize it's not there. I must've left it on the table at dinner.

Fuck.

I stand there like an idiot, all alone, as the music floods my senses and the room spins. Then I spot *him*.

No, not Brett.

It's the dark-eyed god from my dream.

Jack.

He's striding toward me. His forearms flexing as one fist clenches. The other holds my phone.

I smile broadly. He brought me my phone.

I blink once and suck in another breath as the room wobbles beneath my feet.

And before I know it, those strong tattooed arms are around me. His lips growling in my ear.

"*Savannah.*"

CHAPTER TWELVE

Jack

She falls into me like a rag doll. My arms instinctively wrap around her and pull her to my chest. Hold her upright.

"Jack," she breathes out. Her breath is fruity, like she's sucked on a strawberry. Or imbibed an adequate amount of alcohol. "Dance with me!"

I'd only meant to find her. To bring her home. But as she stands there with those eyes... those chocolate brown eyes that appear even alluring in the club... I can't help myself.

I give in. "One song."

Her smile practically knocks me to my knees. *Get ahold of yourself,* I curse inwardly.

The heavy bass thumps through my bones, Savannah twirling around and swiveling her pelvis to the beat.

As she raises her arms overhead, I grab her wrist and twist her against me. I pull her close, pressing my mouth to her ear. "This isn't appropriate, Savannah. I'm—"

"Not allowed to have any fun?" An intoxicating smirk stretches her lips as she raises an eyebrow. Challenging me—again. She leans in, raising onto her toes to reach my ear. "It's just dancing." Her breath tickles the sensitive skin there, and I rear back as though burned.

I move closer again, my lips nearly brushing the skin of her throat. "You've been drinking."

"I'm days away from college," she says as her chest molds to mine. "I've got to learn how to drink..."

My mind goes elsewhere as I imagine what college will be like. This beautiful girl finally having a taste of freedom. Me watching from the shadows as she gets hit on. Flirts. Dates.

Fucks.

I don't like where my head is going. I don't like the feeling in my chest, like my heart is going a mile a minute and I'm helpless to stop it.

So my arms find her waist as I sink my face into her neck. Taking all of her scent, I run my nose along the column of her throat, and she shivers when I reach the tender spot under her ear. "It's time to go, Savannah." Enough is enough.

"Where?" Those dark eyes watch me. Wait for me to make the first move.

But I can't.

"Let's get out of here."

She nods and then leans in again. "I want to go to the beach."

I'd take her anywhere, but I've got to get out of this club. Being this close to her, having to touch her each time we talk... I can't handle it.

"Okay. Beach," I agree.

Savannah stays silent after we settle on the sand. Curling in on herself, she draws her knees into her chest and stares out into the darkness of the ocean. I bite my lip in contemplation as she shivers and shakes, whether from the effects of the alcohol or the chill in the evening air, I'm not sure. I don't want to leave her and go fetch a blanket from the car, but I don't want her to be cold either. So I quickly unbutton the dark collared shirt I'm wearing and drape it over her shoulders.

"You're cold," I clarify when she stares at me with parted lips.

We return to watching the waves roll in. I don't mind the silence. It lets me collect my thoughts and sort them into orderly folders where they're safely stored from the overthinking and analyzing that I'm wont to do.

"Brett ditched me," she finally says.

I figured as much. I swallow thickly and fight the urge to explain how men his age work. How all they want is sex without feelings. It's not what she would want to hear, though, so instead I come up with something trite. "His loss."

With a snort, she finally uncurls. She stretches her long legs in front of her, but keeps her arms wrapped around herself. In my shirt.

In *my* shirt.

"It really isn't."

"Huh?" Because I actually don't understand. My forehead crinkles.

"It's not his loss." She turns to look at me and then, just as quickly, returns her face to the ocean. "It's mine."

I brace myself as I turn my entire body to hers. "You *like* him." I can't help the way judgement seeps into my statement. The way my lip curls in disgust. Not at her— No, never at her. But at him. That he has something she wants. That she *needs*.

"Of course I don't *like* him. But that doesn't mean—" She stops herself, lips clamping shut with an audible *click* as her teeth lock.

My own jaw hardens. What is she hiding? What isn't she telling me? And why do I even care? My eyes trace every curve of her face. From her forehead down to her slightly upturned nose. Over her full lips and across her apple cheeks. She's beautiful. So why on earth does she want some bozo like Brett?

"I love the beach," she finally says, changing the subject after minutes of quiet. "It's the one place I feel like I can breathe." I watch her from the corner of my eye, careful not to stare too hard, else she clam up again.

"Ever since my dad became governor, Michigan just feels stifling. Even in the winter."

I slide my eyes over to her fully. Hers are already scanning me, waiting for me to give her even the tiniest bit of friendship. So I offer what I can without overstepping any boundaries. "I much prefer the cold. The crisp air in Michigan. The way the leaves turn red and yellow and it's chilly in the morning, but warm enough for just a t-shirt by afternoon... It reminds me of playing football on Friday nights and—"

My words die, heart stuttering, as she leans forward, but I stop her with my hand on her shoulder before she gets too close. Even so, she's only inches away.

Her breath still smells fruity, likely from the alcohol that she was served illegally. I'm sure those drinks are the sole reason for her trying to make a move again. Maybe she needs to be reminded of my place... Maybe *I* need to be reminded, too.

Pulling away, I sever the contact between us with a razor blade. "Savannah, we can't." I hold my hand between us. I need something—anything—in between us. To cut the cord that's seemingly pulling me toward her beyond my rational.

Her eyes fill, but she sniffs, turning from me to hide any tears that might have slipped down her cheeks.

"It's just—" I start, wanting to comfort her. To explain. How much I need this job. How much I value my morals and the ethics that make me *good* at it.

"I get it," she says on a dejected sigh, as she stands abruptly, brushing the sand from beneath her thighs. Then she adjusts the hem of her dress that's too near to the curve of her rear end, and I nearly choke on my breath as I imagine running my hand up that thigh.

You're jealous, the voice inside me taunts. *Because Brett can* easily *have what you can't.*

The realization barrels into me like a tsunami, the pressure building in my chest now overwhelming. I need to get out of here and put some distance between us so that I can think straight.

Get my mind right.

"We should get back," I bark at her in an attempt to return to the bodyguard and protectee relationship.

And with her eyes downcast, she simply nods.

And then follows me to the SUV.

CHAPTER THIRTEEN

Savannah

"So you have no idea where he went?" Delia huffs through the phone.

"Nope. Not a clue. And we never exchanged numbers." The morning light streams through my window, and I get up from the bed to close the blinds before flopping back onto the mattress.

"What did you do? Stop it, Frank! You little shit..." The FaceTime video skews sideways, and I spy the victim of my friend's verbal abuse. A massive Labrador puppy has wrapped himself around a mailbox post and is attempting to jump free, but is choking himself in the process.

I wait until my friend's face is back in view. "Seems like the dog-walking hustle is going well."

"Yeah, right. This asshole can't walk in a straight line and won't stop sniffing my crotch. But for thirty bucks a walk, I guess I can suck it up. Only a few more days."

I swallow my chuckle and bite my lip.

"So you never told me what you did after Frat Bro ditched you. Indulge in a carton of ice cream?"

I roll onto my stomach as my mind drifts to Jack and last night. The way his breath tickled along my neck each time he leaned in to talk.

The way he finally opened up about *something* on the beach.

That small glimmer of hope ignites in my belly.

"Actually, I wasn't alone for long." Heat spreads to my core as I visualize the way Jack held me at arm's length. The forbidden aspect of this relationship has me aching for more. "Ja-Jack showed up."

"What?" Delia's squeal startles her companion and he barks loudly. "Shut up, Frank!"

I close my eyes as I feel myself blushing. I'm afraid Delia will see my pink cheeks through the phone, so I bury my face in the pillow.

"Don't you try to hide from me, Sav! Spill. Now." She sits down on a park bench and Frank climbs into her lap. His face takes up the entire screen. "Move, dog!" She pushes his snout out of the way and cocks an eyebrow at me. "Spill the tea, Sav."

"There isn't much to say," I admit honestly. "He was just...there."

Delia narrows her eyes at me. "What do you mean? Did he follow you?"

"I don't know. But I'm glad he was there. I felt safe. It felt right."

"What do you mean *it*? You didn't—"

"No!" I interrupt, shaking my head. "He brought me my phone. We danced."

"You danced." Her voice goes flat. "That's it?"

"Well, no, not exactly." I pause and fling my arm over my face. How can I explain the heat, the desire, the flame that was burning inside me, begging to be released, at Jack's nearness. "We went to the beach—"

"What?"

"I kind of tried to kiss him..." I exhale as the flood of shame washes over me. "He didn't want me." I threw myself at him, and he still didn't want me. He was talking about his weather preference, and I was ready to kiss him, for God's sake.

"Oh, babe. I mean, put yourself in his position. He's employed by an elected official. He could be martyred if something happened and the media found out."

"I guess you're right," I say dully. But that doesn't stop me from wanting him. It just makes me think of a million ways to keep it hidden.

"That's it."

Except it isn't. My mind trails off to returning home. My bodyguard, the man promised to protect me, walking me to my bedroom door.

"Goodnight, Savannah." Jack's throat bobbed and he blinked once. Twice.

"G-Goodnight." My breath hitched as I momentarily forgot to breathe.

And as I closed my door last night and undressed, I ran my hands over my body, imagining it was Jack's hands touching me again.

"I've got to go, Del." I don't even bother waiting for her to reply. I simply click the red button to end the call as my thighs quake beneath the sheets. Tossing the phone off the bed, I reach beneath the covers and find myself already slick and wet.

I part the skin and sink my fingers into my heat as I recall Jack's breath tickling my neck. The way his hand gripped my arm as he pulled me close.

"Savannah."

"We can't."

I roll over, pushing my hips into my hand and grinding against the mattress. As I replay the night, I pretend it went differently. *His hands caressing my curves as we danced. The silkiness of his hair as I run my fingers through it. His nose pressing into the sensitive part of my neck as he inhales, breathing me in completely. The feel of him hard against my hip.*

My nipples pebble, and I ride my hand harder. Pressing my palm into the sensitive nerves at the apex of my thighs, I unravel. Writhing against myself the same way I wished I'd writhed against Jack last night. Wild and unbidden. Chasing the pleasure to its peak and coming down slowly, chest heaving.

With release comes clarity, and as my breathing slows, I know exactly what I want.

I want Jack Keaton, my bodyguard.

Cameras flash, blinding me, as the photographers yell my name.

"Savannah!"

"Savannah, is it true you're the reason your father lost the election?"

"Savannah, why did you fail out of your psychology course?"

"Savannah, what made you decide to wear this dress?"

"Savannah, did you look in the mirror before you left the house?"

I'm back in grade school and a group of students—mostly girls—gathers around Ella Markham's desk. They cackle as she points to something, and then all eyes turn to me.

"Girls, put that away and return to your seats!" Our teacher, Mrs. Link-lighter, stalks to the front of the room. But it doesn't stop one of Ella's minions from strutting past my desk and dropping the offending item right on the surface.

My face reddens as I look at the headline. It's a picture of me stuffing my face with ice cream at an event for my father.

Governor's Tot Enjoys Tubs of Fun at Ice Cream Gala

At recess, Ella and her friends surround me, taunting and poking fun.

"Tubby tot just means fat ass, you know?" the ringleader spews in my face.

"Fat ass and frizzy hair. Not even being the governor's daughter can fix ugly!"

I charge at the tow-headed Ella, swinging my fists and pummeling her face.

In my father's home office, he's packing away his books and awards, his expression crestfallen.

"We've got to move out of the governor's mansion, Savannah. All because you couldn't hold your temper and be the good little girl anymore."

I gasp and open my eyes to find Jack standing over me, his features etched with concern.

"Are you all right? You were having a bad dream."

I blink into the darkness and sit up. As I do, the bedsheet falls, exposing my chest covered only by a thin tank top. Jack inhales sharply and steps away from the bed. Putting distance between us once more.

Delia's words echo from earlier. *"If someone found out…"*

I need to make Jack understand that I wouldn't tell anyone.

His jaw clenches as he slowly moves his hand. My skin prickles in anticipation of his touch. But instead, he only points.

"Your top…"

"Oh, right." I drive my chin to my shoulder as I adjust the tank top strap.

"Well, if everything is okay, I'll—" His feet shuffle against the carpet.

"Bad dream," I mutter, catching his eyes in the dark. I scoot over, hoping he'll sit. But he doesn't.

"What was it about?" His question is so soft. Like a whisper.

Maybe if I tell him, he'll stay. Get closer.

"Just a dream about a girl from school."

He doesn't say anything, but I catch the way his mouth snaps shut. The way his jaw works as he swallows. "D-do you need something? A glass of water?" He fidgets with his hands as he searches for something to do.

"Sure." He spins around and flees the room with the speed of Superman on a mission. I unfurl myself from the tangled covers and follow in his stead as he traipses to the kitchen. The cabinet creaks open, then the faucet spurts to life.

Even in the open, we're shaded in darkness.

"Thank you," I say, accepting the glass he passes to me. I take a hearty swallow and set the cup on the counter. "I-I just don't want to be alone." It's the truth. The nightmare still lingers along the fringes of my mind, as though the second I return to the bedroom and lie back down, it'll claim me again.

We stand there, among the silver appliances and hard granite, wordlessly watching each other.

And I finally break the silence, and tell him what it was like growing up in the shadow of my father's political career.

CHAPTER FOURTEEN

Jack

"The more my father got involved in politics, the more vivid the dreams became." Savannah's hypnotic voice is somehow soothing as she speaks, for the first time to me, about being the daughter of a politician.

"I hate having my photo taken, which became increasingly difficult as Dad started his campaign." Her fingers trail down her bare arm, from shoulder to the inside of her elbow, as she leans against the counter.

"I just want to make him proud." She exhales abruptly, a wheezing sound. "Not be a liability to his candidacy." Her voice grows thick with emotion.

"I can't even imagine. How old were you when he first got into all this?" I should go back to my room. Put space between me and my protectee. But I'm afraid of what my leaving will do now that Savannah has chosen to open up. Even here.

In the darkened kitchen.

Where I shouldn't be, but can't bear to leave.

"Eight."

"That's young, Savannah." My heart aches for her. To know she's had to deal with being in the spotlight for ten years already.

"The first time they took a picture of me and posted it in the newspaper, the kids at school called me fat. Needless to say, it wasn't a very flattering photo."

The thought of Savannah being a child and dealing with the press without any guidance makes me feel more protective of her. I want to reach out to her, hug her close. I want to take away her sadness. Take those memories and all the hurt. That's what you do when you care about someone. You console them. "I'm so sorry." I press my lips together so I don't say anything more. Anything untoward that could give her the wrong idea.

"And then a year later, my mom was gone. Breast cancer," she adds before I can ask.

My throat feels like it's got a needle lodged in it. "That must've been hard, not having anyone to talk to. To shield you from it all." The needle stabs into my esophagus as I swallow. *Let me be that shield, Savannah.*

Her chin wobbles as her finger traces the pattern in the countertop. She nods. "I-I think I'm okay now. Thank you for listening."

I exhale and flatten my lips together, grabbing the glass and setting it in the sink. I half expect Savannah to be gone when I turn back, but she's still there. Her eyes wide, waiting.

"Goodnight, then," I say stiffly, as I pray for her to leave first. The way this might look to someone walking in...

She waits for a beat. Blinks. Bites her lip and inhales like she's preparing to say something.

Please don't... I beg silently.

And she doesn't.

"Goodnight," she says with a curt nod. And then she's gone.

The tension immediately pools out of my body, and I slouch against the counter like I've just run ten miles in the Florida heat.

How much longer can I keep this up? And, more importantly, how long until someone suspects something?

"I haven't seen you around much. Seems like you've been busy." Miranda barely lifts her eyes from her phone as she speaks to me from the back seat of the SUV.

"Just doing my job."

"You seem to be *very* good at your job." Her tone. The way she subtly smirks at me through the rearview mirror. *What does she know?*

"Yes, I try to be."

She tucks a strand of her straight red hair behind her ear, and I gulp down the panic bubbling up my throat.

"I thought I heard voices the other night in the kitchen. Was that you...?" I turn my face to the driver's side window, feigning indifference.

"Oh, yeah. It was just Savannah getting a drink of water. I went to check it out when I heard her."

I'd nearly done more than check it out with Savannah. The flimsy tank top she wore to bed, the way the strap slouched down her shoulder, exposing her bare skin.

Enough, Officer.

"Well, if that's all it was…" Miranda leans forward, and I don't miss the telltale red spots that dot her cheeks as I catch her eyes in the mirror. She's cute when she smiles, which isn't often, but Miranda simply isn't my type.

"Yup. That's it."

The assistant trails her long nail along the curve of the driver's seat. "You know, Jack—"

We both jump as the governor yanks open the passenger door and climbs in, his face dripping sweat. "Hell's bells, it's hot here. Whoever decided to schedule this conference in the bowels of Satan's crotch? I'm of a mind to suggest we move to Michigan next year. At least then we wouldn't all be sweating our tails off in this heat and humidity."

I laugh, not necessarily because I agree with him completely, but because this man's ability to bypass the use of traditional curse words is the epitome of midwestern slang. "I couldn't agree with you more, sir. Do us all a favor, Miranda, and make it happen." I wink at her as I shift into drive and pull away from the curb.

"Fine by me. My complexion hates the Florida sun anyway." She passes the boss a baby wipe, which he uses to clean the sweat from his forehead.

"Where to now?" I tap the brake as we wait to merge onto the expressway. "Back to the house or…?"

"Sir, you've got a lunch with Ms. Prescott at her place in an hour and then I've penciled in some time with your daughter for this evening."

My throat tightens at the mention of Savannah. "Ah, yes." The governor nods from the passenger seat. "I sure feel bad that I haven't gotten away more, but these damn networking events are vital to my yearly budget. I've promised to take her to the amusement park and to watch the fireworks tonight, though. She loves that place," he says as he slides his phone awake. "I already got the tickets and everything."

Miranda clears her throat from the backseat. "Are you sure that's a good idea, sir? You have the Midwest Energy Panel breakfast at 9 a.m. tomorrow."

Paul turns in his seat, his eyes flashing with mirth. "Are you suggesting I'm too old for some amusement park rides with my daughter, Miranda?"

"Uh oh," I laugh. There's nothing our boss dislikes more than being told what he *can't* do. "Remember when that restaurant owner claimed you were too vanilla for our state and you proved him wrong by completing his hot wings challenge?" It had been a major puff piece news story in our area.

"Damn straight. Twenty great balls of fire-flavored wings in five minutes. And my picture on the wall, too. But the best reward was his respect."

"Not his vote?" I joke.

"Well, that too if he actually does vote." With a chuckle, he shifts his attention. "Miranda, please confirm with Savannah for 6 p.m."

My eyes flick to the mirror again, and as Miranda taps at her device's screen, I can't help but wish it was me texting Savannah.

Chapter Fifteen

Savannah

My Apple watch reads 6:05 and my dad is nowhere in sight. I tap my foot as I lean against the kitchen counter. A car drives past the house, filled with a jumble of young teenagers. I sigh heavily and cross my arms.

Of course he's late. He's always late. Or he just doesn't show. I'm not immature enough to believe it's all his fault. As a governor and a politician, I understand that things come up. I get that more than most. But what my father doesn't understand, what he fails to comprehend, is that I'm no longer surprised or even care much when this happens.

I'm used to it.

Life was easier before my dad was elected as governor. Our home was smaller, and we didn't have the luxuries we have now—a house in Florida, for one—but I was happy. *We* were happy. Or so I thought.

"Savannah." I whip my head to the gravelly voice approaching from the garage.

Jack.

The mere sight of him has me clinching my thighs together. The last time we truly spoke to one another was the other night. When I had my bad dream and shared about my childhood.

Funnily enough, I haven't had a single nightmare since.

"Hey," he says, and I clock the bulge under the hem of his shirt. There's something dangerous and seductive about what's concealed there.

"Let me guess. My dad flaked out. Again." I try to temper the disappointment in my voice, but I'm certain Jack caught it. Especially when he saunters forward and, turning his baseball cap around, gives me a small, pitying nod. "So what's the excuse this time?"

"He, uh, threw out his back."

My stomach drops. "Oh my God, is he okay?"

Jack looks everywhere but at me. "Well, you see...he had lunch with Ms. Prescott— Laurel and, ah..."

"Oh ew. Enough." I shiver as the ick factor sinks in. Even my own father is getting some on this vacation. And I can't even *give* it away. A flush spreads up my neck and my cheeks heat.

Not to mention, the awkwardness of my father dating again. Geez...this trip has been *great*.

"So he sent me to let you know."

"Right." Feeling let down, I press my lips together. My dad knows how much I love the amusement park. We went every year together, just the two of us. He absolutely loved the biggest and scariest rides. I begged to go on all of them with him, but I was never tall enough. So when I was, it was a momentous occasion. "I guess I'll just..." I nod to the hallway and my room.

"Unless..." His eyebrows pop up in the early evening light filtering through the open-concept windows.

"Unless what?" I swallow.

"The governor told me how much you love amusement park rides. I could take you?" He clears his throat. "For an hour or two. I mean, the tickets are already loaded on my phone and they're non-refundable, so..." he trails off as his gaze dips to the floor.

"Oh, okay." I nod, a smile quirking my lips. This could be fun.

The ride to the park is quiet. It feels as though we're doing something wrong. Something covert. But even through that slight unease, that danger, there's something else flaring in my chest as my heart pounds over the sound of the radio. We park and, as we saunter toward the ticket counter, Jack hands me his phone. I pass it over to the attendant, who scans the barcode loaded onto his screen. As the attendant returns it, my thumb presses the home button, and it immediately flashes to his wallpaper. An older woman sits on the steps of a dilapidated porch with her arms thrown around a younger version of Jack. His hair is shorter and he's wearing a football jersey.

"That your mom?" I ask as we walk through the turnstile and into the park. I hand him the device.

"Yeah. It's from a few years ago. Or when I was in high school, I mean." Looking at the wallpaper for a moment, he then pockets the phone.

"D'you have any brothers or sisters?" I know nothing about Jack's history. His past before he came to work for my father. He's a locked vault. Not that I've given him much of a chance to get to know each other. My stomach sours at how obnoxious I've been toward him. That's surely not the way to get a man to notice you.

"Nope. It was just me and mom."

The vault stays sealed.

"Can I take your picture?" A photographer approaches us in a bright yellow shirt with a camera slung around her neck.

"Uh, that's—" Jack starts to say.

"Sure. We'd love that," I interrupt as I press into Jack's side.

"A little closer," the photographer requests as she wiggles her fingers at us. I scooch into his flank. My heartbeat pounds in my ears as I glance at Jack and find his honey eyes already on me. His throat wobbles as we inch together.

"Just a little more." I try to remember to breathe as I fit myself snugly against him, wrapped up in the scent of cedarwood and lime. Like the fancy suntan lotion from the volleyball game. My lips part and I lean in...

"Smile!" the photographer commands. I flick my gaze forward and attempt a smile, my mind running wild with the nearness to Jack. She snaps the photograph and passes me the ticket. "Photos can be purchased from the gift shop." We don't even have the chance to say thanks before she's found her next victims. A family of three wearing matching t-shirts.

The father pulls his wife in for a side hug as they both wrap an arm around their daughter, who stands in front and strikes a pose. Her fuchsia glasses match her purply-pink tee. The scene reminds me of the perfect family. Something I always desperately wanted but never had.

"So which ride is your favorite?" Jack's question pulls me from my wistfulness. I pocket the ticket.

Lips pursed, I think for a moment. If Jack is a thrill seeker like me, he'll probably love the biggest and fastest roller coaster at the park. And I want to impress him.

"The Mantis," I exclaim with a huge smile.

"All right then," he gulps, suddenly looking a little pale. "Let's go."

Chapter Sixteen

Jack

I lied.

I lied big time.

I hate roller coasters.

I *abhor* amusement park rides.

The way they toss and turn as your stomach and neck jolt in opposite directions.

The older I get, the tougher it is to recover.

And now as I stand in line with Savannah, who's practically bouncing on the balls of her feet with excitement, I'm fucked and feeling every day of twenty-seven years.

Because there's nothing remotely attractive about a 6'2" bodyguard puking in front of the woman he's supposed to protect.

Or throwing out his back after a ride on the Tilt-A-Whirl.

The coaster roars overhead, and I nearly grab Savannah and haul her ass out of line as the riders scream bloody murder. My bowels go watery, and I swallow down the bile rising in my throat.

"You okay?" Savannah cocks a perfectly arched eyebrow at me as she leans against the paint-chipped railing.

"Yeah. Of course. Why?"

"Because you're incredibly pale and you look like you're about to blow chunks all over the place." Her eyes narrow.

I force out a chuckle and swipe at my brow. "Must be the heat." Running my thumb along my bottom lip, I shrug.

Savannah's gaze zeroes in on my hand and her tongue flicks out to lick her own plump lips. "Come on," she hisses at me as she grabs my arm and tugs me from the line. We dodge around at least a hundred people, apologizing as we navigate the snake-like queue.

I follow until we're away from the coaster's racket and roar. Already I feel like I can breathe easier. "Where are we going? I thought you wanted to ride The Mantis?"

"I did." She shrugs, pulling me along in her wake. "Now I don't."

I dig my heels in and stop. She bounces back against me, and I turn her around, forcing her to look into my eyes. "Savannah. What are you doing? You wanted to ride that monstrosity." I point at the death trap behind us as another group shoots out of the loading area at a million miles an hour.

Their screams of horror drip down the back of my neck like wet goo.

Her eyes skim over my face. "But you don't."

"Of course I do."

"No," she says. "You don't."

"How do you know?"

"I can tell." She's taunting me.

"Oh yeah? How can you tell?"

She reaches up and drags her thumb across my bottom lip. A fire shoots straight to my gut at her touch. "Because when you're nervous, you pull at your lip."

My heart stills in my chest. "I-I do not."

With a smirk, she turns away, pulling me with her. "You do, too. You did it at dinner the other night when—"

Blood rushes to my feet and I suddenly feel faint. "When what?"

Savannah doesn't respond. She keeps moving. I follow in her wake but don't let up. "When, Savannah?"

We walk shoulder-to-shoulder now, and despite the crowd, I still manage to keep my eyes trained on her without bumping into some poor child.

"When you looked at me across the table." Her throat bobs. "Just like that."

She doesn't have to tell me where we were because I already know. At the restaurant. Seeing her in that dress. I swallow, the tightness constricting my airway. She's so right, it's crazy. As I stared at her, tearing apart the roll into those tiny pieces, I was so goddamned nervous that I was going to leap across the table and pull her to me. I thought about it the whole time. Wanted to kiss her so badly that it felt like my lips were on fire with need. It was a completely new sensation and it terrified me.

Almost as badly as the roller coaster.

And now that my protectee knows my tell, how am I going to go back to being the hired help? I stiffen and pull away from her slightly.

By the book, Keaton, I remind myself.

I glance at my watch. "You've got about an hour left. What do you want to do now?"

She blinks at my change in demeanor and narrows her eyes slightly. "Oh, you'll see," she says as her lips lift at the sides.

I gulp and follow a few steps behind her. "The line better not be too long. And nothing with heights."

Biting her bottom lip, a smile cracks through. "Oh, don't worry, Officer. I wouldn't want you to be too *scared*."

Officer.

The way she says it sends a shock of desire to the base of my spine. It unlocks something inside of me.

And as my heart flutters over the way she pushes me, I know that no ride in this park could be scarier than the way I'm feeling about Savannah.

Savannah tentatively turns back to me as I hold the red curtain aside for her to enter first. "I know you love all this scary shit, so after you," I say as she crosses the threshold.

My vision adjusts as we enter the first chamber, a completely dark waiting area. It's hard to acclimate my tactical training with something like this—having *fun* being scared. I had enough people trying to jump me as a cop; I don't need to relive those moments as entertainment.

I can make out a cell with bars and an attendant waiting to let us pass. Savannah stumbles over her feet, but I'm there to catch her from behind. Pulling her against my torso.

Making sure I know where she is at all times.

"Thanks," she whispers as we wait our turn. My hand lingers on her hips. I don't let go, and she doesn't ask me to.

Protecting her. I'm just protecting her.

"You may enter," the attendant bellows as he opens the cell. I tug her back and keep hold of her. Just doing my job.

"I don't like things jumping out at me," I say as I tighten my hold. Who knows what lurks in this dark room?

"Wimp," she mocks, pulling me forward. I nod at the attendant and push into the next room, where a glow-in-the-dark skeleton pops out from behind the door.

Not too bad, I think, releasing Savannah slightly. She laughs, likely finding it hilarious to be startled.

"Come on." She surges onward through the next several rooms, all of which are cheesier than the last. A woman covered in red holding a severed head. An old man in a creaking rocking chair. And lastly, a group of workers who missed their mark and are on their phones as we pass through.

"That last one was the scariest of them all." I lean in and whisper about the distracted workers.

She snorts and holds her free hand out, walking straight into a wall. "Shit!" she mutters, feeling along the passageway.

Searching for our exit, I join her in patting the wall. Our palms collide as we trail over the particle board material. Her soft skin under my rough and calloused hands. She doesn't pull away, but her movements slow. Linger over our connectedness. Her fingers tic up toward my hand, pushing into my touch. It'd be so easy to...

"I think it's down here," I say, breaking the spell. Her thighs edge against my shoulders as I guide her to a tunnel that we have to crawl through, the eerie glow barely visible on the other side.

"Great," she mutters.

"I thought you liked all this stuff?" We're crouched down, face-to-face in the dark room. So close I can practically taste the minty gum she's chewing.

"I'm not a huge fan of tight spaces." Her eyes dart to the tunnel.

"Do you want me to go first?" I cock an eyebrow at the circular exit, wondering how I'm even going to fit through.

"No," she whispers. "I-I can do it." She inhales deeply and moves into the tight space, her rear end right at eye level.

I wait a moment and then crawl in behind her, trying my best to avoid thinking too much about her ass that's right in my face.

Focus, Keaton.

But just then, I face-plant directly into it. "Oh, God... Sorry about that. Why'd you stop?"

Her breathing echoes all around in the plastic tunnel. She doesn't say anything.

"Savannah? Are you okay?"

Arms collapsing, she curls into herself. "I-I can't breathe. It's too tight in here." She's panting between each word.

My training kicks in, and I immediately know what to do. I crawl farther, my body flush with hers. "Savannah, look at me," I instruct. But her eyes are cinched closed.

She continues to hyperventilate, which is made even worse by the cramped space. "Savannah." When I grab her chin, her eyes flash open. "Look at me."

Those chocolate brown eyes are all I see as we lie together, but I feel so much more.

Her chest heaving against mine.

Her body trembling.

And my cock straining against the zipper of my pants.

Fuck.

"Savannah, I need you to breathe in for five on my count."

I start to count from one, and Savannah purses her lips, sucking in air.

"Now out for five," I instruct as she nods.

The minty air tickles against my face, and I feel myself growing harder by the second.

"Again," I direct as we repeat the process.

Her body sags slightly into mine, and it's only then I realize she's gripping my shirt in her fist, holding on to me for safety.

For *safety*.

Because I'm here to protect her.

I'm hired to be her bodyguard.

And the way I feel about her is anything but safe.

A blood-curdling scream pulls us both back to the tunnel, our bodies stiffening once more. "Are you good?"

"Yeah," she whispers against me as her eyes blink once. Twice.

I hold myself against the side of the tunnel as she squirms out from beneath me. Her body writhing along every square inch of mine.

My entire nervous system is on high alert, and as I follow behind her and rise out of the enclosed space, I clear my throat and turn my baseball cap forward once again.

"I think the fireworks are about to start."

"My dad is desperate for me to study international relations," Savannah shares as we sit in the SUV in the amusement park parking lot. "That and political science." The clock reads 9:15, and the fireworks are due to start at any minute.

Savannah had wanted to leave. "It's no big deal if we don't catch the fireworks," she said as we left the park. "I know I'm over my time limit."

"I've never seen this fireworks show. I'd like to watch." Her gaze snapped to mine, and a slow smile spread across her face.

What I'd wanted to say was "I'd like to watch. *With you.*" But that wouldn't be appropriate, even as true as it is. Even truer is that there's nowhere else I'd rather be.

And now, as we wait impatiently for the show, she continues sharing details about her life.

"Is that what interests you?" I grab a handful of popcorn from the bag situated in the console between us. Savannah's leg is hitched up onto the seat as she faces me. Tossing a piece into the air, I expertly capture it between my teeth.

"Of course," she says with a laugh at my trick, although she doesn't sound so sure. "I want to make my dad proud. Make him happy."

"But if you had a choice, it'd be different?" I flick another buttered piece into the air. It lands perfectly once more.

She tucks her lip between her teeth and looks down. Thinking, perhaps? I hope she hasn't shut down. I've enjoyed getting to see more of her real self. The Savannah I was just starting to get to know back in Michigan.

"Catch." I hold a big piece between my thumb and forefinger as she smiles and opens her mouth. Turning toward her, I adjust my height. "Ready?"

She nods as her eyes crinkle. I gently toss the piece to her, and she leans forward, catching it with her tongue. My heart clenches as she releases an excited squeal and claps her hands together.

I've never seen her so excited. Over something so silly. So small.

I did that.

I made her feel that way.

I gulp and grab another handful, shoving it into my mouth.

She blinks and looks out the window. "I think if I had a choice, I'd choose music and business management."

"Those are two vastly different areas of study."

Her hand digs into the bag and pulls out a handful of popcorn. "True," she says as she uses her tongue to pluck a few kernels from her palm. "But I love music—*live* music—and how cool would it be to start a music label? Or even become an agent? I'd get to travel all over, searching for new talent."

The way her eyes light up tells me of her true passion. "Do you play any instruments?"

"No, although my parents tried to get me into piano when I was younger. But I was too active. I wouldn't sit still for the tutor, so they enrolled me in gymnastics instead." She shrugs and munches on a few pieces. "But I've always wanted to learn to play the guitar."

"It's never too late," I add, just as a loud boom rocks the SUV. Savannah lets out a girly shriek and then giggles.

"Sorry." She smiles sheepishly and ducks her head as another firework flashes in the distance.

"It's fine. Part of our police training was being exposed to loud noises."

She blinks at me. "And yet you were afraid of an amusement park haunted house?" There's that mischievousness again. I snort and playfully shake my head. "What made you become a cop in the first place?"

The sparks of light shine in Savannah's eyes as she watches me. "I just always knew I wanted to help people. Make the world a better place and all that."

Nodding, she smiles. "I get that. Very noble." Her lips part as a sparkly explosion goes off. "Oh, I like those ones the best."

I feel my own lips lifting slightly. The colors of fireworks light up her face in various hues of pink, orange, blue, and green. As I watch her watching the show, there are tiny explosions popping off within my chest. A feeling I'm not used to having. A feeling that scares me to my core.

There's no denying, I'm attracted to my protectee.

Chapter Seventeen

Savannah

"You can't be serious." I stand with my arms crossed, glaring daggers at Miranda as she thumbs through her day planner.

"It's what the governor wants, Savannah. Quit being such a child."

My nostrils flare at the affront. "Is this what the *governor* wants, or what my *father* wants?"

Miranda finally looks up and pushes aside the work in front of her. Her eyes narrow as her lip curls. "You do realize they are one and the same, don't you?" She pauses. "Savannah, I'm going to tell you something that nobody else around you will. Because I've known you since you were a little girl. It's high time you at least pretend like you give a damn about your father's position and stop acting like such a spoiled little brat. Plaster that adorable smile on your face the press loves. We're all doing this for him. Got it?"

Before I can come up with a worthwhile retort, she scoops up her work and stalks down the hallway to her room.

Bitch.

My fingers quiver and my heartbeat pounds through my shirt. How dare she speak to me like that? I stomp over to the cupboard and grab a glass, filling it with water straight from the tap. As I slug it back in one gulp, I wish it were something stronger, and slam the cup onto the cold granite countertop.

I stare into the sitting area but see nothing. I only feel the press of the cool countertop against the palms of my hands. Breathing loudly, I inhale and count to five, then continue to ten as I exhale. Repeating the inhale to five and exhale to ten. Just like Jack showed me. When I'm sufficiently calm, I refill the glass and take another drink.

Miranda's not a bitch.

She's right.

As much as I hate to admit it, she's totally right.

My father is the governor, likely to run for higher office in the next four years, and there are expectations of me as his daughter.

Namely, attending a "family-style dinner" with Brett and his mother.

Suddenly, the water in my cup tastes bitter and I toss the rest down the drain. I wish Jack was here. But instead, he's at the conference with my father. My thoughts return to the way he eased my anxiety in the haunted house. His strong body above mine. I'm certain I felt something hard. He clearly wants me as much as I want him. Even during the fireworks, when I sat next to him in the car, I know I saw something in his eyes.

It was the longest foreplay and I only wanted it to keep going.

It's been almost 24 hours and not a single glance or brush of skin.

Even pressing my hips against the hard counter feels better than the nothing that I've become accustomed to.

I roll my shoulders. My nerves ache, skin tingling and eager for his touch. The muscles all over my body beg for release.

It's like I can feel the thrum of energy emanating from my core. I'm a spring wound so tightly that I'm moments away from snapping.

How long will Jack play hard to get?

"Brett shared that you two had a wonderful time the other night."

I cock an eyebrow at Ms. Prescott— Laurel, as she's insisted I call her.

"Oh, yes. It was fun." *After he ditched me, and I threw myself at my bodyguard.* Can my monotone response really persuade her?

I swing my gaze toward Brett, whose face has turned an unflattering shade of crimson. He attempts to bury it behind his menu, but I glare in his direction anyway.

"Laurel, this is the wine I was telling you about the other day." My father pours his newest paramour a hefty glass of the deep red liquid and then returns to his own, swirling the stem between his fingers as he holds it to his nose.

The woman next to me is quite pretty, but she can't hold a candle to my own mother. While Laurel's hair is a deep brown with tasteful caramel highlights, my mother's hair was the color of the Florida sand. A natural blonde. She, too, loved the beach. And red wine. As I watch my father's obsession with wine grow, I wonder if it's a way for him to stay close to her, even in death.

"Miss?" I glance up at the waiter, his smile wavering as he looks down at me expectantly.

"Oh, I'll have the filet medium rare with a side of the roasted Brussel sprouts." I snap my menu closed and pass it over.

"That sounds delicious. I'll have the same." Laurel nods in my direction as her white teeth gleam in the candlelight. It's hard not to like her. She'd be a good fit for my father. I can see why he enjoys spending time with her.

"So, Brett, you have one more year at ECU and then what are your plans after graduation?" Dad spreads his napkin on his lap as the salad course is delivered to our table. I drench mine with dressing and dig in, not much caring about Brett's future.

"I'll be interning with mom's energy commission and then hopefully attending graduate school for environmental policy and energy management." He shoots my father a cocksure grin, and a crouton becomes lodged in my throat.

I cough violently before swallowing a mouthful of water and pounding my fist to my chest. "Excuse me," I manage as the coughing continues. I stand from my seat and wave away my father's worried expression as he, too, rises. "I'll be just a moment." Another cough has me hurrying from the dining area.

As I weave through the tables, I hold in the coughing, and only when I reach the door to the restaurant and burst outside do I release the breath and gasp for air. I hack and wheeze until my throat finally clears.

"You okay?" Startled, I turn, wiping at the tears that have pricked at the corners of my eyes. Jack stands off to the side, his foot propped against the building as he leans against the aged brick. He blows a plume of smoke in my direction and it's only then that I notice the lit cigarette held between his thumb and forefinger.

"Since when do you smoke?"

"It's a bad habit I'm trying to kick. Unfortunately, there are times I just can't help myself."

I saunter closer and reach for the cigarette, wanting to taste the forbidden. The spot that touched his lips, namely.

"Not a chance," he says before lifting it to his lips and taking another puff. He holds it in his lungs before blowing out the smoke through his nostrils. I've never been so turned on by something so dangerous.

"Why not? I'm of age." I carefully join him in leaning against the brick. I press my hands beneath my butt so as not to chafe the same black dress I wore to the last dinner.

"I know. But it's the last thing you need, Savannah." He gulps. "To get hooked on something so bad for you."

He flicks the cigarette into the parking lot and then pulls a small case from his pocket. Taking out a thin square, he places it on his tongue and swallows. His jaw works as he stares at the discarded cigarette still smoking on the ground.

"Go back inside, Savannah."

"But I—"

"Go."

As I retreat to the entrance of the restaurant, he leans back against the brick and pulls another cigarette from his pocket.

"Don't," I call out quietly, my hand on the door but my eyes glued to him. "You smell better without it." And then I swing open the door and go back inside, stomach fluttering at the possibility of him listening.

Chapter Eighteen

Jack

"Let's get out of this heat," I say as Savannah slides under my arm and into the air conditioning. Once her father left with Miranda for some fancy networking event, Savannah had begged to get some ice cream.

"C'mon, you know you want some too." Her eyebrow raised as she widened her eyes in my direction.

I did. And there's nothing inappropriate about ice cream.

Just taking my protectee for a treat.

That's all.

I follow her over to the counter, where she's already standing on her toes, leaning into the glass. My eyes travel up her tanned legs to her ass and the small strip of bare skin along the waist of her jean shorts. I catch a fellow customer's eye and he smiles knowingly, a smirk touching his lips.

Frowning at him, I maneuver myself directly behind Savannah, my fingers coming to rest on either side of her on the counter. She jumps and turns, pulling away slightly, but not before I catch the way her pupils flare.

"What do you want?" I ask gruffly, not taking my gaze off her.

Obviously flustered, she lifts her hand to her chest, her fingers playing with the thin gold necklace that sits at her neckline. *It was my mom's*, she told me the other night as we watched the fireworks light up the sky. It takes all my energy not to drop my gaze, to follow those fingers as they trail along her collarbone, but I keep my eyes up.

"I like the strawberry," she responds, finally breaking eye contact as the teenager behind the counter hands her a double scoop in a crispy waffle cone.

My mouth waters, but not for ice cream.

"Sir?"

I inhale deeply to compose myself, and nod in gratitude as the teen passes me a hot fudge sundae topped with whipped cream.

I follow Savannah to a seat in front of the store's windows. Ever the gentleman, I pull out her chair before taking the one across from her.

Where I can watch her hungrily lick every inch of the strawberry ice cream from the cone.

My.

God.

"Jack? Hello?" I blink, and heat sears along the base of my neck.

"Sorry. I..." I trail off. What can I say to cover my ass? *I was thinking about your tongue on my dick.* I'd sound like some deranged middle schooler.

"Can you hold my cone? I need to use the restroom." I nod, and she passes me the dessert as she sets down her phone and tosses her bag onto the seat. I try my best to keep my eyes lowered as she saunters away, but if she looked back, she'd surely find my eyes glued to her ass.

The *ding* of her phone interrupts my perusal of her derriere. She's left it face-up on the table, and I can't help but notice the message that flashes across the screen.

> **Benji Brett:** Glad we put all the weirdness behind us last night. Want to hang out?

While I have to smirk at the name she's saved him under, my blood boils at the gall of this dude. He had his chance. And he blew it. Royally.

I shove the plastic spoon into my hot fudge sundae and push the dessert aside, my stomach churning. What right do I have to stake my claim on Savannah anyway? Would I really throw my career away for an eighteen-year-old?

What would that even look like? The beautiful and vibrant politician's daughter being photographed fraternizing with *the help*? Me, an almost-thirty-year-old man keeping my girlfriend from experiencing frat parties, tailgates, and all the craziness that college has to offer?

No. I wouldn't do that to her.

These wayward thoughts have to stop.

This can't—

"Thanks for holding my cone. Did you take a lick?" Savannah winks as she grabs her ice cream from my frozen hand and, hooking her bag on the back of her chair, sits back down.

"What?" I blink at her.

"I asked if you took a lick." When she blushes, that sour feeling grows as it travels up my throat.

"No, I didn't." My gaze drops to her phone, which dings again at the unread message. My breathing stutters as she fails to swipe or even acknowledge the text. "You should check that. It could be your dad."

She responds with a slow nod and glances at the phone. Did I mean to kill the mood by mentioning her father? Maybe. Maybe it brings things back into perspective. Maybe she's realizing what we're doing.

But what exactly are we doing?

No, I stop myself before I can go there, and instead get up from the table to throw away my uneaten sundae.

"You're done already?"

I nod solemnly and traipse to the trashcan.

When I return, her head is down as she quickly thumbs over the screen. "Not my dad," she mutters as I retake my seat.

She swipes up and then clicks the side button and the screen goes black. I don't respond.

I'm too focused on her licking the ice cream cone. Her tongue pressing against the cool dessert. Slurping and swallowing the cream, the tendons of her neck flexing the same way my cock is inside my pants.

"Let's get out of here," she says as she tosses her phone into her bag. She stands and takes one last lick before holding the cone out to me. I shake my head, my stomach still unsettled. Pulling the keys from my pocket, she returns from the trashcan and holds out her hand. "Hand 'em over."

"Not a chance," I deadpan as her eyebrows lower.

"Come on, Jack. Please? I have someplace I really want to show you." She reaches across the space between us and runs her hand down my arm. Warmth and desire flood my system at just a simple touch.

You're totally fucked.

I shove the keys into her hand and stalk past her. "You better not mess up the mirrors or change the radio stations."

Reaching the door first, I hold it open for her to pass through. "I'm gonna mess up everything, Jack." She flutters her lashes at me and, with a girlish giggle, jogs to the driver's side of the SUV.

A tightness blooms in my chest, and I can't help but wonder if she realizes she's already done that.

To me.

The windows are rolled down, the sunroof wide open. As we drive along the coastal highway parallel to the beach, the briny sea air tangles through my hair as it whips wildly. Savannah's straightened hair has begun to curl in the muggy humidity, especially along her hairline and the back of her neck. What I wouldn't give to run my fingers under the weight of her strands and up the back of her head. I'd yank hard enough to expose her throat and drag my tongue along the sensitive skin there while my fingers dove beneath her tank top.

"Sync my phone to the Bluetooth, please." She tosses her device at me, and I narrowly catch it before it lands on my thickened cock. Crisis averted.

"Passcode?"

"1-2-3-4."

"Savannah, are you kidding me? You cannot have that as your passcode."

"You told me it couldn't be my birthday because that was too easy, so..." she trails off with a shrug.

I shake my head and type the digits. The screen flashes to life. Her background is set to a photo of her and her best friend on the beach. It must've been taken a few years ago, because Savannah's hair is much shorter and wavier. "I like your hair in this picture."

"Ew, I look awful with my natural waves. Don't even look at that picture."

I frown at her and click on the settings, ready to pair the device with the SUV's system. "You're beautiful, no matter how you wear your hair."

Shit, I shouldn't have said that. My heart palpitates as the nerves disperse in my body, but as the phone syncs, and I slide my gaze to her profile, catching the flush coloring her cheeks, all that regret dissipates. A two-toned noise comes from the speakers, alerting me to the phone being paired. I clear my throat. "Tell me the song and I'll pull it up for you."

"No way!" she exclaims as she grabs the device from me. Her eyes bounce back and forth between the road and her phone as she clicks through her music. Breaking many laws. Settling on a tune, she puts the phone between her thighs and cranks up the volume knob. "I'm really into singer-songwriters right now." She's quiet for a moment before glancing my way. "I hope that doesn't sound too pretentious."

"No, I like this one." I tap my thighs to the beat and enjoy the view. Because the beach is on the driver's side, I get to take in the oceanic panorama and Savannah's profile as she hums along, then begins to sing to the music. My lips part in a smile as I swallow roughly. The way the setting sun highlights her delicate features makes her look like a goddess.

That familiar warmth burns in my chest—

I can't possibly be this enamored by someone so quickly. I'm a grown-ass man, not a hormonal teenager.

"We're here!" Savannah slows the SUV and then turns off the highway into a nearly abandoned beach parking lot. She whips into a spot and parks the vehicle easily. I'm surprised, and impressed, that she can handle the SUV. "Come on, I want to show you my favorite place in the whole world," she says with the excitement of a child on Christmas morning.

CHAPTER NINETEEN

Savannah

As the sun dips below the horizon, the remaining beachgoers wring sand and sea water from their striped towels and pack up their coolers, umbrellas, and kids. Jack and I traipse through the sand, going in the opposite direction as those returning to their cars with sunburns and sandy swimsuits. We dodge tide pools cutting wet paths through the sand and continue walking until the slide of grass on the breeze turns into the crash of waves against the tumbled rocks along the shoreline.

I climb onto the boulders that stretch into the ocean. "Savannah, that's not a goo—"

But with a smirk over my shoulder, I ignore his admonishment and jump from rock to rock. My feet grip the smooth stone like an expert. Seagulls cry overhead as they dip into the crags in search of starfish and crabs. Finding "my rock," I plop down and turn to watch Jack navigate the path.

His tattooed arms lift away from his sides as he balances, his bare feet gripping the rocks. "Careful!" I call out. When he nears, I scoot over so he has enough room. The rock is just big enough for two.

"This is amazing. How'd you find this place?" He leans back on his hands and stretches out his legs, his expression smoothing out almost instantly after the stress I just caused him. A good view has that kind of power.

"My dad used to bring me here. My mom grew up in that little house right over there." I point to a dilapidated yellow beach cottage in the distance.

Jack looks like he wants to know more, but the last thing I want to do is poke at an old wound.

So instead, I tap his exposed forearm and the dark ink that decorates his skin. "Tell me about your tattoos. Do they mean something?"

He points to the various art, landing first on a distinct compass. "Well, this one represents my quest to find the right path in life and staying true to myself. My principles. See how the dial points north?"

I nod, my finger itching to trace over the detailed drawing. "What about this one?" I drag my nail to a quote. "I will remember for you."

When Jack doesn't respond, my eyes flick to his. Only he's not staring at his tattoo anymore. Now his gaze is trained on the ocean. The waves crashing, rolling in the distance. Self-conscious, I pull my finger away from his skin.

"I-I'm sorry. I was being nosy." Embarrassment heats my scalp.

"No, no. It's okay," he responds, as his face turns back to me. "That one's for my mom."

He doesn't share more, and I don't pry. That's one thing I've learned about Jack. If he wanted to, he'd tell me.

"I've always wanted to get a tattoo." I think back to the time that Delia and I snuck out during last year's trip. Our plan was to get something symbolic of our friendship. But as we stood in the parlor, the hum of the needles all around us, we'd both chickened out. "I tried once, but I was too scared."

"You know, they're not as painful as people think. It depends on the location." Jack's eyes dip to my collarbone and he swallows. His cheeks flush slightly, and a smile blooms across my face.

"What would you say is the most painful place?" I lean in as my gaze drinks its fill of his inked muscles.

"W-well, probably someplace sensitive. Ticklish, even." His thumb comes up to trace his bottom lip. My breath hitches at the movement, and he must notice me zeroing in because he immediately lowers his hand back to the rock.

"I'm ticklish all over, so a tattoo would likely be very painful."

He swallows and nods slightly, nothing more than a bob of his head. "Although some people enjoy it. Like the mixture of pain and..." he trails off. "You wouldn't know until you tried, I suppose."

We turn from one another, both of us watching the waves. Only, my mind isn't focused on the water. No, it's focused on the palpable tension building between me and the man sitting next to me. The cord pulling me toward him—the snap as it cinches me closer.

He has to feel it, the yearning and desire. I'm tired of waiting to see if he'll ever act on what we're both so clearly feeling. I don't want to waste an opportunity that, for all I know, could be the last one.

So... I go for it. I turn to him, grab the fabric of his shirt, and pull him into me. I capture his lips between mine as his body surges forward. Melting into me the way the waves melt into the sand. It's all the confirmation I need to keep going.

I slide my tongue through the seam of his lips, and it collides with his. An electric shock lights a fire in my gut. I want—

But then he pulls away, stretching his shirt as I still claim it with my fists.

"Jack, I—"

"No, Savannah. I-I can't be with you like this." His eyes are full of uncertainty, questions, and something else. He rises to his knees to leave. But I reach for his wrist, chest tightening with desperation.

"I'm tired of hearing you say that when I *know* you feel it too!" My eyes well, my body and my heart begging him to stay. "Tell me it's not just me, Jack. Tell me you're in this too…"

I glance down at my fingers wrapped around his wrist. If he truly wanted to leave, to break the hold, he could. But he doesn't.

Instead, he hovers over me, staring into my eyes as he searches my face.

"*Please*," I beg, the whisper disappearing in the waves.

Whatever was holding him back breaks, and he crashes into me. Our lips collide and it's like a storm at sea. Beautiful and dangerous and life-altering. He presses me back onto the rock, my hair tangling with the water beneath us, and claims me wholly as his tongue parts my mouth and enters mine. "*Savannah*." I swallow down my name on his lips as his hands move around to my front. His thumbs track along my stomach, searing me with his touch, and then trail up to my ribs. He gently pushes me away but not before staring me down like I'm a Zagat-rated meal and he's starving. That tongue of his slides along his bottom lip as the hunger flares in his eyes.

I want to beg for more, but I'm afraid if I do, he'll stop.

So I only swallow and nod slightly when his eyes meet mine. *Keep going…*

That same hand covers my breast. Heat shoots to my core as my nipples pebble beneath my bra. I gasp, my hips bucking against his length.

The sea drowns out my moan as he fondles my chest, making me ache for him.

If he were to ask me what I wanted, it'd be this.

With the stars twinkling behind him and the ocean swirling just beyond our reach. What I've wanted for weeks. What I need.

Him.

"I want you," I say, lying beneath him. Flushed with the effects of his touch.

He leans in at the same time a giant wave slams into the rock. "Shit!" I yelp as the onslaught covers me in salty spray.

Jack is up, pulling me along as another wave pounds against the stones. "Hurry," he calls out as he holds my hand and yanks me to safety.

We tiptoe over the slippery stones, no easy feat in the darkness, and return to the dry and deserted sand.

I expect Jack to reach for me, to comfort me as we stand, cold and wet, alone on the beach. My mind is still in this. Wanting more of his touch. Craving him with every fiber of my being.

But he doesn't reach for me. Doesn't touch me.

"You're freezing," he notes as my teeth chatter.

I shake my head, not wanting him to feel sorry for me. Not wanting him to admit that this was wrong.

It *wasn't* wrong.

But the way he's looking at me speaks volumes. It's the same way he looked at that roller coaster.

Terrified.

"We should get back to the car," he says, refusing to look me in the eye.

"I-I'm sorry. I didn't think about the tide coming in."

"It's not your fault. We shouldn't— I shouldn't—"

Tears spring to my eyes, burning more than the salty spray. Chin wobbling, I drown out what he says next as only the ocean's waves and the shattering of my heart reach my ears.

"Savannah, are you listening to me?" He grabs my wrist and pulls me to a stop, running the back of his hand along my cheek and over my jaw. My head tilts slightly as I lean in. Enjoying the little bit of affection he's giving me. Eating it up. "I'm sorry."

I blink up at him. "Why? What do you have to be sorry for?"

His eyes dip to my lips.

And yet, when I lean in to kiss him, he pulls back.

And it's like nothing ever happened.

CHAPTER TWENTY

Jack

"Shh." I pull Savannah through the garage and into her room. Luckily, the governor is out for the night at a networking event with Miranda.

"We'll take an Uber so you can enjoy a well-deserved night off," the governor said as he and Miranda left earlier in the evening in their formal attire.

Savannah carefully closes the door behind her and then clicks on a light that casts a soft glow over the room.

"I think I need help getting all this sand out of my hair," she says, shaking her head with a chuckle.

The way the wet clothes cling to her body. The memory of her lips on mine. The feel of her breast beneath my hand. It's all too much. I can't refuse her anymore. My gaze falls to the compass tattoo on my arm, and it's pointing straight north at Savannah. "Allow me," I say as I take her hand and pull her through the room and into the bathroom.

Her cheeks turn a delicate shade of pink as her eyes flash. She flicks the shower curtain out of the way and turns on the faucet. Then she saunters past me and, with another flick, locks the door.

Before she turns back to me, she lifts the hem of her tank top and pulls it over her head, discarding it on the floor. My body takes over, even as my mind sends out a warning alarm. I'm too far gone, and it only took a glimpse of her bare back.

9403, Keaton. Panic.

I silence that part of my brain as I reach out and unhook her bra. The steam from the shower rolls over the curtain, but as I reach around and palm Savannah's exposed tits, they're already tightened into buds.

"I want to see you," I beg as I maneuver her to face me.

It's not too late to turn back. To stop.

But I don't. Instead, I lean down and pull the pebbled flesh into my mouth. Her gasp sends all the warnings out the window, and as she wraps her arms around my neck and collapses against me, I'm done for.

Her hands dive into the waistband of my pants. I want her to touch me. Stroke me. She unbuttons the trousers and slides her fingers beneath the fabric of my briefs. I hiss as her fingers finally—*finally*—grasp my length.

There's something about the locked door that makes me feel safe. Like no one will ever find out. As I release Savannah's wet nipple with a pop, I turn my attention to her shorts. With her hand still gripping me, I raise my eyebrows at her in question, and she nods.

I unbutton her cutoffs and, as I shimmy them down her waist, toss them to the pile of salty clothing. Then I'm raising my arms and tugging off my shirt, too, before kicking off my pants.

"Shower," I instruct. Monosyllabic is as much as my brain will give me right now. One side is still alerting me to a code 0104—sabotage—while the other side is begging to continue.

Keep going.

I listen to the latter.

We step into the warm shower and immediately come together in a tangle of lips, teeth, and limbs. I've wanted this for weeks. My body won't be denied, even if my head is screaming for me to stop.

My slippery hands are everywhere on Savannah's body. Palming her breasts. Sliding down her ribs to her stomach and then around to cup her ass. And my cock stands at attention, eager for whatever I can give him.

"Has anyone ever touched you here before?" I ask Savannah as my hand trails downward.

She shakes her head, her wet hair slapping against her bare chest. Unexpected pride swells within me as I nod, and then slide my forefinger between her slit. A deep hum rumbles in her throat as I feel her slick desire. Circling her clit with my thumb, her knees nearly buckle before I wrap my other arm around her.

"More," she begs as she leans against me and water sluices around us.

I oblige, adding a second digit but still fingering the sensitive bud as the other slides into her. I add pressure to her clit while moving the other fingers in and out until she releases a long sigh.

"Don't stop."

"I won't."

"Promise?"

"I promise," I respond. Because I'm too far gone now. Fuck it. If I'm going down, I'm going down happy.

And right now, that looks like being knuckle deep in the governor's daughter.

Savannah's hand finds my hard erection and tightens around me. "Up and down, sweetheart," I direct as she uses the water for lubricant.

She grips me harder, and as I capture her mouth with mine, our breathing synced and our bodies warm and slippery, it's only moments before we're both coming. Together.

"Fuck," she whispers as her teeth press into my shoulder. Her muscles pulse around my fingers and suddenly I'm lost to everything.

"Shhh," I remind her as I let loose a gasp and ejaculate into her palm.

"Oh God. Oh God." Her chest heaves as she comes down from the high and regains her footing in the shower.

I bring my fingers to my mouth and lick away her ecstasy as she watches, enraptured. Those dark eyes going pure black.

"Turn around." Her eyes widen as she gulps. "You said you wanted the sand out of your hair," I add with a small smile. With a dreamy exhale, she obliges, and I wash her until she's clean.

"Goodnight," Savannah mutters sullenly as she nearly slams the door in my face. I stand there, my forearm pressed up against the door, for just a moment. Wishing that the shower scene I cooked up in my head had actually happened. Wishing for anything other than the silent car ride home. The distance mounting between us. My dick stands at attention, needing to recover from all the highs and lows of tonight.

I push off Savannah's door and turn toward my own, when a figure steps into the hallway.

Miranda.

I'm rarely ever fazed—part of the job and all—but my gorge rises.

I didn't even hear her and the governor come back.

"Jesus Christ, Miranda. What are you doing up so late?" I pad to my door, feigning nonchalance even as my heart races. She's surely able to hear it beating across the hallway.

She slinks toward me, closing the space between us in a single stride. "I could ask you the same thing." I don't miss how her eyes trail over my wet clothes or the way her lips quirk as she takes in my hard-on straining against my woven shorts.

"Just went to check on Savannah. If you'll excuse me." I enter my own room and nod, closing the door behind myself. But before I can send her on her way, her hand whips out and catches the handle.

"You may not know this, but I've been watching you the last few days."

My blood runs cold, and I turn back to her, narrowing my eyes as a feline smile cuts across her face. "Why would you do that?"

And how did I not notice?

"It's my job to keep an eye on things." She crosses her arms and leans against the door frame.

I swallow the lump forming in my throat. "What *things*, Miranda?" My grip tightens on the door.

"The governor's schedule. His *daughter's* schedule. The finances and bills. *Employees* and their behaviors." Her gaze narrows as she eyes me with the type of suspicion a police officer has for someone he's just caught red-handed. "Shall I continue?"

"It's not what you think. I'm just her—"

But I'm not.

Not after tonight.

Tonight, I crossed the line.

Her eyebrow cocks and she takes another step toward me. I move aside and she stalks farther into the room. "You know, I started to get this little feeling that something wasn't right. Between you and Savannah. But I wasn't completely sure. Until now." She saunters and stares me down as though she can see straight into my soul. "I can see it in your eyes, Keaton. So don't bother lying to me. How do you think the governor will take the news that his new employee—the former East Lansing police officer—has been sneaking around with his barely legal daughter?"

I swallow and nod. I'm completely guilty. I've been inappropriate and broken all the rules of this job. So instead of groveling, I get straight to the point. "You're right. But it's not what you think."

She turns to me and pouts, comically pressing her thin bottom lip out. "She's eighteen, Jack. And your boss's daughter. Can you imagine the headlines?"

Anger radiates from her as her gaze cuts to mine. "I can't have a scandal on my hands. I can't deal with the media storm this would surely cause." She stomps across the small room. "Is that what you want? Because that's what'll happen. You'll ruin that girl, her relationship with her father, and his career."

I sag to the bed and my head falls into my hands.

I've fucked up. Fucked up so badly.

"You're the fixer around here. Tell me what to do. Tell me how to fix this."

CHAPTER TWENTY-ONE

Savannah

I stand in the steamy bathroom, my cheeks pink and my hair clean of the sand. Staring at my reflection in the mirror, I feel like my body just awoke from a long slumber. As though being kissed by Jack ignited something within me.

Unlocked the yearnings I never felt for the boys my age.

A confidence to go for what I want.

I may have settled into disappointment on the drive home, slammed the door in his face out of frustration, but I don't want this night to be over. I'm certain of it.

The way I feel about him is unlike anything I've felt for another. And regardless of him pulling away, I'm certain he feels it, too; he's just torn because of his position, the good man he is.

Wrapping the towel tighter around my chest, I grab my toothbrush, slathering paste over the bristles, my hand shaking.

I know what I want.

When I'm done brushing my teeth, I apply a dab of lip gloss. I rub my lips together and give my reflection one last appraisal before flicking off the light and leaving the sanctuary of the bathroom behind.

I'm going to remember this night for the rest of my life.

As I stand outside Jack's door, I hear voices.

His and Miranda's.

My body goes cold as I press my ear against the wood.

"I can't have a scandal on my hands. I can't deal with the media storm this would surely cause." Then *"Is that what you want? Because that's what'll happen. You'll ruin that girl, her relationship with her father, and his career."*

It's quiet for a moment.

Tell her, Jack, I beg from the hallway. *Tell her that you care about me. That there's something between us.*

But instead, he says, *"You're the fixer around here. Tell me what to do. Tell me how to fix this."*

And then, after another moment of silence, *"This never should've happened. I'm going to lose everything because of her."*

I'm speechless. I wasn't expecting this, and as I bite my bottom lip and my eyes prick, I take a step back. I instantly feel foolish. Stupid. Immature and infantile. I glance down at myself, naked save for a fucking bath towel, and heat sears the top of my scalp. What am I doing?

I turn and flee to the safety of my room. My stomach swirling and heart pounding.

Staring around at my clothes discarded on the floor, the unmade bed, my gaze lands on the picture of me and Jack at the amusement park. As we left one of the happiest places, I pulled the ticket from my back pocket.

"Come on, let's at least see if it's any good," I encouraged as I practically ran to the kiosk.

"No, those are nothing more than a way to get tourists to spend more money," he admonished, even as my belly warmed at the thought of a memento of the two of us. Did he really not want to remember our day at the park?

I passed the ticket to the attendant and, as we waited for her to pull up our photograph, I watched his face. The way it flashed with pain when our picture popped up on the screen. The way he'd turned away from the photo.

"We *have* to get it," I said, pulling money from my pocket.

I stare at the photo and really look at it this time. Seeing everything I was too blind to see before. A girl whose hair was frizzy and a mess. Her face bright red. Her smile so wide.

What an idiot.

Anger courses through my veins. That day means nothing to him. *I* mean nothing to him. I rip it once. And then again. Then I dash the four pieces into the trashcan next to my bed.

It's clear I've embarrassed myself. Thrown myself at him until he had to do something to get me to back off.

I run my fingers across my lips. The lips that Jack only just touched. Despite my hurt and anger, the flame of desire—of being *wanted*—rushes up my throat and leaves me gasping. To know that a single kiss could mean *so much* to me—and mean *nothing* to him?

I'm mortified. Shame and horror bubble in my gut, working their way up my chest.

The tears well in eyes and fall before I can stop them. They trail down my cheeks and cling to the gloss on my lips.

And that's when I decide to pack my things.

I wait as long as I can, my bags packed and sitting near the door as I tap my fingers on the marbled countertop. I haven't been to bed. When my father finally emerges from the primary bedroom upstairs, his brow furrows as he catches my gaze.

"What are you doing up so early, Sav?" He pads to the coffeemaker and clicks a pod in place.

"I want you to drop me off at ECU today." My tone is flat. Emotionless.

Because after a night of shedding tears, there's nothing left inside of me.

"What do you mean? We've got three more days together."

"I looked into it, and I can get into my dorm today. I can get everything set up and be ready when Del comes down. I'm ready to go now."

The coffee drips from the machine as my father stares at me silently.

"And my bodyguard isn't coming with me," I add for good measure and let my face do all the talking.

My face that likely looks haggard and sleep deprived.

"Now, see here, young lady, this has all been negotiated with the college and—"

"I don't care what *Miranda* negotiated with ECU. I need my freedom. I need to be just like every other college student."

"Savannah, you are not like every other college student." His baritone echoes throughout the empty kitchen.

I clench my jaw as my body stiffens. The sting at the back of my eyes has me turning away from him. "I didn't get a choice in your career. But living like this for the next four years is *my* choice. I'm either going without Keaton or—"

"Or what?" my father barks.

"I'll change my major." It's the last option I've got. The last threat that might carry some weight and cause my father to second-guess his decision. "You can't dictate what I study."

"I certainly will if I'm the one paying—"

"I have enough money from Mom's social security that I can pay for a year of my own schooling. And I'll take out financial aid going forward."

My father hasn't bargained on me. He hasn't bargained on my research. He hasn't bargained on this particular chip that I hold. My future. I can get a lot done with no sleep.

He grabs the mug from beneath the coffeemaker and, leaning against the counter, searches my eyes. "What's happened to bring this all about? Is it that Brett fellow? Because he's a nice boy, Savannah."

"I can't believe you think this is about a boy!" My brain doesn't even comprehend how silly I sound, but with my mind running on zero hours of sleep and a broken heart, I'm spiraling. Big time.

"So what is it about, then? What's causing you to cut our trip short?"

"*Our* trip? When has this ever been *our* trip?"

"When you were younger—"

"When I was younger and you weren't the governor, sure. Then it was *our* trip. But this trip hasn't been about me in years. You can't even tear yourself away from some stranger to spend a day at the amusement park with me." I cross my arms, my eyes filling with tears. Who knew I had any left?

"Sav, I—"

"I don't want to hear it. I'm not some political ally you have to coddle or compromise with. I'm your *daughter*." I let the air settle between us, waiting for him to beg me to stay, but he doesn't. No politician begs, least of all my father. My throat constricts and I fight to breathe. "Just take me to ECU. Without a bodyguard. Without any of this." My hand flies around the room. "Please, Dad?" I blink and a tear falls.

The skin around his eyes tightens, but when he presses his lips together and lowers his gaze, I know I've won.

"Okay. If this will make you happy. Let me get the keys."

He shuffles on heavy feet to the sink, where he dumps the cup full of coffee down the drain.

And within minutes, we're speeding away from Jack Keaton and toward a new chapter in my life.

Present Day

Chapter Twenty-Two

Savannah

"You've got to be kidding me, Savannah." Delia leans against the doorjamb, her arms crossed over her chest. "*This* song? *Again*?"

"I like this song." Pink Floyd's "Comfortably Numb" has been my anthem over the last four years, and as I glance around at the clusterfuck that is my room, that's not about to change any time soon.

"Ugh, I understand your weird obsession with listening to the same song over and over—because who *doesn't* have a song on repeat—but this one's been on repeat since *freshman year*." She crosses to my desk and hits pause on the music app. "And what are you still doing with that empty box? You've been in here for hours and it looks like you haven't even started packing!"

I blink and glance around at the mess on my bed, spilling from the closet, and littered all over my desk. And yes, the box next to me is almost empty. *Almost.*

Except for a little black dress.

Delia tilts the cardboard cube toward herself and pinches the flimsy fabric between her thumb and forefinger. Hoisting it up, her eyebrows pinch. "I remember this dress. You bought it for high school graduation and then..." She doesn't continue. *And then I had to retake psychology and received my diploma in early July via the mail.* "It's gorgeous, Sav. Why haven't you ever worn it?"

I don't have the heart to tell her that the dress holds too many bad memories. "I wore it a few times. I just don't think you were around to see it." I can't admit to her that, as I started packing away my belongings, I took one look at the dress stuffed in the back of my closet and emotionally shut down. So instead, I stand and carefully pull down the driftwood curtain rod over the single window of my room.

Delia pushes aside a pile of clothes and takes a seat on the edge of the bed. She looks around at the room I've called home for the last three years. "I don't know why you never invested in blackout curtains. How did you get any sleep?"

I shrug. My crotchet bohemian linen curtains never did anything to dim the rising sun, but I wouldn't have it any other way. "Blackout curtains wouldn't fit the vibe."

"Right. Getting a good night's rest would certainly derail the beachy boho girl aesthetic." She nods to the vintage guitar hanging from the wall next to my bed. "And how are you getting that thing home?"

I shrug again because I don't actually know. My father sent a plane ticket the minute I graduated in May, accompanied by a long text begging me to come home. Fortunately, the lease on our townhouse wasn't up until the end of summer, so I decided to stay put and spend June doing something I never got the chance to do. Being irresponsible and truly blowing off steam.

A heavy sigh from Delia drags me back into the present. "Our summer of slacking has come to an end. I'm going to miss you so much!" She holds out her arms, and I go willingly, wrapping my best friend in a huge bear hug.

"I'll be able to come visit, you know. We'll be campaigning close to New Buffalo sometime in late August, so we can arrange a girls' night out and you can show off your swanky big city apartment."

"The apartment I'm sharing with two other girls."

"It'll be like the TV show *Girls*. Except in Chicago instead of New York," I add.

"Ugh, I can't believe we're both going to be adults with actual real careers." She feigns a pout and swipes away a pretend tear. "What if the people I work with are awful? What if they microwave fish during lunch and stink up the whole office?" Her voice rises an octave.

"I'm sure you'll make friends, what with your shining personality." I chuckle and pat her head. The truth is that Delia is a stone-cold bitch. She hates pretty much everyone except her family, me, and her grandma, an eighty-eight-year-old, who's even more crotchety than her granddaughter.

"Ew. Maybe I'll be the one to microwave the fish. Set the tone that I'm not a people person and all."

I grab a framed picture of the two of us off my bedside table and gently place it in the box. On top of the discarded black dress. Then, for good measure, I dump in my collection of sweatpants and shove a few sweatshirts on top. I push everything down as though I'm trying to fit the last bit of trash in an already overflowing bin.

"What the hell are you doing?" Delia shrieks as she watches me. Mouth gaping open, she shakes her head back and forth.

"Um, packing?" I close the box and haphazardly tape it up before tossing it near the door.

Her hand moves to her sternum as she recoils from me. "What you are doing is *not* packing, Savannah! Mixing dresses with a random picture frame and then adding sweats? You didn't even label that box before you *whipped* it across the room."

I bite my bottom lip and pretend to look contrite. "That's how I've always packed." In truth, the only time I've ever packed my own belongings was when I fled from the beach house. Four years ago. My heart hammers as I recall similarly shoving my belongings into a mix of luggage and trash bags.

Every other time, one of my father's staff, usually Miranda, took care of the packing. I swallow down the irritation burning my throat.

"You're an adult now. With a dual degree in political science and international relations. It's time you learned how to pack your shit properly, Sav. I'll be back." She leaves the room, but before I can even put the next cardboard box together, she's returned.

She lays out stacks of newspapers, bubble wrap, and a Sharpie pen.

"Great," I murmur as I wonder what I'm going to do without my best friend around.

"Tell your dad thanks for upgrading my ticket."

I nod at Delia as we gather our things. "You know he considers you part of the family. Are you sure you don't need a ride home, too?"

She slings her bag over her shoulder. "No, my mom is picking me up and then we're heading straight to the nursing home to visit Nana."

"I still can't believe your parents were able to talk her into selling her home and moving into one of those places." We move at a snail's pace as passengers exit their seats ahead of us.

"Hey, asshole, who taught you the correct way to deplane?" Delia scolds a man who tries to cut in front of us.

The man's face turns an ungodly shade of red as he retreats to his seat. He shoots my angry friend a glare, but she's oblivious as she tugs her carry-on from the overhead compartment.

"At least Nana's in one of those small apartments," my best friend continues, as though she didn't just verbally assault a man for breaking an unwritten rule. "She calls it her condo. She even gets to keep her car and that raggedy thing she calls a dog."

"French Horn is still alive? Jesus, he must be on his last leg." Nana, as even I'm allowed to call her, named her pug-beagle mix after the same instrument that Delia attempted to play in sixth grade, the same year she got the dog. She said the puggle's face reminded her of Delia's when she blew into the giant brass contraption. Like I said, Nana's a crotchety one, but she's always treated me as one of her own grandchildren.

"Yup. He's down to only three legs now, but manages to get around just fine, seeing as Nana carries him everywhere. Anyway, are you sure you can't come visit? I know she'd love to see you."

We finally deplane and scurry up the jetway into the airport. "I've got an early meeting tomorrow with Dad's official campaign crew. But tell Nana I said hello. And make sure to give French Horn a big kiss from me, too," I joke.

We walk down the tiled corridor until we reach the escalator to baggage claim and passenger pickup. Delia only has her carry-on, but I decided to check my guitar rather than ship it back home and risk it being destroyed in the mail.

"Well," I say, turning to her as we reach the bottom level. "It's been great, but unfortunately, this isn't working out. It's not me. It's you."

She smirks. "Honestly, your snoring and personal hygiene became a little too much for me."

My mouth gapes. "I do not snore!"

"You do, actually. I could hear it through the walls. I just didn't have the heart to tell you, so I suffered in silence for four years too long."

Before I can bite back a reply, Delia pulls me in for a hug. As snarky as she can be, she's the best friend I've ever had, and I wouldn't change our relationship for anything. "I'm going to miss you."

"Ew, stop being so emotional. It's gross." She pulls away and sniffs, but not before I catch the glimmer of unshed tears in her eyes.

"Right. I'm the emotional one." From outside the sliding doors, I spy her mom's cherry red sedan. "Your ride's here. I'll call you tonight."

"Sheesh, quit smothering me." Hoisting her carry-on a little higher, she turns away. "But if you don't call me, I'll never forgive you and our friendship will be over."

She retreats through the doors and tosses her bag into the back seat, giving me a little wave to me before ducking into the passenger side and closing the door behind herself.

I inhale deeply, turning to the loud beeping from the baggage claim conveyer belt. Inching closer, I watch as luggage topples awkwardly from the opening, lands, and then begins the carousel ride around the waiting passengers. I bite my lip, worrying about the state of my instrument, just as I spot it through the hole.

Securing my carry-on higher on my shoulder, I maneuver through the crowd. "Excuse me," I say to an older couple as I situate myself nearer to the carousel.

The elongated case edges closer. I stand on my tiptoes as bag after bag is claimed, giving me a clearer view. It appears to be in one piece, with the protective cover still intact. As it rounds the curve of the belt, I lean in and reach for it, when a familiar voice—and forearm—stop me cold.

"I've got it, Savannah."

My hand closes over nothing and tightens into a fist as I turn toward the man now holding my priceless possession. Eyes narrowed, I slide my gaze over his face. The face that kept me awake all those nights four years ago. The one I still see in my dreams as I awake in an unsatisfied sweat with a throbbing core.

Swallowing down the lump in my throat, I work up the courage to finally meet his eyes.

I swipe the guitar case from his grip and do everything in my power to ignore the spark that flares in my chest when our hands touch. "No, *I've* got it, Keaton."

CHAPTER TWENTY-THREE

Jack

I flick my gaze to the rearview mirror in hopes of connecting with Savannah's eyes. Unfortunately, she's refused to even glance my way the entire drive from the airport. Sitting in the backseat was a punch to the gut, but her refusal to even look at me? The ache in my chest intensifies, only catching snippets of her profile as she stares out the window. I'm tossed back in time to her driving us along the freeway. The coast in view as she sings to some throaty indie guitar piece. Her face pointing toward the sun as she belts out the chorus and shatters my world. *God, what I would give...*

"Fuck," I hiss as the car next to us swerves into my lane and I slam on the brakes.

"Jesus Christ, Keaton. Watch the goddamn road!" This time, her eyes meet mine in the mirror, cold and hard. Her admonishment cuts deeper than she knows, especially as she addresses me by my last name. It's the way her father addresses all his employees.

I don't apologize, but rather turn up the volume on the radio and grind my teeth. She returns to looking out the window and, thankfully, avoids commenting on my choice of music.

I navigate the rest of the way safely to the governor's summer mansion. As it's already the middle of the season, he has moved to the Mackinac Island residence farther north. The Arts and Crafts style house sits on a bluff overlooking the strait, and every time I make the trek up here, I'm astounded by the beauty of Michigan.

The moment I pull into the drive and put the vehicle in park, Savannah hops out and retrieves her carry-on and guitar from the trunk. With the bag slung over one shoulder and the case under her other arm, she struggles to close the liftgate. I hurry toward her and pull the hatch down with one hand while the other catches her around the waist and moves her out of the way.

Her muscles stiffen against my palm before she takes a wide step back. "Let me carry something for you. I can put the guitar in your room while you go on in."

Her expression's blank as she looks up at me. "No."

I want to ask her what made her take up playing. Was it the conversation years ago as we watched the fireworks? The knot in my throat grows. If she couldn't be bothered to say thank you, she's certainly not likely to indulge in a conversation about her new hobbies.

She struggles to walk away as one arm raises to keep her carry-on bag from sliding off her shoulder and the other arm hoists the instrument under her armpit. I growl and clench my fists.

This isn't how I wanted this to go.

"That her?" I start as my new assistant, Elijah Jenson, appears from the side of the vehicle.

"Yup. That's Savannah. Miss Smith, as she'll likely request you call her."

"Ah," he chuffs under his breath. "One of those."

My brow furrows as I turn toward him. "What do you mean?"

He slaps me on the back as he takes the keys from my hand. "I've worked with a ton of people like that, man. Too stuck up to fraternize with the help. Just a surprise, since her dad's so friendly and all." Opening the door to the SUV, he hops in and then adjusts the seat. Eli's not as tall as I am, but what he lacks in height, he makes up for in sheer strength. When the governor asked me to hire another bodyguard, I knew my old friend and past partner in the force, Eli, was the man for the job. As a former college wrestler, he's definitely able to hold his own.

"Maybe I'll be able to break her frostiness." With a wink, he slams the door before pulling the vehicle away.

As if I wasn't already in a bad mood, now I have to worry about Elijah attempting to worm his way into Savannah's good graces. If only he knew the real reason she was acting so cold.

"How many more men do you suggest we hire for the campaign trail, Keaton?" The governor's gruff voice cuts through the crowded conference room. We're surrounded on all sides by various members of his staff. From his speech writer to his personal chef, everyone is here for the briefing.

"I believe, sir, that Elijah and I can handle the brunt of the work. However, if needed, I do have a few friends I can call up. But I'd rather hold off until we have a need." I glance at Elijah, who's leaning back in his chair, arms crossed over his chest. He dips his chin in agreement.

"Sounds great, gentlemen. Miranda, I need a finalized schedule emailed to me, Laurel, and Savannah. Please make sure you copy Keaton and Jenson as well." Miranda nods and makes a note on her pad. I have a tendency to tune out anything involving her, especially since she's seen me at my worst. And try as I might to avoid thinking about that day four years ago, I can't stop myself.

It was hard not to blame her for what happened with Savannah, but I know it wasn't Miranda's fault. She was right. I had no business getting so close to my protectee. I'm only grateful Miranda was the one to find out first. Grateful, and ashamed, to be honest. And now that Savannah is back for good, working with her father on his campaign, the memories I'd tried to suppress are bubbling back to the surface.

"*Fuck.*"

All eyes in the conference room turn to me. "Pardon?" The governor sits forward in his seat, his fingers laced together in front of him.

"Oh, nothing. Sorry." I feel a heated flush creeping up my neck. I'm not normally this frazzled. This fazed. I roll my shoulders. *Get your shit together, Jack.*

"Savannah will be accompanying me as my new campaign manager, so you'll need to arrange security for her as well."

It takes a minute to realize the governor is directing his words at me. I blink. "Uh, of course, sir." My gaze catches on Elijah's. "Jenson is more than capable of filling that role with your requirements."

"Actually, I'd prefer you." He closes the folio in front of him and begins to rise from his seat.

My heart pounds in my ears and, as I watch my boss retreat from the conference room, I know I need to speak up now before it's too late. I dodge the other staff who congregate around one another, making small talk over their mugs of coffee, and only catch up to the governor as he slides through the doorway.

"Sir?" He holds up a finger before continuing his conversation with Miranda.

"… I'll need the tickets booked by this evening and a bouquet of roses ordered as well. The card should read…" I tune out, as I've learned to do with anything that doesn't involve my immediate duties. Whatever the governor does during his time is his personal business. Not mine.

I'm happy he's found someone to share his life with, and Ms. Prescott is a kind woman. She goes out of her way to thank the staff, who she knows by name, and she makes excellent desserts, which she shares with all of us. I know the governor has been begging her to move to Washington when he gets elected to the senate, but she refuses. So their relationship continues over the miles between Michigan and Florida.

"Walk with me, Keaton." The governor strides down the hallway, Miranda and I tagging along beside him. I swallow the lump in my throat; I don't want to discuss this in front of her. "Out with it, son."

My breath hitches at the term of endearment. I've observed him with other employees, and I'm the only one he calls that. Palms clammy, I square my shoulders as best I can while keeping pace and let it all out. "Sir, I want Jenson covering your daughter. As the senior member of the team, I prefer to oversee your day-to-day." There. I sneak a peek at him, but instead catch Miranda's slight shake of her head. I bite my bottom lip.

He stops short and turns his back on his secretary. Facing me, he places his free hand on his hip while the knuckles on his other hand go white as he grips the leather folio. "I've said my piece about this, Keaton. Jenson's a good kid, but he's like a dog with a bone when it comes to women, and I don't want him sniffing around my daughter. You're the one I trust. You're doing it."

With a tight nod, he continues his path farther into the bowels of the mansion. But as I watch him retreat, I certainly don't miss Miranda's pinched lips.

And I can just imagine what she's thinking. Because I'm thinking it too. *If only he really knew...*

Chapter Twenty-Four

Savannah

He wraps his hand around her throat while pumping into her.

"Fuck, baby, you feel so tight when you take that di—"

"Savannah?" I snap my romance book closed as my father calls from the other side of the wrap-around porch.

"Over here, Dad." I glance down at the shirtless man on the cover, his abs soaking wet and his deep v-line exposed. I definitely need somewhere to hide my book, but seeing as I'm seated on a slatted Adirondack chair with no cushion, my options are nil. I look around as my heart rate skyrockets. Should I sit on it? Hide it in my shirt? But then something inside me snaps. I'm twenty-two and a college graduate. I can read whatever I want. So, instead of hiding what I like, I place it proudly on my lap, just as my dad rounds the corner.

"There you are." Taking the empty chair next to mine, he lets out a heavy sigh and sinks into the recliner. "Looks like you've got yourself something good to read, eh?" He nods at the book.

I clear my throat. "Yes, it's a, um, great work of fiction." I can already feel my face turning red.

"Ah, nothing to be embarrassed about. Your mother loved to read stories just like those. Called them her smut books."

I blink and relax into the chair. "I-I didn't know that."

"Oh yeah, she loved to read 'em and then we'd get all—"

"Dad! Stop!" My eyeballs practically pop out of my head as I gape at him. "I do *not* need to know that."

"Well, all right then. I didn't realize you were such a prude." I reach over and smack him with the book as he bursts out laughing. "At least tell me what this one is about. Maybe I'll recommend it to Laurel."

"Ew, no. Gross."

He rolls his eyes. I like my father's girlfriend, but that doesn't mean I want to hear about her book choices. That's private business. I certainly wouldn't share my e-reader history with *anyone*. While I may not want to know about Laurel's literature choices, I am curious about my father's intentions. So I take this moment and dive right into the question I've been meaning to ask.

"Dad, are you planning on marrying Laurel? You two have been seeing each other for quite a while now."

"Four years," he sighs as he leans back, putting his arms over his head. "But we aren't in a rush. She's got her company in Florida, and I'm up here doing my thing. We see each other when we can, but we both have big dreams."

"So Brett isn't going to be my stepbrother any time soon?"

My dad chortles and shakes his head. "It's a shame the two of you never worked out, but I'm glad you can get along for the sake of us. It was awfully nice of you to stop by Laurel's to celebrate his engagement party last month."

I smile and nod. While Brett and I never spent any time together at ECU, we've stayed in touch through our parents. He even got accepted into Michigan State for environmental policy and stayed at the governor's mansion in East Lansing for a while.

That was, until he met his fiancée, Anya, a Dutch environmental studies graduate student.

"So what's the plot of your book?" my dad asks as he points to the half-naked man on the cover. "There is a plot, right? I know some of the books your mom read didn't have much of a story. Just pure smut."

"Oh my God, if I tell you what it's about, will you stop?"

He doesn't respond, but his lips press together to suppress a smile, so I take that as a yes. "It's an age-gap romance where the daughter of the mafia boss falls in love with her father's rival."

"Age gap?"

"It's where there's an age difference between the romantic couple. In this story, the gap is fifteen years, but some are less. Some are more."

"You've read a lot of age gap books?" His forefinger taps on the armrest.

I shrug. "Some. Why?"

He doesn't say anything for a minute, but the skin around his eyes tightens. "I'm not gonna have some forty-year-old man showing up at my house asking to take you out, am I?"

I swallow down a chortle. "God no. I much prefer early sixties."

"Savannah Jane Smith, if you bring some geriatric man home for me to meet, I'm going to end up on the news!"

"Geriatric? Don't talk about my boyfriend like that!" I cross my arms with a playful glare.

"Oh, girl, you'll be the death of me, won't you? Not the people of this great state. Not my campaign or the stress of running an election. It'll be all you." He reaches across the divide and pats my forearm before leaning back and closing his eyes.

We sit like that for a while. I set my book down and, instead, flip through my phone. I'm almost certain my dad has fallen asleep, but when I glance over, his eyes are on me. "You've never brought a boy home. Why is that?"

I set down my phone and shrug. "No reason, really." Looking down at the grass, I dig my fingernail into the wooden armrest.

"I figured all those times you didn't come home was because you had a beau at school."

My gaze flicks to his, because who actually says *beau* instead of *boyfriend*? Only my dad. "Nope. No boyfriends." My lips press together.

"Girlfriends?" Eyes widening, I almost guffaw, except the look on my dad's face is purely innocent. Open and accepting of me. Whatever I am, *whoever* I am. He genuinely wants to know.

"No, Dad. No girlfriends either. Can you stop with the twenty questions already?"

"You've got me worried, Sav. You've hardly been home the last four years, save for Christmas and my birthday. Talk to me, kiddo."

Taking a deep breath, I roll my eyes and wave off the concern. "There's nothing to say. I promise. Besides, we met up plenty of times when you were visiting Laurel. We even celebrated Thanksgiving at her house, Dad." Because what can I actually tell him? I've avoided coming back to Michigan because of his bodyguard? I made sure Jack was off duty or with his family before I booked my flights? I'm a twenty-two-year-old virgin who thought she was strong enough to handle seeing the man who spurned her so long ago, but being near him is making my skin crawl and my heart hurt?

"You sure, Sav? There's nothing you want to tell me?"

I swallow the lump in my throat and stand, stretching my arms over my head. "I'm sure. You wanted me to double major, so what did you expect?" I eye him, waiting for a response. But when he doesn't say anything, I press on.

"Everything is fine. I'm going to head inside now." I grab my book and hold it against my chest, ready to flee as quickly as possible. But just as I'm taking a step away from the Adirondack chairs, my dad grabs my wrist.

"I love you, kiddo. I hope you know that I'm here if you ever do want to talk." He gives me a sad, flat smile that doesn't reach his eyes.

"Love you too, Dad. Goodnight." I pull away, even though all I want to do is curl up in his lap like I did as a little girl and have my dad protect me from the hurt of the world.

The election results flash across the screen as the commentator, a floating head, holds back a snort.

"Well, folks, the winner of Michigan's senate seat is none other than Brian Coleman, the young upstart with a social media following of 1.1 million. He ran on a platform based on…"

My ears tune out everything else as my father's eyes flash to me, the rage apparent as his fists clench and his jaw muscles twinge.

"Dad, I'm-I'm so—"

"I don't want to hear it, Savannah." He turns away as Miranda crosses the room to comfort him. Her hand on his shoulder. Laurel stands in the corner, her eyes boring holes in my soul. As if to say, "We all knew you couldn't do it."

My feet propel me across the carpet of the governor's mansion, and I reach for my father. "No, I don't want anything to do with her," he tells Miranda as he refuses to even glance at me. "She cost me this election. My dream."

"Dad, I'm sorry! I-I tried my best. I did everything you asked."

He finally deigns to look at me, but those eyes are cold. Made of glass. "Your best wasn't good enough, was it?"

I gasp awake. It's been ages since I've had these nightmares. Nightmares of being a failure. Being the reason my father lost out on his dream. But coming back to Michigan... Well, it's no surprise my mind would be rebelling against the relocation. Everything is more real here, and I can't escape this anxiety when I'm home.

My body's covered in a cold sweat and, even though the mild midwestern summer air drifts in through my open window, I'm shivering. *Go back to sleep*, I command my body as I shut my eyes against the darkness, but after lying motionless for what feels like forever, I release a groan and reach over to check my phone.

3:12 a.m.

Too early to start my day, but too late to do much else. I pad to the closet and throw on an oversized ECU sweatshirt and decide to wander downstairs and get a drink. Maybe a swig of something stronger than water or milk will calm my nerves.

I use the staircase that deposits me right in the kitchen and immediately stop in my tracks.

"Oh, I didn't realize anyone else was awake," Jack says from his seat at the small cafe table in the corner.

It's weird having so many people living in one house, especially after spending four years with just a single roommate. But since the governor's summer mansion is enormous, most of the staff lives here. "Just getting something to drink. I'll be out of your way shortly." My words are clipped, and I don't even glance in his direction as I pad toward the liquor cabinet in the opposite corner.

The kitchen went through an upgrade during my father's last term. New stainless-steel appliances are now hidden away in polished white cupboards. Everything is very elegant. Almost sterile. It's a far cry from the house we used to live in with dated tiled flooring and mismatched appliances.

The liquor cabinet itself is more of a built-in bar that extends beyond the refrigerator. Cupboards above hold fancy glassware, while shakers, a bucket for ice, and a book of mixology line the countertop. Beneath is a wine fridge and two deeper cabinets with shelves that pull out to reveal the various liquors and mixers. I grab a glass and then open the bottom cupboard to find my favorite whiskey—one from a Michigan brewing company, of course. I've been craving the warmth of the vanilla and cocoa caramelized flavor since I woke with a chill.

But as I tip each bottle back to check the label, I don't see it among the others. I let loose a heavy sigh and glance over my shoulder, finding *my* bottle at the table with *him*.

"Looking for this?" As he holds up the whiskey, I cringe.

"Yes." I saunter over and set my glass on the table a little too loudly. Then, I swipe the bottle and pour, a little too heavy-handed. *Oh well*, I shrug inwardly and go ahead and gulp it all. The alcohol stings as it goes down and my eyes water, but I'll be damned if I cough or sputter. So instead, I swallow the last mouthful and then return my glass to the table to top it off. Once it's brimming, I slide the bottle back across the table.

"I was just *leaving*." I turn and make my way to the stairs, already sipping more of the delicious liquid.

"I wish you wouldn't."

He mutters it under his breath so quietly that I'm not even sure I've heard him correctly, what with it being three in the morning and me on my second glassful in as many minutes. And even though I should come back with some snarky comment, I don't. Because he broke my heart once and I can't go through that again. So instead, I blink back the tears threatening to spill down my cheeks and take the stairs, and another pull from the glass, at the same time.

When I get back to my room, everything is fuzzy and warm and spinning and I have no trouble falling back to sleep.

And this time, I dream of nothing.

Chapter Twenty-Five

Jack

I grab Savannah's bags and put them in the back of the SUV. She doesn't say thank you or even make eye contact with me, not that I'd expect her to. Since she's been home, she's avoided me like the plague, save for the other night—er, morning—when we ran into each other over whiskey. Even then, she didn't come back with some snarky comment. Where is the sassy pain in my ass from four years ago?

The girl who wouldn't take no for an answer?

Has she really changed so much in four years?

Has she gotten over me?

Because now that she's back, I don't know if I can say the same...

I want her to poke my buttons, to challenge me. I want her to provoke me and show me that mischievous smile. Mostly, though, I want to ask her how she's doing. I want to *talk* to her. But the way she avoids even looking at me as she takes a hearty swig of whiskey, passes me in the hallway, or sits across from me at dinner... it's driving me crazy.

"Everyone buckled in?" the governor asks from his place in the passenger seat. I glance in the rearview mirror and see quick nods, so I go ahead and put the vehicle into drive and pull out of the driveway. Elijah's driving the second SUV and follows behind.

The governor prefers a quiet ride, so I've muted the radio. He taps his phone awake and starts scrolling through his emails, typing out responses to some and deleting others. I flick my gaze to the mirror and watch as Savannah puts in her ear buds and then looks out the window.

Is she listening to some cool new musician she just found? Does she still love singer-songwriters? Or has her taste in music changed? I'd love to know her favorite artist so I could download all of their music just so I could have something to connect to her.

I swallow the lump in my throat and then sigh heavily. "Everything okay, Keaton?" Glancing over, I find the governor's concerned gaze meeting my own.

"Fine, sir. Everything is fine."

"Good to hear. It looks like our schedule will be busy while we're at the conference this year. I'm glad Elijah has joined the team. I'll want you helping Savannah navigate all this, since she's still learning her way. We'll be in some meetings together, but she'll need support at the events and fundraisers we're to attend. I'll also want you to be *her* driver while we're down there."

"Sir?" Normally, I'm the only person that Governor Smith trusts to drive him. He won't even let Elijah touch the SUV. Unless it's to clean it.

"Jenson can handle me."

"Are you sure about that?" I send a smirk his way, and he chuckles before taking a sip of his coffee and then returning to his emails.

It's only when I check the rearview mirror as we pull onto the tarmac that I catch Savannah's glare and realize she's heard everything.

"I'll need you to drop me a pin when you arrive at the conference each day and then make sure to document your mileage, too."

Eli rolls his eyes. "I know, boss. You explained all the procedures in last week's meeting, remember?"

I don't, actually. My mind has been everywhere but on the job, and it's got me fucked up. I don't normally make these amateur mistakes, and I'm afraid Jenson's going to catch on that something's up. "Of course I remember. I'm just making sure your dumb ass understands," I joke as I close the folio and slide it into my bag.

"Just because you were the smartest candidate in our cadet program doesn't mean I'm a dumbass. Not everyone scores so high on all the aptitude tests and then decides to become a personal bodyguard for the governor."

I press my lips firmly together to avoid making some sarcastic retort about his *inaptitude*. That wouldn't be very professional of me, and as I'm trying to build something here, I definitely need to mind my P's and Q's.

Just as I zip up the bag, my cell phone rings. I check the caller ID and see my mom's name flash across the screen. "Excuse me," I say to Eli as I stand and hold the phone to my ear.

"Hi, Ma." I carefully make my way to the rear of the plane and lower my voice. Everyone around me is either reading memos or going over the details with one another for the next two weeks.

"Hi, sweetie! I just wanted to call and check in. See how things were going. Are you already in Florida?" I hear the TV in the background and assume she's sitting down to eat breakfast while watching the morning news.

"Not yet, Ma. Remember I told you we'd arrive after ten and I'd give you a call when we landed?" I lean against a beige storage cabinet near the restroom and cross my arms over my chest.

"Oh, that's right! I'm so forgetful, Jacks. I'll let you go, then." I can feel the embarrassment through the phone.

"No. It's okay. I can talk. Did you take your medication this morning?" I'd been able to stop over yesterday and fill up her pill organizer, as well as grab a few groceries to tide her over for the week. I also set up a grocery delivery for next week and spoke to her neighbor, Mrs. Whitberry, a middle-aged woman who works from home and can check in on Ma if needed.

"Of course I took my medication. I'm not a child, Jacks! I just forget things here and there."

"I know, Ma. Don't forget that you have an appointment with your doctor tomorrow morning at 9 a.m. Mrs. Whitberry will drive you."

"I have my schedule right in front of me that you wrote out. I didn't call to be nagged at. You seemed quiet yesterday. Like something was on your mind. Is everything okay?"

"Everything's fine. Just had a lot to do to plan and organize for the trip." I don't tell her that I've been lying awake at night, listening for the sound of Savannah coming down to get a drink. It's been consistent for the past few days. Every morning at about 3 a.m. Her favorite whiskey ran out and now she's switched to other spirits. I wish I'd thought of replacing it. Or, hell, even bringing along a bottle in my luggage. Maybe then she'd talk to me.

"I hope you're not overexerting yourself. Does the governor even let you have an evening off? When was the last time you had a date? You're not getting any younger, son. I'd like to be a grandma sooner rather than later, you know."

With a sigh, I rub the ridge of my brow. Not this again. "Ma, there have been plenty of dates, and I'm sure you'll be a grandma before you know it. Can you give it a rest?"

Just then, the restroom door clicks open, and I'm met with Savannah's stoic face. Her gaze flicks to mine and her cheeks tint as she scoots past me. "Excuse me," she says in a clipped tone. I feel the blood rush to my feet and wonder just how much she heard.

"I gotta go, Ma. Call you when we land." Before she can respond, I press the end call button and pocket the device.

"Savannah, wait," I whisper-hiss as she makes her way up the aisle and back to her seat.

But of course, she doesn't stop. Doesn't even falter in her steps. Instead, she looks over her shoulder and sends me a look that says, *I wish you were dead.*

And at that moment, I wish I were too.

Chapter Twenty-Six

Savannah

The second I'm buckled into the back of the sleek black town car, I shove my earbuds in and swipe open my phone. Searching for something equally calming and upbeat, I scroll until I find my newest favorite song, a ballad by a young singer-songwriter about being broken and bled dry. It's been on repeat lately, for obvious reasons.

I press my lips together and wait as Jack—*Keaton,* as I need to remember to call him—settles into the front seat and buckles himself in as well. He turns on the car and shifts into drive, just as the passenger door opens.

And Miranda slides in.

Fuck. This.

I'm out.

But before I can unbuckle myself and throw open the door, we're driving away from the tarmac and toward the beach. Which means I'm stuck for the next forty minutes in a moving vehicle with the two people I despise the most.

I was so smart

But you made me look like a fool

The lyrics for this song could not be any more perfect, yet as I force myself to look anywhere but at them, shoulder-to-shoulder in the front, I can't help but turn the volume down and eavesdrop on their conversation.

Except they're not talking.

They're not even looking at each other.

Miranda's busy typing on her phone. An email, as it appears from her app.

Jack's using his right hand to steer, while his left, situated against the paneling of the car door, is propped against his temple. His forearm flexes and releases, as do the muscles along the back of his neck. My gaze flicks over the dark ink.

"Tell me about your tattoos."

"Do they mean something?"

God, how stupid I was. Does his new girlfriend know about his body art? Does he have a tattoo for her?

I assess Jack and Miranda from my position, which is hardly perfect, considering all I can see are their profiles. They're clearly uncomfortable, which is surprising, seeing as they conspired together to "fix" Jack's little problem, i.e. me.

"This never should've happened. I'm going to lose everything because of her."

I scoff loud enough that Jack's gaze flicks up to the rearview mirror and catches mine. Only this time, I refuse to look away. Instead, I hold his stare and narrow my eyes.

You were so persuasive

How could you lie without hesitating

He eventually returns his focus to the road, but not before I catch another subtle flex of his forearm against the window.

Good, I think to myself. I hope being in this car makes him as uncomfortable as it makes me.

And then I click repeat on the song.

"You've got to be kidding me," I mumble under my breath as I look at the mess of plaster, paint buckets, and cloth tarps covering the empty room. *My* empty room.

"Oh no, Savannah. I didn't realize the contractors hadn't properly cleaned up and readied all the rooms. Let me go check with your father and see what he'll want to do with you." Miranda pouts at me before clopping down the hall in her kitten heels.

Is this a setup to get me out of the house? The potential problem-causer that I am?

Grinding my teeth, I set my carry-on bag on top of my luggage case and pull my phone from the back of my jeans pocket. Miranda might be wearing a two-piece dress suit, but I'm in white denim and a flowy tank top. I ditched my jacket the moment we stepped onto the tarmac. It's already hot as hell and the humidity has set my waves to frizz mode.

I hear a discussion coming from the kitchen, so I leave my belongings and traipse down the hallway.

"I can call around and see if there are any available hotel rooms in the area, but as it's prime vacation season, and with the conference starting tomorrow, the availability will be limited. It may be best to book something closer to the airport and away from the beach."

Away from us, she means, as though I'm a ticking time bomb ready to blow everything up.

"That won't work, Miranda. Savannah needs to be close enough to attend all the marketing and fundraising events." My father rarely disagrees with his assistant, so I have to relish the way her hollow cheeks tint.

"It's fine, Dad," I say as I reach out and put my hand on his arm. "I can find my own lodgings. I'll call around and see what's available. I'll even Uber so you have enough vehicles for the staff. Elijah can pick me up in the mornings."

He offers me a grateful smile before turning to Miranda. "I don't like this one bit. I expected the renovations to be completed and in order. You ensured me that everything was taken care of."

"My apologies, sir. I'll get in contact with the construction crew right now and see how long they'll need to finish up the repairs." She rushes off with her head tilted down at her phone.

"Dad, there's no reason to get upset. It's fine. I'll call around, book a room, and then Uber my way over there." I offer him a toothy smile and maneuver around him to settle on a stool along the bar.

Flicking through the names and numbers of the nearest hotels, I settle on one with a spa as well as room service. Might as well make the best of the situation.

"Hi, I'd like to book a room for a few nights," I say into the phone as I'm connected with a representative.

"When will you be staying with us, ma'am?"

"Tonight through Monday, at least. Possibly longer." Who knows? If I like this place, maybe I'll just do myself a solid and stay there the entire time. Avoid Jack the entire trip. I feel better already.

"Oh, I'm so sorry. We're all booked up. There's a huge energy conference in town and it's peak vacation season, too." My stomach drops. I was really looking forward to their world-renowned spa and award-winning seafood.

I sigh heavily. "Can you recommend a hotel in the area that might have availability?"

"Oh, no, honey." Her laugh tinkles over the phone. "Everyone around us is all booked up, too. There is the Sandy Sea Dollar down the way from us, though. You might try there."

"Oh, is that an affiliate of your hotel?"

She giggles again. "Not exactly. But it's likely the only place nearby with availability. Good luck."

"Thanks anyway," I mutter as I end the call.

I search up the Sandy Sea Dollar and frown at the pictures. It's definitely dated and looks like there haven't been renovations since the early 90s. But it's certainly better than nothing.

CHAPTER TWENTY-SEVEN

Jack

"You cannot be serious." The sentiment slips from my lips before I have a chance to take it back, but as I glance at Savannah's flattened lips and the way her skin tightens around her eyes, I know she's feeling the same.

"I told you and my father that I didn't need a babysitter. Go back to the house." She tugs her suitcase along the cracked sidewalk and heads toward what I assume is the lobby. There are a few divots in the glass, which appears bulletproof, but there's no way in hell I'm leaving her here alone. Not like that's an option. Her father had demanded, in no uncertain terms, that I was to not only be Savannah's personal chauffeur for the few days she's at the motel, but also keep an eye on her, too.

"Can I help you?" the young woman questions from behind the protective shield. She appears bored or high. Either way, her eyes are bloodshot and at half-mast.

"I just made a reservation. Two rooms for three nights. The name is Savannah Smith."

The receptionist clicks through her dated computer and her brow furrows. "You said two rooms?"

"Yes," Savannah responds as she pulls her ID from the bag slung across her shoulder. She proceeds to place it on the silver tray that slides under the glass.

"I'm sorry, Miss Smith, but we don't have two rooms available. Do you know who you spoke to when you called?"

Savannah leans against the counter and drops her head into her hand. "Seeing as I just called thirty minutes ago, I'm going to assume it was you."

"Hm." The woman looks up and ponders the sentiment for a moment. "I am the only one on duty today. That's strange."

My blood boils, and I inch closer to the glass. "Savannah, there has to be somewhere else we can stay. Or we can go back to the house. You can have my room and I'll take the couch. Hell, I'll sleep in the car." I lean in closer to Savannah and lower my voice. "Anywhere but here. This place doesn't look safe."

Savannah's face turns a shade of red as her eyebrows slam down over her eyes. They darken from their chocolate brown to a midnight black. "As I've said before, I am fine staying here *alone*. Go back to the house. Without me." She turns to the receptionist and tosses down her credit card. "I'll take the room, please."

"Great." She grabs the ID and the credit card and starts typing into the square machine. "Oh, I forgot to tell you both. There's a complimentary happy hour this evening here in the lobby from four to six." She nods to the corner where a box of wine sits atop a greasy table.

Savannah blinks at the boxed wine and then swallows, the cords in her neck tightening ever-so-slightly. She offers the receptionist a faint smile as she takes back her cards and returns them to her purse.

"Your room is around the back. Fourth floor." She passes the key through the tray and Savannah grabs it, then turns to the exit.

"I don't suppose there're two beds?" I ask through the partition.

The receptionist chuckles and shakes her head. "Nope. Just the one. Enjoy your stay at the Sandy Sea Dollar."

"You've gotta be fucking kidding me." Savannah's cry of disbelief mimics my own thoughts as she releases the door handle and stares into the gaping maw that is our home for the next three days.

A queen-sized bed.

A fucking queen-sized bed.

Savannah's eyes narrow as she takes in the bed, and then she turns her head slightly to absorb the rest of the room. I don't miss the way her jaw tics as she slides her suitcase to the side and strides into the bathroom.

"Ugh," I hear her voice echo against the tile.

"That bad?" I'm still focused on the size of the bed and how we're going to both fit without touching.

"Well, it's not good, Keaton." She marches out and catches me staring at the bed.

"I'll call down for a cot. You can take the bed," I add, trying to make the best of the situation. Her lips thin as she moves past me to retrieve her luggage. She pulls it into the room and then, glancing around, decides to deposit it on the side of the bedraggled dresser. Grabbing the handle of a drawer, she pulls, but nothing happens. She moves to the next drawer and repeats the process, but again, the dresser doesn't open. With a deep exhale, she falls to her knees next to her case.

I place my luggage on the other side of the dresser, but don't even bother trying the drawers. I don't mind living out of my suitcase, especially for only a few days. Unzipping the silver hardback case, I pull out a black t-shirt and dark denim jeans. "I'm going to hop in the shower. We're supposed to be at dinner by six." From my toiletry kit, I grab soap, shampoo, and a razor. As I move to the bathroom, I see Savannah glancing at her own luggage with pinkened cheeks. As much as I want to ask her if everything is all right, I already know the answer.

She hates being here.

With me.

I gulp down the guilt I feel and close the door to the bathroom. Cranking on the faucet, I find the water pressure surprisingly decent. The towels, on the other hand, are far from it, and I'm likely to get razor burn from the roughness alone. As steam rises from the shower, I pull my t-shirt over my head and strip down my pants and briefs, too. I climb into the tub and shower combo and immediately soak my hair under the stream.

This is far from the ideal arrangement for the next few days, but perhaps this isolation with Savannah will give me a chance to put things right. Is it too naive to believe she'll ever forgive me? Probably, but I'm nothing if not optimistic. Besides, I can't get the thought of her kneeling beside her suitcase with blushing cheeks from my head. Is thinking of us here *together* causing her to blush?

"Fuck," I hiss as the hot water runs down my face. How am *I* supposed to go out there and not think of her down on her knees, those doe eyes staring up at me?

CHAPTER TWENTY-EIGHT

Savannah

The private elevator dings, and I charge ahead, my high heels clicking on the marble floors. The entryway is spacious, with vaulted ceilings and a giant vase of fresh flowers on the rounded foyer table. Windows reach from floor to ceiling and the enormous room looks out over the Gulf. A pod of dolphins crests in the distance, their backs sparkling arcs in the glass smoothness of the water. Beachgoers appear like ants below, and the view is breathtaking. I step out onto the balcony and inhale the mixture of clean linen from the inside and salt water from the outside. If I could bottle this into a perfume, I'd wear nothing else.

"Are you ready?" Jack's question snaps me from my daydream, and I'm brought back to the Sandy Sea Dollar with a thud.

There are no vaulted ceilings or a vase of fresh flowers.

No dolphins in the distance.

Our room overlooks the back parking lot, and the scent of clean linen and saltwater is replaced with the stale, hot dumpster that stands rusting a stone's throw away.

"I was imagining I was at the Emerald Isle, so no, I'm not ready to acknowledge reality just yet." My head drops back against the plastic chair, but as I inhale the scent of old garbage and asphalt, I realize I, too, now need to freshen up before dinner.

So I stand and slink through the sliding glass door, past Jack and his delicious manly scent.

My nose perks up just as my heart flutters.

Oh, God.

But instead of enjoying the smell of him—it hasn't changed in four years—I grind my back teeth and settle down next to my luggage.

I should've attempted to unpack when he was in the shower, but as the faucet turned on, I could hear the water sluicing over him, and my imagination started to run wild. I had to escape the suddenly stifling room.

So I sat and inhaled humid garbage and watched the comings and goings of the Sandy Sea Dollar parking lot. I counted the number of grease and oil spots. Anything to get my mind off how close I was to a naked Jack.

And now, as I unzip my bag and flip up the lid, I so wish I was inside that dumpster.

Because sitting on top of my clothing is a vibrator. *My* vibrator. And from the way Jack's breath hitches behind me, I know he's just spied it, too.

The silence in the black town car is deafening. I pick at imaginary lint on the pencil skirt I'm wearing and then examine the matching jacket. Anything to avoid looking at, or talking to, Jack.

His gaze stays trained on the traffic along the main drag. We inch forward, but in all honesty, it'd be faster to walk. Unfortunately, we've several miles still to go before we arrive at the venue.

I pull my phone from my clutch and check my messages.

Dad: Just arrived. How far out are you?

I type out the response and click send before shoving the device back into my bag. "Isn't there another way? We're going to be late."

Jack's gaze slides to me, but not before his eyes rake up my bare legs and over the tight pencil skirt. My cheeks heat, but I'm too frustrated with the traffic to give it much thought. "Everyone's avoiding Cermac because of a crash."

I sigh heavily and press my lips together. Feeling as though I'm about to burst out of my skin with agitation, I crank the air conditioning and adjust myself in the sticky leather seats.

"Doesn't this car have vented seats? Who rents a car with leather seats in the middle of summer anyway?" I wiggle again and my skin squeaks across the material.

Jack indicates the appropriate button, but pulls his hand away as I push the blue wavy lines. My ass instantly starts to cool, but I'm still annoyed at the traffic. I take my phone out and check the time, and then toss it right back into my bag.

"Can you chill out? You're driving me insane." He doesn't take his eyes off the road, even as we are bumper to bumper with the car in front of us.

I don't want to admit that I'm nervous. I'm nervous I'm going to make a poor first impression upon these people who my father is depending on. As his acting campaign manager—and *actual* daughter—it's my duty to be on time and professional. Showing up late with sweaty thighs is hardly the picture one wants to project to potential donors.

"Your driving, or lack thereof, is driving me insane," I counter.

He flicks his eyes at me. "Now I see why you needed to bring a toy on this trip," he mutters under his breath.

"What are you talking about? What toy?" But then it hits me. *The vibrator.* A new warmth creeps over my body. One that can't immediately be soothed by air conditioning or vented seats. I'm mortified.

But Jack just chuckles. It's the first time I've seen his smile in four years. I forgot how much I love that smile. *Loved* that smile. His straight white teeth. The way his eyes crinkle at the corners. And then he bites his bottom lip and glances at me.

I blink and look away. Embarrassed to be caught staring. Embarrassed that he knows I travel with a vibrator. I lean against the window, hoping the glass will cool my forehead, but I should've known better. In this humid Florida heat, the window is hot as hell. "Ouch!" I hiss as the glass burns my skin. I flip down the visor and open the lighted mirror, checking my makeup. "Could anything else go wrong on this trip?" I ask aloud as I examine the red spot that's growing on my forehead. My vision goes fuzzy, and I sniff.

Don't you dare cry.

Suddenly, Jack jerks the steering wheel and slams on the gas, zooming down a side street. We bounce over pothole after pothole as we whizz past various condos and apartments. "What are you doing? You said Cermac was—"

"I'm getting you to that dinner. On time." He navigates around a large group of tourists waiting to cross the street and then pulls out onto a larger road.

Where there's no traffic.

"Plug the address into my phone." He passes me the device, and I stall, still mesmerized—and a bit confused—by his sudden detour. "Go on," he prompts, and I type the information into his maps app. When I hand it back, our hands briefly touch, and he glances down at the arrival time. "Looks like you'll be two minutes late. Can you handle that?"

A small smile lifts my lips. "Yeah. Yeah, I can handle that."

Chapter Twenty-Nine

Jack

"Here you go, boss." Eli hands me a glass tumbler of amber liquid with a nod. I take it and sniff, the odor soothing my wound-up nerves.

"Just what I needed. How'd you know?"

His eyes snake to Savannah's back across the room. "You looked a little flushed when you arrived. Late, no less."

I bring the rim to my lips and take a slow pull, appreciating the way the liquid burns as it coats my mouth. "Two minutes."

"Late is still late. Or so you've told me time and time again." He cocks a bushy eyebrow at me and smirks.

"Yeah, yeah, yeah. How's it going so far at the house? Did you get the cameras up and running?" The fucking restoration crew had yanked the wiring clear from the walls and tossed the electronics in a pile, leaving Eli to have to rewire the entire system in an afternoon.

"All but one. The plaster was still too wet in Miss Smith's room to run the wiring, but I'll get on it tomorrow."

"No rush. We've got the motel booked for three nights. Just get it done by Tuesday when we're back."

Eli stills and meets my gaze.

"What?"

His face cracks and his smirk turns into a frown accompanied by the shake of his head. "Nothing, man. You're just using a lot of the plural pronouns today, aren't you?"

I narrow my eyes at him. "Plural pronouns?"

"*We've* got the motel booked. Done by Tuesday when *we're* back. That's a whole lotta *we*."

I just stare at him. What else can I say? Savannah and I aren't a we. She's hardly warmed up to me, but at least the car ride wasn't as chilly as I expected. She took the joke about her little toy pretty well, and she seemed grateful when I navigated the shortcut to get her here only slightly later than expected.

As I take in the banquet room, my gaze immediately finds her. She's turned away, shaking hands with some big wig her father is introducing to her. But in her element, in this environment, she shines. Her shoulders are back, and her chin is held high. She's powerful. Confident. And that, to me, is beautiful. More beautiful than she's ever been. Was she gorgeous four years ago? Of course. But now? Now she's radiant—the sun in a room full of space debris just orbiting around her. Hoping to get closer and begging to be lucky enough for a moment.

Just a single moment.

"Man..." Eli's voice brings me back to my station at the bar. Away from the star that shines so brightly across the room. "You've got it bad." He shakes his head and sets down his empty glass. Beckoning to the bartender for another, he returns his attention to me. "The fuck are you thinking?"

I swallow the dregs of my drink and hold it aloft as well, purposefully ignoring my associate. "What are you babbling on about?" Pressing my lips together, I slide my eyes over to him. The epitome of nonchalance. *Right*?

Within seconds, he's grabbed my arm and leaned in, his lips almost pressed against my ear. "You thinking about fucking her?"

And just like that, the string that's tied me to Savannah all night snaps. I recoil from Eli as my lip curls. "What? No!"

My friend pulls away slightly as his shoulders relax. His facial features smooth out. But in his eyes? In his eyes, I still detect the mistrust. The suspicion.

"I promise I'm not thinking about...*fucking* her." I lower my voice on the last part, else someone hears us.

"I *know* you. We spent how many years together as partners on the force? Roommates in the academy? I know you. I *know* that look."

The bartender brings our drinks and I nod in thanks. I lift the glass to my lips and, this time, take a deeper pull. To dull the nerves? Yes. But also, to buy myself some time to answer Eli.

Like I haven't thought about the consequences over the last four years? I know exactly what would happen to me. I'd be fired. If not sued for breach of contract, too. There's no way involving myself with Savannah would end well for me.

Unfortunately, my friend doesn't take the hint and simply continues to push me. Waggling his eyebrows and jabbing me with his rounded elbows.

"And what if she's thinking it?" Highly unlikely, seeing as Savannah can hardly look at me these days.

Eli blinks. Looking down at his own drink, his body sags. He purses his lips and shakes his head. "You need to remember you have a job to do. She's the type of girl to get you into trouble." When he raises his eyes to mine, they're full of sadness. Regret.

But he's right.

I have to keep my distance from Savannah.

"Oh, fuckin' hell," I let loose as the stale and stagnant hotel room air hits me. And by air, I don't mean air conditioning. Because that has clearly gone out since we've been away.

"Wha—" Savannah begins, until she steps through the doorway and is also assaulted by the heat and humidity. "Oh my God, do you think the AC broke?" Her wide eyes meet mine, a sheen already breaking out along her hairline.

I stalk to the phone and press the office button. It rings twice before the childish woman's voice from earlier picks up. "Hello?"

"Hi, I'm in room 416, and I don't think the air conditioning is working."

"Have you tried resetting the thermostat in the room?"

I point to the square white device on the wall and Savannah goes to it. She flicks it off, waits a beat, and then flicks it back on. We both hold our breath.

Nothing.

"Yeah, that didn't work. What else you got?"

"Let me call our maintenance worker at home and see if he can get down here tonight. He'll give it a look. Fingers crossed he's available and can fix it. It's supposed to be a hot one."

"Right," I respond dully as I swipe my hand across my brow. "Please keep us posted."

"Have a good night," she responds cheerily before the line disconnects.

I replace the phone in its cradle and release a curse. "They're going to *try* to work on it."

Savannah sags onto the edge of the bed and groans. "It's at least 90 degrees in here."

I stand and move across the room to open the sliding glass door to the balcony. Even if it's muggier outside—and smells like actual garbage—at least the breeze from the ocean will feel better than nothing. Then I peel the heavy black t-shirt over my head and toss it beside my bag.

Savannah's eyes widen slightly before she averts her gaze, looking down at her phone in her lap. "Might as well get out of these dress clothes and go check out that box of wine in the lobby." She stands and digs through her suitcase, pulling out a pair of cutoffs and a t-shirt. Then, without another word, she heads to the bathroom and slams the door behind her.

I'm stuck looking at her open case, knowing her vibrator is somewhere within. Staring at her neatly packed luggage, I gulp slowly before my mind starts to spiral. Does she think of me when she uses it? How quickly can she make herself come? I feel even hotter as I imagine the noises she makes. Her mouth popping open as she releases a moan.

"Yo. The bathroom's all yours." My gaze snaps to her, suddenly looking almost like the eighteen-year-old from all those years ago. Face free of makeup. Toned legs highlighted by cutoffs. She hangs up her skirt and blazer, and then, using the mirror, gathers her mass of dark waves into a ponytail. As she raises her arms and loops the holder around her hair, her shorts rise up, giving me a glimpse of the curve of her ass.

I look away and focus on my own suitcase. Pulling a pair of khaki shorts and a polo shirt from within, I cross behind her and slip into the bathroom.

Chapter Thirty

Savannah

"Wait, you don't need the car keys if we're just going to the lobby for a drink," I chastise Jack as we exit the room. We've left the balcony door slightly ajar to get a little bit of air circulating. Hopefully, we don't return to some kind of wild animal infestation. Do they even have raccoons and opossums in northern Florida? I never saw one on campus, but that doesn't mean they couldn't climb up to the fourth floor and trash our room.

"Boxed wine isn't going to do it for me tonight. We're going to an air-conditioned establishment with at least a liquor license."

I glance down at my outfit, ratty cutoffs and a college t-shirt, and hesitate. Should I change? Try to look more professional? The thought of squeezing back into dress clothes sends a panic through me. It's simply too hot!

"What you're wearing is fine," Jack assures me, as though he can hear my thoughts. He holds open the stairwell door and we traipse down, our footsteps echoing loudly. "It's not like it's a date."

My jaw clenches, and I stall on the stairs, nearly losing my footing. Is this a subtle dig at our amusement park "date" from four years ago? Or the time he took me for ice cream? How dare he insinuate I thought *this* was a date? I'm clearly old enough and know better now. I see right through him. Do I *look* like I think this is a date? The only makeup I'm wearing is lip gloss and my hair is tossed into a messy bun, for crying out loud. Rather than come back with some smart-ass retort, I continue in his wake, although even to my ears, my footsteps are louder. More aggressive somehow. When we approach the car, he clicks the unlock button and the sleek black sedan lights up. Even though I desperately want to hide in the back, I slide into the passenger seat. A small part of me considers running back upstairs, but the thought of roasting to death in that stifling room has me buckling my seat belt and waiting patiently for him to start the car.

We zip through the nearly empty lot and are on the main drag before I can second-guess my decision. The air conditioning blasts from the dashboard, and I adjust the nozzle so it's pointing directly at my face. The breeze feels heavenly, and I tilt my head back, eyes closed, and enjoy the cool air.

Moments later, Jack flicks on the turn signal and we slow before navigating into a busy parking lot. "What's this place?"

"Dunno, but it had good reviews. And they have an open mic night." He swallows, and then shifts his gaze across the car. "I thought you might enjoy it."

My pulse quickens. Not only at the chance to listen to some—hopefully—decent music and enjoy a cold drink, too, but also at how thoughtful Jack was in choosing this place. Maybe this night isn't such a bust, after all.

"My lust can't be satiated by anyone. I only want you tonight," the singer croons onstage as a flock of women writhe, their hands in the air, on the dance floor. I have to keep my composure, as the lyrics are hitting a little too close to home tonight. I flick my gaze to Jack's broad back. He's leaning against the bar just in front of me and nonchalantly bobbing his head to the music. Does he know this song reminds me of him?

"So why don't you want me? Other men drool over me and I'm looking at you…"

I bite my lip, my mind wandering to Jack's private call on the plane. Who was he speaking to his mother about? *Ma, there have been plenty of dates, and I'm sure you'll be a grandma before you know it.* Is he with someone now? Are they serious? My mind spirals to Jack in a fitted suit at the end of a flower-lined aisle, turning around as his bride approaches. A smile lighting up his face.

I open my mouth to ask, to reach out and grab his arm.

"You look like you could use some company, baby." The man at my elbow startles me from my thoughts, and I rear back slightly as I take him in.

He's got a backwards cap on and shaggy blonde hair peeking from underneath. He's big. At least the size of a linebacker and with the powerful chest to prove it. Ocean-blue eyes crinkle with smugness as he watches me check him out. "Like what you see?"

I smile politely. "I'm just here listening to the music. With my friend." I nod my chin toward Jack.

"That your boyfriend?" The man takes a long pull from his beer.

"Nope. Like I said, just a friend." Sidling closer, he places his meaty paw over my forearm, which rests on the sticky bar top. I pull away and ease back a little more. "Listen, I'm not really into whatever you're laying out, but thank you. Have a nice night." I look down at my drink, hoping he takes the hint.

But he doesn't. Instead, he leans into my ear. "Someone needs to *lay you out* and fuck the bitchiness out of you." The stench of his alcohol-soaked breath wafts over me.

I stumble back, not fully comprehending what I've just heard. Did he just say—?

Before I know what's happening, Jack's palm presses against my hip, gently pushing me behind him, before squaring up to the brute. "What the fuck did you just say to her?" The muscles in his shoulders ripple with rage.

"Your *friend's* a bitch. I was simply telling her she needed a good fucking. Maybe she'd lose some of that attitude."

Jack's body goes rigid and I'm certain he's seeing red. I ease forward. "It's fine. Don't let him ruin the night." I snake my arm along Jack's and try to pull him away, but he's a statue. Solid. Unmoving. Only his nostrils flare and his jaw twitches.

"Apologize to her," Jack manages through gritted teeth.

"Fuck you," the giant spits.

Jack's in full bodyguard mode. I've never seen him like this. But he's certainly in his element, not fazed at all, as he turns to look at me. "Step back, Savannah. Please." I do as he asks, not due to fear, but because I see the certainty in his eyes that say, *shit's about to go down.*

I take a full two steps back and notice that a group has formed. Several phones are raised and the flashes glow in the dim bar. Someone attempts to chant, "Fight! Fight!"

Fuck.

"Jack, I don't—" But before I can finish that sentence, Jack's got the drunkard in a headlock and somehow also manages to have pulled some evasive maneuver shit with pressure points.

When he adds some muscle, the man squeals like a pig. "I said, apologize." He directs the brute toward me.

"I-I'm sorry," the man mutters through the pain. He's breathing heavily and I'm afraid he's going to pass out. With all of this on video, the optics and implications fly through my head.

Fuck fuck fuck.

"Jesus, let him go already!" I bite out as panic swirls in my chest. What if this video gets out and we're linked to my father's campaign?

Jack's eyebrows furl as his gaze meets mine, but he releases the man anyway. "Fuck you both!" he hurls at us as he rubs his neck.

I blink at him, straightening my shoulders. "Just get out of here, asshole." Then my eyes return to Jack's, his lips flat and a crease forming at his brow. "I want to go."

I storm past him, shoving my way through the onlookers and out into the sticky air. As my footsteps slow, I try to gulp down breaths to ease the worry seeping into my chest, but the muggy air does nothing to help.

"What do you need, Savannah?" Jack's suddenly there, his hand pressing into my lower back as he guides us toward the car. I swallow as the desire pools in my gut and flares up from his point of contact. I don't want to feel like this. Not toward him.

"Nothing. I just want to go back to the hotel. Motel," I clarify, pulling away from his touch. Once the car is unlocked, I slide in and close my eyes, waiting for the cool breeze of the air conditioning to calm my pounding heart.

But Jack doesn't put the car in gear. His hands grip the steering wheel. Knuckles turning white. "What did you expect me to do? Just let that guy insult you?" He doesn't look at me, but he doesn't have to.

"I expect you to act professional and not be a liability to my father's campaign." The words are out before I can stop them.

He snorts. "You sound like Miranda." Then he finally turns to me, those hazel eyes full of hurt. Or is it annoyance at being chastised? It's hard to tell in the darkness of the car, with only the streetlights illuminating in the distance.

"Miranda *is* the fixer. You would know," I add under my breath.

"What's that supposed to mean?" It's like the air is sucked from the car as he waits for me to continue.

"It means, four years ago, you asked her to fix a problem you had. *Remember*?" I drink his features in as they transform from anger to understanding.

"You heard…" The realization hangs in the vacuum between us.

"I heard." I turn my face forward, not wanting him to see the way I'm still affected by his betrayal. But as the back of my eyes sting, I'm certain he can sense my emotions rising. After all, he's trained for all of this, right?

"Savannah, I didn't… That wasn't… *You* weren't…" I shake my head as a sarcastic chuckle bubbles from my mouth. He can't even come up with a decent lie for what he asked Miranda to do.

We sit in silence for what feels like hours, but is likely only a few minutes. I'm just about to demand he take us back to the motel, when he finally slides the car into drive.

But not before he adds, "I handled a lot of things poorly that night. But purposefully hurting you was never my intention."

I swallow the lump in my throat and blink away the pain still throbbing behind my eyes. And only then do I click my seatbelt in place. "Just drive, Keaton."

Chapter Thirty-One

Jack

I fucked up. But what did she expect me to do, let some asshole verbally assault her?

Not gonna happen.

I roll over and sigh heavily as the thick air sticks to every inch of me. We returned from the bar and found the room just as stifling as before. Even after calling down to the motel office—no answer—and opening the balcony door as far as it could go, the room continues to boil. And my mood does nothing to diminish the uncomfortableness.

So instead, I lie on the cot and toss and turn. The sheet kicked to the foot of the child-size mattress and my body refusing to cool.

It seems as though I've just blinked when I startle awake and realize that Savannah isn't in the primary bed nearby. I sit up, but there's only an emptiness. An indent in the mattress where she was.

Scrambling out of my bed, I hurry to the bathroom. When I find it empty, I flick on the lights and discover that the entire room is just that.

Empty.

My heart pounds louder, echoing my footsteps as I race across the room and fling open the door. Barefoot, I race down the open-air hallway and to the stairwell. I take the stairs two at a time, not even registering the mystery wetness on the steps or sticky residue surely attaching to the bottom of my feet.

I've got to find Savannah.

I burst through the door of the ground floor and look out to the beach, spotting her. The long dark hair—turned wavy in the motel room humidity—floats down her back, coming to rest at a place along her spine that I want to run my tongue over. Lights from the motel illuminate her ample curves, her most intimate places covered by the tiniest of bikinis.

I breathe a sigh of relief. She's safe.

As if in a dreamless sleepwalk, I pad along the boardwalk until I reach the beach. My gaze never straying from her. The sand is cool to the touch. It instantly soothes my entire body from the heat of the room. But a part of me, that part deep within my gut, still burns as Savannah struts into the ocean and disappears.

"Savannah! No!" I take off at a run, my legs pumping over the divots and dunes of the sand until I reach the shore. I search the waves, my head whipping from side to side, until she crests beyond the surf. "What the fuck are you doing?" I holler into the night.

She turns slowly, as though she knew I was there all along, and then effortlessly floats back toward the shore. "It was too hot to sleep," she says when she's near enough to look me in the eye. Except my gaze goes everywhere but to hers.

It's been ages since I've seen her this exposed.

I feel myself thickening before I even have time to cover myself. I'm thankful my dark shorts blend in with the darkness surrounding us.

"You shouldn't be out here alone. Or out here at all!"

With a shrug, she walks backward. Taunting me as the water rises from her thighs to her hips and then over her belly. "Who's going to stop me?"

There's that challenge.

It ignites something inside of me, and before I know it, I'm knee deep in the water, my arm wrapped around her waist and her lower body pulled against mine. "Out. *Now*," I command in monosyllables.

She snorts and pulls away, but I flex and yank her back against me. It's then that she must feel my hardness because her eyes widen and her lips part slightly, showing just the bottom of her two front teeth.

As she inhales, a shiver ripples through her. And it's then I realize her tits are flush against my chest. That shiver echoes down to my bones, and I release her.

"You've cooled off enough. It's cold out here." My eyes dip to her chest, the buds of her nipples poking against the fabric of her top.

If it was daylight, I'm certain I'd see an adorable blush tinting her cheeks. But as it's pitch black and in the middle of the night, I'm only afforded a glare and her teeth sinking into her bottom lip.

And then she's stalking past me to her discarded towel. With a "fuck you" dying on the breeze, she leaves me standing knee deep in the waves, sporting a raging hard-on.

Something soft pushes against my crotch, and a groan escapes from deep within my belly. I reach a sleepy arm out and toss it over the smooth skin next to me, pulling that smoothness closer. I haven't felt like this in ages. My dick misses the softness of a woman.

It's cold now, so I pull up the comforter and blanket, cocooning us away from the chill.

Delicate hands explore as my eyes stay closed and my mind simply enjoys. Nails skim up and down my thigh. An ache builds deep in my gut as the softness presses back into my hardness, and I meet it with equal fervor.

My hand slips forward to a hip bone and then trails under a thin shirt. Hungry—*starving*—for the soft skin that pebbles under my touch. My fingers inch higher, to a rounded rib and the outline of a sternum. Until finally they come in contact with the voluptuous curve of a—

"Jack..." The moan of my name slips from her lips and my brain fires awake.

My hand up Savannah's shirt.

Her ass rubbing against my cock.

I pull away so quickly that she, too, startles, and before I have a moment to think about how I got into *this* bed, she's turned, facing me with wide eyes and mouth gaping like a fish as she comprehends what *she* was doing. What *I* was doing.

"What the fuck?" Savannah's shrill squeal tamps down my arousal. "Why are you in *my* bed?" She flees from our cocoon and, standing over me, punches her hands onto her hips, demanding an answer I can't give.

Opening and closing my mouth, nothing comes out. I glance at the smaller-than-twin-sized cot, which has collapsed so only one half stands erect.

And now I remember. My face crashing to the carpet in the night as the flimsy bed gave way. Half asleep, and possibly concussed, climbing like a zombie onto the soft bed. And passing right the fuck out.

Savannah's taut nipples push against her shirt, and it's honestly impossible to focus on anything else, let alone come up with an answer that would make any lick of sense. Especially with how chilly the room is now.

The air conditioning is certainly working.

She looks at the vacated spot on the bed. Narrowing her eyes at me, she realizes what I'm staring at and instantly folds her arms across her chest.

What a shame.

"I'm sorry," I mumble and avert my eyes. "I must've climbed into your bed when I was half asleep and didn't realize—"

"That you were..." Her gaze sinks to my lap while her lips roll together.

Except that I'm pretty sure *she* was the one pushing against me. Rubbing my thigh. It was *my* name on *her* lips...

Ultimately, I am the professional. And I am caught red-handed. Or red-bedded. Shit, I'm exhausted and obviously didn't get enough sleep. "Listen, I'm sorry. I didn't intend for any of that to happen, Savannah. I-I'll sleep on the floor tonight. Now, if you'll excuse me, I'm going to hop in the shower and get ready." I stand and maneuver around her, even as she glares daggers my way. "Oh, and don't forget, your father signed us up to play in the volleyball tournament this morning."

"Lovely," she mutters as I pass by.

On my way to the bathroom, I bend and grab a pair of shorts and a t-shirt from my bag and toss them onto the bed.

"Don't take too long. I have to shower, too."

I flatten my lips and nod. I better make that shower extra cold.

Chapter Thirty-Two

Jack

Watching Savannah compete across from me is the work of the devil. Not only is she in the front row, just beyond the net, but she's also wearing a cropped tee and spandex booty shorts that are proving to be a distraction.

The ref's whistle startles me, and I catch Savannah's icy glare from the opposing team. I hate that we aren't on the same side, but this game is simply for fun. In the last few years, the competitiveness has died down and now the game is only a "networking opportunity." There aren't even true refs anymore. Just volunteers.

"We're down a teammate," a southern gentleman had proclaimed when we arrived and took our places on the blue side. "Would someone care to volunteer to join us?"

Before any other northerners had the chance to speak up, Savannah raised her hand before ducking under the net. "I'll do it!"

Of course, I didn't miss the way she scowled at me as she said it.

Or the way her father thinned his lips from the sidelines as his daughter joined the enemy.

He hasn't been a fan of the "damn reds" since two summers ago, when they'd doused our armbands in itching powder. Needless to say, none of us could hit a volleyball, and Miranda and I were both prescribed steroid cream for weeks.

As though anyone would ever expect a bunch of politicians to play nice.

And now, as Savannah wears that hideous red visor, I want nothing more than to...

Well, to grab her and fireman carry her back to the motel.

Finish the argument we'd started this morning. Call her out for being the one to wiggle her ass into me. As she turns to watch her teammate serve, one long leg extended back, my eyes drift to the rounded cheek and the black skintight spandex barely covering it.

Fuck me, what I'd do to that ass if she were mine.

Images of peeling the Lycra down over the muscled glute, and palming that firm backside before sinking my teeth into the tender flesh, flash through my mind.

The ball flies right past me and lands with a thud in the sand.

"What the hell, Keaton?" my female teammate, a middle-aged deputy director of energy from Ohio, scolds me. "Get your damn head in the game!"

"Yes, ma'am," I respond as I scrub a hand over my face.

Across the net, Savannah shakes her head while smiling and then high fives another red visor.

All right. If this is how it's gonna be... Squatting lower, I keep my eyes trained on the bright white volleyball in the server's hands. He's a decent-looking fellow. Probably early to mid-forties. He's on the younger side, considering some of the living corpses I've seen at these conferences.

But the way his gaze keeps straying to Savannah's rear end has me thinking about putting him into an early grave.

So when he serves the ball directly to me once more, I slice through the air and take a shot. Unfortunately, the middle-aged woman has the same idea, and we collide mid-air. I'm athletic and tall enough to catch myself, landing easily on bended knees, but based on the way the deputy director is clutching her ankle and glaring at me beneath the angry sun tells me I've fucked up. *Again.*

She refuses my help, so I watch helplessly as the other team members assist her off the sand and onto a waiting folding chair. Our team is now down by two and things are looking bleak as the ball is served again. This time, I refrain from going for it, and instead, the blues manage to rally and get the point on a spike from my new neighboring teammate.

"Great job!" I pat her back, and she nods, beaming at me.

"Thanks," she responds as we get back into position.

While I wait for the telling smack of the ball being served, I turn my gaze across the net to Savannah. Her lips, thin and pressed together, tilt down as she assesses me. Before I can ask her what's wrong, the ball goes flying over the net and the game continues.

"What a game," I mutter as I open the door for Savannah. It's the least I can do when our team stomped hers. She slides in without a word and grabs the door handle, pulling it closed with a loud *slam*.

By the time I jog around to the driver's side and sit down, she's typing something into her phone. Very aggressively.

"Want to grab a coffee before we head back to the room and clean up? We have some time before you're expected at the conference."

"Nope." She pops her lips on the *p*, shutting down my suggestion.

"Hungry? We can drive-thru—"

"Just take me back to the motel so I can shower off the stench of defeat, Keaton." She turns her face toward the window, shutting me out completely.

Except I'm not that easily deterred. I'm done letting her dictate how things go between us. I'm done being the one left out in the dark. The one who deals with the fallout. "Savannah, about earlier…" I pause and pull the car away from the curb. It's a quick five-minute drive back to the motel, so I need to get it all out. And fast. Because even though she's facing away from me, it's not like she can run away.

Not in a moving car.

But just to be safe, as we pull up to a red light, I click the lock for the doors.

The noise startles her, and she pulls away from the door before slowly turning to face me. Her eyes wide and full of unasked questions.

Mainly, *what the actual fuck are you doing*?

"Um, so that came off wrong…and super creepy. I just had this fear that you'd—I dunno—jump out into traffic if our conversation got serious and…uncomfortable."

She squints at me, the skin around her eyes tightening. "Why would I jump into traffic?"

I give her the old side-eye complete with a cocked eyebrow. "Just seems like you've been purposefully avoiding me lately."

The column of her throat bobs as she swallows. She flicks her gaze out the window, but when she turns back to me, her features are schooled. "After what happened four years ago, what did you expect? That I'd come back from college eager to be around you?"

I recoil and then chuff out loud. "Four years ago, Savannah? You really want to talk about what happened four years ago?" I thread my hands through my hair as I seriously ponder yanking it out. This woman is driving me insane. For four years, I've been driven insane by her mere presence, even without her around. She lives rent free in my thoughts. Running wild without a care for the torture she is doing to my psyche. I can't take it anymore.

"I *know* what happened four years ago. I don't need to talk about it." She attempts to unlock the door and hop out, but I grab her arm and pull her so close that our breaths mingle with one another's. Only the console separates us, her chest pressed against mine. Her stare hardens as she meets my eyes and pauses, tongue flicking out over parted lips. Full lips with just a slick of gloss.

And I'm a goner.

"I do. I do want to talk about it." I pause and inhale. Readying myself. "Did you think about me, Savannah?" Her breathing stops as the question hangs in the frigid air conditioning between us. The air outside may be sticky with heat, but inside this car, we're suffocating with all the things unsaid. "When you left—for four years—did you think about me?"

"How d-dare you ask me that when you were the one wh-who said..." she pauses. Her mouth opens and closes, but nothing comes out. She blinks at me through eyes that are suddenly watery. Her lashes wet with the dew that threatens to spill down her cheeks.

Fuck, I made her cry?

"I didn't mean—*Jesus, Savannah.* I'm so sorry." I pull her in and wrap my arms around her. Yet that pesky console keeps us separated the slightest bit. If only she'd climb over it, slide into my lap, and…

Having her this close is like coming up for air. She fills everything inside me with life. She reminds me of what it's like to want more.

More than just a career.

The car behind us beeps, and I glance from Savannah to see that the light's turned green. All the cars around us press forward into the intersection.

Savannah recoils from our embrace. Slowly, our contact severs and the heat building in my chest dissipates as another horn farther back blares through the traffic.

My hands find their spot on the wheel, and I release the brake just as Savannah turns from me, her gaze straying to the passenger side window.

And just like that, she's closed off once more.

CHAPTER THIRTY-THREE

Savannah

I step from the shower, almost completely dressed and ready to go and find Jack... *Not.*

He's standing in the middle of the room, bare-chested in only his trousers.

His back to me, his muscles ripple as he presses his dress shirt on the ironing board. I watch, transfixed, as he uses his thumb to activate the steam, and then again as his traps flex when he moves the iron.

How would the pad of that thumb feel on my most intimate places...?

"Sorry, just finishing up and then we'll be on our way," he says as he turns and finds me staring. Probably with my mouth open and drool slipping down my chin.

I shake myself. "It's fine. I just need to fix my hair anyway." I turn away and face the open-concept vanity, which still affords me a decent view of Jack's back and ass. As I gather my unruly hair into a mass atop my head, my eyes stray to him again. The way he glides the iron over the clothes. The way his hips move, ever-so-slightly, side-to-side as he works out a wrinkle.

Who knew ironing could be this sexy?

That heat in my core? *Yeah, it's on fire now.*

He turns and finds my eyes on him. I glance away quickly, focusing my attention back on my hair. It's a giant frizz ball on top of my head, so I grab a handful of pins and start tucking and pinning the strands until I've got a more professional-looking bun.

Then I pull out a few loose hairs and assess my work.

I try not to notice that Jack is behind me, staring at my reflection in the mirror.

I turn around just as he does the same, finally retrieving his shirt from the hook. My eye catches on something—a new tattoo. It looks like a bouquet. I squint to see more, but he quickly covers the body art.

He slides his arms through the holes and buttons himself up while I grab my folio and purse.

We're two people coexisting inside this room, but the tension is thicker than the humidity outside.

Especially after our argument on the drive back from the volleyball game.

"Did you think about me, Savannah?" How could I tell him that he's all I thought about for four years? How could I admit that I stayed away from my own home so that I wouldn't have to see him? Is he really so dense as to not realize?

Being near him brings all those past feelings to the forefront. Feelings I spent *years* burying. Feelings that are now re-emerging as I watch the man in front of me iron a goddamned shirt.

I can't be hurt like that again. So I take a deep breath and mask my emotions. I've gotten good at that, too.

"Ready?" I ask, my eyebrows raised as he rolls up the sleeve of his shirt. I swallow the lump in my throat and refuse to admire those perfect forearms. Instead, I point my chin high and clear my throat.

"Yep." He grabs the keys and his wallet off the side table, along with the accompanying jacket to his suit. Pocketing the wallet, he tosses the jacket over his shoulder with two fingers.

I never thought I had a thing for a thumb or fingers, but apparently, I do.

As I follow him through the door, I wonder why I pitched such a fit at him prowling over my body earlier.

My phone buzzes loudly, startling me from the mindless scrolling I'd been doing in between meetings. Delia's name splashes across the screen, and I nearly squeal with excitement. I click accept and move to a more private area of the building.

"Where are you?" It feels good to hear her voice, even if she's chomping down on something crunchy.

"I'm just waiting for my next meeting to start. And by meeting, I mean lunch with my father and a potential campaign donor." I roll my eyes. "I'm waiting for Dad now. What on earth are you eating?"

"A carrot." She holds up the orange stick before taking another bite with a snap.

My brow crinkles. "Since when have you eaten carrots? I thought you hated all things salad related. Has adulting really changed you so much?"

"Nope. Just too poor to afford things like meat. So I'm subsisting on rabbit food now."

"Oh, Del. Is the pay that bad?"

She cracks a carotene-filled smile. "No, but Chicago is expensive. Did you know this?"

I nod with a side smile, shrugging. "Yeah, I did. Do you need money to tide you over until next payday?" I'd give an arm and a leg for my best friend. Tossing her a few bones isn't anything if it means she can buy groceries.

"No. Friends don't borrow money from friends."

"Says who?" I lean against the wall in a quiet hallway.

"Nana. Anyway, I'm done talking about my financial situation. I'm fine, and plus, my eyesight is getting better every day with these things." She snaps another bite.

"I'm sure." I make a mental note to order a week's worth of groceries to be delivered to Delia's apartment. I never did get her an apartment-warming gift. "Things are fine. Except I'm not staying at the house. There was a miscommunication about the construction and one of the rooms wasn't finished. Guess whose room it just happened to be?" I raise my eyebrows at her through the phone.

"Of course. I wouldn't put it past that twig, Miranda. So are you staying at some ritzy resort on daddy's dime?"

"Well, everything is booked up due to the conference, so I'm at this older motel. It's...quaint."

"Ha! By quaint, you mean not updated since the 80s, right?"

"Precisely." I press my lips together.

"Well, at least you're alone. I can't imagine it's been easy seeing that dick Keaton again."

Heat spreads across my cheeks just as I spot my father striding my way. "Yeah, about that. He's staying with me at the motel."

"What?" Delia's outburst almost causes me to drop my phone. "Why am I just now hearing of this?"

"It's been kind of...challenging to find time to call you. He's always around," I whisper. "Even now, he's waiting in the car to drive us to lunch."

"Ugh, that's gotta be rough for you."

"You're telling me. It's even worse since there's only one bed, Del."

"*What?*" This time, I actually do drop the phone. It bounces twice and lands next to my father's perfectly shined black dress shoe.

He picks it up. "Why hello, Miss Evans. How's Chicago?"

"*It'sgreatMr.SmithcanyoupleasegivemebacktoSav?*" I snort as my father tries to comprehend the jumbled request.

My father passes me the phone with a confused look. "I'll meet you in the car." He strides past me, and I immediately glance back at the device.

"Sorry about that. Your excitement startled me, and I dropped the phone."

"What the hell, Sav? You're sharing a bed with the man who broke your heart?"

I slide my thumb along the volume button. "Whoa, maybe you could *not* screech it out loud? And he's actually sleeping on the cot. Except..."

"Except what?" Her eyes go wide. "I know that look, Sav. What aren't you telling me?

Embarrassment flames in my chest. "Well, this morning, I woke up, and he was...well, he was in the bed. *With me.*"

Delia squints at me, her carrot long since forgotten. "How did that happen?"

I bite my bottom lip as my mind replays this morning's intimate misadventure. "Not exactly sure, but needless to say, the cot was broken, and I was..." I trail off, gaining the courage to admit my wicked ways to my best friend.

"What did you do, Sav?" I'm pretty sure if I glanced at the screen right now, I'd see Delia salivating as she waits like a dog for a bone.

"I rubbed my butt against him." My face heats.

The line goes silent. Then the snap of the carrot and the telltale crunching of Delia chewing comes through the speaker. "That's it?"

"No, that's not it," I add, feeling slightly foolish. "He was *hard*, Del. Like, *really* hard."

"Holy shit! What are you going to do?" The crunching stops again, as I have Delia's full attention.

"I don't know. I really don't know." I shake my head. What can I say? Is Jack attractive? *Yes*. But he broke my heart once, and I'm not about to let that happen again, even if the thought of his hard dick makes my core ache with desire.

"Well, it's probably best that you'll be back at the house soon. I wouldn't want your virtue tainted by such a handsome bodyguard who creeps into your bed in the middle of the night."

"Right," I respond half-heartedly. "Me neither."

Chapter Thirty-Four

Jack

Lunch is a brutal affair. The donor sitting down with Governor Smith is well into his forties and can't take his eyes off Savannah. I sit at an adjacent table, my newspaper and folio laid out before me and my salad untouched, catching snippets of the conversation.

"I would've loved to have attended college in Florida. I'm sure you and your sorority sisters spent so much time at the beach on the weekend," says the pervert as he leans into Savannah's personal bubble.

She doesn't recoil, but I can tell from the tic in her jaw that she's uncomfortable. "My time was spent double-majoring in political science and international relations, so I was much too busy to join a sorority or spend my weekends at the beach," Savannah replies.

"It doesn't sound like you had any fun."

"My goal was to get an education, not have fun, sir."

I always did like a smart girl.

My chest tightens when I realize that I, too, have spent the last four years without any fun. While I haven't been dedicated to studying like Savannah,

I certainly haven't dated. It's the one thing Jenson is constantly giving me grief over. He, on the other hand, is a complete man whore. A new woman every week.

"Women love the whole bodyguard vibe, man. It's like a smut book come to life for them! Once they find out what I do for a living, I can't keep the holster sniffers off my junk."

That's not the type of woman I want.

My eyes track the way Savannah sits up straighter at something said. I can tell she's uneasy with the attention this older gentleman is paying her. Her full, glossy lips are pressed together while her hands wring the napkin in her lap. Her father, on the other hand, doesn't seem to notice the elephant in the room.

"And now that she's graduated, I've put her to work as my campaign manager. There's no better way to get her feet wet." The governor has a twinkle of pride in his eye as he catches his daughter's forced smile. "Excuse me for a moment."

As my boss navigates his way to the restroom, I'm conflicted. Do I follow him, as I've been doing the last four years, or do I stay and watch the lecher devour Savannah with his eyes? After just a second of hesitation, I remind myself that I've been instructed to stay by Savannah's side, so that's what I do. I sit and watch as the man nearly old enough to be Savannah's father leans in and whispers something in her ear.

Her face pales and she visibly flinches.

I'm instantly on my feet, my thighs pressing against the back of Savannah's chair. "Miss Smith, a word, please?"

I step back and pull out her chair for her as she stands. It takes everything in me not to take her hand in my own and tug her away from this rich bastard. Instead, I walk side-by-side with her to the lobby.

We stop and she turns an inquisitive gaze onto me. "What's going on?"

"That man in there. Is he making you uncomfortable?" Lightning flashes through my nerve endings. If she said the word, I'd probably pummel the guy right in front of the lunch crowd.

Her brow furrows and the skin around her eyes tightens. "*What*? Is he making me uncomfortable?"

"What did he whisper in your ear, Savannah?"

"Why is that any of your business?"

"I'm your bodyguard. If he's made you feel uncomfortable or threatened you in any way, I should know."

She chuffs out a laugh. "Y-You think that this is the first time a man has hit on me?" The laughter builds and bubbles, and now she's straight up cackling in my face.

Those lightning flashes roar to life, setting my organs on fire. "He hit on you? What did he say?"

Savannah's laughing subsides, and she eyes me up and down, as though she can sense the change in my demeanor. The aggravation and rage coursing through my blood. "It's nothing I haven't heard before. And, by the way, I took care of myself for four years around guys just like him." Her chest heaves and she takes a step closer. The air around us stills as her breasts nearly press against my chest. Those chocolate irises darken, her pupils enlarging as she studies me. Her lips part and her tongue darts to the corner. "I'll tell you what I told my father four years ago." The skin around Savannah's eyes tightens. "*I don't need you.*"

My lungs feel like they're going to burst.

Mainly because I'm staring at Savannah's ass.

Her cheeks flex one at a time as she runs down the beach, ponytail swinging back and forth.

My body's never been so confused. Gasping for breath in this humidity while rocking a massive boner certainly seems like the recipe for a heart attack.

But if I died here and now? I'd be just fine with it.

Savannah may have refused to share any details about what was whispered in her ear, but I can tell she's upset about something. After we deposited her father at the house and returned to the motel room, she immediately changed and informed me in no uncertain terms that she was going for a run.

With or without me.

I don't need you.

Except that I'm ordered to be by her side during this trip. So here I am. Huffing and puffing the hot Florida air a mere fifteen feet behind Savannah.

And she is fast.

We've gone at least three miles when she finally slows, and then, moments later, comes to a stop. Bending over with her hands on her knees, she gasps for air. I do the same, except my arms are above my head.

She finally stands tall again and canters toward the waves. Her chest still heaves and there's sweat literally dripping down the valley of her spine, but she's never been more beautiful.

Her entire face is bright red. Her straightened hair has returned to its regular mass of crazy waves. But as she faces the dipping sun and inhales the salty sea air, something changes in her demeanor. She turns to the sky and smiles. Really smiles.

When was the last time I saw her smile? Truly smile? I've forgotten how it lights up her face and, before I know it, I'm grinning from ear to ear. Even covered in sweat with her chest heaving, she's gorgeous. Her bestowing that smile on me is like submerging my body in the cool ocean after a hot run. It's refreshing and immediately makes everything right with the world.

I've long since shed my shirt, my own body dripping with sweat, and there's nothing I'd like better than to jump headfirst into the ocean.

So that's just what I do.

I discard my shoes and socks as she watches me with her mouth agape. "What are you doing?" she finally asks, the corners of her lips falling slightly.

"I'm sweating and it's still at least 100 degrees out here. I'm cooling off!" I take off in a run, this time into the waves, and once I'm beyond the sandbar, I jump in. The water's nowhere near cool enough to truly ease the heat—more like a tepid bath—but there's something about being submerged that brings my body back to its baseline.

I brush my hair away from my eyes just in time to catch Savannah lopping toward me. Her shoes and socks left near mine, she splashes past me and then dives under.

When she crests above the water, it's with a smile on her face, looking as though all her cares are gone. And maybe they are. Maybe for her, everything is fine with the world.

I don't need you.

But that statement cuts me. It cuts deep into my core and exposes the emptiness inside of me. I've dedicated years to this job, and it's left me with nothing. It doesn't love me back or fill me with the same joy as seeing Savannah smile.

And that stings more than saltwater in an open wound.

CHAPTER THIRTY-FIVE

Savannah

"Oh my God." My mouth falls open as my eyes widen, my gaze trained on the group of people scuttling toward the ocean's edge. "Are those...?" I squint at the small silver dollars flapping on the sand. "Baby turtles!"

Jack's eyes narrow, and then he spins around, taking in the crowd that's formed. Before he can utter a single word, I'm high-kneeing past him toward the *baby turtles*.

"Savannah! Wait!" my companion calls from behind me as he follows. But even with his height, he can't keep up with the excitement that's propelling me onward.

Baby.

Turtles.

As I near the crowd, my pace slows, and I notice there are several people wearing bright lime green t-shirts. The logo announces them to be the Turtle Trackers. I sidle up to the edge of the group and watch as they walk alongside the hatchlings.

"A group of baby turtles is called a bale, you know." My head whips to the side as Jack's bare torso presses against the back of my arm.

Is there a reason he's so close all of a sudden? The proximity makes my stomach flip. Or maybe it's the three-mile run I just did.

"In my head, I was calling them a gaggle." I shrug and return to the babies. I want to touch them so badly, but as I eye the number of green shirts, I know I'd be caught in an instant. Thrown to the fishes, so to speak. So I keep my arms pinned to my sides, else I accidentally snatch a hatchling and take it home. "Ugh, I want one so bad." I frown, and as my shoulders sag, my back bumps against Jack's chest.

"I'm pretty sure sea turtles are federally protected, Savannah." My sadness subsides as his breath dances across my wet shoulders, nipples pebbling under my sports bra. I don't dare move. I don't know what's got me more excited. The baby turtles, or Jack's closeness.

It's a true toss up, but as I stand, enjoying heaven on Earth, the crowd of onlookers begins to disperse as the turtles reach the surf. Only a few of the green shirts remain and Jack's touch is gone. Striding past me and toward a Turtle Tracker, I follow in his footsteps, my skin begging for his touch once more.

"Sir? Will there be another turtle release?"

The older man, his face shadowed by a fisherman's cap, looks us over. "You and your girlfriend interested in volunteering?"

I'm about to correct the man on our lack of relationship, but Jack speaks up. "Yeah, we are. How can we help?" He reaches out and takes my hand, playing up our togetherness. I'm too dumbfounded to do anything other than hyper focus on his hand clutching mine.

Oh, and watch with glee as the hatchlings roll around in the tumultuous surf as they attempt to swim beyond the waves.

"If you're staying in the area, you can come out just before dawn and walk the beach. If you notice any garbage or larger items blocking the nests, we'd be mighty appreciative of you cleaning up."

Jack nods and, for a moment, I wonder if he's going to release my hand to shake the Tracker's, but he doesn't. "Um, will the hatchlings be okay, being flung around in the waves like that?" I raise my chin toward the remaining babies struggling to get beyond the surf.

"Oh, yeah. They're fine. It takes a couple tries, but they'll be clear of this area soon enough and out to the open sea." The man tips his hat to us and wanders back toward the other green shirts, who are cleaning and passing out pamphlets to other beachgoers.

I return my focus to the sea and realize that the turtles have disappeared. Stepping closer to the edge of the water, I search, but they're gone.

So is Jack's touch.

I keep searching, stepping farther into the ocean, and eventually spot a lone baby turtle. He's flapping his tiny turtle arms so quickly, trying to make it beyond the waves. "Oh, look at him go!" I cry.

"They're faster than they look, huh?" I hadn't realized that Jack followed me into the water, but there he is. Right behind me, watching with enjoyment that matches my own.

I turn away from the hatchling and allow my gaze to travel over Jack. He's changed in the last four years, but at the same time, everything is still the same. His hair's longer. Darker. And he's got some scruff along his jawline. Nothing a razor won't fix, not that I would mind. The facial hair gives him a mature look, more rugged and refined. His shoulders are still wide, but now more defined with muscle. And while he's tall, his thighs must be a source of pride. Because those thighs are definitely made in the gym. Even in his shorts, I can make out the definition that curves around to his rounded butt.

A butt that looks damn good in both a suit and shorts.

And I bet it looks even better in nothing.

Jack cups a handful of water and rubs it over his tanned arm and bare torso. He repeats the same process with the opposite hand and arm before running both through his brown strands.

As the water droplets drip from his hair and then glimmer on his tanned skin, my mind short circuits and my heart takes over.

Or rather, my libido takes over, and with it, a desire that's lain dormant for four years.

"We should have sex," I say with as much nonchalance as I can muster. It must be the endorphins from my run, paired with the joy of watching tiny turtles paddle along fearlessly, that makes me so bold and giddy. Or maybe it was the lecherous way Sam Wilkins, Mr. Richy Rich, looked at me and then practically offered me his room key at lunch. Maybe it's wanting to take charge of my own sexuality and not allow it to be weaponized against me.

"I've put her to work as my campaign manager. There's no better way to get her feet wet," my dad said before getting up to use the restroom.

Once my father was out of earshot, the fucking creep leaned over and whispered, "I'd love the chance to get more than your feet wet."

I think all women are used to being objectified by men in power. I'm not special in that aspect. So sure, I laughed in Jack's face when he got angry.

But looking back at it now, it was admirable that he was so offended for me. He knew I was uncomfortable.

Because Jack is one of the good ones.

I swallow the lump in my throat as it hits me. He wouldn't intentionally hurt me. Even four years ago, he didn't want to take advantage of a girl just out of high school with stars in her eyes and ideas of fairy tale romances in her heart.

He did the right thing.

He *does* the right thing.

I can see that now.

And right now, Jack is laughing and shaking his head. Likely because he can't comprehend what I'm proposing. "Sorry, I don't think I heard you properly. What did you just say?" The line between his eyebrows deepens as he peruses my face.

"I said we should fuck!" This time, I yell it over the waves crashing onto the shore. And he's certainly heard me now as his body goes completely still and his eyes widen.

"Savannah, what are you talking about?" he croaks after a beat. "I can't even—"

Then it hits me. *Ma, there have been plenty of dates, and I'm sure you'll be a grandma before you know it.* "Oh, I'm sorry," I stutter as I back away. "I didn't realize you were seeing someone. I didn't mean..." I dip under the water and smooth my hair back. Ugh, maybe I can just stay hidden here, submerged in the sea like some kind of virginal beach creature.

Unfortunately, my lungs aren't made for free diving and I have to resurface to survive.

As I wipe the salt from my eyes, I realize that Jack has moved closer. His toes nudge mine and my hip bumps against his thigh as a wave crests over us. Even beneath the water, his nearness has me feeling overheated. "I-I'm not seeing anyone." He puffs out his cheeks and just stares at me. "But regardless, Savannah, that's not... It's just not possible for us to... do that."

"Why?"

Like I've popped his balloon with a sharp needle, Jack seems to deflate. His gaze falls to the clear water as he stares at our feet. So close together as I stand before him. Challenging him.

"Why not?" I repeat.

"I'm hired to—"

I cut him off. "Yeah, yeah. You're hired to protect me. You work for my father. It'd be inappropriate." I dip my hands under the water and watch as they appear smaller, smoother than they actually are. "Except that if we were two people who met, say, at a work conference and just decided to have some fun while on this trip, it'd be completely fine." I slowly raise my eyes to his perplexed face.

"But that's not the case, Savannah." His gaze meets mine. Those wet, honeyed eyes are full of sadness and resignation.

The sun glints off my submerged hands. The light dances on the surface. "What if... What if we pretended?"

"Pretended? I don't think I understand what you're suggesting." Even as his voice softens, there's an edge, a hardness about him. Like he's restraining himself from truly letting go.

"I'm suggesting we forget about all the responsibilities and labels between us. I'm just Savannah. And you're just Keaton. I'm suggesting we, *you know*, use each other. Just while we're here in Florida. For the next two weeks."

He pushes away and swims deeper into the water, beyond the waves, where it's calmer. I follow until my shoulders are completely covered. "Savannah." His voice is full of despair. But I can tell he's cracking by the way that edge sneaks in. "Why are you asking this? There must be plenty of guys who would..." He motions toward me with a flourish. "You know."

I laugh a little. "It's not about how many guys are willing. It's about me wanting it to be with someone who cares. Even if that someone is paid to..." I stop.

"Paid to what, Savannah?"

"Paid to care about me."

"*Jesus Christ.*" Leaving me stranded in the middle of the ocean with everything left unsaid between us, he starts back to the beach. Treading water in an ocean of feelings.

So I pursue him. Just like I did four years ago.

"Wait, that's not what I meant. I don't think of you like—"

"Like the hired help?" he asks gruffly, full of growly emotion. It's sexy and terrifying at the same time. I'm scared that I've completely turned him off of this idea.

So I reach out and grab his arm. Dig my feet into the sand and pull tightly. "Please?" The plea hangs between us. "*Please*, just pretend with me."

Maybe he was waiting for me to beg. To really show him how much I want this.

Because he finally presses his lips together and puffs up his mouth with air. "But what if—"

"No feelings attached," I interrupt. "I get it. I'm not asking for more." I inhale and then exhale. Deeply. Focusing my train of thought. As a campaign manager, my job is to organize and provide appropriate details to get the job done—and done well. I can do this. "These are my terms."

"Terms? I haven't even—" He stops and shakes his head, walking back toward the shore. I follow again, the water becoming less and less deep and exposing me more and more. But I can do this. I can negotiate and compromise so that both parties walk away satisfied.

"Our arrangement would last for two weeks and two weeks only. Once we leave Florida, we stop. And no feelings or expectations of attachment. Oh, and obviously, you don't want anyone to know." I hold out my hand.

I should probably type this up and have it notarized.

"*Obviously*, I don't want anyone to know?" As he stares at that hand, his face goes through a myriad of emotions, the waves now pushing us closer to the shore. I struggle to keep my balance, but Jack's sturdier than I am and has no problem.

"Because your job and reputation are important to you," I amend with a smile. "So you don't need to worry that I'll tell anyone."

But he still doesn't shake my hand.

"Please?" I ask, wiggling my fingers. "I'm just Savannah. Recent college graduate. And we just met on this beautiful beach while watching baby sea turtles."

With a heavy sigh, he finally reaches out to take my hand, only just as his fingers touch mine, he pulls away. "Just two weeks?"

I nod, my body suddenly charged and strumming with energy. I ache to clench this agreement as Jack stands before me, skin glistening with droplets of water. Mine for fourteen days. The two weeks we have left in Florida. "Just two weeks. That's it."

That uncertainty flashes in his eyes again, and I panic, thinking this is all for naught.

So I try again. My hand reaches for his. "Hi, my name's Savannah. I'm in town attending a local conference. My hotel's right over there if you'd care for a drink."

A smile lifts his lips. He finally grasps my palm with his and shakes. "Hi, I'm Jack Keaton. I don't like being called Keaton by anyone other than my boss, so please call me Jack."

Something warm and delicious runs through me at the way his fingers tickle along my wrist. "Oh. Okay," I stutter. "I can do that. And I'll get everything typed up so we can both sign it. I'm not sure where the nearest notary public is, but—"

"No," he answers harshly. "We just met and are going back to your hotel room." He stalks away toward his discarded shoes, leaving me standing in ankle-deep water. "So are you coming or not?"

CHAPTER THIRTY-SIX

Jack

"Do you remember that kiss four years ago?" Savannah strolls next to me as we saunter up the boardwalk. Our feet sand-covered and our clothes salt-crusted. "I mean, a lot has happened since then." She approaches the outdoor shower area, setting her shoes on the wide wooden railing. "I'm sure things have changed."

"I remember," I murmur. "And things haven't changed that much." Standing under the showerhead, she cranks the knob. Water pours over her, drenching her from head to toe. My cock strains against my shorts as I watch her hands dance over her body, clearing the sand from her soft skin.

"You must've dated." Droplet-covered lashes assess me, but I only have eyes for her plump, wet lips.

I slide my fingers through my sweaty hair. "There were dates."

"Oh, *plural*. Nice." She sidesteps away from the spray, and I take her place.

"Eli, er Jenson, likes to think of me as his wingman." I scrub my face.

"Did you two know each other before he started working with you?"

"We did. We went through the academy together. He worked on the force much longer than I did, though. But when your da—my boss—wanted to expand his security, Jenson was the only person I trusted enough to recommend."

"Well, he seems nice." She glances out at the setting sun.

"He's not. He's a man whore. Stay away from him."

She chuckles. "Maybe a man whore is just what I need. I mean, once we're done, that is." Her chest rises with a deep breath.

My face falls, and I stand rigid under the running water. I reach out and tug her into me, against my chest and into the spray. Looming over her, the heat radiates off me as she stares up into my eyes. I hoist her up, pulling a gasp from her throat as I lift under her arms and set her on the planked railing. The backs of her legs press against the rough wood, and she swallows.

Her cheeks turn red, and her pupils dilate. I bet if I ran my fingers through her slit, I'd find desire pooling there. She's turned on.

I trace my thumb along her jaw and her thighs tremble against mine.

"I don't share, Savannah. When I'm with someone, I'm with them completely. And I expect the same in return."

She narrows her gaze, and then rolls her eyes. Challenging me to do something about her attitude.

So I do.

Grabbing her chin, I snap it toward me. "I mean it. You said two weeks. Those were your terms. Nobody else, *nothing* else—not even your toy—for two weeks."

My nostrils flare and she tries to look down, but I pin her with my gaze. Shit, is this tough guy schtick her kink? Because I can be that for her. She flicks her tongue out and licks along the bottom of her lip. My eyes track that slow movement and, without waiting another second, I lean in.

Capturing her lips for the first time in four years.

And the beach, the ocean—hell, the entire world—tilts.

Four years ago, Savannah was the one to kiss me.

This time, it's me kissing her. And it makes all the difference.

What if we pretended?

I'm just Savannah. And you're just Keaton.

I'm not her father's employee. I'm not her bodyguard. I'm just Jack.

And I show her exactly what that means.

I suck her bottom lip between mine, parting the seam with my tongue, and she moans into my mouth. I can taste the salt from the ocean on her lips. Like summer sunshine mixed with danger and fear. Throwing caution to the wind and falling into the ocean without a floatation device. I reach around the back of her head and thread my fingers through her wet hair before gently yanking down, exposing her throat. Then I glide my tongue along her jaw and down the column of her neck before releasing her when she whimpers.

Slow it down, my mind warns as my cock presses against my swim shorts.

Both of us breathless, I reluctantly pull away and swallow, knowing once we leave the beach and head upstairs to the motel room, nothing will ever be the same.

"Slow it down?" I huff to myself in the hotel shower. *What the fuck was I thinking?* The confusion in Savannah's eyes had been hard to ignore as I opened the door to our room and immediately fled to the bathroom. But there's no way I can be what she needs—*what she wants*—until I rub one out first.

I stand beneath the stream of hot water with my hand propped against the tile. Fisting myself. I tug at my cock and imagine sliding it between Savannah's pussy. Teasing her with the tip. Rubbing it against her clit. Whatever it takes until she's dripping wet and ready for me.

Savannah wants me. For two weeks.

And I want her.

But—

The door flies open, and I peer around the curtain, surprised to see Savannah there.

Those perky nipples hard and standing at attention under her shirt.

"I just—" But she stops as her eyes follow the movement of my hand behind the curtain. Up and down along the rock-hard erection.

I flip the faucet off, and the water stops, leaving me standing there. Covered, but just barely, by the sheer white fabric. "Did you need something?" I ask as I continue stroking myself, my gaze never leaving her face.

"Y-You just left me hanging. It left me feeling—" She steps back and devours me with her eyes, one delicious bite at a time.

I slide the curtain aside. My body on full display for her. "Left you feeling how?"

How am I supposed to slow it down when she's here? Staring at me like she wants to lick every inch of water from my body.

"I don't just want a kiss," she explains as she leans against the door. "I had that four years ago. I want *more*." Those dark eyes flash with a dare.

"More of what? *Tell me*." I slide my palm up and down myself.

Her gaze dips to my dick still standing at attention. Then the tip of her tongue comes out and licks slowly along the bottom of her lip.

Fuck slowing down. The moment I shook her hand, I was a goner.

I step out of the shower and advance, standing over her as my chest presses against hers. "Touch yourself." Our faces are inches apart. My breath settles over her as she slides her hands into her pajama bottoms. "Are you wet?" I've waited four years to find out.

"Yes," she moans. Her hand moves beneath the soft fabric.

"What do you want to do, sweetheart?" Her lips part and her eyes go glassy. I may be full steam ahead, but she's still the conductor on this train.

"I want to touch you, Jack."

Oh God, is she trying to give me a heart attack? "Not yet." We stand before each other. Me completely bare and her completely covered as we pleasure ourselves. Savannah slumps against the door and my free hand reaches above her, propping myself up as I fuck my palm.

"Tell me what you'd to do to me, Savannah." I dip my toe into the water of our pretend game.

"I'd want to taste you," she says as those chocolate eyes go wide.

"I bet that mouth feels amazing." I stroke myself harder as my hips begin to pump.

"Can I taste you now?"

"Not yet." Because I'm not ready to cross that line. *Not yet.*

"Tell me what you'd do to me, Jack." Reaching under her top, she massages her chest as her head tilts back against the door.

"Lose the shirt first," I order. She quickly pulls the tee over her head, and I'm granted the sight of her full breasts, nipples hard and begging for my mouth.

"Now tell me." Her voice heightens with need.

"I'd put you up on the counter." My gaze dips to the hard surface. "Then I'd guide your hand to jerk me."

Her mouth slackens as I continue.

"I'd spread those legs and slide my finger into your pajamas." My breathing comes faster now. Almost like a pant. "I'd yank those panties aside and find you so wet for me. You're wet for me, right Savannah?"

"Yes, Jack." It comes out as a breathy whisper.

"I'd rub your clit until it was swollen. Begging for me. You like the way that feels?"

"Uh huh." Her eyes drift closed, and she nods dreamily.

"Tell me. Tell me that you like it."

She moans.

"And then I'd sink a finger into your tight, wet pussy. Has anyone ever touched you there before, Savannah?"

She shakes her head. "Not like this. Tell me how to make you come, Jack," she begs as her chin wobbles.

"Not until you come first. I'd add another finger as my thumb circled your clit until your hips were fucking my hand."

"*Oh Jesus...*"

"You'd stroke me harder as I finger-fucked you... And then I'd slide my dick into that wet pussy..."

"My pussy wants that dick, and then I'd kiss you..." she adds as her eyes flash open. We lock gazes and both tip over the edge. She moans, long and loud, her chest heaving, as I come in hot spurts that land on her pajamas.

"Fuck, Savannah. *Fuck.*"

Our eyes don't leave one another, and even if we're not touching, our breathing syncs as we come back down to Earth as one.

I grab a towel from the rack and wipe her clean as she watches me beneath hazy lids.

"Where'd you learn to talk like that?" I ask as I tie the towel around my waist.

She offers a coy smile. "I like to read."

"I got us coffees from downstairs," Savannah says as she re-enters the motel room with her hands full.

She passes me a Styrofoam cup and I take a sip. "Oh, that is…" I pause as the taste gets progressively worse. "Not good."

Glancing at her, I see my own features mirrored in hers: a frown and head shake. I move to take her cup, but she pulls away.

"I'm going to toss them. They're bad, right?"

She takes another sip and shrugs. "Meh, bad coffee is better than no coffee."

I fight the urge to roll my eyes and instead dump the contents down the sink before tossing the Styrofoam cup into the trashcan. "We can hit a drive-thru on the way in, Savannah. You don't have to keep drinking that."

She swallows another mouthful. "Nah, it's already grown on me. I suppose it's an acquired taste for a sophisticated palate like mine." She blushes at the innuendo.

I'm baffled at the overnight change in Savannah. It's definitely changed her attitude—or lack thereof—toward me.

It's like the old Savannah from four years ago is back. The one who fought me at every turn. The feistiness unable to be contained.

I missed her.

Something squeezes in my chest. "Ugh," I burp. "I'm getting indigestion just watching you drink that sludge."

"So don't watch." Grabbing her bag, she slings it over her shoulder and then takes another sip. The column of her neck works as she swallows, and my mind instantly imagines all the things I want to do with that throat.

"I think you'll learn that I love to watch."

She gapes at me, but as I hurry her out the door so she's not late to her meeting, I simply wink.

Chapter Thirty-Seven

Savannah

"**D**ad? Are you ready?" I stalk through the foyer and into the kitchen, where Eli sits with a newspaper and a cup of coffee. "Oh, hi. Have you seen my father?"

Eli doesn't bother to look up from his reading, but instead flicks the paper loudly. "He just got back from his morning jog."

"Oh, all right." I grab the coffeepot and pour myself a cup. "Mind if I sit?"

"It's your father's house," he replies. Again, without looking up.

I press my lips together as I maneuver around the counter and pull out a stool. Eli doesn't acknowledge me, even when I grab a discarded section of the paper and skim through it. I'm wondering what's gotten into him. When we first met, he was so personable. Now? It's like I've offended him. Or I smell. I glance around before leaning over and sniffing my pit. Nope, I definitely don't smell.

"So how's it been going here?"

"Fine." Folding the paper, he sets it on the pile between us. Then he gets up from his stool and walks around to the coffeepot. He pours the remaining coffee into his mug, but it's not nearly enough to fill the whole cup. With a heavy sigh, he glares at me from beneath lowered eyebrows.

"Sorry," I say sheepishly. "I should've put on a new pot."

"No, it's fine," he says curtly before turning around and reaching into the cupboard for more coffee grounds. I swear I hear him mutter "typical" under his breath. My ears go hot in confusion. What the hell's his problem?

"Oh, Savannah. You're back." Miranda saunters in, just as Eli slams the lid closed on the coffeemaker. I jump.

"Just here to get my father before we head to the conference. Are you coming with us today?" Her outfit says yes, as she's dressed in a perfectly tailored sheath dress. I bite my lip as envy crawls up my throat. With my curves, I've never been able to pull off that silhouette.

"Of course." She laughs. "Did Eli show you your finished room?" She flicks her gaze to Eli, who's sullenly leaning against the countertop as he waits for the coffee to finish brewing.

"Oh, I'm sure we were just getting to that," I respond with a friendly smile at the bodyguard. "I'll go check it out myself." Standing, I head down the narrow hallway to the room at the end, just next to the garage. I pass Miranda's room and then the room meant for Jack. My steps falter as I wonder how we'll manage to finish our two weeks if we're back in the house with so many people around.

I press onward and, as my hand hovers over the doorknob, I hear Miranda's voice from behind me. "They just finished painting last night so you could grab your things from that motel and come back tonight."

My smile wavers, but I keep it in place nonetheless and push open the door. The paint fumes are overwhelming, and my eyes squint at the lack of curtains or even blinds. I immediately retreat into the hallway. "You know, Miranda, I just don't think tonight is going to work out. I'll need the blinds re-installed, and the room still needs to be aired out from the fumes. There's no way it's healthy to be breathing in all of that. I should just extend our stay at the motel for a few more days until you can arrange for the contractors to come back."

Her face falls. "I'll get right on that. I'll have them out today, and I'm sure Eli can help with getting the room aired out."

"Thanks so much. That'd be perfect." And then I hurry right past her as my mind comes up with more ways to stall our return. "Let my father know I'm waiting in the car."

"Hello, Miss Smith."

My face snaps up to the man holding open the door. His deep, sultry voice sends a shiver up my spine, and he must assume I'm encouraging his advances because his smile widens when I pass. His eyes clock the goosebumps breaking out along my arms.

"Oh, good afternoon, Mr. Wilkins." I nod politely, but continue my trajectory toward the large reception room just past the vendor booths.

I want nothing more than to get away from this creep.

"I'd love the chance to get more than your feet wet." Gross. Who says shit like that?

A rich man who plans on donating millions to your father's campaign, so play nice, the voice inside my head chastises. I swallow the bile threatening to bubble up my throat. It doesn't mean I have to sleep with him. Just flirt a little. So I plaster on a fake smile and turn back, ready to tell him to have a good day and move on.

Except he's right next to me. "Attending the Federal Facilities and Enhanced Water Resilience training today?" Damn, his legs must be long, or he's just that eager to speak to me. I'm startled he's caught up so quickly.

I glance down at my notepad. "Actually, I'm off to Federal Funding: Options and Leverage today, Mr. Wilkins."

"Oh, please, we're friends now. I think it's only fair you call me Sam." He flashes me a smile with raised eyebrows.

"Right, Mr. Wil— I mean, Sam." A nervous giggle escapes my lips and my face heats. When we arrive at the juncture to the conference rooms, I veer right, thinking my shadow will turn left. Unfortunately, he grabs my arm. My hackles rise, even as his touch is gentle.

"I'd like to invite you to dinner with some of my colleagues this evening. Give them a chance to meet you. We can discuss the merits of your father's campaign and how we can work together to ensure we're all on the same page."

I brighten up and finally feel comfortable enough to offer him a genuine smile. Maybe I read too much into that little innuendo. I mean, rich people often have the weirdest social skills. "That'd be wonderful. I'd love to come."

"Great. We'll see you at Callisto at 7."

He finally releases me, and I stumble into the meeting, feeling extra excited to network and build working relationships without my father.

I'm ready to set out on my own and forge my path.

"What do you mean, you need the car for a dinner meeting?" Jack eyes me from the bed, where he's tying his shoes to go for a run.

He's wearing a sleeveless top and jogging shorts that hug his thick thighs. I recall what's under those shorts... What we did last night.

And suddenly dinner with a bunch of stuffy colleagues isn't very appetizing.

I heave a sigh and return to the mirror, where I apply a fresh coat of mascara.

"I was invited to a meeting to discuss my father's campaign and develop some donor relations." My hips press against the vanity and my rear tilts out. "I don't really need you to babysit me, Jack."

Before I can dip the wand back into the mascara and swipe a coat on my other eye, Jack slides behind me, his front flush with my backside.

"You know that's not part of the terms, Savannah." His hands grip my hips and, before I know it, I'm rubbing my ass against his crotch like a cat in heat.

"How is going to dinner not part of our terms?" I discard the mascara tube and white knuckle the counter as the heat spreads from back to front.

"Not *our* terms," he clarifies. "Your father's terms."

I spin around and he pulls away. "None of that exists with just Savannah and Jack, though. *Two people who just met.*" Winking, I smile wickedly, desperately wanting to get my way.

He pulls his sleeveless tee over his head, and try as I might, I am instantly distracted by the muscled chest in front of me. My mouth waters as I imagine myself running my tongue over the lines along his abdominals.

"Not going to happen. I chauffeur you around. Protect you. Which means we are a packaged deal."

I narrow my eyes at him. "Protect me from what?" He grabs his dark trousers and a white button-down from his traveling case, then marches into the restroom, closing the door behind him.

"Creeps at a bar. Guys named Benji. Take your pick."

I chuckle softly to myself that he remembers the nickname I once called Brett, who's practically my stepbrother at this point. "Fine," I relent before turning back to the mirror and applying the missing coat of mascara.

He flings open the bathroom door at the same time as he finishes tucking in his shirt. My heart pounds, wanting to rip the shirt from his trousers, but I bite my lip and put my hands to good use, adding a tube of lipstick to my purse.

"Let's get this over with," he says, eyeing me up and down.

My nipples pebble beneath my blouse, and a fire simmers in my core. "What's the rush? Got plans for tonight?"

His hazel eyes seem to flash brighter as he smirks. "Yes, *just* Savannah. *We* have plans for tonight."

"And what exactly are those plans, *just* Jack?" Flutters take over my belly, traveling down to my core. I practically need to cross my legs with the way he's eyeing me.

"I'm going to show you what it's like..." he trails off as he grabs the keys and heads to the door.

"What *what* is like?" I saunter over on unsteady legs, my heart in my throat.

"Getting fucked by a man instead of a boy." He swings open the door and holds it for me to go first.

My breath hitches as I force myself to take one step. And then another. Jack thinks I've been with other men—*boys*—before. But what he doesn't know, what I purposefully didn't tell him, is that I'm still a virgin.

Chapter Thirty-Eight

Jack

I love watching Savannah do her thing. She's effortless. Flawless. She leans in and laughs at the most opportune moments. She smiles, flashing her pearly whites, and nods in agreement at the right time. She's amazing.

What I don't love is the way that Sam Wilkins keeps touching her. He's seated right next to her, and I swear he keeps scooting his chair closer and closer. His meaty hands paw at her forearm, pausing against the back of her chair as he leans in to be heard over the din of the restaurant. When he refills her wineglass from the bottle to his left, I nearly stand from my place at the bar and stride over. I'd like to shove that bottle up his ass.

Fortunately, there are two other men and one woman seated at the table, albeit she's old enough to be Savannah's mother. So at least this Sam character didn't lie about the business dinner with his associates. A large part of me wouldn't have been surprised if he tricked Savannah into coming on the pretenses of a lucrative meeting, only to have her show up to an intimate dinner for two.

I swirl the whiskey in my glass and focus on Savannah again. She's wearing a fitted, high-collar red dress. The color looks amazing against her olive complexion. And while she's straightened her hair to within an inch of its life and pulled it back into a sleek bun at her nape, I can't wait until later tonight when she releases it from the style and shakes it out. By the time the night is over, I expect some of her natural waves to pop up along her hairline from our exertions.

I'm hard just thinking of what I'll do to her when we get back to the motel room. We'll be back at the house with the rest of the staff shortly, but at least we have a few more nights together. *Alone.*

Only a little while later, Savannah and the Rich Bitch, as I've taken to calling him in my mind, are standing in the parking lot saying their goodbyes. "Sam, I can't thank you enough for inviting me to meet your colleagues. It was a real pleasure." Savannah sticks out her hand, expecting a handshake, but I see the look of surprise light up her features when this Sam fellow pulls her in for a hug.

Her body stiffens slightly before relaxing and she instantly steps out of his embrace. It takes every fiber of my being to not sock the idiot right in the jaw, but then I'd certainly be in the doghouse tonight. So instead, I wait in the car like the good little pup I am, even as my nose is nearly pressed against the window.

Leaning in, he whispers something in her ear, and her face turns a shade of pink that clashes with her dress. She smiles woodenly, her lips pressed together as she glances back at me. What is he saying to her? I've never seen that look on her face. It's a mixture of panic, embarrassment, and curiosity. My pulse pounds in my ears and I look away.

It's just another moment before the passenger side door opens and Savannah slides into the seat. "Whew," she exhales as she sets her purse on the floor and latches the seat belt. "I'm glad that's over."

I bite back the questions simmering in my mind and tear out of the parking lot with more aggression than I should.

"Whoa, Jack. We don't want to get in an accident."

I worry my bottom lip because she's right. My sole job is to protect, and I'm doing the complete opposite simply because I'm jealous.

I'm jealous.

The thought hits me like a ton of bricks as I pull onto the parkway and drive toward the motel. For four years, I tried to forget Savannah. For four years, I did everything I could to put her from my mind. And now that she's back in my life, I'm suddenly fawning over her and throwing away my priorities and beliefs?

Savannah's words flash in my mind again. *I'm suggesting we forget about all the responsibilities and labels between us.* Can it really be that easy, though? Can I throw away everything I've worked for just for her? But just as I begin to question everything, the two weeks, Savannah, hiding what we're doing...she reaches out and places her hand on top of mine on the shifter. Her thumb circles my skin in soothing motions.

And I'm done for.

I slide the room key into the card reader, but it once again flashes red. "C'mon," I huff as I repeat the process once more.

"Here, try mine instead." Savannah reaches into her bag and fishes out her key before passing it to me. I slide it into the depths of the reader, but no dice.

"Red!" I groan as my forehead hits the door. My eyes close as I imagine what lies beyond. The promise of a bed and Savannah. *Naked.*

The object of my desire nudges me aside, her whole body pressing against mine. If I wasn't already turned on, I'd certainly combust with the way her ass grazes against my pelvis. She sticks the card into the slot.

"What the hell?" A frown tilts down her lips and her brow furrows as she jams the plastic card in once more.

Red.

"Ugh." She rotates and leans her back against the door, her front wedged against mine. A smile plays at her full lips as her dark eyes look up at me. "I guess we're locked out."

"Looks like it," I murmur. The way that dress fits perfectly around her curves has me seeing stars, and I lean in, nuzzling along her throat. "And we had such important plans, too." My lips press tiny kisses against her soft skin.

Just then, my cell phone vibrates in my pants. I let loose a groan, even as Savannah whispers, "Don't answer it."

Except I have to.

We can play pretend all we want, but I still have a job.

For now.

I withdraw the device from my pocket as Eli's name flashes across the screen. "What?" I answer gruffly, annoyed at being interrupted.

"Boss wants you and Savannah to meet him at Bailey's on Third for drinks."

Straightening, I pull away from Savannah. "When?" My gaze bounces between her confused expression and those lips begging to be kissed.

"Now, man. Why? You got plans or something?"

Yeah, kind of... I want to respond. But I clear my throat and put on my professional mask for a little while longer. "We'll be there."

I hang up and, as much as I want to grab Savannah's hand and press it against my dick so she knows the pain I'm in, I pull her away from the door and back to the car. Both of us frowning as we go.

"Well, that was fun," Savannah says wryly as her father waves on his way out of the restaurant. She looks down at her half-finished martini and then raises her eyebrow at my empty whiskey glass before sliding her gaze to the stack of papers between us.

"A brief about the PR firm I'd like you to work with when we return to the campaign in the fall," the governor said as he dropped the folio in front of his daughter. Her face had fallen as she eyed the stack; although I'm not certain he even noticed, as he rattled off more numbers and data points than I could wrap my head around.

"I'm getting us another round." Standing, I head toward the bar.

"Make mine literally anything stronger than this." I turn and find her slugging back the clear liquid in her dainty glass.

On second thought, I return to the table and raise her to her feet. Surprise flashes in her eyes. "What are you—?"

"C'mon," I say, pulling her in my wake as I make my way to the heavy wooden door. "There's a small hole-in-the-wall across the street. And I'm pretty sure I heard some decent music when we pulled up."

"Oh, thank God!" she exclaims, her feet doubling in time as she follows. "This place is way too stuffy."

Moments later, we're standing in the entrance of the Ginned Gator as a honky-tonk band assaults our ears. "I know this isn't quite the type of music you like, but—"

"I love it!" As she flits to the bar, an enormous smile lights up her face. "Two whiskeys!" she hollers over the banjo's trill. "Make 'em doubles!" She slaps down a large bill as the bartender slides the amber liquid her way.

I stand behind her, still deciding whether this dive is a decent place, and accept the thick glass she hands me with a nod.

"Bottoms up!" she proclaims, clinking her glass with mine and taking a hearty swig.

My eyes widen as she licks her lips and then takes another slug, her double now merely a drop. "Savannah, how about I get you a water?"

"Not a chance. Oh! I love this song!" She tosses back the rest of her drink and sets the empty glass on the bar before snatching mine from my hand and taking a luxurious gulp. "Let's dance!"

I haven't seen this side of Savannah in years. Alcohol-infused and already writhing to the sound of the band. My brain flashes back to all those years ago and the way she'd wrapped her body around mine as music pulsed from the DJ booth. Now, given free rein to touch her, I clam up at the chance. "Are you sure you don't want to go back to the motel?"

"Not a chance, *just* Jack! In case you didn't know, *just* Savannah loves to dance!" Before I can persuade her otherwise, she's traipsing through the crowd to the dance floor, and I'm like a moth to a flame.

Except this type of dancing is hardly seductive. Instead, it's line dancing. Complete with intricate footwork, a choreography of kicks and heel-toes, and an insurmountable amount of partner-changing.

I hate every minute of it as I work my hardest to keep track of Savannah. One minute, she's dancing with a wrinkled old man, laughter bubbling up from her, and the next, she's shimmying with a gangly teenager with a beet-red face. I eventually step away from the dance floor and just observe.

Watching her throw back her hair and simply enjoy. And when she finds me in between dances, she continues to swipe the drink from my hand, down it in one gulp, and then cheer excitedly as the fiddle's tune crests over the crowd with the next song.

"It's getting pretty late," I tell her the next time she approaches me and snatches my drink—this time a water—from my hand.

"Is that your code to get me home so you can take me to bed, *Officer*?" She chews on the straw as her eyes work to focus. Her balance unsteady, I place my hand around her waist and hold her upright.

"Sure, baby. How about I take you home and put you to bed?" It's hard not to laugh as she tries, and fails, to wink at me.

Savannah's a lovable drunk. The best kind. "I'd like that. Are you good to drive, or do we need to get an Uber?" She digs in her pocket for her phone and pulls it out, eyeing it with a frown.

"You drank all my drinks, so I'll drive us back." I take her phone from her, and she offers me a beatific smile before coming around the high-top table and sliding under my outstretched arm.

"You smell good," she says as we make our way outside. "You've always smelled good." A grin stretches my face as she sinks her nose into my chest and inhales. It allows me a chance to run my palm higher up her back, tangling in her hair. God, I so want to coil those strands around my hand and yank back, exposing her neck. Lick along the cords of her throat until she's squirming.

As though she can read my mind, she raises her face to me and grabs me around the neck, pulling me down. "You taste delicious too," she mutters as she finds my lips in the darkness of the parking lot.

By the time we reach the car, Savannah's walking like a baby giraffe and sporting a sleepy smile. I settle her in the passenger seat, buckle her in, and then head around to the driver's side.

"You feeling okay?" I ask as I start the car.

And I'm answered only with a soft snore.

CHAPTER THIRTY-NINE

Savannah

"You've got to be kidding me," I groan as the alarm goes off the following morning. Rolling over, the scent of pain au chocolat pulls me from one of the worst hangovers of my life.

"Rise and shine!" Jack's cheerful face greets me with a pink box of my favorite breakfast treats. I peer at him through a haze of crusty eyes and matted, frizzy hair.

"Oh, God," I moan, throwing a pillow over my eyes. "Please tell me you did not just see me looking like a hungover troll."

The bed sags where he seats himself comfortably, away from my hideousness. "One, you do not look like a troll. And two, you are very much hungover and need to get something in your stomach to feel better." He holds a chocolate pastry under my nose to lure me from my hiding spot.

I reluctantly accept the confection and bring it to my mouth. Taking a hearty bite, the bittersweet chocolate coats my tongue and has my taste buds dancing.

Something I also did a lot of last night, apparently.

"How embarrassing was I?" I ask Jack as I finally sit up and attempt to look semi-presentable.

"On a scale of one to ten?"

"*Nooooo*," I moan again as I fall back against the pillows. But Jack grabs my hand and hoists me back to a seated position.

"It was fine. It wasn't until after your dad and Eli left that you really hit the alcohol hard."

"Thank goodness." I take another bite of the croissant. My father's never seen me drunk, and if I have it my way, he never will.

I polish off the last few bites of the pastry and suddenly realize that Jack's been suspiciously quiet. Contemplative.

"Thank you for getting me back here and tucking me in." I glance down at the red dress I'd been wearing last night and am still wearing.

"Savannah, are you regretting what we're doing?" The question comes out of nowhere, and as my wide eyes meet Jack's, my stomach plummets.

"N-no, of course not." I bite my lip and adjust the dress.

"So you getting drunk last night wasn't...?" he trails off. But the look in his eyes tells me everything he isn't saying.

"Not at all," I lie. "I'm not a big drinker, so I don't really know my limit." Shrugging, I look away, afraid he'll be able to see right through me.

His body sags in relief, which I find endearing. That Jack would wonder if I was sabotaging our agreement is outrageous. If only he knew what I was actually nervous about.

Just tell him, a little voice inside my brain hisses at me.

But I can't. I'm too afraid it will scare him away. Make him regret the things we've already done. Make him push me away like he did once before.

And I can't take that again.

So I press my lips together and refuse to tell him that I've still got my v-card.

I mean, he'll find out eventually. In theory.

"Did you still want to go walk the beach for turtle nests?"

"What? When did I...?" And then it comes back. Drunkenly asking Jack to set an alarm so we could take a sunrise walk on the beach and search for more hatchlings. I smile at him sheepishly. "Let me brush my teeth and get changed into something more beach appropriate."

"How's your mom doing?" I ask Jack as we trudge through the cool sand. We stay away from the shoreline and keep our eyes peeled to the longer grasses near the dunes. By the time our motel is out of sight, we're nearly out of breath as we navigate the deeper sand with a slow gait.

"She's doing all right. Not great. But she has a team of doctors who seem to understand the disease. Although they're not world-renowned or anything. The best in East Lansing, at least."

"Is there a better team somewhere in Michigan? I'm sure my father could pull some strings."

"Actually, the best doctors for dementia are right here in Florida, which makes sense, considering the population of the state."

We traipse a few more feet, and I look out at the ocean instead of focusing on the grassy dunes. "Have you ever thought about moving down here? I'm sure you could get a job. Easily. I mean, Laurel would surely hire you."

Jack pauses and picks up a seashell, passing it to me with a smile. "I've thought about it, sure. But I like my job. I like what I do."

I bite my lip, thinking that I'd move to Florida in a heartbeat. If only I wasn't working for my father's campaign.

If I wasn't working for my father's campaign...

What would I do?

"Hey! A nest!" Jack's exclamation pulls me from the musings of a hangover with very little sleep, and I snap my gaze to where he's pointing.

We rush over and kneel together, eyeing the clutch of eggs in awe.

"Good eye," I praise him with a smile.

He beams back, his throat bobbing as he swallows. "Thanks."

We sit and stare at the nest for a time before rising and continuing our walk. This time, we meander closer to the surf, our feet leaving prints in the wet sand.

"Tell me about college." He leans over and picks up a seashell, tossing it into the waves.

"What do you want to know?" To be honest, there isn't a lot to share. I studied. Then studied some more.

"Did you ever run into Brett?"

With a snort, I shake my head. "He invited me to his frat house a few times, but I was always too busy. I think my roommate Delia ran into him once at a party."

He nods slowly and finds another shell, launching it into the water. "What was your favorite class?"

My eyebrows shoot up. "Really? That's what you want to know about the last four years? My favorite class?" I chuckle and plop down onto the sand, my arms coming to rest on my knees.

"Why not? I'm interested in the education of America's youth."

He sounds like my father, but I don't dare mention that, else it ruin the mood. Right now, we seem to be just Savannah and Jack. And while it's easy for me to fall into this pretending, I don't dare rock the boat and cause us to tip over into the truth of our relationship.

Boss's daughter and bodyguard.

"I took an introduction to guitar class," I admit, hoping to steer the conversation to less serious topics that could lead to the real world seeping in. "And then I was able to watch some YouTube videos and learn a few basic songs."

Jack comes closer and sits next to me, our hips touching. It's like that entire side of my body is on fire with his nearness. "So when we get back to Michigan, you'll play me a song?"

"Of course, but by then, the two weeks—" I stop, realizing I'm sabotaging everything.

Jack's quiet for a minute, but his jaw works as he stares out into the abyss of the ocean. Meanwhile, I sneak glances at him. Waiting.

"I'd like to hear you play." A smile breaks across my face just as the sun's rays tip over the horizon.

"I'd love to play for you. But I'm not any good."

He turns to me and blinks once. Twice. "I'm sure you're better than you give yourself credit for."

And then he takes my hand and pulls me to my feet. And we continue our walk as the sun shines on our intertwined fingers, warming me from the inside out.

CHAPTER FORTY

Jack

"I'll just run Savannah by the motel so she can pick up her things for dinner, sir."

Savannah sends her dad a small smile before climbing into the passenger seat as he exits the vehicle. I ensure she's tucked in safely before closing the door and then circle around to the driver's seat.

"Do we have to come back?" she asks as her head falls against the headrest.

"Long day?" The engine turns over, and I reverse out of the drive and into the street.

"The longest. That asshole Sam Wilkins wouldn't stop ogling me during our meeting with my father." Her lip curls as she tilts her face toward me.

"That bad?"

"The worst. If you'd been there, I'm sure he'd be left with empty eye sockets."

A low growl escapes from within, and I clench the steering wheel with white knuckles. "And Eli, where was he?" My co-worker and I had traded off duties today as I was fixing a Wi-Fi issue at the house.

"I don't know." She shrugs and yawns. "Not sitting at the bar, gripping a whiskey and glaring daggers at us, that's for sure."

"I don't do that," I say, even knowing for damn sure I definitely do.

"Yeah, okay." She's quiet for a minute as she scans the busy intersection we've pulled up to. "I like it," she admits softly.

"You like what, Savannah?" My head swivels from left and right as I watch for an opening in the traffic.

"I like the way you watch me. Like at lunch the other day? It kind of turns me on."

My mouth widens in a smile that surely looks devilish. I turn into the parkway and accelerate, my foot taking over as my cock thickens in my trousers. "So you're into being watched, then?"

She bites her lip and shrugs. "I don't really know what I'm into yet."

Just me? I want to ask hopefully, but I swallow the question. It goes down like a lead balloon and leaves me with heartburn. So instead, I say, "Maybe we can *pretend* before we head back to the house. I mean, I love watching you, and you like the way I do it, so...?" I trail off, but look at her with an eyebrow lifted.

She reddens slightly and chews on her lip. Contemplating the idea, perhaps, or imagining all the fun we could have. Either way, I'm having the damndest time keeping myself comfortable as my dick grows harder and harder by the minute. "I guess we should have our fun while we can."

That lead balloon in my gut shifts and suddenly my stomach goes sour. Our two weeks have just begun, yet I can't stop thinking about it ending.

I exhale deeply and push the intrusive thoughts aside, vowing to focus on the here and now.

And what I'm going to watch Savannah do when we get back to the motel.

Before Savannah can walk through the opened door, I grab her gently by the nape and press her against the frame. Leaning in close, I run my tongue along the pulsing skin of her neck and up to her ear. "Get your toy. I want to watch you pleasure yourself."

I release her and, like a newborn colt on unsteady legs, she moves to her suitcase. After rifling through it for a moment, she brandishes a blue and white wand. It looks like a basic back massager, but I know that's likely the only reason Savannah purchased this particular model.

The deniability.

She handles the foot-long vibe while staring up at me through her dark lashes. Waiting for my demands. I decide now is as good as any to show her that I like to take charge in the bedroom.

"Move over to the bed," I instruct as I pull out a chair from the table and set it directly in the center at the foot of the bed. "I want you to plug in your toy and then lie on the bed with your feet toward me."

Savannah complies without a word. Her chest rises and falls more quickly, though, and pink tinges her cheeks. I spread my thighs as I watch her climb onto the bed, my balls feeling heavy and tight in my trousers.

When she's situated, she rolls her lips between her teeth and turns those big chocolate doe eyes on me, waiting for further instruction. "I want you to show me what you do with your toy when you're alone." She blinks once and then lifts her skirt over her hips. Bending her knees, she places her feet flat on the bed. Before sliding the fabric aside, I snag a glimpse of her panties and the wet spot already seeping through the thin material.

Then she powers on the device. It buzzes loudly through the silent room. The vibration pounds through my body, straight to my hard cock. I rub myself through my pants and Savannah's eyes track my hand from her place propped on the pillows.

"Let your knees fall open. I want to see *everything*." She follows my directive, and I'm gifted with a view of her gleaming pussy as the vibrator glides over her lips. My eyelids fall to half-mast as she moves her other hand to her top, pulling down the neckline and palming her tit. "Are your nipples hard?" I ask gruffly.

"Uh huh," she mumbles as her eyes close. Her chin lifts toward the ceiling as her body grinds against the toy. The muscles in her arm flex and her knuckles go white as she presses it into herself.

"Fuck, Savannah." Unzipping my pants, I pull out my dick. The need to fist myself is overwhelming, and I'm afraid I'm going to combust if I don't. I use my thumb and forefinger to jack myself over the swollen tip. As much as I wish I were inside her right now, this foreplay is so much sweeter.

Savannah's eyes dip closed as she slides the vibrator in and out of her cunt. Her body has taken over now, and she bucks against the bed, her thighs shaking as her breathing goes raspy. "*Fuck*," she hisses. "I want you, Jack. *Please*."

I look up from her pussy and find her eyes pleading with me. Begging me to take over. To fuck her. Standing, I drop my pants to the floor, my cock pointing us in the direction of the bed. *He* certainly knows what he wants. But as I fuck my hand and watch Savannah writhe against the rumpled bedspread, I want to make her ache for me the way I've ached for her for four years.

And it was a long fucking four years.

Four years without anyone. It's been four years since I've even looked at a cunt, and I'm not going to overindulge now. I need to savor it. Partition it out little by little, so I have these memories when she leaves me again.

"I thought you didn't need me, Savannah." I knee onto the bed and place my hand over hers, taking control of the vibrator. "I thought you could take care of yourself. Isn't that what you said?" She instantly moves that hand to her clit and rubs the swollen skin with her middle finger. Her other hand continues to pull at her nipple, which at this point could actually cut glass. "Tell me you need me, Savannah. *I want to hear you say it.*"

I withdraw the vibe from her pussy, challenging her to defy me. Those chocolate eyes beg me to keep going as her lips part.

"Tell me, baby." I bring the vibrator to my mouth and take a slow, luxurious lick. Her eyes track me, zeroing in on the way my tongue laps at her toy.

"*Fuck*, Jack. Fuck, I need you. I *need* you."

Satisfied, I return the device to her pussy before sliding it lower. Toward her ass. Her eyes widen slightly, but when the toy slides into place and massages against the puckered hole, her face slackens with pleasure. Just watching her, watching me fuck my hand, is enough to get me off. I jerk myself faster now, rubbing from root to tip while pressing the vibrator against Savannah's tight bud.

Moaning, her legs tremble. "I-I'm coming!" she gasps as she throws her head back and her hands fist the bedspread. I don't stop. I ride the wave of pleasure with her, pumping myself faster, and keep the toy nestled between her cheeks until my own body convulses and I empty myself all over her stomach.

With a pounding heart, I drop the toy and hunch over Savannah, my hand flat on the bed, propping me up as I come down from the high. She lies beneath me, her chest rising and falling as she catches her breath, and a euphoric smile brightens her face.

I lean down and plant a soft kiss to that smile, which is now fading—and fading fast—as we both realize we have to return to the house for dinner, and the pretending is over.

CHAPTER FORTY-ONE

Savannah

"I expect your things to be moved back into the house tomorrow, Savannah."

"But wouldn't it make more sense just to finish out the wee—"

"No, I need you back under this roof so we can begin planning the barbecue and working as a cohesive team. Miranda's had a hard enough time coordinating two separate schedules. And besides…"

My body goes still, and I tune out my father's instructions.

Food left to grow cold, I stare at it with no appetite.

If I looked up and caught Jack's eyes across the table, would I find him also having an internal meltdown about our situation?

Before I know it, dinner concludes, and I'm being led from the house and ushered into the car. "You'll bring your things here tomorrow morning on your way to the conference," my father adds as the door closes behind us. I'm not even sure how I get into the black town car, but as Jack drives the short distance from the house to the motel, my mind is in a tailspin.

"Savannah?" Jack's worried voice pulls me from my thoughts of despair, and I turn to him, finding us already parked at the motel lot.

It's now or never.

Time to tell him that I'm a—

Except he leans in, his hand trailing along my jaw. "Savannah, we don't have to do this. Especially if you're not ready. This shouldn't be something that we do just because there's an ultimatum hanging over our heads."

"What?" My brow furrows in confusion, and I gulp, my eyes seeking his and then raking over his face. All the minute details I've memorized. But the one thing I focus on is his bottom lip. He's running his thumb along it, worrying it between his teeth as he watches me. And in that instant, I know he's just as nervous as I am.

And that makes everything perfect.

"You asked me if I ever thought about you. When I left for college. When I stayed away." I swallow and clasp my hands together in my lap. "When I left...all I ever thought about was what you said that night."

"Which night?"

"That night in your room. With Miranda. You said that kiss we shared...on the beach...it never should've happened." I hold his gaze, begging him to remember. To explain how he could say something so hurtful.

"I said that?" he asks as two lines form between his eyebrows. They're deeper than they were four years ago.

"You said you'd lose everything because of me."

It's like the air is sucked from the vehicle as he looks at me. It's a look that's filled with four years of lust. Four years of anger. Four years of missing. Four years of *desire*.

"I don't want this to be something you regret in the morning."

"I could never regret this. Regret *you*." His eyes canvas my face, and as he does so, his thumb comes up to brush across his bottom lip. "Do you want this, Savannah?"

I tamp down the smile that's threatening to pull at my face and nod, blinking away the wetness pooling in my eyes. "I want this. More than anything."

It's all I need to say before he's pulling me over the console and onto his lap. My legs straddle his waist, and I plant my lips on his, pulling that damn bottom lip between my teeth and sucking it. When he groans, my insides melt. My hands frame his jaw, reveling in this. In him.

I do want this.

I've wanted this for four long years.

I never stopped wanting this.

He pulls away, eyes locking onto mine. "As much as I want to take you here and now, Savannah, there's no way you're getting the best of what I can offer in the front seat of a car."

My heart thunders with eagerness as he flings open the door and fireman carries me to the stairs.

The best of what he can offer? I'm wet already at the promise.

"Put me down, I can walk!" I squeal, playfully pounding on his back as he hoists me into the air. But he doesn't relent. No, he climbs *four flights of stairs* with me over his shoulder before depositing me just outside of the door to our room.

"How are you not winded?" I ask as my mouth falls open.

"Adrenaline. Four years of adrenaline," he responds smoothly before capturing my mouth in his. This time, the door opens seamlessly with the swipe of his key card, and we tumble through, all tongue and teeth. Arms and hands.

"Bed," he demands, and I oblige, the earlier doubt and nerves long gone. Now there's only Jack and the desire burning me up inside.

We drop onto the mattress together, his body flush against mine and mine tingling for his.

"Hurry," I whisper as Jack's fingers dance over the buttons of his shirt. My excitement can't be contained. I don't think I've ever wanted anything as badly as I want Jack Keaton.

"Fuck it," he finally mutters, ripping the shirt down the middle. The buttons fly across the room and my eyes widen in disbelief as he tosses the shirt over his shoulder.

Our lips seek each other again. Tongues colliding and bodies pressing together, hungry for more.

I reach for his trousers and pull the hem of his white tee over his head, exposing his bare chest. My eyes devour him, my fingers twitching to touch. Aching for the feel of his skin against mine. They follow the curves of every muscle. Every outline. "*Jesus*," I whisper, transfixed. I mean, I've seen his muscles before. But to touch them in this way is something else entirely. It's akin to touching a holy relic, and I reverently worship every bit of his chest and stomach. I move to his arms, inching myself up and trailing my fingertips down his forearms, to his strong hands and finally to his fingers, which link with mine.

He grabs the back of my head and pulls me forward, connecting our lips once more. We come together like two crashing waves heading toward shore. I gasp for air as my chest heaves, the heat coursing through my veins making me breathless with need.

"Let me undress you, Savannah," he begs as our lips part. "Please?"

I nod eagerly, and he guides me to the edge of the bed and to standing. As I turn away, he carefully unzips the dress I'd worn to dinner and eases it over my shoulders, then down my hips where it pools on the floor. His fingers graze my skin along the way, his breath hot as he presses kisses along my hip bones. Along the waist of my thong. I jump and quiver at his touch. Each place he kisses warms with wanting. *Needing*. He trails his lips up my spine, that sensitive skin melting as my core clenches. Then over my shoulders and on the back of my neck. Places that only he can reach. Next, he unpins my hair. As it tumbles down my back, his fingers thread through the kinks and waves before falling to the clasp of my bra.

He unhooks it, but immediately spins me around to face him.

"You're beautiful." His voice is low. Husky. I blush, trying to cover myself, but he pulls my arms away and places them on his chest instead. "Don't cover up for me. I want to see all of you."

I lower my eyes, head tipping back, as he bends to lick along my collarbone. My fingers caress through his hair and down to his shoulders, tracing the valleys and trenches of his muscles. When he yanks my bra down and sucks my pebbled nipple into his mouth, I gasp and arch into him.

"*Jack...*" I'm needy, my plea released on a breath. Wanting more of everything only he can give me.

He laves at my chest, from one breast to the other, until the peaks are pointed. Then he gently blows on each, the air hitting the wetness and my body shivering at the new sensation.

I gasp and a lewd noise escapes from deep within my throat as his palms move lower, down to the cheeks of my ass. He grips me, hoisting me against his body—his *cock*—and we fall back together.

My hands sweep down his chest and to the button of his trousers as he grinds against me. I can feel him through the fabric, his length pressing against my stomach. Undoing the button and zipper, I yank his pants over his ass, wanting more than anything to feel him in my hand.

"Lose the pants," I demand. I lie back on the pillows and watch as he does so, tossing the trousers to the side of the bed.

I hold up my hand when he begins to make his way over to me. "And the briefs." He stalls, his hands on the band. My muscles are tense. Dancing and jumping beneath my skin in anticipation.

"Not yet, baby." Before I can protest, he crawls over me, covering my mouth with his and swallowing my objection. His hands trail down my body, the skin that he touches pebbling in his wake. Fingers drawing teasing swirls on my skin until he reaches the apex of my thighs.

"Let me worship you," he asks, his eyes on mine as our mouths part.

I nod, unable to speak any intelligible thought as my body takes over and my brain shuts down.

Jack's fingers slide my panties to the side and part my flesh. "My girl's already wet for me," he says gruffly as he catches my eye. Then his head dips to my breast once again, and he's pulling my budded nipple into his mouth as his deft fingers circle my clit.

I let out a gasp, whether from his mouth or his fingers, I'm not sure. All I know is that my legs are jelly and I've never felt anything more delicious than being covered by Jack.

"You like that?"

"*Mmmm,*" I moan as my hands fist the bedding.

"Move your legs apart. I want to taste you."

I melt into a puddle beneath him as Jack releases my nipple and shifts his face to my core. His tongue finds that sensitive bud and he gently pulls it into his mouth, licking and sucking with such ease that I'm pretty sure I'm going to come already.

"Don't stop," I beg as a tingle begins in my lower back.

"Not yet, Savannah." He pulls away, and I mewl in disappointment, but when he returns with his finger, I practically pant. "So wet and needy." His thumb glides over my clit while he adds a second finger, stretching me.

He works up to a rhythm that has me bucking my hips up to meet his hand. Seeking friction and pressure and *him*. That tingle has become a sweet burn, a tremble that's building like a fire out of control. "*More,*" I beg as I reach for my breasts. I run my hands over myself, pinching and massaging my nipples until they're hard.

Jack obliges, lowering his face once more to lick and suck at my clit while his fingers continue to work my pussy. My knees vibrate as the pressure mounts, and I beg him to stop.

"It's too much. It feels too good." Legs shaking, everything clenches as my body rides the wave.

"Not a chance. Come for me, baby."

As he presses his face into me, I lose it, my lungs heaving and my body convulsing as the orgasm takes control. I squeal and buck against him like an unhinged, wild animal. The throes of ecstasy rage on as Jack continues, not letting up. Driving into me like a man on a mission.

It feels like ages before my body sags against the bedding and my limbs, feeling heavy, fall to the mattress.

"Oh my God…" I take deep inhales as I attempt to catch my breath. And when I look down at Jack, his face is covered in my arousal and his eyes are full of lust. He's also palming his rock-hard cock through his boxer briefs.

"Savannah," he drawls as he stands and moves to his luggage. "If you're not sure about this, I need to know now." He reaches into a pouch and pulls out a foil packet. Then his eyes return to me, exploring my body. From my bare breasts to my wet panties. "Because from here on, I don't know if I'll be able to stop, baby."

I don't answer him. Instead, I drag my fingers to the waist of my underwear. His lids lower as he studies my movements. Lifting my hips, I tug the fabric over my butt and then kick them off the edge of the bed where Jack stands. Those honey eyes turn hungry as he reaches for his own underwear and lowers them over his hips. He steps quickly from them and then crawls over the bed. He's on me before I can blink, and as he claims my mouth, he presses his erection against my belly.

I reach for him as his lips slide over mine and his tongue thrusts through the seam. Tasting myself on his lips is an aphrodisiac. I ache to touch more of him. To feel him in my hand. To *stroke* him. I take hold of his cock and find him even harder than before. I worry if the act will hurt, but as Jack pulls away from my lips and slides his fingers down my stomach, over my pubic bone, and through the lips of my pussy to my clit, the momentary apprehension disappears.

Now there's only Jack, massaging me until I'm swollen—*bursting*—with need again and sopping wet. He gently pushes my knees farther apart, which makes the waves of pleasure more intense. I gasp and grind against his hand. Once wasn't enough.

"*More*." I give voice to my need as I palm my breasts.

He reaches for the foil square and unrolls the condom onto his length. "Ready?"

I nod. I'm ready.

Then he lines up at my throbbing entrance and slowly sinks into me. I gasp past the pain as he seats himself deep.

"Are you all right?" he breathes over my lips like he's holding himself steady.

"Y-Yes," I answer, blinking up at him. "I think so." My body adjusts to the feeling of fullness. My muscles clamp around his length, and before I know it, he's moving his hips. First slowly, rolling forward and back. Grinding his pelvis against my pubic bone. That delicious heat, that thrum, the telltale tingle leading to release, reawakens. And then he's thrusting into me. Gently at first, but as he reaches down between us and rubs my clit, I crave more.

I meet him, raising my hips slightly to match his thrusts until we're moving in tandem. Our bodies taking over and our movements syncing.

"Goddamnit, Savannah, you're so wet and so fucking tight. We fit so perfectly." His dick is buried so deep inside me, I'm certain he can feel my heart pounding as I gasp for air. I'm insatiable, and as I go higher and higher, and Jack thrusts deeper and harder, I explode again.

"Fuck, fuck, *fuck*!" I cry into oblivion as he drives into me with abandon. My body shudders and vibrates as the orgasm carries on, ebbing and flowing when he speeds up and then slows down, dragging out my climax until I'm delirious, begging him to come with me.

He joins me in a mangle of words and phrases I don't recognize from my pinnacle. We ride the high together and then everything blurs as the fuzz in my brain takes over. Groaning the sexiest sound I've ever heard, he gives one final shudder and collapses onto me.

My senses return slowly. I blink against the motel light. Was it always that bright?

Jack nuzzles against me, planting soft kisses along my neck. He slides to the side and pulls me over, hooking my leg over his hip. "My God," he whispers against my hair.

I turn sheepishly as a flush spreads up my chest. I'm suddenly feeling very self-conscious in my own body. My nakedness. My *virginity*. What we just did. My gaze lowers, and I try to turn away.

"Nuh-uh." He holds me tighter. "No retreating into yourself. No running away. Talk to me, Savannah."

I swallow and shake my head.

Reaching under my chin, he tips my head up so I'm forced to meet his gaze. "Talk. Or no more of *this*." He gestures to himself.

My eyes widen, and I gape for a moment. "You'd withhold sex from me?"

"I would. And I know you liked it, so talk."

I narrow my gaze. "How do you know I liked it so much, hm?" I tease as the heat creeps higher.

He leans in and whispers in my ear. "Because I felt your pussy squeezing my cock so good when you came, Savannah."

I'm surely the brightest shade of red as my mouth falls open. But that doesn't deter him. "And we're never going to do it again unless you tell me what's on your mind."

I look away, choosing to stare at the fabric of the comforter rather than his face. "I just wasn't sure if I was any good." Admitting it out loud feels childish and immature, especially to someone who's likely had countless lovers over the years.

But when he grabs my chin again and leans down to plant a tender kiss on my swollen lips, I melt. "It was perfect, Savannah. Just like you."

A knot forms in my throat and, as much as I want to ignore it, I know it's now or never. I have to tell Jack. "Th-that's good," I mutter as my brain searches for the words. "I'm glad you enjoyed it."

He tilts his head to the side as his eyebrows furrow. "What's going on in that mind of yours, baby?" The after-sex high, hearing him call me *baby*, nearly has me second-guessing the decision to tell him.

I'm certainly about to have a heart attack, so I decide to use my last moments on Earth to admit, "I'm glad you enjoyed it—enjoyed me—because I am... I *was* a virgin."

CHAPTER FORTY-TWO

Savannah

I've completely unpacked my suitcase and stowed the luggage in the closet. I suppose the positive to being back in the renovated house is that the drawers of the furniture actually open. Plus, I'm afforded my own bathroom and a bed big enough to sleep like a starfish.

I settle onto the mattress and pull the flat sheet over myself. Still a bit too chilly, I pull the cream-colored duvet over top as well.

I snuggle down for only a moment before I'm burning up. Frustrated, I kick off the covering and the sheet. When I lie back again, I am instantly cold once more.

What the hell? Why can't I get comfortable?

It's because you're not crammed in a queen-sized bed with Jack, you idiot. I let loose a heavy sigh and attempt to close my eyes, but my brain can't seem to shut down.

I'm still too keyed up from what we did last night. And what I finally admitted to him.

"Shit, Savannah? A virgin? Y-you were a virgin?" His eyes raked over me before scanning the rest of the tousled bedding. "*Fuck*." The curse slipped quietly from his lips as his head dropped into his hands.

That knot in my throat grew exponentially larger as the back of my eyes pricked. I pulled the duvet over my exposed body and sat up, unsure of my next move.

Do I reach out and console him?

Do I get out of the bed and get dressed?

But before I could make a decision, Jack reached over and grabbed me, pulling me against him. "*Fuck*, Savannah. Why didn't you tell me? I would've made it so much better for you, baby."

Feeling as though I was in an alternate reality, I gently pushed him away. "Wait, you're not mad?"

A smile lifted his lips. "Of course I'm not mad. I wish you would've told me, but I understand why you didn't. Besides, it wasn't really my place to ask, or expect, that information from you."

Jesus, could he be serious? I gaped at him, my eyes blinking in confusion as my mind worked to catch up.

"But if I had known, I would've been so much gentler with you. D-did I hurt you?"

I couldn't help but snort as I shook my head, the seriousness all too much for me when we were both completely nude. "Jack, it was... It was perfect. Just like you." I smiled as I echoed his sentiment.

And it wasn't long before we were reaching for each other again, our bodies colliding and entwining as the waves crashed on the beach just beyond our room.

Still uncomfortable in the too-large bed, I roll to my side, my core aching with need. I've never felt sexier than when Jack is exploring my body. His face buried between my legs.

My girl's already wet for me.

Not yet, Savannah.

Our breathing synced as we fell over the edge as one.

But only for the next little while.

Because that was the agreement.

Five days have already come and gone, and I know our time is limited, but being back in the house surrounded by my father and his employees is not going to make this any easier.

I sit up, my body as restless as my mind.

And I know what I need to do.

I need to start taking some risks. It's what I did when I admitted to being a virgin. And look how that turned out.

I head to the restroom and check out my reflection in the mirror. My olive skin has a decent enough tan, and while my hair is messy, it has that sultry look about it that I'm sure some people pay thousands of dollars for. All I need to do is roll around on a pillow and I've got frizzy beach waves. I slather on a bit of chapstick and then pinch my cheeks for an additional spot of color, and then click off the bathroom light.

Am I really going to do this? Four years ago, I attempted the same thing. I wonder if I should change into something sexier, but Jack is constantly telling me how beautiful I am when I personally feel I look my worst.

And that means something.

So I push aside the thought of changing and carefully crack open the door. I peer through the narrow slit and, seeing nobody around, step out into the hallway.

I wait a moment, craning my neck to hear any noise from the living room or kitchen.

Silence.

A slow smile lifts my lips as Jack's door opens and he peeks out, catching a glimpse of me creeping toward his room.

"What are you doing?" he whispers as he opens the door farther.

Pursing my lips, I attempt to look nonchalant. "Oh, nothing. Just going for a midnight stroll." I pad closer to him. "What are you doing?"

"Thinking about getting a little snack. I'm starving." His eyes drink me in from head to toe and back up again.

"Is that so? Shall we go to the kitchen?" I try to tamp down the desire fluttering deep in my belly. Leaning against the doorjamb, I cross my arms.

"Nah, I don't think the kitchen has what I want," he responds, never taking his eyes from mine. The magnetic pull between us is so strong. I don't think I could break it if I tried.

"What do you want, Jack?" It's a question exhaled on the lightest breath. Sent out into the charged air between us.

"I want you, Savannah. *Only you*." He reaches out and takes my hand, pulling me into the room.

And as he closes and locks the door behind us, we come together and then fall into the darkness.

Luckily, I'm able to sneak back to my room just before the sun comes up the next morning. As I run the shower and go through my routine, I feel sore in the best way. For multiple days in a row, my body has been worshipped. I've never felt this relaxed. This sexy.

But deep down, there's still a hunger growling beneath my skin. A hunger that simply wants more. She's ravenous, this hunger. And she can't wait until the next meal.

"Savannah?" My father's voice from the hallway shatters my daydreams, and I quickly put the last touches on my face before heading out the door. He has a free day, so I'm off as well. With nothing on the agenda, I'm eager to get caught up on my emails and check in on some of the campaign metrics we've conducted through various social media campaigns.

I find my dad sitting at the kitchen table, a cup of coffee and his laptop in front of him. "Hi, Dad. What's your plan for today?" He's likely off for a round of golf with some of his friends.

"Good morning, dear. Have you seen Jack yet this morning?"

As I lean against the kitchen counter, my blood runs cold. I'm certain my skin turns the color of the white sand just beyond our doorway.

"No, why would you ask?" *What does he know?* Did someone see me sneak into his room last night? I'm suddenly panicking, my heart rate spiking to a million beats a minute.

"Well, you did walk right past his room on your way from yours." As though he didn't almost just give me a heart attack, he hardly glances up from his laptop as he chuckles to himself.

"Oh, um, his door was closed." I clench my fist at my side, willing my body to remain calm.

How the hell am I going to sneak around with Jack when I can't even answer a simple question about his whereabouts without going berserk?

"No coffee this morning?" He slides his eyes over to me.

I eye the coffeepot on the counter, but press my lips together and decide against it. I'm keyed up enough as it is. Adding an influx of sugar and caffeine straight to my bloodstream would surely put me into a code-red myocardial infarction. "Um, no. My stomach is feeling a little funny. Probably best to avoid it."

At that moment, Jack walks into the kitchen, and somehow my blood pressure skyrockets even higher. Being in the same room as him and my father, after what we've been doing, has beads of sweat breaking out along my hairline. I attempt to calm myself by taking deep inhales, followed by slow exhales.

Jack shoots me an inquisitive look, as though to ask, *what the hell's your deal?* I attempt to communicate with him with my eyes, but he simply sends me an odd look and then sits down.

Right next to my father.

"Ah, good morning, Keaton. I have a favor to ask. I know it's not part of your duties, but I was wondering if you'd head to the grocery store today and pick up a few things for our dinner tonight. I've invited Laurel and a few other guests. We'll need a new propane tank for the grill, too." My dad passes Jack a list, which he immediately pockets. Then he leans in, a conspiratorial look transforming his face. "And Jack?"

"Yes, sir?"

I hold my breath, waiting for the other shoe to drop. But Jack, bless his heart, doesn't look fazed at all. If anything, he's more relaxed than ever. As though he couldn't care less that he's fucking the boss's daughter.

"Please take Jenson with you, son. That boy is driving me crazy. I much prefer to golf without my shadow today."

"Would you prefer I accompany you?" Jack asks.

"No, that's not necessary. You and Jenson get the items on the list and then help Miranda with whatever last-minute preparations are needed around here." Bringing his mug to his lips, he takes a steady pull.

I exhale the panic from my body, eager to be in the clear for now. But just when I think everything is going to be fine, my father addresses me. "Savannah, go change. You're coming golfing with me. Sam Wilkins requested your presence. He has a few ideas for the campaign."

My eyes snap to Jack's, and I feel the blood rush to my face. And by the way his jaw ticks at the mention of Sam, he's not particularly excited about it either.

But what can I do? My job is my job.

Right?

So I swallow that pesky lump that's bubbling up in my throat and nod. "All right, Dad. I'll be ready in just a bit."

Chapter Forty-Three

Jack

"This song is complete trash." Jenson's complaint hardly registers with me, my thoughts solely focused on my night with Savannah.

The way she tasted on my tongue.

Her hushed moans leaking through my palm pressed over her mouth.

The way she'd bitten my shoulder as I thrust deep inside her wet cunt.

"Are you even listening to me?" My passenger punches the radio preset, and a popular country song fills the car with a peaceful twang and soft notes.

She needs a warning

But that still wouldn't stop me

"Ugh, can't we get even one song that isn't about love?" Eli clicks over to the next station. This one an alternative lament.

The issue is, I want you like a vice, like I'm an addict

If that doesn't describe what I'm feeling, I don't know what does. "Keep it here," I demand as I smack his hand away from the radio. I hum and tap the steering wheel to the slow beat, the singer's words sinking deep into my bones.

From beside me, Eli narrows his eyes and scowls. "Since when do you like this kind of crap? A few weeks ago, you'd listen to nothing but metal and, for some ungodly reason, Nickelback."

I chuckle because he's right. I wouldn't be caught dead crooning along to some sappy song about losing control and heartaches in the night. Songs like that reminded me of what I'd lost four years ago.

When Savannah left.

But now? Now that she's here, with me, and we're together, there's nothing else I want to do but sing songs about all the moments that matter the most.

The way she laughs. Challenges me with the cock of an eyebrow and a smirk on her face.

The way she falls into me.

How our legs wrap around one another's, as though we can't bear to not be touching.

She's all-consuming, and I'm so ready for her to make a mess of me.

Because at thirty-one, I've finally found the one I want to be with. I tried to forget her, to remember that she's my boss's daughter and *off limits*. And damn if I didn't try. I tried. *For four years, I tried.* I tried to forget her, to move on and put the thoughts and memories of her aside. I tried to enjoy the dates, the casual conversations, the chances at being a wingman for Eli, but none of it worked. Not a single fucking woman could measure up to Savannah.

What I missed when she wasn't around.

I was a shell of myself, simply going through the motions.

I'm not that broken and bitter man anymore.

Savannah may think that this arrangement is only going to last two weeks, but there's no way I'm going to let that happen. There's no way I'm letting her go again.

Damn the job. Damn the consequences. Damn it all.

For four years, I suffered without her.

And this time, I'm not letting her get away.

When Eli and I arrive back at the house, a white delivery van blocks the drive. "Miranda!" I shout, the window of the SUV rolled down and filled to the brim with the groceries.

She saunters through the open door of the property, her face tilted up toward the van's driver. I crane my ear to hear the exchange, but the two seem to do nothing but stare at one another with red-tinted cheeks.

"Oh my God," Eli chuckles, echoing my thoughts. "Is Miranda...flirting with that delivery guy?" He turns to me with a mischievous grin and raised eyebrows.

"It's none of our business," I respond. Regardless, I keep the two of them in my periphery as I exit the vehicle and start unloading.

By the time Eli and I reach the front door, the delivery driver's pulling away and Miranda's waving from the walkway. "What's that all about, boss?" Eli asks as we squeeze past her, our arms overloaded with bags.

"It's nothing." But the way her gaze lowers and slides to the left points to the contrary.

Eli must pick up on it, too. "C'mon, you can tell us. We're all consenting adults here. You got a little thing for the delivery man?" Miranda follows us into the house, but stops as we continue onward to the kitchen.

"He's not *just* a delivery driver, Jenson. He happens to own the winery and personally delivered the alcohol for tonight's dinner."

Eli sets down the bags and turns back toward Miranda as I begin unloading. Go figure he'd leave me to the brunt of it. "Ah, well, surely the winery owner has a name?"

"He does." Miranda steps farther into the kitchen and leans against the refrigerator. She crosses her arms. "Perhaps you'll meet him this evening. The governor invited him to the barbecue."

"Interesting. I didn't know we were bringing dates. Jack, did you know we were bringing dates?" Eli looks over at me, but I purposefully ignore him as I continue unloading and tucking food into the fridge. When I don't respond, Eli presses onward. "Ah, that's right. My good buddy Jack doesn't date."

Miranda snorts and pushes off the side of the fridge, allowing me access to the freezer. I deposit the items and then close the door, just as the skinny ginger comes back into view. My eyes lift and meet hers, and I see the challenge in her face.

I dare you, it says, even as her features remain blank. Impassive.

If the last four years have taught me anything, it's that Miranda knows more than she lets on. As much as I want to contradict her—and Eli—and tell them both the truth about me and Savannah, it's a conversation we need to have together first.

But even as Miranda lowers her smug gaze and then retreats into the other room, we both hear her say, "Your good buddy Jack does more than date, Jenson."

Eli's gaze flies toward me, but I simply turn away and clear my throat, hoping he'll forget.

But chances are, he won't.

I've put away the last of the groceries, when my cell phone buzzes in my pocket. I extricate it and look at the number on the caller ID.

"Fuck," I hiss as I accept the call. From across the kitchen, Jenson shoots me a raised eyebrow. I shake my head and turn away, heading out to the backyard. "Hello?" Closing the French door behind myself, I stand on the patio overlooking the opulent pool and wet bar.

"Jack, dear. It's Angela Whitberry." My mother's next-door neighbor.

"Hi, Mrs. Whitberry. Is everything all right?" I try my best to keep the anxiety from leeching into my voice, but I'm certain it's useless as my throat constricts and a sense of panic trickles down my spine.

"Oh, well, not really, Jack. Your mom was outside watering her flowers and she must've tripped over something. She fell on the sidewalk pretty hard. Busted up her knee and chin."

"Is she okay?" My right hand tingles. Is that a sign of a heart attack? Am I having a heart attack? I clench and unclench my fist, willing the sensation to stop.

"She's fine. We were able to get her to the hospital, and they stitched up her chin. She's resting now, and I'll make sure to check on her later this evening and tomorrow, too. I just—"

"I'll be on the first flight back, Mrs. Whitberry. Thank you so much for everything. You have no idea how much your help is appreciated."

"You don't need to rush home, Jack. Your mother begged me not to call you. She didn't want you to worry, but I couldn't *not* tell you."

With a heavy sigh, I rub my temple. I know at some point I'll need to convince my mother to move into a facility for early-onset dementia patients, but it's not going to be easy. She'll fight me every step of the way, but her health and safety are what's important.

Even if she hates me for it.

"I should be back mid-morning at the latest, Mrs. Whitberry. Again, thank you so much for your help."

"Of course, dear. Your mother was always so kind when I was struggling as a single mother to my girls. I'll let you go now. I'm sure you're very busy with the governor."

We say our goodbyes, and I hang up before stalking back into the house. Bypassing Jenson's questioning expression, I head to my room and open my laptop. I pull up the nearest airport and, within five minutes, have a ticket on the next flight home.

CHAPTER FORTY-FOUR

Savannah

"Wonderful swing, governor!" Sam's voice echoes above the others surrounding my father, all blowing smoke up his ass on his way back to the cart. He slides the driver into the bag and nods at the congratulations from his colleagues.

"You're up, Sav." My father passes me my own driver from the bag of clubs I had to rent from the pro shop. While I've got my own set at home, I hadn't thought to bring them. Plus, I'm quite rusty after only playing here and there over the past four years. Luckily, I was on the high school golf team, thanks to my father's encouragement to find a hobby "fit for the daughter of a politician." Because nothing says business deal like golfing.

I step up to the tee box and pray that my long game can stand the test in front of me. There's nothing more embarrassing than having to be the only woman in a group of men during a sport.

Is golf even a sport?

I'm sure it is. But what these men are playing can hardly be called golf.

They simply tee off, congratulate each other on aiming somewhere in the vicinity of the green, and sip cocktails from the bar cart.

As I line myself up to swing, my pleated skirt flutters in the Florida breeze. At least the weather is nice. The humidity isn't as high as it's been, and my hair has actually remained straight, tucked neatly in a ponytail under my visor.

I widen my stance and choke up on the stick, keeping my eye on the bright pink ball. And no, I didn't choose the color. That was all Sam. He figured I'd love a set of bright pink balls.

I'm not sure if that was his idea of a romantic gesture, but at least I'll be able to find it when I hook the ball into the trees just next to the green.

Keeping my elbows straight, I swing through, knocking the ball directly into the sand trap. The gentlemen behind me chortle among themselves, and I'm pretty sure I hear something along the lines of "poor girl." As though I'm a toddler who skinned her knee.

I plaster on a fake smile as I retreat from the tee, back toward my father. As I pass him the driver, he pretends to examine it. Likely looking for defects.

"It's simply been a while since I've played. I'm out of practice. There's nothing wrong with the driver." I pat him on the arm and hope I haven't embarrassed him too badly.

I take out my scorecard, just for something to look at, and lean back against the far side of the cart. I've no interest in watching yet another man guffaw over some dirty golf joke as he tees off. Instead, I exhale, close my eyes, and simply try to enjoy the feel of the warm sun on my exposed arms.

"Your game may not be the best, but your tan is top-notch."

My eyes snap open, and I find Sam staring at me, his arm propped dangerously close to my face as he leans against the cart. "Excuse me?"

"I just mean that your golf game could use some work. I can help, if you'd like." He shoots me a smile.

"Oh, sure." I shrug innocently. Pocketing my scorecard, I smooth down my skirt.

"Why don't we ride over together to the next hole. I'll give you some pointers." He hops in the golf cart and pats the seat next to him.

I glance around, looking for my dad. "Well, I guess that'd be okay." When I realize he's already driving off with another gentleman, I climb in and hold on to the side as he turns on the engine and floors it down the pavement.

"I thought for sure it landed somewhere in this area." I keep my eyes peeled on the bright green grass as we leave the paved trail and head toward a copse of trees. "You'd think a bright pink ball would be easy to find."

Sam chuckles as he slows the vehicle. We drive parallel to the tree line, our eyes skimming over the rough, in the search.

"Thanks, by the way, for the balls. Pink's one of my favorite colors." I've learned that flattery goes a long way, especially with potential donors and campaign associates, and even if I don't *actually* have a favorite color, a white lie won't hurt anyone.

"Maybe it went farther into the trees. Let's see." Sam spins the wheel before I can grab hold of the handle, and I nearly fall from the cart. Luckily, he grabs onto my wrist and pulls me back inside. "Sorry about that." He grips tightly as he navigates to an open area between two larger trees and hits the brake.

Powering off the cart, he pulls me through the driver's side, my wrist still captured in his hand. Smiling politely, I try to pull away, but his grip holds strong. "I'll look this way if you'll check over there." But what I really want to do is rip my arm from his grasp. Everything inside of me is screaming, *warning*!

Instead, he releases me from his clutch, but not before I'm pressed up against the side of the cart by his body.

The length of him is flush against my front, and as the situation comes into focus, my heart rate speeds up. "This isn't appropriate, Sam." I press my lips together in an attempt to sound and look harsher than I am.

"What's so inappropriate, Savannah?" His eyes scan my features as his tongue darts out and slides along his bottom lip. "You're unattached. I'm unattached. Right?"

That niggling feeling at the base of my skull screams louder. *Warning. Warning. Warning*! "Whether I'm single has nothing to do with this relationship staying professional." I duck beneath his arm and extricate myself, but my senses are still on high alert. I don't feel safe hidden in this grove of trees. I need to get out in the open. Back to the group.

"That's unfortunate. Really, it is." He pouts in my direction, the skin around his eyes tightening as the frown tugs at his face.

"I'm certain we can continue to work alongside one another throughout this campaign, Sam." I force merriment into my voice, lightening my expression. "Now I'm sure the others must be wondering where we've gotten to." Trekking around the golf cart, I retake my place in the passenger seat, ready to put this awkwardness behind us as quickly as possible.

Sam slides back into the driver's seat and turns to me. His fingers tap the wheel. "Unfortunately, I don't think I'll feel comfortable working alongside you any further. I'll be forced to let your father know that you've cost me the opportunity to contribute to his campaign, both as a donor and an advisor. Unless..." his words trail off as he starts the engine. He presses the gas pedal, and we lurch forward, my breath caught in my throat.

We whip through the trees, and I flinch as some come extremely close to the cart.

"Unless what, exactly?" There's a pounding in my ears, and I'm certain there must be a drum of some sort on the course. It grows louder and louder. "Um, maybe you should slow down?" I suggest as a limb slices against my bare arm.

"We'll speak more this evening at the barbecue, darling Savannah. I'm sure you'll come to your senses before then."

As we zoom out of the trees and into the open course, the pounding doesn't subside. If anything, the pace increases.

And it's not until we spy the remainder of our party that I realize there's no drum.

It's my heart.

CHAPTER FORTY-FIVE

Jack

Fastening the last button of my white collared shirt, a soft knock interrupts the quiet of the room.

I take a quick pull of the amber liquid in the glass on my desk. "Come in." I adjust the collar of the shirt as the door opens.

Savannah.

She's wearing a sapphire silk cocktail dress that glides over her curves like liquid metal. The thin spaghetti straps barely contain her ample chest, making me want to dive straight into her cleavage. "My God, Savannah..." I'm speechless. I can only stare at the beautiful goddess standing before me.

For once, her hair isn't straightened to within an inch of its life. It's pulled into a messy—dare I say, sexy?—low bun at the nape of her neck. I haul her toward me and press my lips to the exposed skin under her ear.

"Careful," she goads as she turns into me. "Someone could see us here. I know how much you value your position."

Is she taunting me? Challenging me to take her right here in my room while the catering staff set up just down the hall in the kitchen?

I'm already too deep into this thing, so I throw caution to the wind and tamp down the little angel on my shoulder who tells me to back off.

"If you wanted me to be careful, you shouldn't have worn a dress like that, baby." My tongue darts out and licks along the corded muscles of her neck. She tastes like vanilla and smells like a tropical flower. Heaven on Earth. Pulling away, I meet her gaze. "I have to be gone for a few days, but I don't want to forget this, so I need to indulge as much as possible."

She stiffens and leans back slightly, leaving my mouth hanging open. "Is everything okay?" The lines deepen between her perfectly plucked eyebrows.

"Everything's fine. My mom…" I pause, not sure how much I want to divulge. Savannah says we're only in this for two weeks, but I want more. More than just the timeframe and more than just the sex. I want to share everything with her. The truth of how difficult it's been dealing with my mom recently. The fact that I don't know what will happen if the governor is elected to a position in Washington. "My mom fell, and I need to check on her."

"Oh." Her doe eyes widen, and she takes my hands in hers, squeezing slightly. "Is there anything I can do to help?"

Come with me, I want to ask. Beg. But I hold back. Something inside stops me. A protective instinct that burrows into my gut in case she takes off again.

"No. Just…" I run my thumb along my bottom lip, thinking over my choice of words.

Her chocolate gaze zeroes in on that motion. My tell, as she reminded me so long ago.

"Just be here when I get back?" That protectiveness is overridden by the need to know that she's not going anywhere. That she won't run away again. That this all isn't for naught.

She smiles slowly. "Of course I'll still be here. We've still got another week left."

It's a punch to my gut that she's aware of our time limit. That she sees this as nothing more than another planned arrangement.

"Right," I say, stepping away. "I should finish getting ready."

She blinks once. Twice. Pressing her lips together, she raises a hand to fiddle with the necklace at her throat. "Oh, okay then. I guess I'll see you out there?"

"Of course." I turn to the mirror and finish getting ready as she slinks from the room with her head bowed.

As much as I'd like another glass of whiskey, I know better than to indulge when my mind is already racing. I can't get Savannah out of my mind, and as she slinks around the room in that perfect blue dress, I want nothing more than to pull her into my arms and claim her mouth right in front of everyone.

I can't stop the thoughts that spiral. It's simply because I'm exhausted. Worried. My mother's health is first and foremost in my mind, and not being near enough to take care of her is affecting me in ways I'd rather not divulge.

So, until I can control myself, the liquor stays in the bottle.

I saunter over to the grill, where Eli appears to be bothering the cook. "You know, you should really turn the meat every two to three minutes."

I roll my eyes. Only Jenson would have the audacity to interfere in a professional chef's grilling methods. "Hey, man," I say as I throw my arm around his shoulder. "How about we take a walk and leave this talented grill master to it?" I spot the relief in the cook's eyes as he nods, his lips pursing as he returns his attention to the meal preparations.

"Ah, fine. He wasn't taking my advice anyway." We amble away from the outdoor grill and kitchen area and over to the pool. Rounded white candles float on top of the clear blue water, adding additional lighting to the tiki torches that flame around the lawn. "Miranda did a fine job with the setup," Eli adds.

"She did," I admit. Taking a swig of the long neck in my hand, my eyes circle the premise. I don't spy Savannah anywhere, although her father is chatting animatedly with the governor of Florida. They laugh uproariously over some shared joke.

"You know, our next president could be at this very party." Jenson's eyes trail to our boss and his companion.

"I'm not sure about that, but I do know that our boss has his gaze set on the senate seat. We may have our work cut out for us over the next several years, my friend."

Eli takes a pull of the clear liquid in his glass. He's been a gin man since our time in the academy. While we didn't get out too much during our training, Jenson was the type of officer who knew how to have a good time. But he never let his love of partying affect his work performance, which is why I trust him with my life.

"I bet there are some good parties out in D.C."

I shake my head, even as a chuckle bubbles up. "I can't believe I'm thinking about all the security and personnel implications of a senator's safety and you're thinking about ass and clubs."

Eli simply shrugs and brings his tumbler to his lips once more. "Perhaps if your priorities were a little more focused on ass and partying, you wouldn't be alone at night."

I don't have the heart to tell him that I'm certainly not alone at night. At least not until Savannah and I really know what we are. "Listen, I have to fly home early tomorrow to check on some things. Can you keep an extra eye on Savannah while I'm gone?"

His gaze narrows. "Of course I'll do my job of protecting Mr. and Miss Smith, Keaton."

"I know that. I just... I need to know that you'll handle things while I'm away. In case—"

"In case what, exactly?" He takes a step back and looks me up and down. I do my best to appear calm. Reassuring.

"It's nothing. Forget I asked." I turn my attention back to the party. I search for Savannah, but still don't see her anywhere.

"Are you two...?" His eyes widen as his mouth drops open.

Where the *fuck* is Savannah? My heart rate speeds up slightly as my neck cranes around the lawn.

"Are you two fucking, Keaton?"

When was the last time I laid eyes on her? It's been at least twenty minutes. If not longer.

"Keaton, are you fucking the governor's daughter?"

I don't even bother responding as I take off, my strides growing longer as I cut through the guests and couples gathered around the pool area.

"*Keaton!*" Eli's voice echoes off the stucco house, but I ignore him. My mind is focused on only one thing.

Where's Savannah?

CHAPTER FORTY-SIX

Savannah

"Ah, the beautiful Savannah Smith. There you are!" Sam's voice sends ice down my spine, but I plaster on my practiced smile as I pull away from my father and turn around. Welcoming him.

"Good evening, Sam." Before I can situate my face into demure and polite, he's pulling my hand toward his mouth and planting a kiss on my fingers. The blush that creeps up my neck and into my cheeks flares hot as I realize everyone around us is watching.

"Oh, none of that." I pull away and subtly swipe my hand against my thigh. "We're pretty laid back here at Chateau Smith. In fact, can I get you something to drink?"

I would direct him to the bartender, but I need any chance to escape from the way he's eyeing my dress. "Oh, no, I don't drink at these events. I prefer to keep my wits about me." His smile slices across his face. I never realized how gummy his mouth was or how small his teeth, but as he inches closer, it's all I can see.

"Is there someplace quiet we can continue our discussion from earlier? I'd love to hash out the *details*." The obvious innuendo has me shivering in my heels. I glance around, hoping for any reason to avoid pairing off with him, but most everyone has removed themselves to the back lawn.

"If you'll follow me, Sam, I'm sure we can find a seat outside with the rest of the party. And my, doesn't that food smell delicious?" I inch closer to the French doors. But of course, he doesn't take the hint.

"I'd actually love a tour of the house. I'm thinking of purchasing property in the area myself. My realtor's constantly trying to find places that fit my specifications." Without waiting, he simply stalks farther into the interior.

"Well, uh, this is the kitchen. Obviously," I add as I follow quickly behind. I try to maneuver into the busy space filled with the hors d'oeuvres and waitstaff.

"Ah, yes. What's down this hallway?" He continues onward toward the private rooms, specifically mine, Jack's, Eli's, and Miranda's.

"Those are simply the bedrooms. Nothing to see." I flap my hand lazily. "I could show you the amazing outdoor kitchen area we've had installed?" I linger within eyesight of the last staff member, who is currently organizing a tray of bacon-wrapped cheeses.

Don't go. Don't go, I beg internally, even as she hoists the tray onto her overturned forearm and exits the kitchen.

"And this hallway here leads to the garage, yes?" Sam saunters farther into the darkness, his eyes perusing the beach decor on the walls as his form darkens.

When Sam Wilkins is around, my sense of control flies out the window. He makes me incredibly uncomfortable. I want to rebuff him, but I know that my father needs his financial contribution for a successful campaign.

To top it off, Sam is from Michigan. So any misstep could have further ramifications in our own home state.

Especially if he speaks to any of his rich friends about me.

I have to tread lightly.

"Yes, the garage is just through there." I take a step. Then another. I disappear from sight of the French doors and kitchen. My eyes adjust slightly to the lack of light in the hallway as I take another step.

I'm still within earshot of someone. Surely, I'm safe in my own home.

"Won't you show me the garage, dear? I'd like to assess its size and compare it to what I would need to fit my...well, my toys."

"Toys?" My brain short-circuits as I creep farther into the hallway. Closer to Sam.

"I am a man of wealth. I have a vast array of pursuits, including restoring cars. I'll allow you to lead the way." He beckons me forward and leans against the wall, giving me enough space to pass.

"I-I don't think this particular garage has the space for anything like that." My feet still.

"Perhaps. Perhaps not. I'll be the judge of that. Please. Show me." His eyes glint against the lack of light.

I take a deep breath and prepare myself to speed walk past him—

"Miss Smith. There you are." The voice from the other end of the hallway is a godsend.

Jack.

I pivot on my heel and rush toward him. Surely, he must notice the relief on my face. "Yes, Ja-Keaton?" I correct myself. "What is it?"

"Dinner is nearly ready. Your father wishes to speak with you about the toast." Even as Jack addresses me, his eyes never leave Sam, who stalks back into the light and comes up behind me. I feel his presence like an evil spirit. The chill down my spine is certainly noticeable.

Thank you, I mouth to him. "If you'll excuse me, Sam," I toss over my shoulder as I flee toward the lawn.

Bursting through the open French doors, I gasp for air. My hands are shaking as the adrenaline high, that fight-or-flight urge, suddenly bottoms out.

I think I'm going to be sick.

"Savannah, are you all right?" It's Miranda's voice at my side that brings my focus back to the party.

"Yes. Yes, I think I'm fine." I exhale and look around at the guests, ready to fake happy the rest of the night.

Back to simply being the governor's daughter and campaign manager.

While the ocean isn't in the backyard, it's not far. The waves crash onto the shore, echoing off the stucco houses surrounding us. Their natural white noise lulls me into a sense of relaxation and calm, which is only heightened when I realize that the hired staff have left. Miranda, the last person in sight, flicks off the overhead kitchen light and meanders down the hallway, her strappy sandals hanging by her forefinger.

And my father? Well, I'm pretty sure he snuck off with Laurel back to her place at least an hour ago, leaving me and Miranda to deal with the cleanup.

From my solitary spot huddled on a lounge chair on the darkened patio, I finally release the breath I've been holding since Sam cornered me in that very hallway.

I reach to the messy bun at the back of my head and pull pin after pin from the mass of waves. So much time and energy to get a look that was supposed to scream effortless. I shake my head and the dark tresses tumble around my shoulders. Massaging my temple, I lean back against the cushioned lounge chair and close my eyes.

What would have happened if...?

Nope. I don't want to think about that. If anything, I'm good at pushing the negative thoughts from my mind and refusing to spiral into the endless abyss. I force myself to standing and pad, barefoot, around the edge of the pool. I surely look like a ghoul haunting the place. My hair hanging down my back in stringy waves, eye makeup long-since smudged beneath my eyes. But as I near the pool's edge, I want nothing more than to submerge myself in the water. Float on my back and relax among the remaining candles that flicker their last flames, the wax burning lower and lower.

The zero-entry pool allows me to walk into the shallows before it becomes deeper and deeper on a slight incline. As my feet submerge, I undress. First, the jewelry, which I set on the edge of the pool. Then the dress itself. I hoist the silky blue fabric over my head and discard it along with the accessories. Clad in only a strapless bra and thong, I step farther into the depths.

As the humid air hugs me a little too tightly, the pool needn't be heated. The cool water feels refreshing. Necessary. My arms sway as my hips, and then belly, are submerged. When I reach the middle, I finally lean back and allow myself to float. Let my eyes fall closed and simply shut it all out.

After hours of schmoozing, I certainly need to decompress and shut down.

With my ears under the water, I don't hear him approach. It's not until the water shifts that I blink open my eyes and find him standing over me, his gaze raking over my body.

I don't cover myself. And I don't stop floating. I stay like that, my lids at half-mast and my arms and legs starfished. "It was a long night," he whispers, closing the inches between us.

"Hm," I answer as my eyes close again. I've no idea what he actually said with my ears underwater.

His movements are slow, as is expected with the candles. Too much agitation and they'll topple over, spilling their melted wax. He moves through the water until he's standing near the top of my head. "What are you doing?" I ask sleepily. The calmness of the water is enough to put me to bed.

"Hush." I keep my eyes closed, but the mix of cigarette smoke and mint that he breathes out has my eyes popping open.

"You—" I start to shift to standing, but he grabs my shoulders gently and presses into the tight muscles there.

"I did. It won't happen again. Now hush." My brow furrows, but I oblige nonetheless, settling back against the weight of the water.

He moves his hands along my shoulders and up the back of my neck until he's cupping my skull. Then, as he holds the weight in his palms, he uses his thumbs to massage the area behind my ears. My mouth falls open as he presses with more force, massaging the tension from my neck.

"So good," I murmur quietly. He doesn't respond, only slides the pad of his thumb up the middle of my skull to the top of my head and then drags it down to my ears.

He repeats the same process, from behind my ears to the top of my head, over and over, until I'm so relaxed I could melt away into the pool.

"I don't like that man you were with, Savannah." He says it softly as he continues to massage the base of my skull. Instantly, the tension in my neck is back. "Relax, sweetheart."

I do as he says, forcing my shoulders to lower and my mind to quiet once more. "I don't like him either. Just so you know."

"Hm," he hums. "I do know."

My eyes open and I meet his gaze. Were his eyes on me the whole time? There's something sensual about that—him watching me, and my nipples harden beneath my bra.

I turn over and find my footing. Facing him, I realize he, too, is in his underwear. His black boxer briefs do nothing to hide the obvious erection, even with the water's coverage.

"Come." I take his hand and pull him through the pool, higher and higher up the incline until we're once again standing on the stone patio. "It's time for bed."

CHAPTER FORTY-SEVEN

Jack

I follow a dripping wet Savannah through the darkened house and into her bedroom. She closes the door softly behind us and immediately pushes me against it. Pressing her wet chest against me, the water runs down our bodies and onto the carpet at our feet.

"I've never been so relaxed and so turned on at the same time." Her dark eyes shimmer with lust.

I lower my mouth to her neck, tasting all the chlorine and dampness from her hair and then lick my way along her jawline until I find her lips in the dark. Already rock hard and weeping, my dick is begging to be set free from the boxer briefs. *Not so fast, pal.* Instead, I hoist Savannah up and grind into her, stepping away from the wall. Her hands find my hair, and she holds on for dear life as I thrust against her.

She gasps, and I flip us both around so that she's against the wall. "Touch me," she demands, her body vibrating with need.

I slide my hand down her torso, her gasps coming faster as I caress the sensitive flesh, until my fingers find the waistband of her thong. Watching her ass as I followed her out of the pool had been a test of both endurance and restraint, as I wanted nothing more than to bury my face between her cheeks. But now, as I pull the thin strip of fabric to the side and slide my fingers into her heat, I only want to be *inside* her.

She moans as I add another finger, curling them against her inner walls and strumming her clit with my thumb at the same time. Her breathing comes faster now, and as her pussy clenches around my fingers, I use my teeth and lower her bra, freeing her bouncing damp tits.

Pulling a mound of flesh into my mouth, I savor the way her nipples tighten against the cool air. As she rides my fingers, all I can imagine is her sopping wet body riding my dick.

"Bed," I muster before my mouth finds hers, swallowing the moan of ecstasy that bursts from her lungs. Swinging us around, we topple onto the soft mattress. I hover over her, my fingers still thrusting deep while my thumb rubs circles over her clit. "Savannah, do you see what you do to me?" Her eyes drop to my wet boxer briefs and the erection poking through the slit in the fabric. Pushing down the waistband, I pull myself free before guiding my fist up and down the fleshy length. Those pupils dilate ever-so-slightly before her lids fall as her mouth slackens.

"Fuck." She draws out the word, watching me stroke myself. When she reaches for me, I push myself into her waiting hand, my cock now begging for her touch. As she jacks me, I thrust into her hand with my pelvis, pretending her palm is the wet pussy I'm finger fucking.

My little finger dips past her sweet cunt and finds its way along the sopping wet fabric splitting her ass in two. The image of those two rounded mounds brushing against one another as she led me into this room urges me forward, and I press my pinky gently against the rosebud flesh.

I watch Savannah for any signs of discomfort, but as she moans "more" and her hand tightens around my dick, I press onward. My digit circles the sensitive area, now wet and lubricated from her weeping pussy, and it's not long before she's coming undone on my hand. Her body tightens as pleasure overtakes her, but I don't stop pressing into her until she's gasping for air, eyes wide and toes curling. "I-I-I—" She can't even get the words out as her eyes snap shut and her body pulses around my fingers. Her free hand palms her tits, pulling at her peaked nipples with her thumb and forefinger. Finally, she crests over the top of the orgasm and her moans and stilted breathing subsides.

But that doesn't stop me from continuing. Once she's done, I flip us once more until I'm on my back and she's straddling me. "Do you have—"

She slides off me and, like a sweet baby deer on wobbly legs, disappears into the bathroom before returning with a tiny foil packet. The look she gives me is anything but innocent as she uses her teeth to rip the packaging. I close my eyes, committing the image to memory, and then she's back on top of me, rolling the condom over my length.

"I want to see you ride me." My cock stands at attention, but her dripping juices make easing down onto me seamless. As she takes all of me within her, inch by excruciatingly slow inch, I release a breath through my teeth. The sensation is mind-melting. The feel of her impaled on my dick short circuits my brain and, before I know it, I'm thrusting up into her while grabbing onto her hips and yanking her down my length.

She uses her knees to ride me, gliding up and down my wet cock, but I can't focus on anything except the way her tits bounce. I reach for them, palming one and then the other until I'm sitting up and pulling a hard nipple into my mouth. I suck and nibble at the bud before turning my attention to its twin. Savannah brings her hand around the back of my head and holds me in place, arching her back until our torsos are flush against one another.

The sensation builds in my lower back and circles under to my balls. I bring my arms around her back and, holding her against me, flip us over one last time until I'm on top. Driving into her, thrust after powerful thrust.

Throwing her legs over my shoulders, I pound into her until I'm certain she's sunken into the soft mattress, but as she reaches around and fondles my balls, everything goes blank. I look into those chocolate eyes, the parted lips, and that's the last thing I need to push me over the edge.

I see fireworks and flashes of white and lust and love and a family, coming so hard and fast, the world tilts. Lowering my mouth to hers, she bites my lip, moaning my name through the fog of euphoria like the prettiest song. Breathing in one other, our lips don't break apart until long after I collapse beside her.

Chapter Forty-Eight

Jack

"So we're just going to avoid the elephant in the room, then?" Elijah asks from the passenger seat.

"What room?" I glance around at the interior of the auto.

"Quit fucking with me, man. Tell me the truth. Are you banging the boss's daughter?"

My grip tightens on the steering wheel, my knuckles turning white. "No," I lie. Eli can't know. He may be my friend and co-worker, someone I trust to have my back at all times, but I'm not ready to admit the truth to him yet.

At least not until Savannah and I have *the talk*.

I'd meant to sneak away last night, to return to my own bed, but instead we fell asleep curled around each other. Our bodies still damp from the evening swim, but satiated nonetheless.

As I woke before sunrise this morning, I looked at her sleeping face and the urge to wake her pulled at me.

Just tell her. She was brave enough to initiate this agreement, and you're not even brave enough to tell her how you feel?

It's laughable that the world believes men to be the stronger ones. We may look more muscular at times, but it's women who possess that inner strength to tackle whatever comes their way.

And in that moment, I was too much of a coward to put myself out there.

So I slunk back to my room, gathered my luggage, and, with Eli in tow, headed for the airport.

"Listen, I need you to run a check on this Sam Wilkins guy. Something feels off about him. I don't want him around Savannah without you right by her side either."

Jenson looks up from his phone. "If you're so concerned, why haven't you done your due diligence?"

I swallow the guilt climbing up my throat. "It's been a little difficult with going back and forth between the motel and the house." *And you've been too busy banging the boss's daughter*, as Elijah so eloquently put it. "So, can you handle the extra responsibility or not?"

"Of course I can. My head is completely in the game. Nothing else on my mind but work and the safety of our employers." His gaze slides to mine and I'm sure my cheeks turn red at his insinuations.

"I appreciate it. With my mom's illness and all..." I trail off as the audacity at what I'm doing sends a shot of pain straight to my chest.

I'm using my mom's ailment to deceive my coworker.

What a new low, you piece of shit.

"Ah, man, it's no problem." Elijah's expression softens. "How's Ma doing anyway? D'you think she's getting the best care in Michigan?"

"I honestly don't know. It's the best situation for now, though."

"What will happen if the governor gets elected to the senate seat in D.C.? Have you started thinking about that?"

I have, but I don't tell Elijah that. In all honesty, there's no way my salary can afford the kind of housing and care my mother needs in a city like the capital. Luckily, I avoid continuing the conversation as we pull into the airport. "Listen, I'll text you my return flight information."

"No problem. Tell Ma I said hi and take all the time you need. I've got things under control."

I exit the vehicle and grab my bag from the trunk as Elijah scurries around to the driver's side. I nod in his direction, but tamp down the urge to remind him to keep a watchful eye on Savannah. It'd only heighten his suspicions.

"Let me know what you find out about that Sam guy." I pray I haven't overlooked something serious. That I haven't put Savannah in danger.

"Ma?" Staleness coats the air of the small Michigan house that I called home for so long. "Ma, where are you?" I stalk across the original hardwood floors, now scratched and worn from years of raising a terror of a teenage boy, and enter the kitchen. A pile of dishes soak in the sink. "Ma?"

"In here!" Her voice comes from the small laundry room off from the kitchen and dining area. I set down my pack and push open the door, finding my mother bent in half as she rips a washcloth from the dryer's clutches.

"Let me get that!" Gently scooting her out of the way, I grab the offending fabric, tearing it in half as it comes free from the rubber gasket. I stand and make to pass her the torn material, but the way in which she rubs her back—the lines etched across her brow—tells me she needs to sit. "Why didn't you wait for me to get here?"

I lead her by the elbow to the small kitchen table for two and settle her into a rickety old chair. My eyes assess her for further injury or ailment.

"Oh, stop looking at me like that! I'm fine." She leans back against the chair and hums in appreciation for the respite. "Besides, I didn't know if you were truly coming home or not."

My lips turn down at the affront. "Why wouldn't I come back? I said I would, Ma."

"Well, I never know with that man...if he'll let you actually leave or if he'll work you to the bone."

I roll my eyes because this has been a source of contention since I started working for the governor.

"Besides, I didn't vote for him," she adds as she crosses her arms over her chest.

"You didn't vote for anyone!" I chide in response. I traipse to the refrigerator and am pleasantly surprised to find it stocked with all the necessities, from juice and milk to lunch meat and microwaveable meals. Pulling the OJ out, I uncap it and take a swig before returning it.

"Stop that! Get a glass." When she rises from her seat and goes to the cabinet, I brush her off and close the door.

"Sit back down and let me see your knee." She follows my orders—for once—and rolls up her pant leg. Her knee is fairly swollen. "Does it hurt?" I ask as I inch my hand closer.

She retreats with a hiss and immediately lowers the fabric. "No."

Liar. Eyes narrowed, I sit back on my haunches. "Well, your chin doesn't look too bad." The stitch work could be better—she'll have a decent scar—but it appears to be healing well. "Where's the ointment? You should be keeping it slathered on so you don't get an infection." My gaze falls to her knee and the way she props her foot up on the leg of the table.

"On the counter in the bathroom." I head down the hallway to the small room and find a tube of antibiotic cream. I double-check the expiration date because I know my mom, and find that it's expired.

"Ma, this is old." Returning to the kitchen, I hold out the tube for her to see the prolapsed date.

"It works just fine, Jack."

"I'm going to the store to get you a new one. Do you need anything else?" I make a mental note to grab new bandages and other wound care items, as well as something to prepare for dinner.

"I don't need you making a fuss over me."

"Well, if not me, then who will?" I check my pocket to ensure I have my keys. "I'll be back in a few. I want you on the couch with your leg propped up and watching TV when I get back!"

CHAPTER FORTY-NINE

Savannah

It's Sunday, so there's no required meetings, training, or schmoozing on the schedule. Yet something is off. Something is...missing.

Jack.

His presence has become a boon, a security blanket, to me over the last few days.

And I feel his absence like a paper cut on my heart.

We'd immediately fallen asleep last night, our arms and legs still clinging to one another in a tangle of temptation, the smell of chlorine lingering in the air between us. When I woke, he was gone, but a text on my phone alerted me to his arrival in Michigan.

And yet I can't help but think of his question last night. *Just be here when I get back?* The way his eyes pleaded with mine, his fist clenched around the empty tumbler on his desk.

As though I could leave.

I hoped this wouldn't happen, but I should've known better. Of course I'd catch feelings—*deep* feelings—especially for Jack.

After all, I'd spent the last four years trying to forget him.

And look how that turned out.

In all my smutty romance books, the male love interest has always been dark. Brooding. Kind of an asshole. While the spice is nice, those characters never set my heart to flutter. And while Jack has his moments, he's anything but a compilation of those villain and savior traits.

He's the protective one with a kind soul who just wants to make the world, and himself, better.

And I don't think two lifetimes, let alone two weeks, will ever be enough for me when it comes to Jack.

"Sav? Are you there?" Delia interrupts my thoughts and brings me back to the sunny sky and the ridiculously large float that supports my languid body. Between the regular sex and the copious amount of vitamin sunshine, I'm not sure I can ever leave Florida.

I'm fairly certain I never want to.

"I'm here," I answer over the FaceTime video. Delia's got her phone propped in a grocery cart as she wheels around the market. "Didn't you used to hate people who were on their phones in public places?"

"Yep," she answers, popping the *p* loudly like bubble gum. "But everyone in Chicago does it. Besides, it's not like I can talk to you while lugging my groceries back to the apartment. So in the shopping cart you go, my friend." She folds her arms across the handle and leans down to eyeball me through the screen. "Looks like daddy's campaign is treating you nicely."

"It's all right. I guess." I'd rather not talk about anything work-related on such a gorgeous day, but the whole Sam situation is weighing on me. "Remember that Sam guy I told you about? He's some millionaire who wants to donate to my father's campaign."

"I remember. Tall, dark, and rich? How could I forget?"

Right. "Well, he's being super creepy. And I'm afraid if I don't play into his flirtatious games, he'll back out of donating to the campaign."

Delia pulls the shopping cart to the side as she murmurs "excuse me" to another shopper. Then her face fills the screen, her eyebrows lowered and her eyes tight with concern. "How is he being creepy?"

I sigh. "You know that movie, *Indecent Proposal*? Where the millionaire basically pays to be with Demi Moore?"

"Of course. It's a classic."

"Well, that's how it feels," I respond, raising a single eyebrow as my stomach churns. "Like he can just buy me because he's rich."

"Ew, that is not a vibe. Have you told your dad?"

"I mean, no." My throat squeezes, chest tightening at the thought.

"And why not, might I ask?" Her deep golden eyes stare through the screen like she can sense my emotions rising to the surface.

"Because I know that my dad's campaign could really use the money. And I don't want to be the reason he loses out. Just because I'm creeped out by some rich asshole."

"It sounds like you're more than just creeped out, Sav. You need to tell your father. He should have all the information before he decides to get into business with someone like this Sam character."

"Fuck," I breathe out. She's right.

"What?" Tossing the phone back into the cart, she begins to move once more down the aisle.

"You know I hate having heart-to-hearts with my dad."

"You and me both. But it's time you put your big girl adult panties on. Besides, if you don't, this Sam fellow could have a major influence on your father's campaign, and you could be stuck working with him in D.C. Is that what you want?"

"Ugh, no. I need to get rid of him now." If only I could figure out a way to not involve my father.

The butterflies in my stomach go bananas when I get the text from Jack. Granted, it's at the same time that I'm getting ready for dinner with my father, Sam, and his colleagues, so who's to know if I'm eager for Jack to return or simply nervous to see Sam again.

"This never should've happened. I'm going to lose everything because of her."

The memory from four years ago flashes into my mind. Is Jack regretting this arrangement? Am I being selfish, potentially ruining his career? Have I pushed him into doing something that his heart isn't really in?

"Just be here when I get back?"

What if he's coming back to tell me that this whole arrangement has been fun, something to pass the time in Florida, and that's it? What if he's going to have 'the talk' with me?

Everything I thought I felt from him four years ago was all completely one-sided. It could certainly happen again.

Perspiration prickles along my forehead and I curse as I look in the mirror and see the frizzy curls along my hairline. I reach for the straightener, luckily still plugged in, and pull it through my hair again and again.

Singeing the waves until they're straighter than Jack's perfect nose.

What the hell? I can't even primp without thinking about him.

I add a dollop of straightening balm to the front pieces and pull my fingers through the strands. I've always hated the way the Florida humidity took my straightened hair and turned it into something akin to a tumble-weed. I look in the mirror once again and focus on the dry ends. Then I shake my head back and forth, as though I'm miming 'no.' My hair doesn't move. It's as straight as a board, the strands stringy and lifeless.

I bring my fingers up to my hair and feel along the bottom, along the ends. They're sticky with the straightening salve and brittle to the touch.

Disgusted by what I've done to my hair, I frown at my reflection. The hair my mom loved. The hair she "always wanted." She was the one with pin-straight hair while I inherited my father's crazy waves.

Before I know it, my head is in the sink and my hair is drenched from the tepid water pouring from the faucet. I run my fingers through the mass, making sure each straightened strand is now soaked before grabbing my shampoo and conditioner bottles from the shower ledge and going to work.

As my waves take shape in the sink, I feel the butterflies settle.

CHAPTER FIFTY

Savannah

"We'll have the 2019 Riesling for the table."

"Yes, sir. And how many bottles?"

Sam looks around the circular seating, his eyes assessing everyone, before stopping on me. "We'll start with three, but put two more on ice."

"That's a fantastic varietal, Sam." My dad compliments our host from his seat next to mine as he opens the thick leather-bound menu and peruses the entrees.

"Nothing but the best for our future senator." His slow smirk and wink have me edging to the far side of my chair. Away from him.

Because, of course, he seated me directly to his left. A seat that should've been reserved for my father. The man of the hour.

Instead, my father is partnered with Sam's colleague. A woman wearing an obnoxiously low-cut blouse who can't seem to stop peppering him with questions about Michigan's weather.

Has she really never traveled to a state with four distinct seasons?

I frown, drowning out her gasps over the magnificent fall foliage, and turn to my own menu. The restaurant is clearly upscale and pricy, as detailed in the multi-page booklet before me.

A single eight-ounce filet costs an eye-watering $125. I gulp at the prices.

"The A5 Kobe beef has the highest level of marbling and tenderness." Sam leans across the divide between our chairs, a gorge that I continue to widen without his notice, and whispers in my ear. "You haven't lived until you've tried it."

I smile politely. "I think I'll stick with the lobster tail." Snapping my menu shut, I set it on the table before digging my hands into my lap.

I itch to take the sleek cotton napkin and pull it to pieces, but instead I furl my hands together as my shoulders stitch themselves to my ears.

I've never been so uncomfortable in my life.

Not only have I worn my hair in its natural state, but I've also outfitted myself in my most modest dress. The sleek satin material keeps me cool in the southern heat, but the cap sleeves and round high-neck style cover my chest. Unfortunately, the slit in the hem rides up as I cross my legs, a detail Sam clearly notices as his eyes widen and a flush creeps into his cheeks.

"That's a beautiful dress, Savannah."

"Thank you," I murmur as I hold my wineglass aloft to another of Sam's colleagues. The older gentleman, a mustached man about my father's age, smiles kindly as he fills the cup with an appropriate amount.

"Ah, Daniels, that's hardly enough. Top it all the way!" Sam takes the bottle from his coworker and proceeds to flood my glass with the blood-red liquid. "Don't worry, there's plenty more, so drink up. It's an award-winning bottle, after all."

I awkwardly bring the glass closer to me, careful not to spill the contents on the table or down my dress, and lean forward to take a sip. While the flavor is lovely, I much prefer the taste of whiskey.

Especially on Jack's lips.

The thought radiates through my brain, sending a tidal wave of serotonin directly to my nerve endings.

"So you like it." Sam mistakes my flush of arousal for an affinity for his wine selection.

"Of course it's wonderful. Thank you for making the selection. My father is still learning the intricacies of...the wines," I mumble stupidly as I try to engage my father in the conversation. Unfortunately, he's discussing a political adversary with the rest of the table. I cock my head and try to listen so Sam will shut up, but he doesn't take the hint.

"I'm quite the oenophile myself. Perhaps I can teach you some things?"

"Oh, I'm not the wine connoisseur in the family. I find the drink much too sweet on most occasions." Sam's eyes flash with annoyance. "Although this particular...vintage...is quite, um, delicate on the palate?" It's clear to anyone listening that I'm floundering. But the line I'm trying to walk is precarious.

Thankfully, the waitress returns, ready to take our order. I patiently wait my turn until the waitress comes to Sam.

"I'll have the Kobe filet medium rare, as will the lady." Sam gestures to me with a wink.

A sour taste permeates my mouth. Whether from the overpriced wine or the overpriced filet, which I didn't especially want, I'm not sure. But it gives me enough of a prod to the gut that I speak up. "Actually, I'll have the lobster tail with the vegetable medley. Thank you." I pass the hefty menu past Sam, careful not to smack him straight in the face with it.

"But the filet—" Sam begins before I stand from the table, smoothing my dress down.

"I'm sure you'll enjoy your Kobe steak well enough while I enjoy my *own* choice. If you'll excuse me." My eyes dart around the table before I stalk toward the restroom.

I pray there's a window I can climb out of. But if not, spending a few minutes away from Sam will be gift enough.

On my way to the restroom, I pass the bespoke bar and find Eli, or rather, Jenson, as my father so affectionately calls him, nursing a clear drink and a plate of stuffed mushrooms.

The dining room is elegant, but as I enter the bar area, I'm actually impressed with the architecture. Floor-to-ceiling windows rim the outer walls with gold columns supporting an ornate white ceiling, backlit by fluorescent lights set into curved recessing. A marbled plaque at the entrance mentions that the Brat Pack once frequented this very establishment.

"This place is something," I murmur as I lean against the teardrop-shaped bar.

Eli swirls his tumbler and shrugs. "Seems like you'd know better than I would."

"Right," I chuckle. "Because there are so many places like this back home in Michigan."

Raising his fork, he stabs the soft flesh of a mushroom before gulping it down in one bite. His teeth grate across the metal utensil. "I certainly wouldn't know," he responds as he chews.

My eyes narrow. "Funny that you think I would."

He shrugs and pokes another gooey fungus onto his fork, repeating the scraping of his teeth against the tines. The sound grates along my spine. It's like nails on a chalkboard, putting me on edge and irritating my already frayed nerves.

I roll my eyes and shake my head. Whatever. If this prick doesn't like me, it's not like I even care. I make eye contact with the bartender, and he approaches.

"I'll have a whiskey. Neat."

He nods and saunters off to make my drink. The wine Sam ordered may be expensive and award-winning, but it's got nothing on my drink of choice.

"You copy his preferred drink, too?"

"Excuse me?" I turn to face Jenson, who assesses me with a cold gaze. His lips are flattened, nearly curling into a snarl.

"Isn't that what girls like you do to keep a man interested?"

"Girls like *me*?" I'm dumbfounded and pretty sure my mouth hangs open. What is this asshole getting at? The bartender sets the glass of whiskey in front of me with a flat smile. "Thanks," I mutter before pulling a large bill from my purse and tossing it down on the bar.

"You don't have to pay for my meal," Eli sneers as he eyes the money like it's tainted.

"I wasn't. That was for my drink. And a solid tip for the man who brought it to me." I lift the glass to my lips and attempt to savor the smell. The flavor. The emotions that I associate with something so simple as a fermented drink.

Jack.

Despite the animosity I have for being in Jenson's presence, I allow a small smile to tilt my lips as I take a swig. It goes down smoothly. Smoother than the wine. And at a fraction of the cost.

"That's very rich of you. Tipping the bartender, what, four times what the drink cost?" The annoying little bug in my ear begins to whine again.

I knock back the rest of the drink and slam the glass onto the white granite. "What the *actual* fuck is your problem?"

Jenson stares at me for so long, I think he might truly regret his tone. But then, as he raises a single eyebrow and shakes his head, I know he's just an asshole. "You know, Jack worked really hard to get this job."

"I know that." My eyes narrow as I await the accusation that is surely coming. The thought of it makes me uneasy.

"As a police officer, I saw a lot of women like you. We called them holster sniffers. They got off on being with a man in uniform."

"And I'm sure *you* never took advantage of these...women?" I arch an eyebrow and remember what Jack told me about Eli, that unease turning right back into annoyance.

"What I did couldn't get me fired." He swallows the rest of his drink and stands.

My blood boils at his presumptions, but as he stalks away, I'm speechless. Maybe a little nauseous.

What does Eli Jenson suspect about me and Jack?

I really did need the facilities, so after my refreshing beverage—minus the company—the bartender points me toward the ladies' room. A silky warmth spreads through my belly as the whiskey heats me from inside. I pull out my phone and, as I saunter toward the lavatory, attempt to type out a message to Jack.

> Hurry back.

No, I think, as I delete the letters one at a time. Sounds too desperate. Like I'm already hung up on him.

Aren't you?

I try again.

> Can't wait!

Ugh. An exclamation point? What am I, twelve?

Gross. Next.

> See you soon.

I lean against the wall leading into the alcove of the restrooms as I ponder any dilemma with the third attempt. It's hopeful without being too needy.

It's perfect. I click send and tuck the device back into my handbag as a shadow falls over me.

"You've been gone a while. Now I see what's taken your attention from me." Sam eyes the curved line of the phone as I attempt to button the bag.

Whoever invented these tiny clutches didn't account for the size of smart phones. I jam the device farther into the leather reticule and attempt to zip everything up.

"Oh," I laugh nervously as my phone beeps in protest. Hoisting the purse higher onto my shoulder, I cross my arms over my chest. "Just answering some pressing emails. A campaign manager's job is never done. Especially when she's related to the candidate," I joke. I glance at the sleek gold door handle just an arm's reach away as my bladder cringes.

"Hm, I suppose if you finally gave me a moment of time to speak of my offer, I could ease the burden of your position, Savannah."

I blink up at him. "Offer?"

He leans his forearm against the wall at my back. Looming over me as he inches closer, he presses his hips against me. My body freezes, and I turn as cold as the marbled bar top. "I mentioned at our golf outing that I wanted to speak with you more, but that opportunity never arose at the barbecue. You seemed to avoid me."

My jaw hardens as I force myself to stand up straighter. I'm not going to be bullied by some rich prick who thinks he can buy me like he buys everything else. "I think you're mistaken, Mr. Wilkins. It would be highly inappropriate of me to accept *shady* offers for my father's campaign."

Sam doesn't take the hint, and as he sinks deeper into me, my skin itches and stings. As though I'm allergic to his mere presence, I raise my shoulders and try to turn away from him. "Oh, I'm sure there are plenty of shady things your father has done. And if not, I'm happy to make some up for the media."

My eyes snap up to his hard gaze. It's cold. Calculating. "Wha—"

But before I can get the exclamation out, his thin lips are covering mine as he presses his hips against my stomach. Caging me in. I attempt to push against his chest, but he yanks my arms up and holds them overhead as his other hand slides down my side, cupping my breast.

I crane my neck and manage to pull away from his mouth just as Eli exits the men's room and spies us. His eyes widen and he jumps into action.

"Get the fuck off of her!" He grabs Sam and instantly shoves him against the wall, and I take a breath of relief. The police training has certainly come in handy as he holds Sam's hands behind his back. As Sam attempts to wrest himself free, Eli buries his hand into the tender flesh between Sam's trapezoids. Suddenly, as I take in the scene before me, I start to panic.

"Stop that!" I admonish Eli as I attempt to pull his arms off Sam. My gaze flies around the perimeter, catching on servers and guests who do their best to look away when they meet my eye. My father's campaign doesn't need a scandal right now. And Sam Wilkins seems like the type to cause a *major* scandal. I can see the headline now. *Senate Hopeful's Bodyguard Thrashes Millionaire Donor.* No matter what the truth of the story, the media will always put a spin on it that we can't control. My father's aspirations could be ruined. "This isn't—"

"What are you saying, Miss Smith?" Elijah's raised voice coils down my throat and leaves me gasping for air. I need time to think. To see how this looks and fix it.

"Just let—"

I need to see this from all the angles. Be able to figure out how to fix this without ruining everything.

"Just let him go? You've gotta be…?" His face falls before the skin flushes and his brow wrinkles. "Fine."

"Elijah, that's not—" But Elijah releases Sam. He rolls his shoulders and adjusts his suit jacket as his hand rubs the back of his neck.

"You'll regret this," Sam snarls at us as he stomps away.

Shit. What does he mean by that? Is he going to follow through on his threat to send stories of my father to the media?

"Whatever you do, don't tell my father." My eyes meet Elijah's, pleading seeping into my tone.

His face softens. "You need to let your father know, Miss Smith."

My jaw tightens as I shake my head. "No. Not yet. And please don't tell Jack either," I add. At that, Jenson's eyes harden again, and he shakes his head.

"I knew it. Jack wouldn't admit it, but I knew there was something going on between you two."

Elijah stalks off, muttering a slew of curses under his breath.

And I'm left standing alone, my body quaking as at the adrenaline seeks an outlet. There's no way I can go back to that table, so instead I push into the ladies' room and seek the solace of a quiet stall.

CHAPTER FIFTY-ONE

Jack

That simple text has lived in my mind rent free for hours. From the moment I got it last night, I don't think my heart has calmed its steady thrumming.

"What's got you in such a good mood?" Mom asked as I stared at my phone once more. We abided by a no-devices-at-dinner policy, but I couldn't help breaking it for just one more peek.

I cleared my throat and set the phone face down on the table. "Nothing, Ma. How's the chicken?"

"It's delicious, Jacks. You're a great cook. But you could've just picked up a frozen pizza or warmed up something in the microwave. You didn't need to make this whole meal just for us. We'll never eat all this food." Her fork circled around the table at the mashed potatoes, salad, and homemade macaroni and cheese.

"Then you'll have leftovers for the rest of the week. I like cooking for you. Keeps me busy."

"Mmhm," she murmured over a bite of mashed potatoes. "Keeps you from thinking about somebody. Maybe the girl that texted you?" Her eyes gleamed with mischief. Early onset dementia be damned. My mom wouldn't let a single thing slide when she was being nosy.

"It's nothing." I turned my focus back to the chicken. I'd tried a new barbecue glaze that had caramelized perfectly. But even as I assessed my culinary skills, my mind wouldn't stop thinking of Savannah.

Was our arrangement really about using each other for just two weeks?

Or was it more?

And now, the following morning, as I glance at that message for the umpteenth time, I'm no closer to an answer.

"Sir?" The TSA agent raises his eyebrows at me as he waits for me to place my phone in the bin.

"Oh, shit. Sorry." I drop it into the container, along with my shoes, belt, carry-on, and watch. Then, on socked feet like a toddler, I walk through the security checkpoint.

If only that digital metal detector could transport me to Florida, I'd be one happy man.

"Thanks for the ride, man!" I settle into the SUV passenger seat and toss my bag into the backseat. He hits the gas, and I'm jerked into the back of the seat before I've even buckled the seat belt. "Whoa. Are we in a hurry?"

Jenson's gaze doesn't stray from the road as we navigate past taxis, shuttles, and resort buses on our way from the airport lot. If anything, I notice a tic in his jaw as he signals and then merges with the flow of traffic.

"Okay, what's going on? You get ghosted by another girl?"

He shoots a puff of air from his flared nostrils and then slams on the brakes as we come to a stop at the red light. "You know, I've always looked up to you. I trusted you. I trusted that you had my best interest in mind when I left the force and took this job." His knuckles turn white as he grips the steering wheel, still not making eye contact or deigning to look in my direction.

"Elijah...I have no idea what you're talking about or what's brought this on. Care to fill me in so this isn't just a one-sided argument with yourself?" I slide my phone from my pocket and turn it on. No messages, but that doesn't stop me from sending one to Savannah.

> On my way. Eli's in a mood.

An audio file pings in the message box. Curious, I hold the phone to my ear and listen. A cold frost covers my body, starting at the top of my head and freezing its way downward as the message plays. "What happened? Why am I listening to an audio message of that dickhead harassing Savannah? I told you to *watch out for her*." My harsh tone must snap Jenson out of his nasty attitude because, for the first time since I got in the car, he finally looks at me.

Eli shakes his head as the car accelerates. He zips and zooms around slower vehicles, dashing in and out of the lanes. "What do you know about Sam Wilkins?"

I keep my eyes trained on the roadway and try to put my faith in Elijah. We both went through the same training at the academy, so I trust that he can handle the advanced speed. What I don't trust is the other drivers on the highway. "Self-made multi-millionaire who wants to invest in Michigan's renewable energy resources. What else is there to know?" My heart races at the puny answer. Is that all I know about the man who's been ingratiating himself into the Smith campaign?

"Sam Wilkins isn't exactly a self-made multi-millionaire, Jack. He's the stepson of Giacomo Zanotti."

"The fucking head of the Detroit Syndicate?" The fucking *mafia*? How the hell did I miss this?

Fuck, I've been distracted.

By Savannah.

And not only has it affected my job, but also the safety of the Smiths.

"Why would the Detroit Syndicate have an interest in Paul or Savannah?"

Jenson's gaze flicks to me as his eyebrows furl. As though to say, *are you kidding me, idiot?* "Paul was head of the Michigan Power Company before becoming governor, right?"

He's quiet while I form my own conclusions. "You don't think Paul has a connection to the Syndicate, do you?"

The entrance to the neighborhood lies ahead. We've made record time from the airport. A testament to Elijah's driving, as well as his eagerness to figure out what the hell is going on.

My heart thunders as we pull into the drive and Jenson cuts the engine. "What's the plan?" he asks as I fling open the door.

"Get some answers."

Elijah and I find our boss sitting on the patio with a folio of papers fanned in front of him. Miranda sits across from him, scrolling on her phone while simultaneously eyeing the governor's documents.

"Welcome back, Keaton. How is your mother doing? Is she feeling any better?" It's hard not to trust a man who has treated me so well the last four years, but as I scan the paperwork laid out on the table, I wonder what exactly our governor has been up to.

"She's doing much better, sir. Thank you for asking." My gaze swings to Elijah, who stares at the papers as well. Likely trying to make out what they're actually for.

"Sir, wha—" Jenson begins, just as I clamp my hand around his shoulder and squeeze. He snaps his mouth closed but gives me a look that says, *what the fuck*?

"Miranda, can we speak with you for just a moment?"

She seems taken aback by my request and blinks at me.

Before she can refuse, I've pulled out her chair and Jenson's hoisted her up, albeit gently, and we're traipsing as a trio around the side of the house.

"What's going on? Why are you both being so strange?" She eyes her phone, thumb scrolling over the screen.

I cross my arms. "Miranda, what do you know about the governor's involvement with the Detroit Syndicate?"

Her eyebrows squish together as her gaze flicks back and forth between mine and Eli's. "You mean the mob? Are you asking me about the mob?"

"That's right. Does the governor associate with any of them?" Jenson leans into her, his hands on his hips and his gaze hard and calculating. He's in full-on police mode and loving every minute of it, even as my heart pounds in my ears.

I'm the rookie here, and I don't like it.

"You think the governor...and the mob...?" She bursts out laughing. "You've got to be kidding me." She makes to leave, going so far as to dip around Jenson's burly form, but I pull her back.

"Cut the shtick, Miranda. It's *us*, not the media. We're serious. That Sam creep, he's—"

"Related to the Syndicate. I know. So does the governor." Now it's her turn to cross her arms and stare at us with an eyebrow cocked.

"Wait, you both already knew?" The confusion and shock lick their way up my throat.

"Of course we did. Figured you did too. Or, you should, if you were doing your job properly."

"So the governor's not—?"

"In cahoots with the mafia? Not directly." Her eyes dip to the freshly cut grass. "But what the public doesn't know won't hurt them. The key is to maintain anonymity when dealing with *those* types of people." I swallow the lump in my throat as I realize that everything I thought about our governor could be a lie. Could he really associate himself with the *mob*?

"So that's why this Sam Wilkins character thinks he can fondle Savannah and get away with it?" I cross my arms, else my fists start pummeling the privacy fence separating us from the neighbors.

"What?" Miranda's face pales and her mouth falls open. I pull out my phone and play the recording as my eyes trail to Elijah's. Biting his lip, he frowns.

I narrow my gaze at him as the phone falls to my side. "What aren't you telling me, Jenson?" I worked with the guy on our beat for four years prior to taking this job. Besides spending every day together in the academy, we're brothers in blue. I *know* that look.

"Savannah didn't want me to tell her father. Or you."

Now Miranda's eyes are colliding with mine, and I don't miss the distrust or anger flashing in them. She shakes her head at me before turning her attention to Elijah. "You knew about this and didn't tell the governor or me? What the fuck were you thinking?"

Jesus Christ, this situation is getting out of hand.

"Listen, we need to tell the governor what we know. And then you can come up with a plan to fix this, Miranda."

The fiery redhead composes her features and rolls her shoulders like she's mentally preparing for battle. "You're right, Keaton. Let's go."

I fall back, allowing Eli and Miranda to approach the governor first, as the feeling of missing something so crucial and important lingers in the air.

I swallow over the lump in my throat. The bitter taste of failure on my tongue.

And at the same time, the gravity of what I know I need to do weighs heavily on my shoulders.

"We need to get out in front of this before Wilkins carries through on his threats," Miranda says as I stalk up to the outdoor seating.

"I've got it all recorded here, sir." I hold up my phone as proof and play the audio. Except I forgot to restart the recording, so it plays from where I last left off.

Elijah's voice fills the air. *"You need to let your father know, Miss Smith."*

"No. Not yet," Savannah says. *"And please don't tell Jack either."*

"I knew it. Jack wouldn't admit it, but I knew there was something going on between you two."

Three sets of eyes snap in my direction as I click the stop button. The phone falls to the table with a *thunk*.

"I need that entire recording sent to my phone, Keaton," the governor demands gruffly. He stands and gathers the papers, tidying them into the leather folio. "Miranda, give me fifteen minutes and then meet me in my office."

He stalks to the French doors before turning back. My breath catches in my throat as his eyes bypass me and fall to Jenson's. "Eli, son, let my daughter know I need to speak with her. Immediately."

As the door slams behind him, my eyes snap to Jenson's. "Give me five minutes with her first. Please?"

Eli's jaw flexes, and I see the dilemma all over his face. But I don't give him a chance to answer before I'm sprinting around to the garage and entering the door nearest Savannah's bedroom.

I've got to get to her first.

CHAPTER FIFTY-TWO

Savannah

I reread Jack's text.

On my way. Eli's in a mood.

A heaviness settles in my stomach, and I wonder what they're talking about on the ride from the airport. Is Jenson telling Jack what he saw at the restaurant? I pace across my room, wearing a path in the plush carpet as I stalk from one wall and then turn, repeating the process.

A ruckus in the hallway pulls me from my trance, and I rush to the bedroom door, throwing it open at the same time that Jack appears. I take him in, from the purple grooves beneath his eyes to the stubble along his jaw. My ribs feel tight, like they're suffocating me.

Something is wrong.

My lips part, but before I can ask Jack all the questions that have been running through my mind, he grabs me around my waist and hauls me against his warm body.

"I missed you," he murmurs just before his mouth finds mine. I barely get my lips tilted up in a smile of satisfaction before he's pushing his tongue past them and slamming the door behind us. Locking it. "Savannah..." He breathes my name through the small gaps in time when our lips break apart, devouring one another again. Our kisses are hungry, a last-ditch effort to feed the desire that aches between us. I circle my arms around his neck, begging him to stay in this embrace, but somewhere deep in my gut, I know it's too late.

Our kisses slow, coming to a stop. Our mouths part. My gaze strays to his lips, puffy and coated in my lip gloss. I swipe my thumb along the bottom one, pulling at the skin to lighten the heavy mood hanging over us.

"Savannah," he repeats as his eyes soften. They scan over my face before a grimace pinches his features. "We need to talk." He pulls out his phone.

I gulp slowly, though I'm still determined to make the best of the situation. After all, while it hasn't been quite two weeks, I'm sure Jack has realized that his job is at risk.

All because of me.

"Okay." I force my voice to remain strong, and maybe only I can hear the subtle tremble in it, but tremble it does. I take the few steps to the bed and sit on the edge, my back ramrod straight as I brace for the inevitable.

The end.

Jack follows, but rather than sit, he stands before me. His white Henley is wrinkled from the flight, yet his pectoral muscles flex through the fabric as he inhales. Like he's preparing himself. He's holding his phone up in front of him. Did he write out a breakup speech? "There's no way to say this delicately, so I'll just come out and—"

"It's over," I finish for him. I've never been the intrepid type. I always yank the Band-Aid right off and deal with the sting later.

"*What?*" His eyes widen as his voice cuts through the awkwardness between us.

"It's over," I repeat as my head nods slowly. "That's what you were going to say." The backs of my eyes prick as my tear ducts activate. *Hold it together, Sav,* I admonish myself. At least until he's gone. I blink in succession to stave off the flow.

"What the fuck are you talking about, Savannah?"

I look at him with pinched eyebrows. Does he not understand that I'm trying to make this easy for him? "You had a change of heart, right? I mean, I guess I get it. I always knew how important this position was to you." I'm rambling. "Besides, we're closing in on two weeks. Per our agreement, it's over."

He chuffs and places his hands on his hips. Staring at me strangely, he bites his bottom lip. Then he turns and sinks onto the bed. He keeps his gaze trained on the wall in front of us, as though turning to look at me is too...difficult? "Is-Is that what you want, Savannah? For this to be *over*?"

With him so close, so close that the entire length of our arms is pressed skin-to-skin, my nerves inflame. Ache for more contact. It'd be so easy to lie. To save face, harden my heart, and allow that Band-Aid to flutter into the trash.

Four years ago, I hardened my heart and ran from my emotions. I fled to dodge the heartbreak I knew was coming.

But a lot has changed in four years.

And as my gaze peruses Jack's face, searching for the right answer that will leave us both with the least amount of pain, I find nothing.

Those dark circles under his eyes could be from agonizing over ending things...or just as easily agonizing over continuing things.

"Savannah." He reaches out and takes my hand, pulling my soft palm into his calloused one. "What do *you* want?"

I can't remember the last time someone asked me that, if ever. My life has been mapped out for me since my father decided to become governor. It was always a given that I'd become a part of the political machine, even as I was never directly asked.

And now, as I glance around the room at the discarded business-casual clothes on the floor to the suits hanging over the bathroom door, I wonder if, given the choice, I'd have come to the same ending.

The "no" bursts forth from my lungs with a sob as the tears well in my eyes. Beside me, I feel Jack stiffen as the word hangs over us. But my own body feels lighter than it has in years. And as I turn to him, a smile lifting those just-kissed lips, I find my voice.

"No, that's not what I want. Not at all, Jack." I blink back the moisture that threatens to spill down my cheeks and squeeze his hand. "Two weeks was never going to be enough for me. And I'm sorry if you feel differently, and I've made this conversation awkward and harder on you, but—"

Before I can continue, he hauls me onto his lap and grabs the back of my neck, pulling me down to meet his mouth once again. Then his hands are everywhere. Scorching the skin across my back, curling under my breasts, and trailing up to my cheeks. I grind into his lap and wrap my arms around his neck, tugging us closer.

He lifts my t-shirt over my head and tosses it to the floor before releasing my lips and pulling my nipple into his mouth. The wet tug sends sparks straight to my core, and I gasp. I reach between us and, with deft fingers, flick open the button of his jeans. Diving into the waistband of his boxer briefs, I free his thickening cock.

"Savannah, wait," he says as he releases the tight bud with a pop from between his lips. "I need to show you something."

He pats the bed next to him, and I crawl off his lap and settle onto the mattress. Then he pulls his shirt over his head and turns away from me.

My gaze catches on the tattooed bouquet on his shoulder blade. The art I'd spied at The Sandy Sea Dollar. "I got it two years ago. When I couldn't get you out of my mind. I knew..." he trails off as my fingers reach out to touch the inked skin. "Forget-Me-Nots."

"You got this for me?" The crystal blue blooms shudder as my nail traces the petals.

He turns back around and inches closer. His thumb moves across his bottom lip, pressing and dragging the soft flesh from side to side. "I-I need you to know that..." he pauses and takes that same thumb and tips my chin up. "Savannah, I'm in love with you."

My heart stutters and crashes into my gut. My limbs feel frozen, but every molecule in my body is firing energy straight to my brain, which is going haywire. Did he just say—?

"*Love.*" Without any context, Jack's eyebrows squish together. I shake my head, clearing the chaos, and try again. "I feel the same way about you. I'm so in love, too, Jack. With *you.*"

A goofy grin spreads across his face, likely matching my own. Then our mouths are seeking each other out and we're falling—him backwards and me forwards—onto the covers of the bed. I rise onto my knees and straddle him as I yank his Henley over his head. The waffle knit goes flying in the general direction of my own discarded top, and then we're pressing against one another, my breasts flattened by his broad muscular pectorals. At the same time, he inches his pants and briefs down, wiggling through my long legs.

There's an urgency to his movements. A rush I match.

Then he's undressing me from the waist down, exposing my ass in the afternoon light that peeks through the closed curtains. I feel self-conscious. Like every imperfection has a spotlight shined on it. Instinctually, my arms stray to the way the skin sits along my hips and belly, like a shield protecting me from the light. But even if I could dive under the duvet and hide, would

I really want to? Jack entwines his hands with mine and pulls me forward, into his embrace, and any insecurities fly out the window.

"Ride me, sweetheart," he says as he reaches for himself. He's thick and large and as greedy for me as I am for him. I rub myself along his length, wetting the shaft with the consequence of my desire. His eyes dip low, the lids covering so far that he almost appears asleep except for the smug smirk that tilts his lips. "Watching your pussy glide over my dick has to be a core memory."

His words spur me onward, and I grab the tip and ease him to my entrance before sinking down quickly.

"Fuck, Savannah. We forgot the condom." A gasp escapes his pursed lips, whistling through those two mounds of flesh that I want to take in my mouth. I should be scared. I should stop. But I don't. I wait until my body acclimates to the feeling of fullness from this new position. As I swivel my hips, a spark of desire shoots straight to my core and my nipples pebble.

"Sav—"

"Just wait," I beg. It feels so good like this. "I want to feel all of you inside me. *Bare.*"

We stay still for a moment, just feeling one another without anything between us.

"Feel good?" Jack finally asks, pushing his hips up and nearly sending me over the edge. I hold on tight and nod dumbly, speechless, as I grind into him.

"I-I love it." My hands stray to his shoulders and, as I match him thrust for thrust, the pressure builds quickly. He slides a single hand between us and anchors it, pressing his thumb into my clit. I work myself harder, grinding down on his cock and pressing into his thick thumb, until I'm so close I'm trembling. "*More,*" I beg as the tempo increases.

We move in tandem, but at any moment, any millisecond, really, one of us might adjust or shift ever-so-slightly and send the whole rhythm off its hinges. So I keep going, even as my thighs burn and my ass clenches from the exertion. Sweat breaks out along Jack's brow, but as the muscle in his jaw flexes and he reaches for my chest with his free hand, I know he's thinking the same thing.

Don't stop.

Our labored breathing is the only sound in the room as we force ourselves to silence. Even the springs of the mattress are in on the act. It's not until I'm so close—nearly there—that a rush of air, accompanied by a low moan, escapes from between my lips.

"Oh my...*fuck*," I manage before Jack's hand moves from my chest up to my throat. He slides his fingers around the taut tendons and squeezes.

"Shhh," he demands. I follow orders and press into him harder. Everywhere. Harder onto his length. Harder into his thumb. And I force my neck into his grip. He's consuming me, wrapped around me everywhere. Invading me down to the very core.

And I love it.

"I-I-I love you," I whisper as I come, gripping onto his shoulders. Everything explodes all at once. The air seems to be sucked from the room just as my nerve endings combust. And I'm floating on a high as my thighs go numb and the world goes white. The orgasm keeps going as Jack utters a curse, following me onto this explosive white plane. He withdraws from me and jacks himself, coming all over my belly and thighs. Even as he finishes, the after-effects of my climax flicker through my limbs as I watch him. "Oh my God," I mutter, languidly kissing his lips as I disentangle myself and curl into the covers. "Fucking amazing..."

My eyes close and my breathing returns to its baseline.

And that's when the knock on the door pulls me from all that is perfect in the world.

CHAPTER FIFTY-THREE

Jack

My leg jostles with anxiety as I wait outside the governor's office. I've tried numerous times to stop the fidgeting, but I know what's coming. And even so...

I'm so in love, too, Jack.

With you.

Her words drip down my chest and a sense of calm settles over me. They fill me with a feeling of euphoria.

And my leg settles.

She loves me.

And I love her, too.

Everything seems right with the world.

Except it isn't.

The oath I took is broken.

Because, ultimately, I've failed to do the one task I was assigned to do by Governor Smith.

Protect him and his daughter, his only family. From guys like Sam Wilkins.

Of course, any governor in a state with a history of mob presence would be aware of, and likely have come across, one of the associates. Hell, even the Syndicate's boss, Giacomo Zanotti, attends gubernatorial events and donates to his chosen candidate, too. But all of that is hush-hush, as Miranda said. What goes on behind closed doors is not for us mere mortals to know.

What I do know is that I was too busy falling in love with my protectee, and that is certainly a fireable offense.

My actions, my job performance, is now FUBAR.

Totally fucked.

I run my fingers through my hair, which has grown long over the last several weeks. I'm due for a haircut.

Yet another task that's gone unnoticed.

The door to the governor's office opens and Savannah steps out. Her face is pale and streaked with tears. Her eyes are unreadable, and she avoids looking at me as she takes the stairs, leaving me alone to face her father.

Shit. I gulp down the anxiety bubbling up in my throat and stand.

"Come in, Keaton," the governor calls out from inside the spacious room. It's light and airy up here in the boss's quarters. The walls are painted a professional beige and his desk, while more modern than the one at the mansion in East Lansing, has a heavy glass top.

I stand before him until I'm instructed to take a seat. He stands, his back to me as he glances out the floor-to-ceiling windows at the view of the ocean from the backyard.

I wait patiently for the firing that I know is liable to come. Steeling myself for the admonishment and berating I'm due.

After all, I broke the rules.

Even if I'd do it all over again, I deserve the consequence for my chosen action.

"How long have you been sleeping with my daughter?"

Jesus, the man comes right out with it. I have to force down the smile that's blooming on my lips, as I now know where Savannah gets her forthrightness.

I clear my throat and sit forward, perching my elbows on my knees. "Just a few days, sir."

He hums. Or growls. It's hard to tell as he's still facing away from me. Refusing to look at me.

"She tells me that she's the one who propositioned you. That you don't deserve to be fired for your...*indiscretion*."

I chuff out a breath. There's no way I'm admitting to this man that his daughter asked me to fuck her. It doesn't matter who initiated it. All that matters is that I agreed. "Sir, it's true that I broke protocol. But I'm in love with your daughter."

He finally turns to me. His brow creased as his eyes search mine. "In love? After a week?" He snorts and shakes his head.

"I... Well, it's been going on longer than a week."

His gaze hardens. "How long, exactly?"

I swallow. "Nearly four years, sir."

"Four years? Four *fucking* years, Keaton?" The rage in his eyes is no joke, and as he clenches his fists and puffs up his chest, I steady myself. Just in case.

"Sir, it wasn't like that. It was nothing but a crush then. A *mutual* crush. We never—" I snap my mouth shut before I go any further. Better to leave the past in the past on this one.

The governor hangs his head and his shoulders sag. "So you agree with her?"

"Sir?"

"You don't think you deserve to be fired." Crossing his arms over his chest, he assesses me once more with narrowed eyes.

"I didn't say that. I deserve to be fired for breaking your trust and doing...what I did. I accept that."

The governor makes a low noise in his chest. Then he stalks around the desk toward me and perches on the edge. "Except if I fire my daughter's...bodyguard...then I'm the bad guy in her eyes."

Ah, now I see where this is going. I lean back and allow that smile to stretch my face. He may be politically powerful, but he's certainly afraid to break his daughter's heart.

So I let him off the hook. After all he's done for me, it's the least I can do. Make his life a little easier and keep his and Savannah's relationship intact. "Sir, I think it's best if I put in my notice, effective immediately." There's not much else to say, so I stand and offer him my hand.

Man to man.

Father to daughter's boyfriend.

And we shake.

"You can't be serious, Keaton!" Elijah trails after me as I stalk toward the town car. I try my best to ignore him, but when he catches up and grabs my shoulder, I know I've got to deal with him.

"I guess it's a good thing you're here. You're driving." I pass him the keys I'd palmed from the basket in the foyer and shove them into his upturned hand.

"What the fuck happened?" His voice rises an octave, face as white as the towel I'd used earlier to dry off with.

"Get in the car and drive," I instruct as I move to the passenger side. "And then I'll fill you in."

I'm in the seat and already buckled by the time Eli finally comes to his senses and flings open the door. He slides into the driver's seat and starts the ignition. "Listen, man, you've done a lot of fucked up shit in your life— No, wait, that was me." I half-heartedly listen as we back out of the drive, and then accelerate out of the division. "Where are we going anyway?"

"Follow the GPS," I instruct as flatly as possible as I hand over my phone. The address on the screen means nothing to Elijah, as it shouldn't. In fact, it meant nothing to me up until twenty minutes ago.

"Who's staying at The Oasis?" As we approach a stop sign, his eyes flick up from the phone. He glances both ways as he slows, but never comes to anything close to resembling a stop before accelerating through the intersection.

"That was a stop sign. You're supposed to, you know, stop."

"Yeah, well, *you're* supposed to inform your best friend before you fuck the boss's daughter, dick."

I release a chuckle and lock eyes with him. "Don't talk about Savannah like that. And you're not my best friend."

"What the fuck? *I'm* not your best friend? Then who is?" His grip loosens on the steering wheel as we roll through yet another stop sign. I shake my head, wondering how long it'll be before he's pulled over with the governor in the car if he keeps up this entitled driving.

"I don't have a best friend. Mainly, because I'm not ten years old. Or a girl," I add for good measure.

"Psh, whatever," he grumbles as his eyes flick back to the phone's GPS. The resort isn't far from the governor's palatial mansion, so we're nearly there. "You still could've told me before you quit, Jack."

"Oh, we're going to use first names now? Is this in an attempt to bring us closer?" I joke because it's not the time for the conversation. Maybe after...but not right now. Right now, I need to be angry. Riled up. Not emotional and sappy.

"Listen, I don't know what's going on with you and the governor's daughter, but if that bitch is the reason you—"

"Savannah's not a bitch, and if you call her that again, I'm going to have to rough you up a little bit. Possibly a lot. So stop it now, before our friendship is irreparable."

Elijah clamps his mouth shut; whether from my threat or the look he spies on my face, I don't care. Because nothing could be farther from the truth. Savannah isn't the only reason why I tendered my resignation.

Sam Wilkins is.

"So are you finally going to tell me who we're here to see?" Eli asks a few minutes later as he follows me through the sleek glass doors. They're automatic, parting for us like we're royalty, and as we walk through, I'm hit with a waft of lilac and lavender.

This place sure beats The Sandy Sea Dollar, which feels like ages ago.

Even though it's been mere days.

I spot the bank of elevators and hurry toward them, pushing the up button and tapping my foot while I wait. I scan the shiny marble floors, the bespoke lighting and decor, and even tip my lips into a frown at the chic staff uniforms.

Savannah really did deserve all of this and more.

And yet...

And yet that grubby little motel, with its busted air conditioning and filthy stairs, will forever rate higher for me than this Zagat-worthy resort.

The elevator arrives on the ground floor and dings open. Jenson and I both step aside to allow the occupants to pass and then stalk through the wide door shoulder-to-shoulder. He stands with his hands clasped in front of his pelvis while I punch my thumb over the number.

Floor 27.

"All right. Floor 27. Wonder who's all the way up there. Guess I'll find out soon enough, then." As he rocks back and forth on his heels, Elijah refuses to look at me. Instead, he looks out at the street and watches with a bemused spark of curiosity as we rise higher and higher.

I, on the other hand, keep my gaze trained on the silver door. While it could be because I hate heights, it could also be because I'm keeping my mind focused and ready.

As the elevator passes floor five, it accelerates. My stomach rebels like it's on a roller coaster, but I swallow down the nerves and take a deep breath.

We edge higher and closer to our destination.

Floor 21 quickly morphs into 24, and then, before I can blink, the car decelerates and comes to a stop. I blink, catch my bearings, and step through the door before Elijah.

I turn to him. "It's best if you stay here. Maybe hold the elevator?"

The bright-eyed look in his eyes instantly dulls as his mouth falls open. "Are you kidding me? I've never seen you this serious. This secretive. And now you want me to stay behind? No way!" He gives me a playful shove, which doesn't even jolt my feet from their planted position on the tiled floor.

That's how steady I am.

How certain I feel.

"Really, Eli. I don't want your position with the governor affected by my actions." I hold up my phone and access the saved audio file. It plays aloud, my blood boiling at what that fucker did and said to someone that belongs to me.

"So you're risking everything for *her*?" Elijah's shocked tone tells me he still doesn't get it.

"I fucking love her, Jenson."

With a snort, he shakes his head. "You've gone and gotten yourself involved with one of *them*. A holster sniffer. Did you learn nothing from the academy?"

I stare at him and feel nothing but pity. Because he may not want to admit it, but all Elijah's ever wanted is the type of woman Savannah is. The type of woman I *have*. "She loves me, too. And that's all I need to know."

"How long has this been going on? A few days? You're going to throw everything away for a *few days* of pussy?"

I grind my teeth and shake my head. "It's been four fucking years, man. I've thought about her for four fucking years."

Understanding dawns on Jenson. His shoulders slump and he cocks his head, allowing it to roll forward into his hand. "Jesus, man. You're really going to go through with this, aren't you?" He doesn't even wait for my response. He just knows. "God-fucking-damnit, man."

"Like I said. Stay here." I turn and eye the plaque on the wall, which lists all the room numbers. "Room 2-7-1-9," I mutter out loud as I scan which direction to go. Why are these things always so confus—?

My arms are pinned to my side as I'm hoisted off the ground. I try to wiggle free of my restraints.

Jenson's big fucking arms.

"What the fuck are you doing? Put me down!" I roar as I'm hauled back toward the elevator. He kicks at the button, but misses because his flexibility is shit, before trying again and cracking the plastic cover as his aim lands true.

"You're not fucking everything up just to punch some spoiled little prick in the face." As he says this between grunts and exhales, I continue to wrench my arms free or find purchase with my legs, to no avail.

Fuck, I guess I should've learned some of the wrestling moves he was always trying to teach me. Because he's got me in some strange hold I cannot escape.

Finally, the elevator dings and—*lo and behold*—Sam Wilkins appears.

"Motherfucker," I hiss as my adrenaline kicks in at the sight of the rich prick. My feet find purchase, and Elijah suddenly releases me just as Sam realizes who we are.

"What are you two doing here? This is for hotel guests only!" I don't miss the way his eyes flick back and forth between mine and Jenson's. It's what a guilty person would do when they know an ass-kicking is coming.

Before I can initiate, Sam flies past me and lands a cheap shot right in Eli's face. "That's for the other night, you rent-a-cop!"

Nobody calls my buddy, a former police officer, a *rent-a-cop*, so I grab Wilkin's from behind, my arm going around his neck. "And this is for assaulting my girlfriend, you fucker!" I squeeze as hard as I can as Sam claws at my forearm. He ducks suddenly, and as I lose my balance, he wrenches my arm backward. I hear the telltale pop as my elbow dislocates, and I grit my teeth through the pain.

Jenson, out of nowhere, grabs Wilkins around the middle and tosses him to the ground like he's a child's toy. "If you ever fucking come near the governor again—"

"Hands in the air, hands in the air!" My blood runs cold as Eli and I both turn and take in the security guards standing in the open elevator doorway. While they're not armed, they do have tasers and an impressive baton hanging from each of their waists.

"We said hands in the air, assholes!" I flick a raised eyebrow to Jenson, and we both nod, following orders.

Except my elbow is shot to shit and I can only raise one hand, but I still oblige.

CHAPTER FIFTY-FOUR

Savannah

I pull the SUV into the tiniest parking spot known to man.

"You're crooked," my dad says from the passenger seat.

I blow out a deep breath through pursed lips, the frizzy curls along my hairline fluttering out of the way. Checking the rearview mirror and both side mirrors, I put the giant tank of a vehicle into reverse and then pull forward again, straightening everything out.

"Too close on this side." I snap my neck toward my father, the muscle in my jaw probably able to cut glass at this point, and bare my teeth.

"So. Suck. It. In."

The snort from the backseat has me lifting my eyes to the rearview mirror, where I meet Miranda's pinched red face.

She's attempting to hold in a giggle, but failing miserably.

"What are you laughing at?" I turn in my seat and face her full-on like a cat with her claws exposed.

"Now I know why your father chose campaign management for you. Your driving is awful!" Her burst of laughter is accompanied by my father's wheeze as he joins in.

"Joke's on you," I say as I turn my attention back to my father. "You're the one who taught me how to drive!"

"I admit I did a shit job." He chuckles as he releases the seat belt and opens the door. I follow suit, hopping to the ground and locking the doors once everyone is clear of the vehicle.

We meet as a trio on the sidewalk in front of the sleek back SUV, and I stare at the tan building before me. The insignia shines in the bright Florida sun.

Emerald Coast Police Department.

Miranda had been the one who received the call. My father and I were going over the itinerary for our last few days at the conference, as well as setting up meetings for when we returned to Michigan.

"I'll need to have a sit-down with the Lieutenant Governor on Tuesday and then we need to set up a photo op on Wednesday morning with her campaign manager," my father directed as I took notes.

"Oh my God, you're calling me from where?" Miranda's shrill voice cut through the burbling of the pool's filter. "Jail?" She held her hand over her mouth and snapped her face to my father's.

"Who is it?" he inquired as his face sank and his shoulders slumped. Like he already knew.

I watched as Miranda informed him that not only had Elijah been arrested for assault, but so had Jack. Elbows stacked on the table, my father's head dropped into his hands as he muttered "*fuck*" beneath his breath.

I don't know that I'd ever heard my dad curse before.

"Let's get this over with," my dad says warily as Miranda and I follow in his stead.

Luckily, we don't have to wait long in the drab and dirty lobby. After giving our information, including picture IDs, a uniformed officer immediately leads us into the holding cells. As I round the corner of the hallway, I instantly spy Jack, his left arm tucked against his stomach. Elijah leans against him, his hand wrapped in blood-soaked gauze.

While Miranda's eyes light up with glee, obviously tucking this mental image away for another time to hold it over them, my father's jaw works as he grinds his teeth loud enough for us to hear over the metal key clanking in the lock.

My lips part as Jack stands and his eyes drift to mine, but the subtle shake of his head stops me from saying anything.

"Come to bail out your goons, Governor?" A voice from the next cell sends a familiar chill across my collarbone. The same place he'd manhandled only days ago.

Jack's eyes darken, and his good hand clenches at his side. "Not worth it, man," Elijah mutters as he guides Jack from the cell.

"You come near me or any of my employees again and I'll punch you in the face myself!" I gasp when I realize that my own dad has stalked to the neighboring cell and is pointing his finger through the bars at Sam Wilkins.

Sam, his nose crooked and cheek bruised, simply chuckles as though he hasn't a care in the world. From his reclined position on the metal bench, he eyes my father with disgust. "Just one more thing to add to my lawsuit. Assault and now threats." He makes a checkmark in the air. "Looks like we'll be having a new senator from Michigan. One who will work with people like me."

My father's face pales and his index finger slowly falls back to his side. As I glance around at the people on our team, from Jack to Elijah to Miranda, the hatred I see directed at this piece of garbage is palpable. I can taste it permeating the stale air of the jail.

"File a lawsuit against them and I'll counter-sue for sexual assault, you fucking pig." Before I know what I'm doing, I'm wrapping my hands around the cold metal bars and glaring through, wishing I had the upper body strength to yank them apart like Superman.

That certainly shuts him up, even as he adjusts himself a little straighter and sniffs. "Like anyone would believe you."

My gaze slides over to Jack before returning to the dick in the cell. "Giacomo Zanotti is all about the optics. And financially supporting a sexual abuser certainly won't be well-received by the Syndicate."

"And there's also the audio file of you assaulting Savannah and threatening the governor." Jack holds up his cell phone and clicks play, the ominous words playing out loud for everyone to hear.

"Oh, I'm sure there are plenty of shady things your father has done. And if not, I'm happy to make some up for the media."

Sam's mouth slams shut as his face pales.

I reach for Jack, tears welling in my eyes as he pulls me into his embrace. He hisses as I press against his injured arm. "Oh, I'm sorry," I begin before he releases me.

"Sav..." His voice is strained. His body rigid. And that's when I realize my father is standing right behind us. I pull away and swipe the tears that have begun leaking down my cheeks.

"Dad, I—"

"Let's go." The skin around his eyes is tight, even as his warm palm across my shoulder blades pulls me away from the cell.

"Our lawyer will contact you," Miranda directs at Sam as I follow Jack and Elijah around the corner and out into the lobby.

"I still can't believe you kept all of this from me, Savannah." My father's voice is hollow. Empty and emotionless in the town car as he drives us back to the house.

I don't remember the last time he drove himself, let alone me, anywhere.

"I wasn't keeping anything from you." My defense is just as empty as his question. "I just…didn't tell you."

From the passenger seat, I watch as his lips flatten. When was the last time my father was angry with me?

We travel a good five miles in silence. My mind is on Jack, mostly. Miranda was assigned to take both him and Elijah to the emergency room, while my father had told me in no uncertain terms to get in the damn car.

So, once again, I followed suit and did as I was told.

"When did you start keeping things from me?"

My gaze snaps across the divide between us. He doesn't look at me. Simply keeps his eyes on the road as we navigate through the evening traffic. "I-I don't really know," I admit. "I just always felt like I had to be perfect. I couldn't disappoint you."

His knuckles turn white as he grips the steering wheel. "I never expect-ed…" He trails off as he clears his throat. "I'm sorry you grew up feeling that way."

My eyes grow bleary as renewed tears well. "It probably wasn't anything you did. It was likely just who I was. Who I *am*," I add. "The governor's daughter and all."

The car rolls to a stop as we come to a red light. We sit in silence, both of us staring at the intersection. I will the light to turn green.

"So...you and Jack?" He coughs out the last bit of the question, clearly uneasy with the way this conversation is headed.

I look down at my hands clasped in my lap. My fingers are clenched together, the digits bent at odd angles as I fight the anxiety coursing through my body. "Yeah, Dad. Me and Jack."

I glance at my father's face. It's turning an unnatural shade of red as he puts the pieces of the puzzle together.

"Was he the reason...?"

I nod, swallowing over the giant lump in my throat. "I didn't mean to upset you, but I couldn't... I couldn't be around him. Not when I felt—"

"Do you love him?" My dad's question sucks the air from the car. But despite how much I still want to be his perfect little girl, it's time for me to be honest with him.

"Yes. Yes, I love him."

He hums to himself. Or maybe it's a growl. I'm not sure. So I continue on in an attempt to make the situation better. "And he loves me too, Dad. He said so."

I roll my eyes at how immature I sound. Like a teenage love song gone wrong. Except I'm not a teenager and neither is Jack.

"I suppose it really is for the best that he quit, then."

"He *what*?" My body temperature instantly plummets. The icy chill saps the warmth from my body, even though it's over 100 degrees outside. "H-He quit?"

"Earlier today. I guess it all makes sense now," my dad says. "I mean, I would've knocked the spit out of any man who treated your mother the way that bastard Sam Wilkins treated you, Savannah. Because I loved her."

The lump in my throat grows exponentially and my chest burns. The reality of Jack's actions—his feelings for me—sink in.

He's given it all up.

Everything.

For me.

"Sav?" My father's concerned tone snaps me from my inner turmoil. I glance over and attempt to pull a breath through my nostrils. Do I look as panicked as I feel? "I just want you to be happy."

My lips lift slightly, and I nod before returning my gaze to the road. I am happy. But as we continue the drive back to the house, my chest heaves and my mind spirals, and I can't help but wonder if Jack will be happy. With me. Have I ruined everything for him?

I fall heavily into the passenger seat of the air-conditioned town car.

"Long day?" Jack asks, his right hand on the steering wheel and his left tucked against his stomach in a sling.

"The longest," I groan as my head tilts back against the seat and I close my eyes. "Dad has dinner with Laurel, so Elijah needs to pick them up at Callisto at 7:30. I told him I'd pass along the memo when I got back to the house." My eyelids flutter open and slide to Jack, who's holding his cell phone in one hand while also trying to thumb out the text message to Elijah. The device wobbles and then falls between the seat.

"Shit."

I offer him a small smile. "I got it." Sitting up straighter, I roll onto my knee before shoving my arm into the tight area between the seat and the armrest. "I almost…" My index finger touches the tip of the phone before it tips farther back, out of reach. "Damn."

I'm just about to get out and walk around to the adjacent seat, when Jack uses his good arm to grab me and presses his mouth to the exposed skin of my neck. "Leave it," he says, licking me along the flexed tendon there. A flash of desire slices down my sternum. "Buckle up. We've got plans. We'll retrieve the phone when we get there."

I pull away and give him a playful pout before following directions. "We're not going back to the house?"

"Nope," he says as he pulls away from the curb. Then, as though my heart couldn't be any fuller, he clicks the radio over to the Bluetooth feature. "Play whatever you want, baby."

I blow him a kiss and take him up on his offer as I pull out my phone and connect to the town car's sound system. "What are you in the mood for? Pop? Country? Alternative?"

His gaze flicks to mine briefly before returning to the road. We're heading away from the metropolitan area. "Doesn't matter. I'll love whatever you pick."

I keep my eyes on him for an extra beat, simply savoring the man next to me. Not only is he amazing in bed, but he lets me choose the music?

He beats all the book boyfriends I've read over the years.

"I love you."

His eyebrow cocks as he glances my way once more. "I love you, too, Sav."

I allow the smile to crack across my face as I scroll through my new music. Debating between a few songs, I finally settle on a crooning country duet about two ex-lovers remembering the best parts of a relationship.

I've tried not to think about our past—or our future—over the last few days. I'm living in the here and now, which, as far as I can see, is all that Jack and I have at the moment.

Because when he explained why he quit, I couldn't argue with his logic. He didn't want to continue at a job where I was a distraction to him.

I couldn't blame him for making me feel so loved that I *was* that distraction.

So for now, we're here. Enjoying one last day in Florida before Jack flies back to Michigan and an unknown future.

I watch as the palm trees and ocean pass by, savoring the last vestiges of a vacation I never want to end.

And as Jack sings along to the song we've listened to a hundred times in the last two days, I can't imagine a more perfect person to have spent the past two weeks with.

CHAPTER FIFTY-FIVE

Jack

I pull into the familiar lot and slide the gear into park. Facing the ocean and watching from the driver's seat as the waves roll over one another, my stomach follows suit. Rolling and bubbling. Only it's from nerves, not the wind or rotation of the Earth.

Or whatever the fuck causes ocean waves.

I glance over at Savannah. Her head's tilted against the seat and she's curled in on herself, her hands tucked under her chin. Her eyes closed.

I wonder if she's exhausted from work. Or from thinking.

If she's anything like me, she's spending her nights staring at the ceiling as the thoughts whip through her brain, one after another in succession. And then suddenly, it's morning.

But the thoughts don't stop.

Except now, as I reach for her and run my thumb along her jaw and over her bottom lip. Only then do the thoughts seem to slow to a manageable pace.

Only when I'm with her does the world make sense.

"Where are we?" she asks without opening her eyes. A small smile spreads across her lips, and I pull my thumb away.

"Your favorite place."

She sits up like I've lit a firecracker under her and glances around, coming to terms with her surroundings. "I haven't been here in years! I can't believe you remembered." Her gaze turns to me, the softness making her eyes sparkle. She's rarely like this, soft and sleepy.

Mostly, she's headstrong with all hard edges.

I'd take her either way, all her personalities and charms.

We exit the car and walk hand-in-hand down to the beach, to the rocks that jut into the sea. Our shoes long gone, we hold our arms wide, fingers still linked, and balance our way until it's just us and the salt.

As we settle onto the flat rock—that same flat rock, if memory serves correctly—I pull the picnic from the bag slung across my back.

"Where did you find it?" Savannah squeals when I pull out her favorite Michigan brand whiskey from the pack. She reaches for it with greedy fingers, and I pass it to her with a smile as she cracks the seal and immediately takes a long pull.

"I brought it back when I went home."

She lowers the bottle and holds it out for me. I follow suit, taking a swig. "It feels like forever since I tasted it," she says as she licks her lips. "But it's really only been..." Her eyebrows crinkle as she tallies.

"Almost two weeks," I finish for her as I cap the whiskey and set it down. I pull out two sandwiches and pass one to her. She unwraps it and takes a small bite, chewing as she stares out into the blue-green waters.

"Two weeks isn't a very long time," she finally says after swallowing. Her gaze darts to mine before returning to her sandwich.

"Not really," I admit between bites. I watch her, waiting for her to say something. When she doesn't give me any indication of what's going on in that spiderweb of a brain, I continue. "Although, to people like my mom, two weeks is a lifetime."

"What do you mean?" She reaches for the whiskey, and I pass it over.

"Well, my mom's condition means that she doesn't remember more current events. Even things that happened in the last twenty to thirty years are sometimes hazy for her. So, no, to her, two weeks *could* mean nothing if she couldn't remember any of it."

Savannah's eyes lower as she sets the whiskey down by her lap and stares at her sandwich. Her lip starts to quiver.

I reach for her, taking her hand in mine and pulling her against me. "But, on the flip side, there are things my mom remembers from years ago, the smallest events or something so insignificant to someone on the outside...and it's stayed with her throughout the progression of her dementia. Through it all, those memories have meant the most to her."

I don't have to see Savannah's face to know she's crying. I can feel her body shuddering every time she sniffles. She swipes at her cheek and the back of her hand comes away wet. "Jack, did I ruin everything for you?"

My mouth gapes. "Sweetheart, why would you think that?" I hold her hand against my heart, hoping she can feel it beating for her.

"What you said...four years ago. And now...? Now you've quit your job..." Her chin wobbles, and as she looks down, the tears stream from her eyes and crawl over her cheeks.

I push her away from me, if only to turn her around so we're face-to-face. She needs to see me. Know that I'm serious. "Savannah, baby, that was then. This is *now*. I've lived that life. Without anyone. I thought that job could be enough. I thought I didn't need someone. Thought I didn't need *you*. But when you came back, I realized what a fool I've been. What a fool I *was*. Because I'm not that person anymore. And I want you—I want *this*—so much." My eyes flick back and forth over hers, and I feel her relax slightly.

"What does this mean for us?" she asks so softly that I can barely hear her over the crash of the waves against the rocks.

"I don't know. But I can't work for your father anymore. Especially not with a potential lawsuit. And my mom needs me around more, too. I can't... I can't go to Washington."

She nods before swiping at her cheek again. I take her sandwich and set it down on the hot rock before turning her so she's facing me. With my thumbs as guides, I angle her chin until we're at eye level. All chocolate brown sadness and uncertainty filling my own vision. "All I know is, I love you, Savannah." I reach for her lips, pulling them to mine. She wraps her arms around me and pulls away from my mouth before curling into my neck, dragging her nose along the artery. The source of my life blood that beats for her now. "I've loved you for four years."

"We'll make this work, right?" she asks. Her words tingle against the sensitive skin.

"Of course we'll make this work, but for now, I have to go home."

As she leans back to look at me, tears well in her eyes once again. Her chin wobbles. None of this is easy, but we've been apart before—for four years—and found our way back to each other.

God help me if another four years of separation is before us.

But I don't believe that.

Not when I feel this way after just two weeks.

Savannah eyes her sandwich before picking it up. She brings it to her mouth, and then, without taking a bite, lowers it back to her lap. "I'm not hungry anymore."

"Me neither," I admit as I pull a piece of the bread from my sandwich. I toss it into the ocean, where a seagull swarms to grab it from the surf.

A warm smile tilts Savannah's lips. She follows suit, tossing a tiny piece into the water. A few more seagulls dive for the bread, cawing at each other as they fight for it.

And that's how we spend the rest of our evening. Tossing unwanted food to the gulls and sipping on vanilla-flavored whiskey while the waves splash us with their salty spray.

Chapter Fifty-Six

Savannah

"I'll meet you at the airport with plenty of time, I promise." I drag my luggage across the marble floor and set it with the other cases, all zipped and buckled and ready for boarding.

"I just don't understand why you can't come with us. We can stop wherever you need, Savannah." My father's reading glasses are perched on the bridge of his nose as he slides his thumb over the screen of his phone.

"I'll be shoved in a tiny private plane with you all for hours. I just have a quick errand to run." I hoist my purse higher on my shoulder and tap my foot impatiently. Miranda appears behind me, adding her carry-on to the pile of luggage before pressing her phone to her ear and traipsing back down the hallway in the opposite direction. She squeezes past Jenson, his broad shoulders taking up most of the space as he holds two duffel bags like a soldier carrying weaponry.

"At least take Jenson with you," my dad demands as he, too, catches sight of the burly bodyguard.

His only bodyguard now.

"No," we both blurt out at the same time as I divert my gaze back to my dad. Pleading to be left alone.

Even after I learned that Elijah had nothing to do with the Sam Wilkins tussle, I still haven't forgiven him for the way he spoke to me at the bar that night. He's never apologized for his part, either. Our truce is shaky at best. Built on a shared love of Jack, but nowhere near solid.

So while we've both shared the same orbit the last few days, we've also retreated to our own spaces to miss Jack alone.

"I just need some time, Dad." This time, I don't take no for an answer as I grab the keys from him.

"The plane leaves promptly at 3:30, Savannah Sue. Not a minute later." I blush at the childhood nickname, but don't glance back.

At least not until I hear my dad ask Jenson for the resumes for the new bodyguard hires. Only then do I pause, my heart stuttering momentarily. "When we move to Washington, we'll need a larger team. I'm thinking five, maybe six. What are your thoughts, son?"

When I checked last night, my dad was up by twelve points in the polls. It'd take a miracle for his opponent to win. Or a lawsuit, which is unlikely, given that Sam Wilkins hasn't responded to our lawyer's inquiries.

And so, a move to D.C. is on the horizon. Where I'll continue to manage my father's campaign, help Miranda run his staff, and do God knows what else in the nation's capital.

It should be a dream come true for a double major in political science and international relations.

But all I can think about are those cold metal bars and how much the idea of Washington feels like a life sentence.

I saunter through the soft sand, my flip-flops dangling from my index finger, past the rocky quay that juts into the Gulf. I already said my goodbyes days ago as Jack and I shared sips of Michigan's finest whiskey among the seagulls. But now, my gaze strays farther along the sand. To the paint-chipped house in the distance. I don't know when I'll be back to my favorite place in the whole world. And that scares me.

The faded yellow color has worn even more throughout the years, until it's hardly noticeable unless you're right on top of it. But even as I approach, it isn't the peeling paint or the splintered railing that catches my eye.

It's the *For Sale* sign.

I blink as I get closer, certain that my vision is failing me.

But no, the wind picks up and the sign swings in the breeze, creaking menacingly as a realtor's Cheshire Cat smile gloats from the image on the board.

My pace increases until I'm attempting to run through the sand, which is almost impossible unless said sand is wet. I get close enough to see the tiny printed website and, as I hold the sign steady with one hand, type it into my phone with the other.

As the page loads, I glance at the house. It's in decent condition.
Decent-ish.

Sure, it could use a fresh coat of weather-resistant paint and probably a new roof. But as I stagger closer and peer through the windows and take in the beautiful wood floors and curved arches, something sparks in my chest. The kitchen appears updated, with stainless-steel appliances and granite countertops.

I glance at my phone as the listing loads.

And just then, the device in my palm vibrates and rings. Jack's name flashes across the screen.

Pressing accept, I hold it to my ear. "Are you on your way home yet, sweetheart?"

I can't help the smile pulling at my cheeks as I stalk back over to the *For Sale* sign.

"Not yet. I'm actually at our beach..."

Epilogue

Chapter Fifty-Seven

Savannah

"All right, everyone scoot in and smile when I count to three!" I count down and snap the photo before passing the phone back to its owner.

"We just had the most wonderful time, Miss Smith!" the middle-aged woman says as she drops her phone into her bag. "Our friends are coming down to the Emerald Coast in a few weeks, and we'll definitely tell them about this place!"

"Thank you so much. Word of mouth is the best recommendation besides Yelp," I hint with a laugh. "Please tag us in your pictures if you post on social media!" I add, waving goodbye to the large group of tourists.

They traipse carefully through the sand and, as I watch them go, my shoulders begin to sting.

"Shit!" I mutter, realizing it's been nearly five hours since I reapplied my sunscreen. "Joe! Where's the bag of sunscreen?"

A familiar fellow in a lime-green t-shirt saunters over. His Turtle Tracker logo identifies him as part of our group. "It's with the cooler up by the tree line. I told you to reapply every two hours. Now your shoulders are beet red, Miss Smith." He glares at me like the upset grandpa I never had.

"I know, Joe, and for the millionth time, it's Savannah." Even if my white polo shirt reads *Emerald Coast Parks Department*, I've worked with Joe and his organization multiple times over the last few months to bring tourists and media attention to his cause.

"Right, Miss Savannah," he says apologetically. I purse my lips and shake my head, realizing this is the best I'll get.

"If you're calling me Miss Savannah, I'm calling you Mr. Joe," I toss back as I stalk toward the sunscreen bag.

"It's weird you don't already," he mutters under his breath, and I snort. Florida people are strangely stuck in their ways, but I love it here.

When I'd told my father that I wasn't going to make it to the plane on time, he'd nearly had a conniption. "I told you the *exact* time and you still couldn't make it? Now we'll have to pay a fine, Savannah!"

"No, Dad, I'm not making the flight at all. I'm staying here. In Florida." As much as he threatened to get off the plane and come get me, I stood my ground. And while inwardly he still wishes I'd pursue campaign management and politics, outwardly he's content to allow me to find my own path.

Using my education in public relations, campaigning and fundraising, along with Laurel's political affiliations, afforded me several job opportunities. It was only after I sat down and thoroughly thought about what *I* wanted that I decided on the EC Parks Department. And who knows, maybe running for office one day might be in my future. But for now, I'm happy to work with the local government to bring awareness to the various causes that are important in the community.

And Miranda proved to be a quite-capable campaign manager in my stead. My father won the senate seat handily and is living out his D.C. dreams.

We check in almost daily, and he hasn't stopped asking me to come visit. But with the energy conference coming to town in a few weeks, I know we'll get together. It'll be nice to see everyone again.

My phone buzzes in my pocket, and I wipe my greasy hands onto my legs and then pull it out and unlock the screen.

A smile tilts my lips as my heart beats faster. I type out the response and then return the device to my shorts. "Hey, Joe! I'll see you in a few days, okay?" I wave across the sand at the older man, who hardly looks up from his work.

"All right, make sure you send me those pictures so I can share them with my daughter on the Facebutton."

"It's Face*book*, Joe, and I will!" I laugh as I gather my things and trudge to my car. It's nothing special, an older soft-top Jeep Wrangler, but it's mine.

Long gone are the town car and chauffeured drives.

I slide the key into the ignition and crank the radio, my new favorite singer-songwriter blasting through the audio cable.

And I head home.

The Jeep's brakes squeal as I pull into the sandy driveway and shift into park. Taking out my phone, I call Delia.

"Thank God you called. Kayce won't stop crying, and I don't know what to do, Sav!" I peer carefully into the phone's screen at my disheveled best friend. Her deep red hair is thrown into a messy bun and there's a circle of saliva—or spit-up—on her shoulder.

I bite my lip as my brow crinkles. "Del, I don't know the first thing about a baby. But, um, did you make sure he was fed? Changed?"

Tears pool in her eyes and she sniffs. "I-I did all the things the book said. Nothing's working!" The squalls from baby Kayce echo in the background.

"Have you called your mom or dad? Maybe they'll know what to do..." I feel like a real Judas mentioning Delia's parents. They practically disowned her the moment they found out she wasn't marrying Kayce's father.

"Are you serious right—" a loud knock interrupts Delia's tearful outrage as her face swings to the left. Then the screen is moving, and I hear the telltale unlocking of her apartment door.

"Who is it?" My heart speeds up as my friend's face instantly changes from despair to expectant. That look, it's almost—

"Del, let me take him across the hall and you can have a break." A bulky torso crosses behind Delia and momentarily returns with a cooing baby in his arms. Lean arms swing the diaper bag over a rounded shoulder. "I'll bring him back in a few hours. Get some sleep."

The sound of the door closing echoes through the video as Delia's eyes return to the screen.

"Was that—?"

"Dane, yeah. He's so good with Kayce." She tucks an errant strand of hair behind her ear.

I hum noncommittally and stop myself from smiling. Delia doesn't need my prying right now. "He's right. Go take a nap and call me when you're feeling more like yourself, mama."

The purple half-moons crinkle under Delia's eyes as she nods. "Okay, and don't forget to send me those financial papers."

I shake my head. "Del, you've got enough on your plate. Dealing with my pipe dream shouldn't be another obligation for you. I can find someone here to—"

"Hush. You've wanted to work in the industry for years. Opening your own nonprofit to work with musicians isn't just a pipe dream. I'm happy to do what I can, Sav."

I swallow thickly and nod as the back of my eyes prick. "Okay, I'll email them tomorrow."

My best friend blows me a kiss and ends the call. I toss my phone into my bag and exit the Jeep just as the sun dips below the horizon.

As I traipse up the patio, I keep my Keds on, less I get a splinter in my heel. There's still so much work to do on the house. The roof will definitely need to be the first task, as I've already had a leak in the sunroom.

I enter the code on the smart-locked front door and open it wide as I kick off my shoes. "Anyone home?" I shout, carefully closing the door behind me.

Jack appears from the guest room, a huge grin on his face and his hair much shorter than the last time we saw each other. He's also sporting a more rugged beard around his jawline. It suits him.

"Who is this stranger in my home?" I ask coyly as I slink my way over. His arms go wide, and he wraps me up into a huge bear hug, lifting me off my feet.

"I thought you said this was *our* home," he adds, nuzzling into my neck. I hum with appreciative glee and wiggle back to the floor.

"Of course it is. But I get to make all the decorative choices. And music choices. Oh, and pet choices, too." I flex onto my toes and press a kiss to his lips. "I'm so glad you're finally here."

"Me too," he murmurs between chaste kisses. "The flight was awful."

I pull away and haul him over to the couch before shoving him down onto the cushions. "I'm sure flying coach was fine." Straddling his legs, I take a seat on his lap, facing him. I press more kisses to his neck, so hungry for him.

"Coach is only good for short, thin people," he murmurs in my hair as he grabs the ponytail and pulls with gentle strength.

My head is yanked back, my body arched against his, while he uses his other free hand to slide up my stomach and over my breast. "God, I missed this. Missed you." He thrusts his hips up, and I gasp as the desire for him skyrockets.

"Oh, I thought I heard someone else out here. Hello, dear, you must be Savannah." My eyes widen, and I swivel around Jack until I'm face-to-face with his mother.

"Hi, Ma." I smile cheerfully as the heat creeps from my sunburnt shoulders up to my face. When we'd met at Christmas, Jack's mother had insisted I call her Ma, too.

"Everyone does, dear."

I climb off her son and stalk around the couch to pull her in for a hug. I play along that it's our first-time meeting, as per the doctor's recommendations. "It's so nice to meet you!" When I glance back at Jack, my eyebrows raise in horror at being caught canoodling by his mother.

"I thought you were going to lie down for a while, Ma?"

"Oh, no, I was too excited, and I wanted to meet the girl you've been going on about for months, Jacks!" She assesses me up and down and smiles kindly, her eyes a warm honey brown that matches her son's. "But I think I'll go sit out on the porch for a bit. Listen to the waves and enjoy the sunset." Sending Jack a wink, she gives me a gentle pat on the arm as she moves toward the door. "You two let me know when dinner's ready."

Then she's gone and we're alone again, our bodies instantly coming together like two magnets. His hands are in my hair and my nails are scraping down his back before he hauls me up. My legs wrap around his waist as he carries me to the bedroom. We barely make it through the door before my top is off and his trousers unbuttoned.

Our mouths meet, tongues dancing across the divide, as we unbutton, discard, and pull every piece of fabric from one another. "Fuck, Jack," I hiss as we collapse onto the bed. He knees my legs apart and enters me fast, but I'm ready. My body needy and wet for him.

Moving in tandem, we kiss and thrust and moan as we climb the mountain together. We reach the apex so quickly, my body spasming and toes curling as his cock pulses inside me.

Going on the pill was worth it to feel him come inside of me.

"Jesus, Sav," he breathes as we collapse next to one another. "I've never gone that quick before."

We lay side-by-side, content just to be with each other in our most vulnerable state, and breathe one another's air. "Ar-Are you..." I begin, as the vulnerability comes pouring out of me. "Are you glad you've brought your mom here? To Florida?"

Jack's lips part, like he can't believe I'm asking him something so stupid, before he closes the distance between us and pulls my bottom lip into his mouth. "I'm. So. Glad. Baby," he says in between kisses. Then he pulls away to look into my eyes. "The last few weeks have been torture without you. Selling my mom's house. Applying to the retirement community that she chose..." The new wrinkles at the creases of his eyes tell of his worries.

"You know she can stay here. With us." I offered months ago when Jack officially moved in, but his mom wanted to be with people her own age. And "maybe meet a man friend," she'd said.

"I told her, but she is excited about water yoga or whatever those places offer. Plus, I think she hates my cooking."

"What? Your cooking is great!"

"Thank you, sweetheart." He chuckles and playfully shoves my shoulder. "But I'm more of a grill man."

"Ouch," I hiss, glancing down at the red orb that is my sunburnt body part. "I need to be better about applying sunscreen every two hours, according to Joe."

Jack presses a soft kiss to the angry skin.

"And Laurel? She's good?" Laurel's been staying the summer in D.C. with my father as he settles into his new role. I trace my index finger along his jaw.

"Yeah, she's great. And the doctor she recommended for Ma is amazing. I meet her team on Tuesday and everything is set."

Laurel had originally asked me to work for her, too, but I didn't think it'd be wise with Jack also coming on board as her head of security. Besides, a part of me felt like she was only offering because of my dad.

This—finding out what my dreams are and then following them—was something I needed to do on my own.

And while starting a nonprofit for musicians and songwriters to work with business mentors and industry professionals should scare me, it doesn't.

I've gone nearly my whole life with my career laid out in front of me by my father. Now it's my turn to choose.

And I'm simply excited.

"Where'd you go?" Jack asks, tipping my chin toward him.

I smile, taking in his features and then allowing my gaze to circle over the room. The sound of the waves just outside my window. "I'm just glad we're finally here."

The End

Sneak Peek at Delia's Story

COMING SOON

The ice cold water slices through the chilly February morning. Daggers pelt against my bare back like razor blades, and I release a yelp as I jump away from the shower head's assault.

"*Fucking fuck*!" My profanities echo off the crisp white tile.

"Mom, no swearing!" Kayce hollers from his place in front of the toilet.

I peak around the shower curtain at the mop-headed kindergartner. "Aim straight or you're cleaning up the mess this time, kiddo." As he turns to catch my eye with a sleepy smile, he loses focus of himself and the yellow stream sprays across the toilet and wall.

"Kayce!"

"Sorry..." His gaze turns back to the toilet and the mess now dripping down to the floor. When he finishes, he grabs a towel— my *hot-out-of-the-dryer* towel— before smearing the pee all over in an attempt to clean up.

I grind my teeth together and flick the shower curtain closed. Nothing like drying oneself with a piss-covered towel after taking the coldest shower known to man.

I manage a quick rinse and then hop out. I grab a decorative hand towel and dab myself dry before tossing on my robe and diving under the sink to fetch the all-purpose cleaner.

Shaking the bottle, I realize it's almost out, but send up a prayer of thanks as there's just enough left to cover the mess. Then I use the still-warm towel to wipe up the urine.

"You've got ten minutes, buddy! Put the iPad away and eat your breakfast!" I don't even have to look into the tiny living space to know that Kayce's face is glued to some ridiculous cartoon while his waffles go cold.

Instead, I stalk down the hallway, deposit the dirty towel in the basket on top of the stacked washer and dryer, and head into the room I've occupied for the last five years.

Discarding the robe in a pile on the floor, I step into a matching blush pink panty and bra set that I'd selected a few weeks ago from the Target clearance section. Looking at the black skirt I'd laid out the night before, I frown. I'm still shivering from the shower and there's no way I'll ever feel warm, even with tights, if I stick with the skirt. So instead I don a pair of sleek navy pants and a soft creamy white sweater.

"Five minutes, kiddo!" I call out again as I catch my reflection in the mirror. Surprisingly, the icy shower has lent a rosy glow to my cheeks. Or maybe it's a bit of frostbite. Either way, I forego the blush and simply apply a quick coat of mascara before throwing my unwashed and slightly greasy hair into a high ponytail. On my way out, I kick the discarded robe toward the hamper and raise my fist in victory as it lands true.

As a single mom of a five year old, I'll take my wins as they come.

And today I need a win.

* * *

As Kayce and I tumble from our apartment and nearly roll down the steep stairs to the sidewalk, a bright yellow bus pulls to a stop in front of the building.

"Wait!" I call as I grab him by the book bag, yanking him back against me. I press a quick kiss on his soft blond curls and then release him to the wild. "Have a great day, buddy!" I'm not even sure why I bother with the wave, as he's already charging down the aisle of the bus and not paying a lick of attention to his affectionate mother on the curb.

"Did he even comb his hair today?" As the bus pulls away from the curb, my focus snaps to the man standing next to me, his own hair a mess of tousled light brown waves.

"Did you?" I ask, cocking an eyebrow in his direction as I slide past him and into the Italian restaurant in front of our building.

Dane, our landlord and owner of the eatery, chuffs as he follows me. "Of course I did." I grab a seat at the counter as he slides his fingers through his hair, pulling it back from his face. But as he leans over and flicks on the coffee pot behind the counter, the strands fall forward once more.

"When's the last time you had a haircut?"

He pulls two mugs from beneath the till and sets them between us. "It's been a while. Why? You offering?"

"I mean, I'm no stylist, but I can trim and shape pretty well. Would you be willing to take a look at the water heater while you're over?" My chest tightens as I toss the question into the empty restaurant. As though my half-assed hair styling would even come close to an even trade.

Dane's jaw tenses as he grips the counter. "Delia, is the water heater out again?"

"If the icy shower I had this morning was any indication, then yes." I eye the brewing coffee behind him as my stomach gurgles.

"Fuck, why didn't you come over and take a shower at my place? I'll stop by tonight and see what needs to be done to get it up and running."

My teeth dig into my bottom lip, the thought of accepting charity giving my heart a run for its money. "I can pay. For whatever parts. Or repairs." The lie slips out so easily now.

"I'm the landlord, Delia. This is part of the rental agreement." He says it slowly, like I haven't heard it enough in the last five years.

"But, see, you don't actually charge me the full rent, so it's not—"

He turns away and yanks the coffee pot from the machine. "— I told you when you moved in. Pay what you can. I'm not worried about it."

Dane passes the steaming mug of coffee to me before replacing the pot. He pulls two sugars from a box under the counter and then heads to the back. I tear open a sugar packet and add the contents to his mug before repeating the process with my own. He returns with a carton of half-and-half, adding a hefty amount to my cup and then his own.

We each take up our spoons and stir in silence, the only sound the cutlery clinking against the ceramic mugs. "So tonight then?" He asks as he brings his mug to his lips and blows softly.

"Oh, um..." I look down at the swirling caramel-colored liquid before me and purse my lips. "Well, I actually have a date tonight. But tomorrow would work. And I could give you that trim, too." I shrug and raise my eyes to meet his.

Except his brows are pulled together and he's holding the mug away from him as he eyes it with a pinched expression. "I think the half-and-half has gone bad."

I frown, but, my stomach still rumbling and reminding me to feed it something— *anything*— I bring the mug to my lips and take a slow sip. "Seems fine to me."

Dane ignores me and heads to the back again. Through the food window, I'm able to see him toss the coffee down the drain and then wash the mug, his lips pressed together as he shakes his head. I eye my own cup and take another delicate sip. I hold the liquid in my mouth, testing it for something off. Anything strange.

Nothing. It tastes like coffee.

"I really think it's fine!" I call to him over the din of the running water. I grab the carton still sitting on the counter and check the expiration date. "You've still got another week left. Maybe it's you?"

Dane cuts off the water and sets the mug on the rack to dry. He towels off his hands and then stalks back around to the counter. "Don't you have work today?" He checks his wrist for a watch that isn't there. "Wouldn't want you to be late when you've got rent to pay."

I flatten my lips and roll my eyes before taking a final hefty swig of the coffee. "Just because you have awful taste doesn't mean you have to be a jerk about it," I mutter as I dig in my purse. I slap a few dollars onto the shiny counter and hoist my bag onto my shoulder.

I drape my coat over my arm and head for the exit.

"I'll come by tomorrow after work to fix the water heater. And for that trim," Dane adds just as my palm connects with the door handle. "And the offer's still open to use my shower in the meantime, too."

That's very generous of you," I reply as I swing the door open. "But I prefer a cold shower to your grumpy ass in the morning."

Acknowledgements

Here we are with book three — my very first contemporary romance. As I sit, thinking about who to thank, the first person that comes to mind is my very closest and best friend, Sarah. She has been my go-to alpha, beta, and ARC reader from day one. My biggest hype girl. The person who's read every single one of my books without fail and given me the cold hard truth. Thank you, my friend, for standing by my side and supporting me through this journey. I could not have done this without you.

A second hearty thank you to Jackie, my spirit animal and beta reader. I'm so grateful to your friendship and support. Without your sass and jokes, my life would be incredibly dull. I hope this gives you enough spice for your itchy biscuit.

Of course I could not have completed this journey without my family. My husband, my rock, and my children. They may not understand why I write— the need I feel to get the puzzle in my head onto the page— but they give me the time and peace to do so. They are proud of me, support me, and love me.

A big thank you to the two professionals who made this book come to life: my editor, Mackenzie @nicegirlnaughtyedits and cover designer, Kate from Ya'll, That Graphic. They've ensured that my story was polished and at its best. Thank you for your hard work!

Lastly, I'd like to thank you, the reader, for taking a chance on my story. This book was a long time coming and I hope you love it as much as I do. Thank you for reading!

If you enjoyed reading *Just Two Weeks*, please consider leaving a review or recommending it to a friend. Your support, through reviews, word of mouth, and social media shares, helps readers find my story.

Follow Jenn Lynn Adams on social media:

Instagram @jennlynnadams

TikTok @authorjennlynnadams

On the web www.jennlynnadams.com